A Death in the Dales

Also by Frances Brody

Dying in the Wool
A Medal for Murder
Murder in the Afternoon
A Woman Unknown
Murder on a Summer's Day
Death of an Avid Reader
Death at the Seaside

A Death in the Dales

A Kate Shackleton Mystery

Frances BRODY

Minotaur Books

A Thomas Dunne Book

New York

This is a work of fiction. All of the characters, organizations, and events portrayed in this novel are either products of the author's imagination or are used fictitiously.

A THOMAS DUNNE BOOK FOR MINOTAUR BOOKS.
An imprint of St. Martin's Press.

A DEATH IN THE DALES. Copyright © 2015 by Frances McNeil. All rights reserved. Printed in the United States of America. For information, address St. Martin's Press, 175 Fifth Avenue, New York, N.Y. 10010.

www.thomasdunnebooks.com
www.minotaurbooks.com

The Library of Congress has cataloged the hardcover edition as follows:

Names: Brody, Frances, author.
Title: A death in the dales / Frances Brody.
Description: First U.S. edition. | New York : Minotaur Books, 2017. |
    Series: A Kate Shackleton mystery ; 7
Identifiers: LCCN 2016043770 | ISBN 9781250098825 (hardcover) |
    ISBN 9781250098849 (ebook)
Subjects: LCSH: Women private investigators—England—Fiction. |
    Murder—Investigation—Fiction. | BISAC: FICTION / Mystery &
    Detective / Traditional British. | FICTION / Mystery & Detective /
    Women Sleuths. | FICTION / Mystery & Detective / Historical. |
    GSAFD: Mystery fiction.
Classification: LCC PR6113.C577 D425 2017 | DDC 823/.92—dc23
LC record available at https://lccn.loc.gov/2016043770

ISBN 978-1-250-09883-2 (trade paperback)

Our books may be purchased in bulk for promotional, educational, or business use. Please contact your local bookseller or the Macmillan Corporate and Premium Sales Department at 1-800-221-7945, extension 5442, or by email at MacmillanSpecialMarkets@macmillan.com.

First published in Great Britain by Piatkus, an imprint of Little, Brown Book Group, an Hachette UK company

First Minotaur Books Paperback Edition: January 2018

10 9 8 7 6 5 4 3 2 1

For Jill Hyem, champion friend,
fine scriptwriter and trailblazing stalwart
of the Writers' Guild of Great Britain

The heart may be misplaced from birth. I have seen a case in which it lay upon the right side, and had always been in that position. Its action was natural.

A variety of causes may tend to push it out of its place.

Virtue's Household Physician, Volume I, 1925

A Death in
the Dales

Prologue

Langcliffe, 29 April, 1916

The wax candle burned brightly in its brass holder. Freda Simonson sat at her dressing table brushing her hair. Ever since she was a girl she had brushed her hair one hundred times before going to bed. Now her arm ached more easily. She switched hands. Over the years, more and more hair found its way onto the brush. Each morning, she would comb through the bristles and take small grey bracelets into the garden, placing her gifts on the shrubs. It pleased her when sometimes she spotted a bird carrying off the trophy for nest-building.

Once, her hair was dark. The first grey streaks appeared days after Lucian went to war, as if the worries and fears she tried to suppress found their way into her locks. She gave a small smile at the speed with which this process had accelerated. Soon her hair may turn silver, as had her mother's.

The bedroom curtains were open. Above the three mirrors of her dressing table, she watched a cloud float across the heavens, briefly hiding the crescent moon, tonight in its last quarter. Now, at her grand age, she preferred this final phase of the moon. There was something too bold and unsettling about the moon when full.

A commotion from outside brought her to her feet. She walked round the side of her dressing table and looked through the window. Across the street, she saw quite plainly in the light from the bracket lamp on the wall of the White Hart, a man being ejected from the alehouse.

She recognised the man doing the throwing out. It was Rufus Holroyd, alehouse keeper, wiry and slightly hunched. The drunk was the bigger man but unsteady on his feet and in no state to resist. Mr Holroyd gave him what seemed an unnecessary shove. The man fell in the gutter. Still, he probably felt nothing. Holroyd turned and was halfway back to the door when another figure came round the corner, looking dark and imposing in a long coat and pulled-down hat. He came close to Holroyd, so close that Freda could not see what happened, but Holroyd fell.

The man in the gutter struggled to his feet and stumbled towards the alehouse keeper who lay very still. The drunken man leaned down towards Holroyd, and then knelt over him. The night stood still as Freda watched, waiting for the man to help Holroyd to his feet.

The man shouted, 'Help! Murder!'

Freda turned from the window and, faster than she had moved for a long time, she ran down the stairs.

One

Killingbeck Hospital, Leeds

April 1926

'Kate! Watch where you're treading or you'll ruin your shoes.'

I stepped carefully around bright daffodils. The flowerbed was under the big window that looked onto the girls' ward at the fever hospital. My sister Mary Jane and I were visiting her daughter. Harriet was recovering from diphtheria and we were very lucky that she had pulled through. That dreadful illness brings death to so many. I say 'visiting' but that is something of an exaggeration. We were not allowed entry to the hospital. Under my arm, I had the latest newspaper that carried information about patients. Alongside Harriet's patient number was the word 'Comfortable'. What a relief! She had previously been marked 'Very ill' and 'Serious'. To be described as 'Comfortable' meant that she was finally on the mend.

My reason for stepping onto the flowerbed was to tap

on the window and hope to gain attention. Once patients are 'Comfortable' they are able to come to the window and smile at their parents and relatives through the glass. After several taps and careful mouthing of Harriet's name to another young patient, our own Harriet finally appeared.

Mary Jane forgot her intention to keep her shoes pristine. She stepped up to the windowsill, her feet sinking into the damp soil.

We signalled encouragement through the glass. None of us is very good at lip-reading, so our conversation was somewhat limited. But I did make out when she said she was glad to be isolated as she would not want to infect anyone. It was horrible. She patted her chest and panted, showing how hard it had been to catch a breath. 'Is Austin all right?' she asked anxiously, and was relieved when we said that her younger brother was well. 'And the baby?'

Mary Jane beamed. She held up a photograph of the latest addition to the family and pronounced each word with great clarity: 'Baby misses you.'

Our visit was cut short when a nurse, who at least did not glare at us too frostily, escorted Harriet back to her bed.

As we walked towards the gates, Mary Jane let out a great sigh of relief. 'Thank God she's recovered. And I'll be so glad to have her home. I'm run off my feet without Harriet to give a hand. She's so good with the baby.'

The rose bushes at the side of the path had been cut back and were all green stems and sharp thorns. Harriet would be out soon, well before the roses bloomed. 'Mary Jane, Harriet will need to recuperate. I'm going to take her to the Dales for a fortnight. A friend of mine has offered me the use of his late aunt's house in Langcliffe. It will be just the ticket for Harriet.'

'But . . .'

'You see how pale she is, and those dark rings under her eyes. She needs a holiday.'

She gave me a quick glance, as if trying to assess whether there was some ulterior motive behind my words. 'Who is this friend?'

'He's the doctor I met at Bolton Abbey.'

'Ah.'

'What do you mean, "ah"? It's nothing like that. I just happened to mention the last time we met that I needed a holiday. His Aunt Freda died six months ago and her house has stood empty since then. It's the perfect spot for Harriet to recover. Don't deny her that.'

'I know you're fond of Harriet, but I wish you wouldn't be so bossy.'

'I'm not bossy. I'm right, and you know it.'

Langcliffe would be the perfect solution to Harriet's and my need for rest and recreation. I hoped.

Two

After stopping in Skipton for lunch, we made good progress until negotiating our way through Gargrave. It was a fine Saturday, the first day of May. Slowing the car to a snail's pace, I carefully avoided market stalls, meandering shoppers armed with sturdy baskets, gawpers, and children playing marbles in the gutter.

We had driven all the way from Leeds with the canvas down, enjoying the breeze that made our faces tingle. The river, when it put in an appearance, tumbled angrily, ready for trouble.

Every few miles, I stole a quick glance at Harriet, keen to make sure the journey was not tiring her. She bore up well, valiantly struggling with the map, folding and re-folding as she traced our route. At fourteen she is thankfully too old to keep on saying, 'Are we nearly there?' She is a bright girl and practising her navigating skills gave her something to occupy her mind.

'Follow the sign to Settle, Auntie. After Settle, it'll be a right turn to Langcliffe.'

On the approach to Settle, I noticed the whiteness of the

roads, due to the limestone formation. Sharply defined hills, boulders and rocks stood out against green foliage. Castlebergh came into view, towering over the town. We would not be able to climb the great rock but Lucian had told me there were sometimes funfairs there.

Being Saturday, and a market day in Settle, the whole town and inhabitants from miles around colluded in walking on the little strip of road not taken up with stalls selling vegetables, baskets, sheepskin rugs and itchy cardigans. Had I known the area better, I might have tried to find another way and avoid the crush.

Feeling a sense of achievement at not mowing down a single inhabitant, we left Settle behind. As we drove along the narrow road, Harriet gazed at the scenery. Fields and meadows stretched to the hills, their dry stone walls penning in sheep and cattle. 'It's going to be very quiet round here, Auntie.'

Oh dear. Was she disappointed that we had not stayed in smoky Leeds, where we could visit music halls and theatres and stroll about the shopping arcades?

'There'll be plenty going on in Langcliffe. There are May Day celebrations today. And there's the Kirkgate Kinema in Settle.' I tried to make it sound as if this would be the best picture house for a hundred miles, which perhaps it was.

'What's the house like?'

'Wait and see.'

'How long has it stood empty?'

'Since November when Dr Simonson's aunt died. She was his father's sister and brought him up when his parents stayed in India and sent him home.'

'Are you two courting?'

'Harriet!'

'Mam says you are.'

'Well, if your mam says that it must be true.'

Harriet laughed. She gave me a mischievous look that told me she would soon find out how matters stood between me and the doctor.

Lucian and I had seen each other only a dozen or so times in the past couple of years. Each time, I liked him more. We made each other laugh. He is kind, thoughtful, and has that rare knack of making a person feel she is the centre of his world. Between our trysts, he sends me picture post-cards, snippets of rhymes and the occasional bunch of flowers.

Although the words had not been said, we both knew that this fortnight's holiday would decide our future. Lucian has his own cottage in Embsay but also has a share in a practice in Settle. Being left his aunt's house meant big changes. He had asked me to take a look at the place, but that suggestion implied so much more than 'a look'.

'Slow down, Auntie! Here's a right turn coming up.'

I turned more suddenly than intended and was taken by surprise at the steepness of the bumpy cobbles.

How long must Lucian have been standing there, I wondered. There he was, waiting a little way up the street. I brought the car to a halt.

Lucian leaned towards us and raised his cap. He wore tan and green tweed plus fours, a Norfolk jacket and highly polished brown shoes. Undeniably handsome, he looks younger than his thirty-seven years, with a fine head of hair and a slightly weather-beaten complexion.

'Hello, Lucian.'

I felt glad to see him as his face lit up with a beaming smile. 'Hello, Kate! And you must be Harriet.'

'Yes.' Harriet spoke rather stiffly, eyeing him cautiously.

I introduced them.

He reached into the car to shake hands. 'How do you do, Harriet.'

She smiled. 'How do you do, Dr Simonson.'

He glanced at our valises that were behind, in place of the dickey seat. 'Not much luggage.'

'We have a trunk coming by rail.'

'Glad to hear it! I'm suspicious of ladies who travel light.' He waved with the stick. 'Straight up into the village. You'll see a fountain with a memorial cross. The house is to the right of that, the one with my motor parked outside.'

'Do you want a lift on the running board, Lucian?'

'Best not. I'll cling to my shreds of dignity.'

I smiled. 'Right. See you up there.'

Passing terraced grey stone cottages with tiled roofs, I continued towards the top end of the village.

Harriet turned back and waved to Lucian. 'He's nice.'

'Yes he is.'

'You didn't tell me he has a limp.'

'It's not polite to mention a person's limp within seconds of seeing him.'

'I expect he was in the war.'

'You expect right.'

'So you were both in the war.' She made this sound as if The War had been a fine opportunity for romantic assignations. 'Is that where you met him?'

'No.'

She was suddenly diverted. 'Oh look! There's a band and everything.'

The Langcliffe Brass Band played a stirring tune from their spot between the large sycamore tree and the war memorial with its fountain base. 'Well of course! They're celebrating our arrival.'

Harriet's eyes widened. 'Do they know we're coming . . . ? Oh, you! I fall for it every time.'

Harriet and I spotted Lucian's Bugatti at the same moment.

She pointed. 'That must be the house.'

Aunt Freda's cottage was a substantial house constructed like the others roundabout of local limestone, fronted by a neat garden, planted by someone who had loved lilac and lavender, hence the name Lilac Cottage.

I drove just beyond Lucian's car and parked by the corner from where we could see the village green. Children played around the maypole, adults chatted, some sitting on the grass enjoying the sunshine, others gathering around the Morris dancers. Music, laughter and children's high-pitched voices filled the air.

On the other side of the green was the parish church, stone with a slate roof and a porch. At the top end of the village was the school.

Harriet climbed from the car and went to sit on the low wall at the front of the house. 'I like it here. It's not as bad as I thought it would be. There's a fair few shops.'

I joined her on the wall and we surveyed the scene.

Back the way we had come was a most strange-looking building, a narrow three-storey house that did not seem to fit with the other houses. Somewhere nearby was Threlfall

Hall, home to Langcliffe's landowning squirearchy including, according to Lucian, a girl of Harriet's age.

Green hills surrounded the village. Cloud shadows and shafts of sunlight formed a still picture, contrasting with lively laughter and friendly voices from the village green. There would be no urgent calls upon my investigative services here.

After all my enquiries into dastardly goings on, it was a great relief to arrive in such a peaceful spot.

Some of the children sidled over to look at the new car that had arrived in their village, and at us. Harriet explained to them that the car was called a Jowett and that her aunt liked blue. She did not deign to move from her spot on the wall, being so much older than the children who congregated to gaze and admire.

Twisting her hair around her finger, one little girl asked, 'Have you come to live here?'

'Just for a short time.' Harriet drummed her heels on the wall. 'We are on holiday. My aunt is a private investigating detective and needs to rest her brain.'

Thank you Harriet, I said to myself, for announcing my occupation. Fortunately, the little girl had not the vaguest notion of what Harriet was saying, although she looked impressed.

As Harriet saw Lucian approaching, she picked up her case and lugged it along the path to the front door.

After a few moments, he was leaning into the car to pick up my valise. He called to Harriet. 'It's not locked, Harriet, you can go in!'

Harriet flung open the door.

Lucian smiled. 'Watch out, Kate, she'll commandeer the best bedroom.'

He stood back to let me walk along the path. 'I hope you like it. I've had the place cleaned. My aunt didn't believe in throwing anything away, though she did have new sash windows installed so it's much lighter here than when I was growing up. Oh and the room that was mine, that's been redecorated and has new furniture.' He spoke to Harriet who had already walked through the house and back. 'Take a look at the back bedroom. It has new furniture called fumed oak. See what you think.'

Harriet carried her case upstairs, refusing Lucian's help.

He took my hands. 'I'm so glad you're here. Come on, I'll show you round.'

It was just the kind of house I like, with a central tiled hall, an off-centre staircase, and rooms on either side. The hall was decorated with Anaglypta paper in brown and cream. An attractive grandmother clock stood on one side and a hall stand complete with coat hooks and walking sticks on the other. A raincoat still hung there.

We paused in the hall. 'The kettle has been on so it shouldn't be long in boiling.' Lucian carried my valise upstairs.

I glanced into the parlour, crammed with old-fashioned furniture and ornaments, and a rocker that I could have sworn moved. I could imagine Lucian's Aunt Freda looking up, a lace cap on her head, her long skirts brushing the footstool.

I walked on through the hall to a large kitchen at the back. A curtained alcove contained a maid's bed. In the centre of the room stood a sturdy table covered by a patterned oilcloth. Covered with white tea cloths, the plates held sandwiches, pork pie and cakes. Dishes gleamed on the Welsh dresser. The gas cooker looked as new as the day it was bought. I imagined that Aunt Freda had been suspicious of gas.

Nothing about the house prepared me for the miraculous view through the kitchen window. The wall enclosing the garden was constructed of those tiny dark red bricks favoured by the Elizabethans. A tree near the solid wooden arched gate shimmered with delicate apple blossom. Earthenware pots of herbs cast shadows across the path. Aunt Freda must have loved this patch of earth. Someone had gone on tending it in the months since her death. I felt a stab of sorrow that she was not here to see the phlox, snapdragons, Canterbury bells, sweet peas and carnations. In between the flowers were vegetable patches, marked out with string and with flutters of paper to discourage birds. The crooked garden shed had been patched and mended over the years.

I opened the door and stepped out. On the garden bench under the window lay a new skipping rope and a couple of tennis balls.

By the time I went back inside, Lucian had made a pot of tea and he and Harriet had settled themselves at the table. He presented her with a sixpenny compass and encouraged her to take it with her when we went for walks. They went into the garden and he showed her how to use it while his cup of tea went cold.

'Who's the gardener, Lucian?' I asked when they came back inside.

'I am, for the time being.'

'I didn't know you were a keen gardener.'

'You didn't ask.'

'You're a man of hidden talents.'

'Well of course, and talking of that, I've stupidly prom-ised to help set up our photographic society exhibition in Settle Town Hall tomorrow, before we fixed our dates. I can cancel it if you want to do something special.'

'No, you stick to your plans. Harriet and I will do a little exploring on our own.'

'Come in to Settle if you have time. You should take a look, since you'll have a couple of photographs on display.'

'Oh good! I didn't know whether my entries would pass muster.'

'Stop fishing for compliments! You know very well they would.'

Harriet looked from one to the other of us. Was she making mental notes of how we got on, to report back to her mother?

She bit into her egg and cress sandwich. 'Is that skipping rope for me?'

Lucian frowned. 'What skipping rope?'

'The new one someone must have bought for me, along with the tennis balls and compass.'

'Oh that skipping rope.' Lucian pushed the cake stand towards her. There were iced buns, vanilla slices and cur-rant cake. 'I suppose you won't believe me if I say it was left by the fairy of the Dale.'

Harriet groaned. 'I'm too old for that sort of remark!'

'Excuse me!'

When Harriet had gone out to explore, Lucian showed me round the house.

14

The front bedroom was spacious, decorated with fading William Morris patterned wallpaper. Aunt Freda must have had a mixture of tastes, traditional and modern. The oak bedroom suite, dressing table, wardrobe and tall boy in the front bedroom looked the kind of thing a couple might buy, or be bought, for their wedding. Their wedding in 1860. I wondered about Aunt Freda, and whether taking care of Lucian had been a reason why she never married. From what he had told me, she was thirty-four years old when she started to care for him when he was six. She was sixty-four when she died last year.

Against one wall was a big brass bed covered with a white candlewick spread.

Lucian threw open the wardrobe and grumbled. 'I'm sorry, Kate. All her clothes are still here. I asked Mrs Holroyd whether she would take them for some of the women in the village. They're all good quality and clean.'

'Don't worry. I'll manage.'

He tutted as he opened a drawer. 'Mrs Holroyd saw to the cleaning of the house, and she brought in provisions but she hasn't moved Aunt Freda's belongings.'

Lucian lifted out a coat from the wardrobe and began to fold it. 'I'll bring up the washing basket, and find a couple of suitcases. If you wouldn't mind emptying the dresser drawers . . .'

'Harriet and I will sort it out.' I smiled. 'I'm guessing that's partly why I'm here, to help you decide what to do about the house.'

'Yes.' He continued to fold the clothes, pausing over a long tweed coat lined in mustard-coloured silk.

'Lucian, we don't have to do this now. Leave it and show

me the rest of the house.' This would be something Harriet and I could do, when it rained.

We went onto the landing.

'This was my room.' Lucian opened the door to the back bedroom that was refurbished, and would be Harriet's. The smoothly plastered walls and ceiling had been painted palest primrose and were quite bare. It was the kind of room a person might imagine putting her stamp on.

Having a bathroom at all in a house this old was a bonus, and it was very nicely kept, with a geyser over the bath for hot water.

'It's all gas.' Lucian turned on the geyser, to demonstrate that it worked. 'Eventually, I'll have electricity laid on.' He indicated stairs to the loft. 'You can look up there at your leisure. It's a bit of a mess but there is the old bed up there, for emergencies. And there's the usual cellar with the cold press and stocked with food, thanks to the good efforts of Mrs Holroyd.'

'You've thought of everything, Lucian. Thank you!'

'What do you think to the house?'

'It's a good solid house, and I love the garden. This must have been a splendid place to grow up.'

'Yes it was, and I had the privilege of going to the local school until the age of eleven, far better than being packed off as a boarder. My aunt was very good to me.'

'What are your plans for the place?'

He hesitated, and there was just the slightest of blushes. 'I'm thinking of keeping it on. The room at the front might make a good consulting room.'

'As well as your cottage in Embsay?'

'That's rented and the practice doesn't keep me busy,

Kate. There's no doctor here in Langcliffe or in Stainforth. I've been helping old Dr McKinley in Settle. He plans to retire soon and I could have a practice in both Settle and Langcliffe and make this my home.' His hand brushed mine, but he held back from saying what I knew he was thinking: 'Our home.' Instead, he said, 'The loft would make a decent space for a housekeeper, even one as particular as your Mrs Sugden.'

'Well, it's a lovely house.'

'I think you said that already.'

'I need gloves.' I went back into the main bedroom, to take a pair of gloves from my case, having worn motoring gloves for the journey.

'Sorry. Didn't mean to sound as if I'm making assumptions.' He waited on the landing while I searched for my gloves. 'I wouldn't necessarily turn the parlour into a consulting room. There's a cottage next door that's a little ramshackle but might be converted, if I can tempt the occupants to move elsewhere in the village. It's all a little up in the air.' He watched me draw on my gloves.

'I'm happy for you, Lucian. It's always good to make a change.'

'It wasn't a great wrench to leave your investigations then?'

'Not at all. We have a fraud case and a dognapping in hand. Jim Sykes and Mrs Sugden are more than capable of minding the business while I'm away. Now come on. I want to keep an eye on Harriet and it's too fine a day to be cooped up.'

As we walked down the stairs, there was a knock on the door.

Lucian went to answer.

When I reached the hall, he was saying, 'Yes of course. My bag is in the car. You may as well jump in and you can show me the way.'

He turned to me. 'Terrible timing, Kate. I'm so sorry. I have to go to see a patient in upper Settle.'

'Then off you go! Harriet and I will manage perfectly.'

We exchanged a quick kiss, and I followed him to the gateway and then walked to the corner. From there, I spotted Harriet on the village green. She was watching the dancing.Lucian started the motor. As he climbed into the car, he called to me. 'Ah, here comes Bradley Wigglesworth. I told him you were coming.' He waved in the direction of a man who was strolling up the road. 'He's an old friend of Aunt Freda's.'

Mr Wigglesworth came to a halt as the car moved away. When it drew level with him, he and Lucian raised an arm in mutual salute. Making no haste, the old gentleman continued his walk towards the cottage. As he drew close, he smiled cheerfully, showing a row of small teeth in a pleasant moon-like face. He raised his hat revealing grey hair with streaks of the original ginger, cut as short as a well-kept bowling green.

'Mrs Shackleton I presume?'

'Correct, Mr Wigglesworth.'

'Sorry to land on you the instant you arrive, but May Day you know, May Day, a good excuse to come here. Lucian had to scoot off did he?'

'Yes. A patient needs him. The man in the car is the relative I think.'

He nodded, as if knowing all about it, which perhaps he did.

I wanted to go across to Harriet who just at that moment

looked rather forlorn. Yet here was this man, only an inch or two taller than I, rocking on his heels, clutching a brown paper carrier bag with string handles, obviously waiting to be invited in.

'I am so very happy to make your acquaintance. Freda had hoped to meet you herself you know.'

'She knew about me?'

'She did, she did.' He gave a nervous and somewhat pained laugh as if to hide embarrassment. 'Lucian spoke of you, spoke highly of you. She had great hopes.'

'Oh?' Great hopes of what, I wondered. Seeing Lucian settled, I supposed.

'There was something Freda wanted you to see you know, something, well this as a matter of fact.'

He looked down at his carrier bag, swinging it a little, towards me and away.

'What is it?'

'You'll see. If I may?'

He indicated the front door.

I could hardly refuse. 'My niece is with me,' I said, hating the apologetic tone in my voice. 'She is on the green. I don't want to leave her alone.'

'Of course you don't. I'll be very quick, simply want to hand this into your safe keeping, and I have brought a tonic for your niece, the girl who is recovering from diphtheria. Lucian may have told you my trade.'

'I'm sorry. He may have done . . . '

'I'm an apothecary, well *the* apothecary, in Settle, opposite the Market Place.' In the hallway, he took a shoebox from his paper carrier bag and handed it to me. 'It's Freda's papers, you know, the papers regarding the trial.'

'What trial?'

'The murder trial.' A sudden dismay turned the corners of his mouth and widened his eyes. 'Lucian did not mention it?'

'No.'

'Ah, then I am sorry to spring it on you like this, but Freda was most particular that you, being in your line of work, would be the person she had waited for.' He folded his carrier bag carefully and put it in an inside pocket. 'Perhaps I should say no more about it, at least not yet.'

I stared at the box, and then lifted the lid to see papers, newspaper cuttings, letters, typed sheets. It took a great deal of restraint on my part not to tell him that I was here on holiday and would rather not look. Lucian had spared me this information, perhaps with good reason.

Mr Wigglesworth saw my hesitation and moved as if to retrieve the precious shoebox. That decided me.

'I'll take it through now, for later.'

That sounded idiotic, the kind of thing one might say if presented with a stale seed cake.

'Yes, yes, you do that. I see that you are anxious to join your niece.' He took a dark bottle from his inside pocket. 'This tonic is my own recipe. It will buck her up no end.'

'That's very kind.'

He followed me into the parlour, sighing as he opened the door of a corner cupboard. 'In there, eh?'

I placed the shoebox in the cupboard. He put the bottle of tonic on top of the cupboard and turned to leave.

'You say there was a murder trial?' I asked, walking towards the door, pausing until he followed me back into the hall. 'Who was murdered?'

'The alehouse keeper at the White Hart.'

We stepped outside into the sunshine, along the path and back to the gate which we had left open. The brass band had moved on.

He closed the gate behind us. 'You see that house, with the lamp on the wall?' He indicated a building across the square, about thirty yards away.

'Yes.'

'That was the White Hart. Mr Trevelyan had it closed down as a public house after the murder, though the out-sales continued under the new owner, for a time at any rate. It's privately occupied now.' He turned back to Lilac Cottage and looked up. 'Freda saw the murder, from her bedroom window.' He pointed to the front bedroom.

I followed his gaze. It was the room that would be mine for the next fortnight. I continued towards the green, wanting to catch up with Harriet. Mr Wigglesworth kept pace.

'Freda gave evidence at the trial. It was a constant sorrow to her that the wrong man was convicted and hanged.'

'How dreadful!'

'Yes. Young chap called Flaherty, a Dubliner who worked at the Hoffman Kiln. He was caught with the knife in his hand and said he had withdrawn it. Freda backed him up. She swore she saw a different man do the deed and run away, but she wasn't believed.'

'Why not?'

'She asked herself that until the day she died.' Mr Wigglesworth paused at the corner. 'Take a good look, there's no one paying attention to us, all too caught up with their own enjoyment.'

So they were. The Morris men began a new dance. A

crowd gathered round. I lost sight of Harriet as Mr Wigglesworth warmed to his theme , saying, 'You wouldn't know now that was once the alehouse.'

He seemed eager that I should picture the event. 'Rufus Holroyd, the alehouse keeper, wasn't a big chap but he had been a boxer and could handle himself. Flaherty was younger but the worse for drink. According to Freda, who heard a bit of a commotion, Holroyd manhandled Flaherty round to the kerb and gave him a good shove. Holroyd was on his way back inside when a big fellow appeared, tapped him on the shoulder and knifed him. Freda didn't see the actual knifing, just how close the man came, and that Holroyd dropped to the ground. The man then disappeared around the other corner. Flaherty was struggling to his feet and cried out. He went to Holroyd and the worst thing he did was withdraw the knife, so it had his fingerprints on it.' He touched my elbow. 'Better keep walking. If we dawdle too long someone may guess that I'm giving you chapter and verse on what's become unmentionable in this village.'

I was glad to keep walking, especially as I once more spotted Harriet, and she me. We waved to each other.

She was my reason for being here. I did not want to hear from Mr Wigglesworth about a long-ago murder any more than I felt ready to respond to Lucian's sudden haste regarding our future.

Mr Wigglesworth had slowed his steps. It would be impolite to stride off, and unkind to ignore his distress when he spoke about his friend.

'You were very fond of Freda?'

He nodded. 'She was my oldest friend.'

In spite of my impatience, there was something quite

touching in his words. Freda had never married, perhaps due to circumstances or fierce independence, but I knew from Mr Wigglesworth's manner and his voice that it was not for want of opportunity.

'I had a bit of a hand in the events myself, Mrs Shackleton.'

'How so?'

'Being apothecary in Settle, Licentiate of the London Apothecaries' Society, I was sent for. We had an absence of doctors in 1916. When I arrived at the White Hart, Rufus Holroyd was dead. He had been carried inside. His wife said he died in her arms, but I doubt he lasted that long.'

'How dreadful. But I'm sorry, you must excuse me. There's my niece.' He suddenly looked like a lost boy. 'Come and say hello to Harriet.'

He coughed. 'Yes, yes, thank you. But just let me say, you see I've screwed up my courage to speak to you about this. Freda hoped you would take an interest in the case, because of your occupation. She hoped you might look for the truth of what really happened.'

Three

Harriet was already on the village green when she saw Dr Simonson drive away. Auntie Kate was just about to come across when an old man called to her. The two of them went inside, but not for long. Harriet kept an eye out until she saw them leave the house. The old man was slowing Auntie Kate down.

The two of them walked towards the maypole where Harriet had been watching little kids playing about, grabbing ribbons and jigging even though their dance had ended. Going to meet her auntie, Harriet had to step sharply to avoid a little lad who'd thrown himself on the ground pretending to have been choked by ribbons, clutching his throat and laughing, and then other boys flinging themselves on top of him.

Grown-ups stood about chatting, ignoring the children.

She was so proud of her Auntie Kate who looked the tops in her silk and cashmere turquoise dress and coat, with a hat that shouldn't match but somehow did. People turned to look as she walked across the green. The old chap with her looked like someone who would feel obliged to hand out sweets or compliments but when he spoke, he was just very friendly and said he hoped Harriet would not mind but he knew that the Trevelyans of Threlfall Hall were keen to meet them.

'They have a daughter of your age, Harriet.' He led them in a beeline towards a man, a woman and a vicar on the far side of the green.

Auntie Kate already knew the Trevelyans. Dr Simonson had introduced them at a New Year dance they attended in Skipton. The dance was to raise funds for the hospital. Mr and Mrs Trevelyan were patrons.

Harriet did not want to meet them, but saw that she had no choice. They looked pleasant enough, Mr and Mrs Trevelyan, both plump and fair and pink. Harriet understood from their talk that they owned farms nearby, and land that hadn't already been nabbed long ago by some duke or other.

When it turned out that the daughter of her age had gone home, Harriet sidled away. She looked about her. Was there anyone here worth talking to? Several soppy-looking girls wore white dresses and garlands of flowers on their bonces. Well, let them get on with being soppy and garlanded.

'I saw you arrive in a motor.'

Harriet turned to see who had spoken. The girl was standing a few feet away, on the edge of the green. She was about Harriet's height, her dark hair scraped back from a broad, cheerful face. Clever eyes. She was a little older than Harriet, perhaps fifteen. She wore a grey skirt and a white blouse with red collar.

'I came with my auntie,' Harriet said, feeling silly and young. 'We're on holiday.'

25

'All right for some,' the girl said, not unpleasantly.

Harriet did not know why she felt the need to explain herself. 'I was in hospital with diphtheria and my auntie said I needed to convalesce.' She took a bag of liquorice allsorts from her pocket and offered it. 'I'm not infectious.'

The girl searched through for her favourite, but not in an obvious way. It was one that Harriet didn't like, the flat liquorice covered with tiny pink sweet dots.

She popped it in her mouth. 'What's your name?'

'Harriet. What's yours?'

'Beth, Beth Young.'

Harriet did not say her last name. It was a cause for argument. Her mother had married Bob and wanted them all to have the same name. Harriet liked Bob, but she also liked her own name. So why don't I say it, she asked herself. It was in case she lost the argument, or gave in.

'When you came along in your motor, did you anywhere on your travels see a boy of thirteen, hair same colour as mine, a likeness to me, and as tall? He might have been walking along the road.'

'I don't think so.'

'Oh.'

'Who is he?'

'My brother. Him and me came here two weeks ago and they sent him to work on a farm. I was expecting him to be let off for the May Day celebration, but I don't think he'll come now.'

'Well where's the farm?'

'They say it's on the tops but I don't know where. I went looking, but I got lost.'

'Have you asked someone?'

26

'Aye, but they say he'll be settling in and leave him be.'
She sat down on the grass with a sigh. 'I've been standing up
all day, waiting to see him, looking up beyond the school,
watching for a figure coming down the track. And I don't
even know if he'd come that way.'

Harriet sat down beside her. 'Why were you brought
here, and where did you come from?'

'We come from Pendleton, in Lancashire. We were
fetched by the blacksmith on his cart.'

'Why?'

Beth stroked the grass, running her fingers back and
forth. 'Our mam died and our dad was away, so we were
packed off here for work. I'm a doffer in't mill.' She gave
a quick smile. 'I've made pals. They're off walking by't
river, or into Settle for first showing at picture house. But
I stopped here thinking Martin might turn up. Martin's my
brother.'

'It's sad that your mam died.'

Beth stopped stroking the grass. 'I know. It was appendicitis and they're supposed to be able to do summat about
it, if it's caught in time.' Her hand made a fist.

'My dad died.' It surprised Harriet to hear herself speak
those words because usually she could not say it. She had
never said it to the girls at the new school.

'When?'

'Three years ago.'

'So you were how old?'

'Ten.'

'I was fourteen when Mam died, just a month ago. I'm
fifteen now.' Beth spat on her hand and held it out.

Harriet spat on her hand. They shook.

'Which is your auntie?' Beth asked.

Kate looked towards the group at the far side of the green. 'She's there with that old gentleman and Mr and Mrs Whatyoumacallthem.'

'Trevelyans, from the big house.' Beth looked from the group to Harriet and back. 'She's very smart, your auntie. You look a bit like her.'

'Do I?'

'Yes you do.'

Harriet felt pleased. She wouldn't mind being like Auntie Kate, having nice clothes and a motorcar and looking into things. She wondered where the doctor had got to. Her mother had told her that Kate and the doctor were keen on each other and that it would be grand to have a doctor in the family. Harriet must give them time to themselves to do a bit of courting and get on with it. Harriet had not yet worked out how she was supposed to give them time. Go to her room, perhaps. That would be all right. She liked that room.

Beth narrowed her clever eyes and stared at Harriet. 'She's posh, your auntie, and she's with posh people.'

'But she's nice.'

'I'm not saying she int. You're alike, but you're different aren't you?'

Harriet was never quite sure what she was supposed to tell and what she should keep quiet about. Her mother had drilled her in what not to say, and now she could not quite remember. 'If in doubt, keep your trap shut,' her mother had instructed before she left. Harriet hardly knew this girl. Auntie Kate had said not to be blathering to all and sundry about her being a detective. But it wouldn't hurt, would it, to say that her aunt was adopted at birth and grown up in a very different better off family and that they had never met her until a few years ago? All the same, Harriet thought of something else. 'We lived in different places. My auntie was married to someone who didn't come back from the war. He would have been my Uncle Gerald.'

It did not really answer Beth's question but had the advantage of truth. Harriet also knew that it was searching for news of her husband who went missing in 1918 that turned Auntie Kate into a detective. She kept to herself that Kate had a 'mother' who was a lady and a high-ranking police officer father, even though Kate's real mother was Harriet's granny. The whole thing gave her a headache.

Fortunately, Beth was more interested in herself. She told Harriet about the small farm she once lived on and how her father always took it into his head to go travelling for work, leaving her mother, Beth and brother Martin to take care of the farm.

Beth looked so sad when she spoke about Martin. Kate almost said about Auntie Kate being a detective, but she held that back. 'If he hasn't turned up by tomorrow, your Martin, do you want me to help you look for him?'

Beth jumped to her feet and held out a hand to Harriet, pulling her up. 'Thanks, but I think he'll come tomorrow. I have a plan you see.'

Before Harriet could ask what kind of plan, Beth was walking them to the Village Institute. 'There's tea and buns, scones and all sorts, so we might as well. Mrs Holroyd is on't cake stall. She'll give us a couple of buns.'

'Who's Mrs Holroyd?'

'My landlady. I live in a house on New Street, opposite the washing green.'

'I'll tell my auntie where I'm going. She might worry if she can't see me.'

Harriet was glad that Auntie Kate excused herself from the group and came over to be with her, meaning that she did not have to barge in and interrupt. They moved across the green a little way.

'I've made friends with a girl called Beth and we're going into the Village Institute. Do you want to come? Beth's landlady, Mrs Holroyd, is in charge of tea and buns.'

'Mrs Holroyd?' Auntie Kate's eyes gave that sudden flicker that showed she had thought of some idea, but it was gone in an instant and another person might not have noticed. 'Yes I'll come with you.'

'What is it?' Harriet asked as they crossed the green. 'What did that old man want from you?'

'How do you know he wanted anything?'

'I could tell from the way he was looking at you and how you were talking.'

Harriet watched her auntie, wondering if she would tell her the truth. Kate put her head to one side. She's going to fob me off, Harriet thought.

'It seems my reputation arrived in Langcliffe before we did. Mr Wigglesworth wants me to look into something that happened in the village a long time ago, something bad.'

'How bad?'

'Very bad.'

'A murder?'

Her auntie's eyes widened, surprised by how quickly

Harriet had guessed. She came to a stop and said very firmly. 'Yes, it was a murder, but you and I don't have to think about it.'

Harriet felt a cold shiver as she remembered finding her dad's body in the quarry. She took a deep breath. 'You should investigate. I'll help you.'

Certain things must run in families, Harriet thought. Her dad had been a stonemason, like his uncle. As little as he was, Harriet's brother Austin wanted to be a stonemason, too. Harriet might be a detective. She would watch how her aunt did it. Harriet glanced across to the group that they had left. The old man, Mr Wigglesworth, stood alone. 'Don't turn round now, Auntie, but Mr Wigglesworth, is looking at us. Why is he so sad?'

'Perhaps he's just tired.'

'Who was murdered?'

'Harriet! Not so many questions.'

'I'm only asking. Who?'

'A Mr Holroyd.'

'That's why you looked interested when I said Mrs Holroyd was in charge of buns.'

'Yes.'

They set off walking again and reached the edge of the green. 'Does that mean we're investigating?'

'No! But it did cross my mind to have a tactful word with Mrs Holroyd, if she is the widow. She saw to the cleaning of Lilac Cottage and brought in our groceries, so I have a reason to speak to her, to say thank you.'

'And ask a few questions.'

'Possibly. You see, Harriet, there's never just one version of a story.'

'So we are investigating. I'll be your assistant. I'll take the place of Mr Sykes.'

At the door of the Village Institute, Harriet hesitated. 'Mr Sykes has a pair of handcuffs.'

'He does.'

'Do you think we ought to send to Leeds for the hand-cuffs?'

'I hope that won't be necessary.'

'But it would be handy to have them, just in case.'

Four

The Village Institute hummed with chatter. Excited children sat at trestle tables and under them. A toddler, happily amazed at the vastness of the space, tottered along the centre of the room drawing as much appreciation and admiration as a star stage performer.

Harriet's friend waved. She had secured a place at a table and indicated there was tea and a bun for Harriet. I went to meet her. A friendly girl, she got to her feet straight away. 'I'll fetch you a cake, Mrs Shackleton. What would you like?'

That would defeat my purpose. 'You sit down, Beth. Which is Mrs Holroyd?'

She pointed out a tall, thin woman, all angles and big pinafore, at a table near the wall, presiding over a tea urn.

Don't expect too much, I told myself. She won't talk about her tragedy to a total stranger. I would simply attempt to be on good terms. That would be a start.

Everything about Mrs Holroyd was severe. The set of her jaw, the unrelenting thickness of her dark straight eyebrows, the nose with flared nostrils, the tightly shut grey lips, dry

33

and with tiny white cracks. Yet she must have been attractive once, with her sharp cheekbones and thick hair braided and wound over her head.

I am five feet two inches and had to look up to her. 'Mrs Holroyd, how do you do. I'm Mrs Shackleton, staying at Lilac Cottage.'

'How do you do.'

'Thank you for getting in provisions for us.'

'It was no trouble. I sent my daily woman with a list.'

That put me in my place.

'Was it your daily who did such a fine job on the house?'

'She did her best. I went in only to inspect her work.' Her snort indicated she would rather not have set foot in the place. She picked up a thick cup. 'Tea?'

'Yes please.'

She placed the cup under the urn tap.

I took a plate and chose a bun. 'Did you bake these?'

'I did.'

'They look delicious.'

'That'll be tuppence.'

I paid her. Take the chance, Kate, I told myself. Break through her defences. 'I think I understand why Dr Simonson's request that you help with the house may not have been welcome.'

She put my pennies in the tin. 'I would always oblige Dr Simonson. He's a fine man and a good doctor.'

Foolishly, I pressed on, giving voice to what was unsaid. 'But Miss Simonson's house is not a place you would willingly set foot in. The doctor did not realise, being away at the time of that tragic event.'

Idiot! Why had I said that?

She twisted her mouth to the right and bit on her lower left lip. 'You know then.'

'Yes.'

'We don't talk about it.'

'Understandably.'

'Miss Simonson persisted in her delusion. She knew what she thought she saw. Without her testimony that man – I cannot say his name – would have pleaded guilty and spared me the ordeal of a trial.'

'I'm sorry to have brought it up.'

She looked across at Harriet and Beth. 'Is that girl yours?'

'She is my niece.'

'Tuppence for her tea and cake. Church funds.'

I slid a thrupenny bit across the counter. 'I'm glad to have met you, Mrs Holroyd.' And that was true. It reminded me that some you win, some you lose. This whole desperate business was not my concern.

That would have been enough. I should have turned away. Picking up my tea and plate, I looked at her again. I had caught Mrs Holroyd off guard. Was she hostile and angry because of that? Might I extend some olive branch that would allow me to speak to her again under more favourable circumstances?

She spoke first. 'If you're going to ask about that woman's clothes bursting out of the wardrobe, don't. I've a lot of time for Dr Simonson and I wouldn't want to hurt his feelings. But you might as well know I wouldn't touch his aunt's clothes with the washing pole. Don't you know what damage she did?'

She must have seen by my face that I was taken aback by her vehemence. I opened my mouth to speak, but she stopped my words with hers.

'I held my husband in my arms as his life ebbed out of him. That Fenian would have pleaded guilty if Miss High and Mighty hadn't stuck up for him. Sergeant Dobson as good as told me so. She wanted attention, that's all. Who was it she thought did the deed if not the man caught with the knife in his hand? I sat in that courtroom every day. And the worst day was when she spoke. The worst day of my life. It's unchristian to speak ill of the dead, but she was an old fool, a silly woman with too much imagination. No one in this village will ever forget. If you ask anyone what to do with her clothes, they'll tell you to keep them till Bonfire Night, dress Guy Fawkes in them and toss him on the fire. She poisoned this village, insinuating it was one of our own men that killed my husband.'

The venom in her voice made me feel sick. What had Freda Simonson felt if this was the general attitude of the villagers? How she must have suffered for her integrity, and alone, too. I imagined she had protected Lucian by not telling him about her ordeal, by tolerating the ostracism of the village without a murmur.

She was not my relation. I had not known Freda Simonson, and it was not up to me to defend her. I looked into Mrs Holroyd's eyes for a sprinkle of doubt, for a dash of compassion. Nothing. Hard, grey nothing.

Another villager was approaching, picking up a plate and doily. I spoke softly, but she heard. 'I expect Miss Simonson did what she thought right.'

*

After the excitement of the May Day celebrations, Harriet, Lucian and I shared a quiet supper. Harriet was pleased at having made a new friend.

She took herself off to bed early, saying she had to write her diary.

I went up to make sure she was comfortable and took her a cup of cocoa.

'Did you find out anything from Mrs Holroyd?' she asked.

'No. I didn't do very well at all.'

'There's plenty of time.' She took a sip of cocoa. 'We have two weeks. If I think of anything, I'll write it in my diary so I don't forget.'

Downstairs, Lucian had carried a shovelful of coal into the parlour. We sat on the sofa. He brought out the family albums, which I had asked to see.

For an hour or more, we pored over albums, looking at pictures of Lucian as a baby and toddler in India with his parents and his ayah, of the ship that brought him to England at the age of six, in the charge of a returning officer and his wife.

He and Freda had walked the hills and there were pictures of each of them, squinting into the sunlight, standing by a tarn, picnicking on a flat rock. Then there was Lucian at university, holding up his medical qualification and beaming into the camera.

When it grew dusk, he lit the gas light and tonged more coal onto the fire.

'She took a good picture, your aunt.'

'She did, in both senses – as a photographer and as a subject. It's odd looking at these now. She was thirty-four when she took me in, and she seemed so ancient.' He turned to a studio photograph of Freda, aged about nineteen, smartly dressed in black skirt and white blouse, a shorthand notebook in her hand.

'She was so proud of being a shorthand typist, and a good one. I never thought about it at the time, but she had given up her job to take care of her parents. Then I came along. By the time I was old enough for her to return to work, there was no job for her. Not until war broke out and she worked at the Town Hall in Settle, until the men came back.'

'I wish I had met her.'

'I'm sorry you didn't but she was very poorly towards the end, and not at all her old self in those last months.'

He sighed. In that moment I could see the little boy in him, the puzzled child sent on a long voyage away from everyone and everything he knew.

He returned the albums to the sideboard and took out two shoeboxes decorated with *découpage*, hats and gloves carefully cut from picture papers. The first box contained postcards, birthday and Christmas cards.

'I'm spreading out my life for you, Kate. Try not to yawn!'

'I love looking at histories trapped in shoe boxes.'

A second decorated box held maps of the local area and some drawings – very good drawings – by Lucian as a boy. I took out a map that would be useful for our walks.

He had not seen the plain box brought by Mr Wigglesworth. I wanted to mention it, but he was being quite restrained, unusually so. I realised that after his earlier confidences about our possible future in this house, he did not want me to feel pressure or obligation at being under his roof.

We sat side by side, feeling comfortable and quietly happy.

Finally, he stood up and stretched. 'I'd better be on my way or we'll be the subject of gossip.'

'That wouldn't do your reputation any good.'

He laughed. 'I know you're joking, but a doctor has to think about these things.'

At the door, he said, 'Did old Wigglesworth have much to say for himself?'

Now I had to tell him.

'He told me about the murder your aunt witnessed.'

'Oh. I wish he hadn't.'

'When were you going to tell me?'

'Not on your first day here.' He sighed. 'That whole business upset her greatly. Towards the end, she was supposed to be resting, but she would go to the window and look across, as if re-living that night. It was most distressing.'

'Lucian, what made you ask the murdered man's widow to see to Lilac Cottage and order groceries?'

He looked totally surprised. 'I'm not sure. I happened to bump into her. She's a stalwart of the church, Mrs Holroyd. She takes in lodgers that she prefers to call guests. I thought she might need the money.'

I did not have the heart to tell him how deeply Mrs Holroyd resented and detested Freda Simonson.

When I had waved Lucian off at the door, I went back into the parlour and put a log on the fire. The miners were on strike and I had not thought to ask Lucian how much coal there was in the cellar.

I lifted out the shoebox and sat on the floor where I would be able to spread out the papers. I had not previously noticed the writing on the lid. It was a quotation, but I could not place it.

A better lad, if things went right,
Than most that sleep outside.

There were newspaper cuttings; a coroner's letter demanding the attendance of Miss Freda Simonson at the inquest into the death of Rufus Charles Holroyd; what appeared to be Freda's hand-written witness statement; solicitor's letters, and a judge's summing up that had been typed. By whom, I wondered. And then I thought of the photograph of Freda with her shorthand notebook. Had she sat in the courtroom, taking down the judge's words? Or had she copied it from some newspaper?

There was enough here for me to reconstruct the trial. I hesitated. Now was not the time to look through these papers. But when would be the time?

The coroner's letter demanding Miss Simonson's attendance at the inquest was so formal that it read like a threat, giving a hint of what must have been a dreadful ordeal to follow.

Until late, I sat looking at the papers. There was the article from the *Craven Herald* giving an account of the 'Committal of Lime Kiln Worker for Murder at Langcliffe', stating that Joseph James Flaherty, a native of Dublin residing in Langcliffe and lately employed at the Hoffman Kiln, had been in custody since the sixth instant charged with the murder of Rufus Holroyd, a beer seller at Langcliffe. He was brought up before J Birkbeck, Esquire, Reverend H J Swale and H Christie, Esquire. The reporter rather sniffily commented on the proceedings being conducted behind closed doors, the public being excluded for reasons the reporter did not glean.

There were notes in two sets of writing. Freda's notes were in shorthand, with the occasional longhand word. I soon realised that the other person's hand must be Mr Wigglesworth's and that they attended the trial together. It all felt too much for me to make sense of, after today's long journey and the effort of being in a strange place.

I folded the sheets of paper, ready to return them to the shoebox. As I did so, I noticed that the bottom of the box was lined with thick crepe paper, and there was something under it.

I removed the crepe paper and took out two foolscap sheets filled with neat writing from a broad nib. The ink had turned brown. The passages, in the form of letters, had been written a year apart from each other over a period of ten years. Freda, showing her Yorkshire thrift and acknowledging the wartime shortage of paper, had left narrow spaces between each entry.

These were messages that would never be sent through the post. Each one was addressed to Joseph Flaherty.

It took me a moment to realise that her chosen day of writing to the man she had failed to save was each anniversary of his execution. Although the fire burned brightly, I felt a chill and reached for the shawl that was draped across the back of Freda's chair, and then I began to read.

41

Third Thursday in June 1916

Dear Joseph

It is now five minutes past that fateful hour. The terrible and unjust deed is done. I failed you in court. I failed today. I should have kept watch by the wall of Armley Gaol when you took your last steps on this earth. My friend Wiggy and your priest were there. They took the train to Leeds when I was too knotted with stomach cramps to leave the house. My body let me down. That long night I was on my knees, praying and doubled in pain. As if we have not wasted enough young lives with this war.

Third Thursday in June 1917

Dear Joseph

My nephew Lucian is home on leave. When I came home from work we sat in the garden. What he has seen and lived through I can only guess but when he looks at the anemones, snapdragons and marigolds, he is mesmerised into silence. He does not smile as often as he used to. When he does, the smile does not light his face. It hurts me to see him. When I ask what it was like over there, he names places and changes the subject. At least he is alive, I hear you say, if you could speak. When I told him about the murder, he showed no curiosity, as if it had happened centuries ago. A neighbour came apologising but asking him to examine her little boy who has broken out in spots. Thankfully it is not measles but a heat rash. The sun shines, just as if everything in life should be perfect. You must have been so hot working in those harsh conditions at the lime kiln. How I wish you worked there still.

Dear Joseph James

I have not forgotten you. You are in my thoughts and prayers.

An odd thing happened today. No one mentions you. On this day I do not go out and of course no one calls. But today someone did, and had such a pleasant and sympathetic visit with me that I wonder whether my friend Wiggy told him how I mark the day. It was Gabriel Cherry, whom I have known since he was a boy. He is on leave and brought a set of picture postcards of Arras. He said he appreciated my letters and the little oddments I send. The poor chap has no one else. I asked him if he would like to have Lucian's room but he says he will stay on the farm as the Gouthwaites need help. He brought a friendly little mongrel back from France and I have agreed to take care of Nipper until Gabriel comes home. Gabriel has always liked to read and I gave him the pick of books as Lucian said he would not read them again. He chose Treasure Island, Tom Sawyer and Huckleberry Finn. After visiting me he was going to see the gardener at Threlfall Hall whose son will not be coming home from the war. I wonder, would you have enlisted, or been called up? Gabriel is a corporal, a well-deserved promotion.

Dear Joseph

Wiggy came today. I am now surplus to requirements at the Town Hall and no longer have Nipper to walk because, mercifully, Gabriel Cherry came home in one piece. The days are long. Our nation has chosen its day of remembrance but Wiggy and I have this extra day that we must mark, your day, Joseph's Day. We walked by the Hoffman Kiln, once more fully fired like the furnaces of hell. From there we made our way along the riverside. Wiggy said, 'We are like the River Ribble, you and I. We flow in another direction.' Well why should a river not flow east to west as well as west to east?

Wiggy and your priest have become friendly, an odd pairing, atheist and believer. Father Hartley told him that your family will have masses said and make the Stations of the Cross to ensure your passage from purgatory to heaven. I asked how long that might take. Wiggy had asked the same question. The priest was not very forthcoming regarding Time. It might be a hundred thousand years or the twinkling of an eye. I prefer to think that you went straight to heaven, innocent and wronged as you are.

What would your life be like now, with the situation in Ireland such as it is?

Third Thursday in June 1920

Dear Joseph

I went to your church and lit a candle for you. Afterwards I sat with Wiggy in his shop and helped with tinctures.

Lucian finds it hard to settle. In spite of the injury to his leg, he is determined to keep up his walking and is off on some long hike today. He cannot ride his bike but says he might manage some kind of adapted motorbike. We will look into it. Sometimes it strikes me that the war was not against nations but against young men.

Third Thursday in June 1921

Dear Joe

Were you called Joe sometimes?

I am not forgotten by some of my neighbours for giving my evidence and trying to make the truth known. Today in the Village Institute preparations are in full swing for the summer fete but my services are not required.

Third Thursday in June 1922

Dear Joseph

Wiggy and I made a grand pilgrimage today. He is a great one for consulting Bradshaw. We managed all the connections to take us to Morecambe where we stood and looked across the Irish Sea and skimmed pebbles into the waves. The tide was so far out I thought we must have walked halfway to Ireland just to find the water's edge.

Third Thursday in June 1923

Hello Joe

You must have reached heaven by now. I refuse to believe otherwise.

Lucian is over at Bolton Abbey. After last year's mishaps it seems that those who matter are determined to have a doctor in the vicinity. Lucian has his eye on renting a property in Embsay where he might provide a surgery for the surrounding hamlets. Did you know that one of the Devonshires (they have the estate at Bolton Abbey) was murdered in Phoenix Park? He was not the intended target having gone to Dublin to Do The Right

Thing regarding the Irish Question. Is that not a tragic irony?

Third Thursday in June 1924

Dear Joseph

You would like Gabriel Cherry. I told you before that he visits me and the gardener at Threlfall Hall. Today I gave him more books. It does not surprise me that he likes Henty and Conan Doyle but I was surprised that he has taken a fancy to Jane Austen.

Third Thursday in June 1925

Dear Joseph

This will please you. It pleases me. Lucian has found a friend, a widow but still young. Her name is Catherine Shackleton. I like that name. When I am gone, this house will be Lucian's. She must want children and so must he though he gives no indication. I won't tell her about you straight away, not on first meeting, or she will think me strange. You are wondering why I should tell her about you at all, after all this time. She is a private investigator. Is it too much to hope that so far on, she might clear your name? If a soul can move from purgatory to heaven in a hundred thousand years or the twinkling of an eye, anything is possible.

If my plan to clear your name succeeds, Judge Mr Justice Pelham will eat his words, the jury will hang their heads in shame and angels wipe their tears.

I folded the letters away. What store Aunt Freda had set by me, expecting that I would find out who really did kill Rufus Holroyd. How I wished I had met Freda. She had almost six months of life left to her when she wrote that final note. I felt upset with Lucian that he had not told me she was ill and wanted to meet me. But perhaps he did not know. From the way she wrote, they had not been close to each other after he came back from the war. Yet I knew how fond he was of her.

I have had some strange requests for my professional services over the years but this was the first time the summons had arrived from beyond the grave. Would I take on the case, I asked myself, and if so how would I explain myself to Harriet and to Lucian?

If I did, it would have to wait. Nothing must be allowed to interfere with Harriet's recuperation.

It gave me a surprise to hear the volume of my sigh.

Later, in the bedroom that had been Aunt Freda's, I tried to sleep. Freda must have grown accustomed to sleepless nights during that desperate time. I could understand how the events of that evening gnawed away at her.

Sleep escaped me. There was not a sound to be heard in the village. Yet as I listened to the silence, I heard the faint rustle of wind down the chimney and the slight rattle of the window pane. The rattle took my attention. It was easier to blame the rattle for my sleeplessness than the unease of my mind and spirit.

Aunt Freda had made a list of the witnesses for the defence. There was herself, of course; Flaherty's parish priest; his foreman and workmates, including Matthew Walsh, the friend who was with Joseph on that fateful night.

47

Her papers included a note from Bradley Wigglesworth, signing himself Wiggy, arranging to travel into Leeds with Freda for the trial. If I were to re-investigate this murder, which was what Freda had hoped, I could do worse than talk to these people. Mr Wigglesworth had made it plain he wanted to talk to me. As for the others, I could not imagine they would welcome the subject being re-opened. Some of them may have died or moved away. My failure with Mrs Holroyd rankled, and so did her accusation against Freda. 'She was a silly woman with too much imagination.'

The window frame rattle grew more frequent. I looked in my bag for some card or paper to jam in the space between the window and the frame. The letter Lucian had sent to me giving directions for the journey to Langcliffe would do the trick.

A floorboard creaked as I went to the window. My eyes were drawn to that building, that former alehouse where Holroyd had been fatally stabbed. What a scene of horror Freda had witnessed a decade ago. Did she suffer nightmares ever after?

It was no use pretending I could ignore Aunt Freda's wish. No doubt this would be the wildest of goose chases and would make me permanently unwelcome in Langcliffe, but I must find out whether there truly had been a serious injustice done to Mr Flaherty.

I took out my writing case and, sitting at Freda's dressing table, wrote a note to Jim Sykes, telling him of Freda Simonson's cuttings, and her concern, and asking whether there was anything else he could uncover about the trial of Joseph James Flaherty at Leeds Assizes in June 1916.

As I sealed the envelope, the grandmother clock downstairs surprised me by beginning its midnight chime. When I looked out of the window a ghostly figure in white appeared from nowhere, crossed by the war memorial, and disappeared from view.

Five

Beth Young shivered. It was strange to be out when every-one else in the village slept. She chuckled to herself. If any curtain-twitcher caught sight of her crossing the village at dead of night in her long white nightgown and black shawl of invisibility, they would think a headless ghost walked through the village. They would tell the tale of her and create a new story, a legend for all time.

It had been her intention to stay awake until midnight. That didn't happen. After working at the mill Saturday morning, she had hung about at the Mayday celebrations into the evening, watching and waiting for Martin to come. After supper, she played cards with Mrs Holroyd and Madge.

Beth and Madge shared a big iron bed that put Beth in mind of a raft that would float away through the ceiling and sail to the stars as roof slates dissolved into air. Once she climbed into bed, she felt suddenly tired and knew she must shut her eyes just for a little while. Once settled, she banged her head on the pillow eleven-and-a-bit times, to be sure of waking before midnight.

'What you doing?' Madge asked.

'Reminding meself.'

'What about?'

'I forget.'

'You're mad, you.'

She opened her eyes just before the witching hour. In the moonlit room everything took on an air of strangeness. Beside her, Madge slept. Beth would have liked to tell her the Big Plan, but Madge would only blab and then all the girls at work would take the mickey. 'Beth and her magic. They hang witches, you know.'

On a night like this, witchery must work. Witches knew a thing or two. She once watched her mother empty a teapot on the grass and chant a wish, so there must be something in it but only a fool would let the world know what she was up to.

She slid from the bed. Quietly, she picked up her shawl, clogs and the bone-handled bag that contained all the paraphernalia she would need to cast her spell, and her dad's letter of course, which she carried about with her like a talisman. She reached her fingers into the bag and touched laurel leaves, lavender, rosemary and mistletoe. To give herself strength for the task in hand, she took out the rosemary, held it to her nostrils and breathed in. It was a sharp, no nonsense smell, clean and clear but with a terrible longing mixed in – a heartfelt longing for now to be then, when everything, which was never really all right, at least seemed to be.

Most of all, she wanted her mam back, longed for her, could barely believe that she was no longer here, even though Beth and Martin had watched the coffin swallowed into the earth.

It was no use wishing for her dad. He would come back when he was ready, and find everything changed, and his wife and children gone.

All she could do is what she would do. Find Martin. This coming morning, by fair means or foul, Beth would find her brother. At first, she had been persuaded to believe that it would be good for him to live on a hill farm. Surely to be on a farm, once again in the open air, with hens and pigs and plenty to eat, would suit him. It would not suit her, not now. The mill was to her liking. She chummed up easily with the other girls and women. They liked her face and that she had a bit of life in her and wasn't afraid to answer back. They were all in the same boat, ready for a laugh and a joke, and no going outdoors in all weathers.

All the women at the mill said the same thing. She should not be surprised if Martin didn't come to the village. He would be busy during lambing time. Young stock would be turned out for the first time. There'd be cows calving, grass to harrow, muck to spread. As if Beth didn't know all that.

The feeling that something was wrong had nibbled night after night into her sleep, causing bad dreams, even with the lavender under her pillow. He ought to have managed the May Day celebration. He ought to have managed church last Sunday.

With no work today, Sunday, she would make it her business to find him.

She decided against leaving the house in the usual manner. Mrs Holroyd slept in the kitchen alcove, her bed by the wall, claiming she never shut her eyes, never caught a wink these days. Beth could believe it for though Mrs Holroyd never spoke of the terrible thing, one of the girls at the mill had told her, having earwigged when her elders did their whispering. Mr Holroyd had been brutally murdered outside some alehouse by an Irishman, a wicked Fenian.

Beth could hear Mrs Holroyd snoring, but decided not to risk tiptoeing down the stairs.

The sash window rattled as she raised it. She put her clogs in the bag carefully so as not to crush her herbs, and then hung the handle over her wrist. Now to shimmy the drainpipe.

The windowsill looked wide until the moment she needed to swing her backside onto the sill, and then suddenly it seemed too narrow. It looked slippery from the rain. Balancing carefully, holding the bottom of the window frame, she reached for the iron drainpipe that was further off than she thought. Her legs still in the room, her bottom on the cold sill, she leaned, and reached. The drainpipe looked so solid but creaked and moved. One of the black nails attaching the pipe to the wall had come undone. This might be where she tumbled to her death.

If she fell, breaking a bone or cracking her head, who would find Martin? And who would pay her bed and board to Mrs Holroyd while she recovered? Sweet nobody. She would end up in the workhouse.

So she must not fall, must never fall. It was up to her. She would make sure she and Martin stayed hale and hearty until Dad returned to say he had found work. She would keep the promise to their mother.

That sliver of a moon would be her friend tonight, now that the rain had stopped and the sky turned clear.

She clutched the rocking drainpipe with both hands. Her

legs and feet dangled. She swayed and then swung a leg. Her thighs tightened on the pipe, her feet pedalled the wall. All was well. The drainpipe had agreed to help. Her mother must be looking down.

She slithered silently, passing the dark kitchen window. Her bare feet touching solid ground, she came into a crouch.

It was silly to bring her clogs. Putting them on would wake the wide world. She took them from the bag and set them by the door.

Mrs Holroyd's house stood square-on to the washing green. One of the wooden posts of the washing line leaned in her direction, making a courteous bow. She walked along the street, turning towards the centre of the village, not minding the hard touch of the cobblestones on the soles of her cold feet.

She glanced towards the three-storey workhouse building, where, a month ago, the horse and cart had brought them from the village of Pendleton to Langcliffe. No one had called the place they were taken to the workhouse but she knew right enough what it was. She was marked down for the cotton factory and lodgings with Mrs Holroyd, the tragic widow.

'It's lucky for you there's an opening at the mill here in Langcliffe,' the clerk in the stiff collar said to her when she signed her name. 'You've Mr Trevelyan of Threlfall Hall to thank for that. And it's lucky that you have the makings of a farmhand, my lad, and that a farmer is willing to give you work.'

This was to Martin who looked pleased. He wanted to leave school and now he could.

They were too strict in the mill these days, the clerk said, especially since that bad accident when the over-keen factory inspector put in an appearance and checked birth certificates. Otherwise Martin could have gone there.

Beth told the man that Martin should be at school. She felt her fists clenching tightly and wished for the man to say that Martin could stay at school for as long as possible, and that they would stay together. That he could also come and lodge at the same place.

The clerk adjusted his metal-rimmed spectacles that had broken and were held together with sticking plaster. 'He's near enough fourteen, and you're in farming country now.'

Beth and Martin exchanged a look. They had been in farming country before, but the less said the better. She could see that Martin was glad he would have a job.

'Now where's he going?' The clerk glanced at his note. Beth thought she saw something like dismay in his look. 'Ah.' He bit his lip. 'Well, it'll be a roof over your head.'

Beth conjured an odd picture in her mind's eye of Martin, standing on moorland, with a roof hovering above him and nothing else, no walls or doors. In her vision, his head was tilted to one side as he watched rain fall everywhere but on himself.

'Mam says we're to stay together, sir.' Beth reached out to touch Martin, but he moved himself just out of her reach. She explained to the man in the stiff collar that their dad had what he named 'ports of call' where he was given work, but it was in vain.

'Your father's on the tramp is he?' the man asked, getting it all wrong.

'He's not on the tramp. He has a skill and people pay

him. He'll be upset to come back and find Mam dead and buried and Martin and me sent away, but at least if we're together . . . '

The clerk had looked at her pityingly. His glance betrayed that he did not believe her dad would return. 'He hasn't left us.' She spoke as firmly as this strange situation would allow. 'He'll be back. He allus comes back.'

The clerk picked up a square of well-used blotting paper and pressed it cautiously onto the column where he had entered their names. 'Then it's lucky for you that in the meantime we in the good Parish of Langcliffe can give you a home.'

When he said that, she expected the farm was nearby. Only later did she learn that Langcliffe was a large parish including hills and dales and that the farm was some miles off. She waited until a sly-looking man came on a horse and cart to collect Martin. Martin suddenly seemed smaller, but he held his head high and said, 'So long for now,' and gave her a wink.

The man on the cart had a doleful look. He reminded Beth of the undertaker in Pendleton, a stillness about him. But this man had kind light blue eyes that belied his slyness. 'Come on, kid. You'll soon learn to be a farmer's lad.' He picked up Martin's bag with big swollen hands that were sore and marked. 'You'll be fattened up.'

When he said that, Martin looked at Beth. For a moment she thought they would both start to laugh. She used to tell him the story of Hansel and Gretel and the witch who fattened up children for the pot.

Beth took a few steps alongside the cart, telling Martin she would see him in church on Sunday. She said it more sternly than she meant, hoping to stiffen his backbone because neither of them had mixed with strangers until now.

Beth banished these thoughts from her mind as she walked barefoot through the deserted village, passing the fountain with the memorial stone cross inscribed with names of the village men who would never come home.

The trickle of the fountain broke the silence of the night. Somewhere not far off an owl hooted, searching for something to kill.

In the churchyard, the lozenge shape of the headstones made her feel the dead wanted to speak, offer advice, tell her the right words for the job in hand. Here was an old man who had lived over eighty years. Given half a chance, his corpse would rise and offer her a mint imperial.

She wished one of these was her mother's grave and then she could ask her what to do. But perhaps her mother was nearby in spirit, because Beth heard her voice. Find Martin.

'How am I to find him?'

No one answered, only the wind disturbing leaves on the yew tree, made a sound. A branch creaked. Leaves fluttered. They danced. That was what the leaves did, they danced and so must she. She shook off her shawl and draped it on a tombstone.

Everything she needed for her spell was in her bag: bay leaves for Martin, for victory and good fortune. Hawthorn to protect from harm. Lavender, always lavender to conjure the fulfilling of a promise. Mistletoe so as not to fail. Rosemary to bring good spirits to her aid. Thyme to ward off sorrow. Sage to speed his way. She hoped such abundance of herbs would not confuse the spirits.

The hem of her nightie was splashed by puddles. She hitched it up to her knees. Dip and scatter, dip and scatter herbs around the church porch, to make him come. From the porch, she danced, skipping and turning, spinning along the path.

Martin, Martin, hear my words and my calling song and come here this Sunday, dancing along, church spirits bring him to me. It's been two weeks since him I did see.

She hoped spirits did not object to poor rhymes.

Half dizzy she stopped by a grave as the apology for a moon slid behind a cloud before appearing once more and lighting the inscription on a nearby gravestone. This was the resting place of a boy, aged nine. There were other names, too, but it was only the boy aged nine that made her gulp for breath, let go her nightie, and stare as if this name held some message.

The little boy in this grave might be Martin's guide. 'Fetch him to me, sweet spirit, fetch him back. Someone is keeping him from me. Show him the way, or show me the way to him.'

She knew things in this place and understood that something felt deeply wrong, yet she could not put it into words. In the daytime, she had thought about how she might wangle Martin back to Langcliffe by finding someone to take him in, or speaking to the schoolteacher. But no one she spoke to saw her point of view. Mrs Holroyd said she had left school at twelve. Even Madge told Beth she should not make a baby of a big boy.

The spirits would understand. But would they like plain English? Probably not on the grounds of a lack of magic. They would prefer something witch-like, something that could be recognised as a proper spell.

Without effort, the spell came from her lips.

Hubble de bubble de, brother me here with me, clod a lee lotter lee, bringle him back to me, river run rapidly never turn back on me. Amen.

That was more like it.

Spell almost cast, she took the oak twig from her bag and the moss that had grown on the oak. She showed it to the boy under the earth.

Where shall I place it?

In the gateway, where the living come and go.

And so she did.

This is where you must come tomorrow, Martin. I'll be here, watching the day long, until you come.

She pictured him waking in the night to hear her. She pictured him at this gate, turning his head to look at her. She heard him say her name.

Work done, she left the churchyard as a cloud hid the moon.

By the fountain memorial she took the last of her herbs, shaking the dust and stalks from her bag and spreading them round the top of the little wall, patting them into place, watching the trickling water splash over them.

She circled the memorial three times, chanting.

Then came the rain, teeming in earnest, plastering her hair to her head, soaking her nightgown. Half blindly, she retraced her steps to the cottage.

A leak in the gutter by the drainpipe caused a whooshing flood of water to baptise her. The drainpipe was slippery and the rain beating down. Looking up she saw that Madge had closed the window. Madge! She should have looked and seen that the place in the bed beside her was empty.

Suddenly dizzy at the thought of the strength it would take her to push up the window while balancing on the sill and holding the drainpipe, she stood and stared.

As she looked up, she saw the window of the house next door open. A man's head appeared.

'Ye took yer time.' He peered across and saw the window was shut. He held up a hand to signal help, leaned halfway out the window and reached over. It did not work. He came out further. He would fall and hit his head and everyone would blame her and say what was she doing, standing there in her nightie in a pool of brains from the lodger next door.

But easy as anything, he pushed up her window and then went back inside his own. He watched as she climbed the drainpipe.

When she reached the window and climbed inside, she looked out. 'Thank you.'

He looked back. 'Ah sure it's no impediment. Goodnight and God bless, miss.'

An Irishman, like the Fenian who murdered Mr Holroyd. Mrs Holroyd would not like him being next door.

She hadn't meant to say it aloud. 'You're Irish.'

'Not a bit of it, miss. I put on the blarney, for a bit of a lark.'

He closed the window.

Leaning over the windowsill, Beth looked down, saw the dim outline of her clogs by the back step, and knew they would be full of rainwater.

As she closed her window, she realised that she had put down her bag and forgotten to pick it up. Someone would find it and read the letter written by her dad. They would link the herbs to her and know she had been casting spells in the churchyard. Her mother had warned her always to be careful of others' opinions. Women of Pendle had been hanged for casting spells.

Having felt so good about doing something definite, she now felt horribly miserable and low. People could do anything to you. Make you leave your farm, your home, separate you from your brother, take you to a mill to work forty-eight hours a week and think yourself lucky, legs and arms aching, and at night dreaming about bobbins of cotton, fluffs of cotton, clouds of cotton, mountains of cotton, filling your eyes and ears, threads of cotton, choking your throat and stopping your mouth.

Six

Harriet was sleeping when I went out for the Sunday papers and to post my note to Sykes, asking him to find out what he could about the trial of Joseph James Flaherty. On the way back, I spotted a black cat on the ground near the fountain war memorial. It lay very still. A stray cow galumphed towards the memorial but the cat did not move. My eyes had played tricks. Coming closer, I realised that the 'cat' was a black velvet bone-handled bag. I snatched the bag before the cow mistook it for fodder. After a polite, almost affectionate glance in my direction, the animal began to drink from the base of the fountain, sloppily and with great concentration.

Inside the sodden bag was a damp letter. The dust of herbs gave off a powerful scent of lavender intensified by rain, and the sharp sorrowful aroma of rosemary. Whoever dropped the bag had also sprinkled herbs around the fountain's ledge.

People do strange things. Perhaps the herbs were meant as an offering for the eleven men whose names were carved on the cross. Did the men know? Were they looking down and thinking, *Our loved ones remember us in such peculiar ways.*

It was early, and still raining. I decided to take the bag back to the house, dry it, and return it to its owner.

Stepping into the vestibule, I took off my mackintosh. By now the kettle had come to the boil and I made a pot of tea. There is something about being away from home that is very relaxing. Not only was the house without a telephone, but so was every other house in the village, excepting the post office and the police house. No one would disturb us here. This gave me a wonderful sense of freedom.

My assistant Jim Sykes and housekeeper Mrs Sugden were back in Leeds, taking care of any matters that might arise. Sykes was only too pleased to be left in charge of our current cases. Meanwhile Mrs Sugden had booked a seat on a mystery charabanc day trip, having arranged with a neighbour's boy, Thomas Tetley, to keep an eye on our cat, Sookie, who graciously tolerates Thomas's attentions.

I set the black velvet bag on the fireguard to dry and placed the damp envelope on the mantelshelf.

I carried my tea into the parlour where I sat in Aunt Freda's chair and turned the pages of the newspaper. It reported a rousing speech by Austen Chamberlain, on overcoming burdens, and difficult days. Enough of that. There were pictures from the Royal Academy exhibition. Not missing anything there then. Miners have walked out of their pits, refusing a cut in wages. Yesterday's news. I thought about Harriet's late father, Ethan, and how this walk-out would have brought him to his soapbox on behalf of the hardworking pitmen. There was an appeal for funds for Jane Austen's old school. If I'd ever thought about Jane

Austen's education, I would have guessed it to be undertaken at home.

I put down the paper and looked around the parlour. This was the room that Lucian thought might make a good consulting space.

On the walls were a couple of watercolour paintings of country scenes. On top of the piano was a Japanese vase. Bookcases contained volumes of Shakespeare and other English poets alongside Goethe and Schiller. Aunt Freda had been working on a tapestry when she died and there it was, an unfinished country scene. A tray sat on the sideboard, neatly set with a doily, delicate glasses and a decanter of sherry.

On the window ledge were a few ornaments that may have been given to Freda as presents, perhaps by Lucian. They looked the sorts of pieces that would be chosen by a child. One was a boy in blue playing a bugle, another a little shepherd boy with lambs, one black, one white.

Aunt Freda only had to look across to the window to bring back the memory of that night.

Freda's cuttings and account of events felt fresh and vivid in my thoughts. But the murder of Mr Holroyd and the conviction of Joseph James Flaherty had waited a decade. A few more weeks, months or years would not matter to Freda, at rest in the churchyard, or to Flaherty in his unquiet grave within the walls of Armley Gaol. Yet I knew with every fibre of my being that I would take on this case, futile as my efforts may prove. So I had decided. Why the sudden resolve continued to surprise me I could not say. Making notes about who to see should have given me a clue that I was hooked.

I looked again at my notes from last night.

The parish priest of St Mary and St Michael of Settle had given a character reference. He must have heard the condemned man's last confession. If Flaherty valued his immortal soul, he would have told the truth. Might I extract that truth from the priest somehow? Matthew Walsh, the workmate who stood by his friend, was he still employed at the Hoffman Kiln? It seemed to me suspicious that during the crucial moments, he was absent, and yet so sure of Flaherty's innocence. Mr Wigglesworth, Freda's apothecary friend, would be only too anxious to talk to me again. According to Freda's notes, they had travelled to Leeds together to be present at the Assize Court. For her own sanity, Mrs Holroyd must believe that the true culprit was executed for her husband's murder. But was there some titbit of information she did not know she had, something that might shed new light? Her husband may have had enemies.

Where I had failed with Mrs Holroyd, someone else may succeed.

Had the accused man compatriots to visit him, family over here to offer comfort, if there was comfort at such a time?

Upstairs, I heard Harriet moving about. She would be down shortly.

I closed the door on the parlour and made my way into the cellar for a couple of sausages and rashers of bacon.

Back in the kitchen, there was a basket of eggs on the dresser, and a solid-looking loaf of bread in the crock. Even all this time after the war, it seemed a privilege and a pleasure not to worry about shortages, at least here in the countryside.

Soon the bacon and sausages sizzled in the heavy frying pan. When the rashers crisped, I cracked two eggs. Perfect timing. Harriet sauntered in, dressed in her blue flowered frock, her long brown hair still in its bedtime plait. She is tall for her age, and swiftly becoming a young woman. I smiled at her and she smiled back. If I had anything to do with it her cheeks would turn rosy before the end of our stay.

'I thought we'd go to the church service, Harriet.'

She put knives and forks on the table. 'If you like.'

'Probably Susannah will be there.'

'Who?'

'You know, Mrs Trevelyan's daughter from Threlfall Hall. You were supposed to meet her yesterday.'

'Oh yes, I'd forgotten about her. I was thinking about our investigation. Did Dr Simonson know anything about it?'

'No and it might be best to keep it to ourselves for now, that we might look into it I mean. A country doctor wouldn't want to be classed as a busybody and since we are staying in his house, we must tread carefully.'

'I suppose so.' Harriet spotted the bone-handled bag which was now almost dry. 'Whose is that nice bag?'

'I found it by the war memorial when I went out earlier. There was a letter inside.'

'What did it say?'

'I don't know. One doesn't read other people's letters.' I took plates from the dresser. 'Oh cut us a couple of slices of bread, eh?'

She picked up the bag from the fireguard and sniffed. 'It smells of herbs.'

'The bread knife's in that top drawer.'

'Mam doesn't let me cut bread.'

'Just keep your fingers and thumbs out of the way of the knife.'

She looked at the envelope on the shelf. 'It's to a Mrs Young in Pendleton, Lancashire.' Cautiously, she put the bread on the board and picked up the knife as if it might bite. She cut a thick, jagged slice. 'Beth is from Pendleton and that must be her mother. But I don't know who would send Mrs Young a letter because she died of appendicitis.'

'How sad. When?'

'Recently, and people shouldn't die of that now, not in the twentieth century.'

I picked up the letter. The postmark was no longer legible. 'It's been opened, so someone has read it.'

'Beth probably. I'm glad you found it.'

I ladled the bacon, sausage and egg onto the plates. 'If that is Beth's bag, we may see her at church and give it back to her.'

Harriet's mood changed in an instant. Suddenly she was full of energy and joy. She wanted a friend of her own age. 'I'll be happy if we see her. Can she come on the picnic?'

'Of course.'

The rain had stopped. I opened the kitchen window to let out the smell of cooking. 'I do like this room, and looking out onto the garden.'

Harriet dipped bread in her egg. I cut into the sausage, hoping they were done all the way through.

Harriet frowned. 'But do you think this house . . . would you say it's a sad house?'

'I don't think so. It has stood empty for six months.

Perhaps it just needs people to be here for a little while.'

'Did Dr Simonson's Aunt Freda die here?'

'Yes, she died in the bedroom where I am. Does that upset you?'

'No. Everyone has to die somewhere. Probably there isn't a house in this village where someone hasn't died.'

The sadness was coming not from the house, but from Harriet, whose father did not die peacefully in his bed. I tried to lighten the mood. 'And I expect every house has had someone born in it too.'

Harriet smiled. 'I know. I have to cheer up. This is our holiday, to rest your brain.'

'I thought it was our holiday for your recovery. I didn't know my brain was tired, but now that you mention it . . .'

'Where will we go for our picnic? I want to try out that camera you gave me.'

'There are caves nearby.' I reached for Aunt Freda's map which I had opened at the path that led out of Langcliffe towards the caves. 'But you must tell me if you start to feel tired.'

'I'm not tired.' She looked over my shoulder at the map. 'I'd like to see caves.'

'Let's go to church first. You might see Beth and we can tell her about the bag.'

Harriet put down her knife and fork, forgetting the food on her plate. 'She might not want to come with us on the picnic. She's hoping her brother will turn up in the village today.'

'We'll see.'

'She thinks he'll come to church because everybody's supposed to be let off work on Sunday, aren't they?'

'I suppose so. But it may be that people on remote farms forget what day it is.'

The Neo-Gothic stone-built church of St John the Evangelist stood on the far side of the village green. With its modest grey slate roof it fitted perfectly in this workaday village. The iron gates stood open. People were already arriving in their Sunday best for the mid-morning service.

Inside, the church's stained-glass windows, lit by the sun, gave it a lovely brightness. The organist played some stirring but unfamiliar hymn to hurry people into the pews. There were the usual flags and banners that I came to hate so much in the aftermath of war when they had grown dusty, and the hymns of sacrifice and patriotism made me feel nauseous.

I led us to a pew near the front where we could see the pictures on the windows to either side of the sanctuary. One of them made me smile, thinking of Harriet recovering from her illness. It was the raising of Jairus's daughter, with the inscription, 'The maid is not dead, but sleepeth.'

When the service began, Harriet whispered, 'We should have sat at the back, then we would have seen who's here.'

'People will congregate outside afterwards.'

The vicar sped nicely through the service and then came to the pulpit. He was an elderly man with sparse hair, a fine girth and a booming voice.

He informed us that this was the fourth Sunday after Easter and the Epistle came from St James on the Life of Faith.

Harriet whispered, 'My dad didn't believe in any of this, you know. Do you?'

'Shhh.'

After the Epistle and Gospel, the vicar announced banns of marriage, looking directly at the people in the pew opposite ours, a middle-aged couple and the engaged couple, who exchanged a smile. In a sonorous voice, he said, 'I publish the banns of marriage between Derek Pickersgill of the Parish of Giggleswick and Jennifer Murgatroyd of this Parish. If any of you know cause or just impediment why these persons should not be joined together in Holy Matrimony, ye are to declare it. This is for the first time of asking.'

It had never struck me before that there was a similarity between this announcement and the patter of an auctioneer. Going once, going twice, gone to the couple in the second pew.

Having completed that little bit of business, the vicar's manner changed in an instant. With a solemn glance, taking in the entire congregation, he straightened his cassock, and adopted a stern countenance, waiting as though expecting some culprit to own up in advance of an as yet unspecified charge. 'Some person, no doubt some young female buoyed up with May fever, has strewn herbs in the church porch, along the path and on the hallowed ground of the churchyard. This person or persons caused the verger the extra work of sweeping. I am told our sacred war memorial is now also littered with herbs.' He paused, his glance lighting on a small group of girls who wore bright bonnets trimmed with cotton flowers, and in his view the likely culprits. 'Pagan practices will not be tolerated in this parish.'

Seamlessly, having made his remonstrance, the vicar began a sermon about certain pagan practices that had been swallowed by Christianity, and how Christianity would always prevail.

Given that the bag smelling of herbs belonged to Beth Young, and had been found at a scene of the 'crime' –herbs strewn around the war memorial – I guessed that the vicar had picked the wrong culprits. If anyone had cast spells, it was likely to be Beth, trying to conjure her brother.

The final hymn was 'Father, hear the prayer we offer'. Harriet did not sing. It struck me that this was an appropriate hymn for the place we were in. It spoke of green pastures, rugged pathways, still waters and rocks along the way.

When we left the church, Harriet glanced about her, looking for Beth.

She spotted her new friend, standing sentry on the edge of the village green. I gave Harriet the bag with the letter inside. 'It must be hers, Harriet. But don't give it to her straight away, just in case. Ask if she's lost something.'

Harriet nodded sagely. 'I suppose a detective shouldn't take anything for granted.'

A small group had gathered by the church door and were chatting to the young couple whose banns had been read.

After a few moments, Harriet came back. 'It is her bag. She was hoping Martin would have come to the service. He's at that farm she told me about, somewhere up on the hills. She doesn't know where. She hasn't seen him for two weeks.'

'It is lambing time. Farmers are very busy at this time of year.'

'Yes but she has this bad feeling, and he's younger than she is.'

'How old is he?'

'Thirteen. They've never been apart before. It's not fair, Auntie. If it was our Austin, I'd be frantic.'

'Then if she's worried, we must do something to help. His name's Martin you say?'

'Martin Young.'

'Take Beth back to the house. She can sit on our wall and look out for him. You get a picnic ready.'

'What are you going to do?'

'I'll speak to Mrs Trevelyan. Mr Trevelyan will know where the boy is, and if he doesn't know he'll be able to find out.'

'Is anyone else coming with us on the picnic?'

'No. Who were you thinking of?'

'Dr Simonson.'

'Not today. He's helping to set up a photographic exhibition in Settle. We'll explore on our own.'

'So Beth can come?'

'Yes, I said so. If the farm where her brother works is not too great a distance, we'll go there and seek him.'

I walked to where Mrs Trevelyan stood, at a little distance from her husband who was talking to two men by the side of the porch.

'Mrs Shackleton! There you are.'

'Mrs Trevelyan, just the person I want to see.' It was the wrong thing to have said. She looked happy at my words, as if no one ever did or ever had wanted to see her.

'That's nice.' She glanced across at the betrothed couple. 'I was just congratulating Jennifer and Derek. They're here with his parents to listen to the marriage banns.'

There was something in the way she said 'his parents' that

made me curious. I felt I was supposed to enquire about the bride's parents. I hoped it would not be some story of a terrible tragedy. 'And her parents?' I asked politely.

She mouthed rather than spoke. 'Not here.' She edged me away to the other side of the porch, saying in a rather public voice how lovely it would be for the village to have a May wedding, and so near Empire Day. When we were safely out of hearing, she spoke in a low voice. 'Between you, me and the gatepost, Mr Murgatroyd is not happy at the match. He would have preferred his daughter to marry a young farmer. A trainee solicitor will be no help at Catrigg Farm, but I did think Mrs Murgatroyd would have put in an appearance.'

'Speaking of farms,' I said, as if we had been speaking of farms, 'something has come up regarding a girl who works at the mill. Harriet chatted to her yesterday.'

'I saw them together. The girl from Pendleton?'

'Yes. Her name is Beth Young. She was hoping to see her brother who works on a nearby farm, but she does not know which one.'

'Oh, yes, he was sent up to Raistrick Farm. I don't suppose you know it?'

'No, but I have the ordnance survey map.'

'It's about five miles north as the crow flies. Are you thinking of going there?'

'It would be a destination. We're to take a picnic. Perhaps Susannah would like to come?'

'If she feels up to it.' Mrs Trevelyan glanced about. 'Oh dear, she's done it again. Slipped away. She'll have her nose in a book by now.'

'Another time then.'

'Your best way to Raistrick Farm is to go via Stainforth. There's a track leads up from there. It's farmed by the Gouthwaites.' She frowned. 'They are not the most hospitable people.' She looked as though she might say more but thought better of it.

'We won't trouble them for hospitality but it would set Beth's mind at rest if she knows her brother is safe and sound.'

'You're very kind, Mrs Shackleton. And I suppose this kind of thing is second nature to you, given your line of work.'

There it was again, for the second time. She had referred to my work yesterday. This time, I did not let the remark pass. 'Was it Dr Simonson who told you I am a private investigator?'

'No. Dr Simonson is discretion itself. Word went round the area when you were over at Bolton Abbey not so very long ago.'

'Ah, yes.'

She glanced about, and drew me a few yards away from the porch, out of hearing of those dawdlers just leaving the church. 'The thing is, Mrs Shackleton, I have a rather awkward situation that I need to discuss and I don't know where to turn.' She smiled as she spoke. Anyone observing us would think we were discussing the weather. 'This is a terrible imposition, but we did get on so well at the New Year dinner dance for Skipton Hospital.'

'It was a lovely evening.'

'I feel we have a certain . . . well, we can trust each other I hope.'

'Yes of course.'

'I wish to consult you in a professional capacity.'

My first instinct was to say no, because this was a holiday, away from all responsibilities except that of taking care of Harriet. But of course I did not say no. I hesitated.

She took advantage of the pause. 'We can't speak here. The vicar will pounce at any moment. He comes back with us for sherry and lunch. Might you call tomorrow for a private word?'

'I'm sorry, Mrs Trevelyan, but I'm here for Harriet's sake. She is convalescing and I do need to take care of her.'

It was best not to mention that I also needed to keep an eye on her. She can be too independent for her own good.

Mrs Trevelyan was not ready to throw in the towel. 'Bring your niece with you. Let me give you lunch. Susannah will show Harriet the garden.'

'I can't promise to help you.'

The vicar came beaming towards us. As I was introduced, I hoped he at least would not have some private matter to discuss with me. After less than twenty-four hours, I had been swept up in Aunt Freda's guilt and pity regarding the condemned Irishman and the murdered alehouse keeper and offered to help a mill girl locate her young brother. That was plenty to be going on with.

I excused myself as soon as politely possible.

Mrs Trevelyan called after me. 'Till tomorrow! About noon?'

My only consolation as I walked away, defeated, was that Harriet would meet a girl of her own age. I hoped that she and Susannah would take to each other.

Slowly, I made my way back towards Lilac Cottage. When I found myself outside the former alehouse, I looked down, half expecting to see a bloodstain. Mercifully, the pavement was clear and clean. Even being in possession of the facts, it was difficult to believe that a murder took place in this peaceful setting. The shock of witnessing such a dreadful act might easily make the mind play tricks. Perhaps Aunt Freda was mistaken when she believed some sinister figure wielded the knife and ran away.

I arrived at the cottage gate at the same moment as Beth Young. She wore a black skirt and cream blouse dotted with forget-me-nots. Her eyes sparkled with excitement at the prospect of a motorcar ride. She was swinging a dark blue bonnet by its ribbons.

'I just went to tell Mrs Holroyd that if our Martin comes when I'm out looking for him, she must tell him to wait. And look what she lent me. This is a motoring bonnet. I can't wait for Martin to see me in this.'

Harriet was standing in the doorway. 'If my auntie and me can't find him, no one can.'

Her confidence made me uneasy. I remembered the way Mrs Trevelyan had frowned when she told me the name of the farmer and it struck me as odd that a young lad had not been allowed to come to the village on May Day, lambing time or no. According to Harriet, Beth had a 'bad feeling' about her brother. I knew from experience that such forebodings often turned out to be justified.

Seven

I had spread Aunt Freda's map on the kitchen table and traced the route to Raistrick Farm with my finger, trying to commit it to memory. Harriet's new friend, Beth, seemed a sharp, clever girl but her eyes glazed over as she looked at the map.

Harriet wrapped cheese sandwiches in a teacloth. 'Where is this farm then?'

'Here.' I pointed to Raistrick Farm. 'We'll drive through the village of Stainforth and then follow this lane. It's not the first farm, but the second.'

Harriet put the sandwiches in the wicker picnic basket. She pulled a face. 'What kind of name is that? Goat Lane!'

'Probably named because it's steep and would take a goat to climb it. First it's Goat Lane, then Silverdale Lane.'

Beth put one forefinger on the farm and the other on the village. 'Here, to here. How do you know it's steep?'

'These wavy lines tell you the height above sea level.'

'But we can do it?'

'I hope so.'

Harriet came to look. 'Auntie, it's miles away. How

could they take Martin so far from Beth? That's cruel!'

'No, look at the scale. It's about four miles, that's all.'

Harriet lost interest in the map, corked the bottle of cold tea and put it in the basket.

Beth traced a line. 'What are Shake Holes?'

'Nothing terrible. Just dips in the ground.' I pretended greater confidence than I felt. This trek up a narrow lane with the possibility of rolling boulders, holes in the ground and stray cattle was not what I'd had in mind at all. My plan had been for a gentle stroll up to the caves just above Langcliffe. That would have to wait for another day.

Harriet added slices of currant cake to the picnic basket. She fastened the straps.

'Everybody ready?' I picked up my motoring coat. 'Ready for our big adventure?'

Beth put on her bonnet, tying the bow carefully. Harriet preferred a silk square fastened under her chin. She took some persuading to put on her coat. I found a chunky Fair Isle jumper of Aunt Freda's for Beth. 'It'll be cold when we climb the hills.'

Because it was Beth's first time in a motorcar, Harriet insisted that she sit in the front beside me, while Harriet took the dickey seat and held onto the picnic basket. I always enjoy taking someone out for a ride for a first time. As we set off, Beth became absolutely quiet, looking about her, sitting up straight, storing up memories.

The way to Stainforth was quite straightforward, the road running parallel to the railway line. When we heard a train, both girls turned to look. Although the trees and bushes between us and the line must have prevented any passengers from seeing them, the girls waved energetically until the train overtook us.

Having got the knack of navigating, Harriet called out when she saw the turn-off to Stainforth. We entered the village, which like Langcliffe was built of the local stone. At the sound of the motor, people came to their windows to look. We passed the Craven Heifer where, according to Lucian, the landlord pulled a good pint.

Hills edged closer. Lucian had told me how he used to climb as a lad, Penn-y-ghent, Ingleborough and Whernside, sketching flowers and rocks, and wondering whether he might become an explorer.

As we left Stainforth behind, the lane became narrower and bumpy. The dry stone walls were perfectly done, like elaborate puzzles with each stone in place. I marvelled at the prodigious amount of time, effort and skill that had gone into the building of these walls. Without mortar to hold the stones, they withstood winds, rain and snow, built by men who had long since found their resting place in the earth. Their descendants had replaced stones that fell and kept the walls in good repair.

Beyond the walls, sheep grazed in the meadows, a few black sheep and lambs among the white. Lambs turned to look at us. One was black and white and would make a wonderful photograph. I would like to have stopped and encouraged Harriet to take her first picture, but it would be best to press on, find the boy, and put Beth's mind at rest.

Beth called out when she saw a farmhouse and barns.

'That's not the one, Beth. Raistrick is further on. We just keep going.'

'Well I wish it was this one. He'd be nearer and I could walk to see him.'

As we left the first farm behind, the walls became a little more dilapidated. Stones had fallen and not been replaced. There was a gap in the wall. Sheep had wandered through onto the lane, reluctant to move, and I had to edge my way among them, inching forward.

The wind rose. On our left was a tall structure, a little like the remains of a windmill.

'What's that?' Harriet shouted to be heard above the wind and the sound of the motor.

Beth answered. 'It's a lime kiln. There are big lime kilns near the mill but before they were built there were all sorts of little ones round about. That's what the foreman said. He was trying to scare us, saying how dangerous everything is – the potholes and caves, the old quarries and disused mines. I think he says it so we'll stay near the mill and not use up our energy walking about the moorland.'

A half-open broken gate hung off its hinges. A small herd of bullocks crowded together beyond the gate. The solitary bull, tormented by flies, flicked its tail in irritation. For one anxious moment I thought the monster-sized creature might pick a fight with the car, but it merely tossed its head and pawed the ground as if rehearsing a coming engagement with a matador.

I drove into the farmyard across deep ruts. My poor Jowett would need a good wash after this journey. 'Will you two wait here, while I go and enquire?'

Too late. Beth was already out of the motor, her clogs squelching into mud.

'We'll come with you, Auntie,' Harriet said, quite

unnecessarily because they were already leading the way to the farmhouse door.

I picked my way carefully but not very successfully around the puddles.

I knocked on the door.

No one answered.

I knocked again.

'Who's knocking?' It was a gruff male voice.

'A visitor, Mrs Shackleton.'

'Who?'

'Shackleton.'

'What?'

I pushed open the door a little way, to be greeted by a smell of bacon and stale tobacco. I peered in. The kitchen table was piled with dishes. A horsehair sofa stood sideways-on to the range where a fire blazed. On it was a man in his fifties. Everything about him was, like the broken gate, undone. He was unshaven, shirt unbuttoned, and topped by a moth-eaten woolly waistcoat. He wore old tweed trousers. One trouser leg had been slit top to bottom. His leg was bandaged.

'May I come in?' I took a few more steps into the room.

He glared. 'Thah's in already, and uninvited.' He sat very straight for such a slovenly man and I realised that a padded splint had been applied to his leg, reaching from his buttock to the heel.

Not wanting to appear to stare, I glanced away. On one side of the hearth was a smashed teapot, tea leaves spread out from it. On the other side was a basket where a tiny lamb slept on a blanket. The entire kitchen was in a state of disarray, not just untidiness, but squalor.

'Excuse me. I'm sorry to disturb you. Mr Gouthwaite?'

'Who are you?'

'My name is Mrs Shackleton. I'm staying in the village.'

'Have you come to buy milk, eggs, piece of beef?'

'No.'

'Then sod off. I don't give directions to trespassers.'

Charming! Mrs Trevelyan had said he was not hospitable. The man was downright rude.

I was close enough now to see that the bandaging on his leg had been skilfully applied, with triangular bandages above and below the knee.

A pair of crutches lay within his reach, one along the back of the horsehair sofa and the other propped against the sofa's arm. Reassuring. He wouldn't be able to fight back if I hit him on the head with his crutch.

Sweetly reasonable, that would be my response. 'I'm a friend of the Young family, in the area for a short stay. I wonder if Martin is nearby to say hello.'

'No he's not.'

'Do you know where he is?'

'I do not.'

'But he does work for you.'

'Not any more he doesn't.'

'I should like to see him.'

'Aye and so would I.' He reached for the nearest crutch, and waved it as if challenging me to a duel.

'Is Martin on the farm somewhere?'

'I've no knowing where he be. I can tell you he did me this damage.' He pointed to his leg. 'He's a vicious lad. If I never see him again it'll be too soon.'

'What happened?'

'What happened? What happened is that he set about me, tried to kill me, turned violent.'

I was suddenly aware of someone behind me. Beth had been listening. In a flash, she stepped forward, her cheeks flaming. 'Martin wouldn't hurt no one. What have you done to him?'

He stared in disbelief. 'Is she yours?'

'Beth, leave this to me.'

She was shaking.

The man growled. 'I did nowt. I could bring a charge against him. If it hadn't been for my farmhand Gabriel who fixed this leg, I'd be in hospital mithering doctors and running up bills that Master Martin Young would spend his life paying off.'

'He wouldn't cause trouble. He never causes trouble.'

'Beth!' I should have made them stay in the car.

The man's nose twitched in anger. 'Are you calling me a liar? He tried to do me in. Put me out of action at lambing time.'

Beth stiffened with rage. She rushed towards him. 'What have you done to my brother?'

'Beth, leave this to me.' I put my arm around her, as much to keep her under control as to comfort her. 'Mr Gouthwaite, Martin's sister is naturally upset. If Martin isn't on the farm, where is he?'

'I don't know and I care less.'

'He was in your care, and he is a minor.'

'Then let him descend into a pit and stay there. I won't have him back.'

'When did this happen, this altercation between you and Martin?'

Gouthwaite stared at me and then at Beth. He put a hand on his injured knee, as if to protect it. 'Yesterday. He was after the easy life, wanting to run off to the village when we're up to us elbows in newborns.'

Beth was ready to start again, to explode. He realised it and reached for the crutch that was balanced on the back of the sofa. It fell to the floor.

We were getting nowhere. 'Very well, I'll make enquiries elsewhere.'

'You can enquire till you're blue in't face.'

I took out my card and offered it to him. He did not take it.

'I'm staying in Langcliffe, in the house that belonged to Miss Simonson. If you hear news . . .'

'I don't want no news of him.'

'The boy is thirteen and a newcomer. I shall notify Mr Trevelyan and the local constabulary. I regard his going missing as a matter of urgency.'

'You can regard it as what you like.' He leaned forward.

I moved towards the door, having no wish to try and pick him up if he fell. 'You must send word if you hear anything.'

'Send you word? You send me word. I'll have the law on him for assault and battery.'

I stared at his injured leg. 'Be careful, Mr Gouthwaite. If you fall again you might do further damage to your knee.'

'I've all't advice I need about that from Gabriel Cherry who was a stretcher bearer in't war so you can keep your sneck out.'

I took Beth's hand. 'Come on, Beth. We'll find Martin, don't you worry.'

As we left the house, he called after me, 'Don't go pestering Selina or the men.'

Harriet had been listening from the doorway. Her face was white, her fists clenched. 'I'm glad he has a broken leg. What a horrible man.'

'Harriet, take Beth back to the car. I'll find someone else to ask.' I glanced about at the outbuildings. There were a couple of barns, a pigsty, a hen hutch. There must be someone else about who might be keeping Martin out of sight until the fuss died down. 'I'll find Mrs Gouthwaite. She'll be more reasonable.'

Harriet's look was full of doubt and concern. I had done the wrong thing in bringing the girls here. This convalescing holiday was taking an unexpected and unwelcome turn.

'Do as I say, go back to the car. I'll be with you shortly.'

Harriet took Beth's arm. 'Come on, Beth. Let Auntie Kate sort them out. She'll get to the bottom of it.'

The first barn contained bales of hay and farm machinery. A ladder led up to a storage area.

'Martin! If you're hiding, it's safe to come out. Beth is here.'

There was no reply. I listened for a movement, in case someone came from the upper area of the barn, to peer down. Nothing. No one.

Noises from the second barn that I approached were both animal and human, a cow's moo and a woman's moan of effort.

This outbuilding was more ramshackle than the last, the kind of place that could not make up its mind whether it was to store broken bits of farm equipment or to house animals. There were bales of hay and two stalls. A broken-down cart stood between me and the stalls so that I had to walk past it to see where the sounds came from.

In one of the stalls a cow was in labour. A big, sturdy woman, leaning in towards it, seemed almost part of the animal, somehow entangled with it. She had her hand inside the creature and was moving, talking, murmuring to it. This must be Selina Gouthwaite, whom I had been warned not to pester. As I watched, a calf's head appeared, bloody from the womb, and then the rest of it, wobbling out, swaying unsteadily, dizzily, onto its feet.

The woman leaned back. She was crouching. She too began to sway as if in time with the movement of the calf. Pins had fallen from her hair and long grey, greasy strands of hair lay over her shoulder. It was such an intimate moment that I felt embarrassed to be there and wanted to turn and go but, rooted the spot, I kept on watching. She brought her sleeve to her nose and wiped it, speaking gently to the cow. 'I'm weary as you, old girl.'

Perhaps I made some sound, but she suddenly became aware of my presence and turned, looking at me, making me feel that one of us was not quite real, an apparition, and that might be me. Only the woman, the cow and the calf were real: bloody, snotty, each complaining in their own way.

Finally she spoke, not to ask me who I was or why I was nosing about. She wiped her hands on an old cloth. 'Well that's done. Another life in't world.'

Selina Gouthwaite was overworked and tired. It was for her that politicians made rousing speeches about overcoming burdens and difficult days. But I doubted Mrs Gouthwaite ever read the words of Austen Chamberlain.

'I'm very sorry to disturb you, Mrs Gouthwaite. You have your hands full.'

It was a ridiculous thing to say. Her hands rested on her thighs. She leaned back against the wall of the stall, exhausted, not speaking.

I stepped closer. 'I'm here about Martin.'

The cow began to lick its calf. Mrs Gouthwaite rose to her feet, keeping her back to the wall. 'Martin.'

'Yes, your farm lad, Martin Young. I'm looking for him.'

She sighed, lifted her pinafore and wiped her eyes. 'Who might you be?'

'A friend of his family. Kate Shackleton's my name. I'm concerned about Martin, and sorry your husband was injured.' I added this for good measure, hoping to have her on my side in the matter.

'What did Abner tell you?'

'It seems they came to blows, and Martin ran off.'

'Aye that's it. The lad got the wrong end of the stick.'

The word stick came out harshly. I thought of a walking stick and that the boy must have been fighting back, warding off a beating.

'When you say the wrong end of the stick, do you mean Martin misunderstood something, or that your husband was chastising him and he resisted?'

'Don't be questioning me. I'm weary. Whatever Abner says is right.'

'Do you know where Martin may have gone?'

She turned back to the cow and its calf and gave the cow a pat, speaking softly. The calf was suckling.

She stepped out from the stall and came towards me, a tall, big-boned woman, her shoulders stooped, yet she could not be much more than thirty-five. Her cheeks were weathered, and lined with tiny veins. 'Martin ran off. For all he knew, he'd left Abner for dead, lying in the mud.'

'What happened?'

'I wasn't here. The lad wanted to be away. He had it in his head that May Day's a holiday. There's no holiday when you've animals to care for.'

'When was this?'

'Well yesterday, May Day, when do you think?'

'He hasn't been seen in the village.'

She shrugged. 'He's a big lad.'

'He's a child.'

'Big enough to send Abner sprawling. Happen he's gone back where he came from. All he'd have to do is follow the Ribble and he'll be back where he belongs, in Lancashire. They can keep him.'

'He may be afraid, because of having hurt Abner.'

'So he should be.'

'Is there anywhere he might be hiding?'

'Why would I know? Lads run off. That's what they do.'

'Might any of your other workers know where he may have gone?'

She shrugged.

I persisted. 'What about Gabriel, who bandaged your husband's leg?'

She looked defiant, as if being criticised for home doctoring. 'Gabriel was a stretcher-bearer in't war. There's not much he dunt know about injury.'

'Might I speak to him? Perhaps he has some idea where Martin may have gone.'

'You don't need my permission. He's out working't sheep. Seek him out.'

'And is there anywhere you can think of where Martin might go, a den, a favourite spot?'

'He wasn't here long enough for favourite spots. Folk hide best in full view. Try Catrigg Farm. They could use a lad, they was after having him. They've more land, better pasture. If we had that, we'd thrive as well as them Murgatroyds. Happen he's got his feet under their table, and is scoffing them out of house and home.'

'Thank you.'

I left the barn. She followed.

Without another word, Selina Gouthwaite walked back towards the farmhouse with heavy tread, as though weary enough to fall asleep standing. I remembered the feeling, from when I had been nursing all night and felt ready to drop, and I sympathised.

Back at the car, Beth looked at me, full of expectation.

'She doesn't know where Martin is, Beth, but don't worry. We'll go on looking.'

'What do we do now?' Harriet asked.

'Leave this farm and enquire at the one we passed earlier.'

I dreaded to think what kind of welcome we would meet there. This was a different race of people. We had entered a hostile land.

Eight

High spirits fled. The mood in the car had flattened. Both girls were silent after the encounter with Abner Gouthwaite.

There was something slightly ridiculous in this venture, a woman and two girls scouring unfamiliar countryside for a runaway boy who knew very well where to find his sister if he chose so to do, and for a farm labourer, Gabriel, who might be able to tell us something.

The most sensible idea was to head for the farm we passed earlier and enquire there. Martin Young must have slept somewhere. If I were a boy on the run, I would prefer a farm building to laying down my head on some grassy bank, especially with the amount of rocks around here.

Plenty of sheep took an interest in us as I drove back along the lane, but no humans came into view. On the short journey between the two farms, Harriet looked to the right and Beth to the left, hoping to spot some person who might have seen Martin, but without success.

I brought the car to a stop a few yards from the entrance to Catrigg Farm whose wooden nameplate was nailed to the five-bar gate. Unlike the previous gate, this one was attached to the post, and bolted.

'You two girls wait here this time. I won't be long.'

I let myself in, shutting the gate firmly. Noisy hens showed a particular interest in me. The farmhouse was a little way off, just visible between several buildings. This looked promising. Perhaps Martin had found refuge here, either by invitation or stealth. I was tempted to go into each building and call his name but it would be better to enquire first and enlist the family's help.

I passed two structures and came level with a third, a shippon with the door standing open. I paused, and listened, hearing the mooing of cows, but also a young female voice singing 'Greensleeves'.

Gentle splashing sounds accompanied by singing gave me an odd feeling of having stepped into another world.

I looked inside and saw a young woman seated on a three-legged stool next to a cow, her face resting sideways against the creature. She wore a floral frock, a large pinafore, a hood and pattens over her shoes. Milk squirted from her fists into a pail below. I had stepped into a Thomas Hardy novel, with musical accompaniment.

She was the young woman whose banns were read in church this morning. What was her name? Murgatroyd, that was it. Jennifer Murgatroyd. It was the same print frock she wore at church but she had discarded her bonnet for the hood. The cow turned to look at me, a pretty animal with dainty horns.

I ducked out of sight, thinking that the cow might stop yielding, through bovine embarrassment.

After a few moments, Jennifer patted the cow, rose,

picked up the stool in one hand and the pail in the other.

When she had tipped the milk into a churn, I spoke.

'Miss Murgatroyd!'

She gave a small cry of surprise and then turned to face me.

'I startled you. I'm sorry. It is Miss Murgatroyd?'

She gave a tentative smile. 'Yes, that's me.'

'I was in church this morning and heard your banns.'

'Oh, thank you.'

She seemed suddenly shy, so I encouraged her. 'Such a lovely morning for your banns.'

'Yes.'

'I should introduce myself. I'm Mrs Shackleton, staying in Langcliffe.'

We were still speaking across a wide space. Now she came towards me. 'How do you do. I saw you talking to Mrs Trevelyan and I heard you are staying at Lilac Cottage.'

'With my niece, Harriet. I don't like to bother you but I wonder if you might be able to help me.'

'Are you lost?'

'No. I'm taking Harriet and a girl from the village on a picnic.'

'You should go to Catrigg Force, that's a lovely spot and popular for picnics.'

'Thanks for the suggestion, but first of all we're looking for the girl's brother. She's Beth Young and works in the mill. Her brother Martin was working at the farm up the road, until yesterday. I don't suppose you've seen him?'

'No. I've been staying in Settle at my fiancé's house. Mrs Pickersgill has baked the wedding cake and made my dress, you see, so there has been a lot to do.'

'That must have been enjoyable.'

'Yes. Mrs Pickersgill is very good. Mother has been that busy with lambing and doesn't have time. I suppose we should have done it all sooner.'

'Well you have another three weeks. You have the cake, the dress and the fiancé, that's the main part seen to.'

She smiled. 'I hope so.' She turned back to the cows, telling them she would let them out soon.

'Might I look round the outbuildings to see if Martin is hiding here? It's worrying because he is only thirteen. And perhaps then I could talk to your parents. They may have seen him.'

'I'll look round out here. You wouldn't know where to start or where to look. I do know about Martin working for the Gouthwaites, poor lamb.' We stepped out into the sunshine.

She waved towards the house. 'You go speak to Mam. Dad's in bed poorly. I couldn't understand why they weren't in church to hear my banns. They said they would be, even though it's lambing time. But Dad took sick.'

'I'm sorry to hear that. What's wrong?'

'Oh just overwork I suppose and a tummy upset. Mam said to let him rest so I haven't seen him. We're short-handed. That's why I'm doing the milking.' She paused and waved her hand in the direction of the farmhouse. 'Just knock on the door and go in. It'll be all right. I have to turn out the cows but I'll take a quick look round for Martin first.'

'Thanks then.'

She smiled.

Her smile was infectious. I smiled back as the hens spotted her and came clustering round.

Just knock on the door and go in, she had said. I knocked and waited. No one answered. I knocked again, and stepped inside. The kitchen, with its spotless surfaces and shining brasses, was deserted. I called out hello. A baby lamb lay curled on the hearth in an apple box lined with a strip of blanket. A ginger cat, lying on top of the lamb, looked up at me with big marmalade eyes. Deciding I was no threat and of no account, it shut its eyes.

Footsteps sounded on the stairs. A door opened.

The woman who stood there was an older version of Jennifer, with a broad, pretty face and bright blue eyes. We took a few steps towards each other.

'I'm sorry to disturb you, Mrs Murgatroyd. Jennifer said to come in as I wanted to ask you something.'

She stared at me as if she had not understood a word. She came to a halt by a bentwood chair and gripped the wooden back with her hands so hard that her knuckles turned white.

'It's nothing terrible. I just wanted to know whether you'd seen the lad from the farm up the lane.'

'Oh.' Her mouth opened a little. She tilted her head to one side. Was there something wrong with the woman, I wondered. Perhaps she was the one who was sick.

'Is something the matter, Mrs Murgatroyd? Jennifer said your husband is unwell. You probably don't need any help, but I did nurse during the war.' I thought about Harriet, ready for her picnic lunch, and hoped this would not take long.

She bit her lip. 'I wondered when someone would come. I thought the future in-laws might come back after church, but they've better things to do than muddy their shoes.'

'What's wrong?'

'You're a nurse you say?'

'Yes.'

'Will you come upstairs? It's my husband.'

I followed her up the creaking stairs. The landing floor was uneven, with bumps and dips, the floorboards having made their own decisions over the years about what was a good shape to take.

She led me through a door into a bedroom at the front of the house. This, too, had uneven floorboards that were spread with a sheepskin rug. A four-poster bed dominated the room. Mrs Murgatroyd gently moved her husband's arm which lay on top of the eiderdown. She lifted back the bedcovers, revealing a sleeping figure. He faced us, away from the direction of the light, lying on his right side, his knees drawn up. He wore long underpants and a striped shirt. At first, he looked as though he slept but there was no rise and fall. He was curiously still.

Mrs Murgatroyd sat down on the bed. She took his hand. There was no movement, no flicker of the closed eyelids. Gently as I could, I took his hand from hers and felt for a pulse. She already knew the outcome. The hand was as cold as any stone.

'I'm so sorry, Mrs Murgatroyd.'

'It's true isn't it?'

'Yes.'

She began to weep, flinging herself onto his body, sobbing. 'What were you thinking of to go dying, you daft beggar. You've no business dying.' She shook him. 'Do you hear me?'

I held her by the shoulders and led her to a raffia chair. 'He can't hear you now, Mrs Murgatroyd.' A stupid thing to say. 'He looks peaceful.' A second stupid thing to say.

She stayed in the chair where I had placed her while I lifted the blanket and eiderdown over his body. 'When did he die?'

'I don't know. What kind of wife doesn't see her husband is dead, but thinks he's sleeping?'

'I might have thought that, too.' Lie. How could she not know? It must be shock, or denial.

'I didn't realise how bad he was. I thought I was letting him sleep this morning. I didn't tell the men. I knew my mister here would say, Let them get on with their jobs. I did everything meself, thinking I was doing him good to let him rest, and that when he woke, he'd be his old self. But he won't.'

'No.' I murmured the reply under my breath, because no answer was required.

'I can't tell our Jenny. She's come back that full of her-self and delighted about the wedding dress and the cake, telling me how the villagers were full of congratulations over the banns.' A slight note of bitterness crept into her voice. 'And what a marvel her future mother-in-law is, and how in Settle the sun shines out of everybody's backside. I couldn't burst her bubble.'

'Has Mr Murgatroyd been ill?'

'He's never ill. He took a bit poorly last night, but it was summat and nowt. Or at least I thought it was summat and nowt, and so did he. We're not used to being poorly.'

'Mrs Murgatroyd, I'm so sorry. What a most horrible shock.' I almost put my hand on her shoulder, but did not.

It would be too familiar, too intrusive. 'Let's go down-stairs.'

She nodded. 'I have to tell her.'

'Yes, and the men, and the doctor.'

'Nay, doctor's no use now.'

'Let me make you a cup of tea.'

This time, I led the way.

The kettle was on the hob, boiling. I spotted a brown teapot on the table. 'You sit down. Tell me where's the caddy and the cups.'

'There – on the side.'

I took down the caddy and spooned tea into the pot. The shelf above was packed with home remedies, in bottles and jars. Had he dosed himself with something and had a bad reaction?

Minutes ticked by as I made the tea. I remembered Harriet and Beth waiting patiently outside. Beth would imagine I was finding information about her brother. It would be too much to hope that Jennifer had found Martin hiding in a barn.

I spooned three sugars into a cup, poured in the milk, gave the tea in the pot a couple of stirs. When it was strong enough, I poured.

'Take a good drink. You need the sweetness for your shock.'

She picked up the cup and drank.

'I'll find Jenny and send her to you.'

She shook her head. 'No!'

'Mrs Murgatroyd, it must be done. One of your men must go into Settle for the doctor.'

She gulped and then played with the handle of the cup, as

if testing whether it might come off in her hand. 'He came in feeling sick. When he vomited, I thought he'd fetched up whatever ailed him and he'd be better for a rest.'

'Is there someone you can send for?'

She was not hearing me, but speaking half to herself as if explanations might bring him back. 'He felt sick and dizzy, he complained he wasn't seeing right.' She tapped her chest. 'He felt right fluttery. I made him get himself into bed and take a drop of morphia. I took up hot water bottles and a mustard plaster for his tummy. I thought that'd ease him, that and a dose of laudanum. He said if he could sleep a little he'd be all right. So I left him in peace.' She began to cry. 'Peace, call it peace. Forever peace.'

'I'll go fetch Jennifer.'

'Jenny?' She spoke more to herself than to me. 'What's to be done? What will we do without him? She loves her dad.'

I squeezed her hand. This was no time for words, at least none that I could think of.

I left the farmhouse, to find Jenny. She saw me first. That smile again. 'Martin isn't in any of the barns. I'll ask the men to look out for him.'

'Are any of the men nearby?'

She shook her head. 'Out in the fields, seeing to the sheep.'

So there was no one to go for the doctor. 'Jenny, I'm going now but your mother wants you.'

'Oh all right. Had she seen the boy?'

'I didn't ask, but don't worry about that. I'm sure he'll turn up.' She would have plenty else to think about now.

'Did Mam say what she wants me for?'

'She'll tell you.'

Something in my voice alerted her. I felt I had to warn her. 'You'll need to be strong to hear what your mother has to say.'

'What . . . ?' The smile faded.

'I'm going to Settle. You won't be alone long, you and your mother. Go to her.'

'But . . . '

'I can't say more. I'm very sorry.'

All colour fled from her face. She hurried towards the house.

Harriet and Beth watched eagerly as I arrived back at the car.

'Any luck?' Beth looked up hopefully. 'You were a long time.'

'He's not there, but there's no reason to believe he's come to harm.'

Harriet wasn't fooled by my soothing words. 'What's the matter, Auntie?' She looked pale and wan.

'Are you all right, Harriet?'

'I'll be all right when we have our picnic.'

'Have something now.'

'No! We have to do it properly. Find a good spot.'

'We're near a lovely waterfall that Dr Simonson told me about and Jennifer Murgatroyd just mentioned. It's called Catrigg Foss or Force.'

Beth cheered up. 'I've heard of it. The foreman from the mill goes there sometimes with his family.'

I unfolded Aunt Freda's map. It was a little awkward but I spread it on the bonnet, and looked for the area I wanted. We were very close to the waterfall. At the same time, I tried to work out how long it would take to drive to Settle for Lucian. Poor Mr Murgatroyd would be going nowhere. It seemed callous to leave Mrs Murgatroyd and Jennifer alone any longer than necessary but my duty was to Harriet who needed my care. She should eat little and often and it had been hours since breakfast.

I closed the map, making a bit of a mess of the folding. Harriet reached out and took it from me. 'I'll do that.'

I started the motor and drove back along narrow Goat Lane in the direction of Stainforth. The waterfall was just outside the village. Lucian had mentioned a gate and a narrow footpath. I stopped the car near the gate. The water-fall was accessible only on foot.

Harriet stood up and looked around. 'Where's this waterfall then?'

'Listen and we might hear it. There's a footpath. Come on, I'll show you.'

I carried the picnic basket. Harriet took the blanket.

Beth picked her way down the path, calling back to us. 'We might see Martin. He'll think it's such a surprise to see me with a new friend and an auntie with a motorcar, and sandwiches.'

She spoke so cheerfully that I encouraged her, to keep up her spirits. 'Yes, wouldn't it be good to bump into him without even trying.'

'But we are trying, aren't we?'

'Of course we are.'

Without the noise of the car's engine, the place was still, its silence broken only by the call of a curlew and the grow-ing sound of rushing water. We descended on rough and crooked limestone steps towards the waterfall. I trod carefully, watching the girls bound ahead, stopping myself from calling out that they should be careful on this steep and stony path.

The sound of the falls grew louder. The girls had stepped onto enormous limestone slabs and were walking to where the water teemed over high rocks.

Harriet looked all around her. 'It's so lovely here, and peaceful, like a secret grotto, but wild as well. This is perfect.'

Beth laughed. 'What a racket that water makes. It makes a whisperer of the mill pond.'

I joined them and looked down. The view was dizzying. Catrigg Force was an apt name. The sheer drop into the river took my breath away and made me anxious that the girls go no closer to the edge. There was no one else here. A popular picnic spot, Jenny Murgatroyd had said. Well, not today.

Beth had taken the picnic rug and was looking for a good spot.

Harriet stood beside me. We were standing on massive uneven slabs that had been here since the ice age. She said quietly, 'What's the matter? What happened in the farmhouse that you stayed so long? I saw you in the yard, talking to the girl who was in church this morning.'

'I'll tell you later. You need to eat something.'

'Tell me now. I'm your assistant aren't I?'

I glanced across at Beth who had taken off her shoes and socks.

Harriet followed my glance. 'I won't tell her. She's not curious, except about her brother.'

I could not pretend nothing had happened, or lie to her.

'The farmer died during the night. His wife didn't realise, and no one has gone for a doctor. After our picnic, we'll go to Settle and report the death. All the men are out on the hills, with the sheep.'

'You want to go now don't you?'

'No! I want to see you eat something, enjoy the fresh air, and have a rest.'

'You go. We'll save some food.'

'I don't want to leave you.'

'Honestly, Auntie! We're not kids. She's fifteen and you know you can trust me.'

'If I do, you must promise to be careful. Don't go too close to the edge of the falls.'

My thoughts of this holiday being 'educational' returned to mock me as I half-recalled titbits about strong white limestone, weak grey limestone, Stainforth Beck and the River Ribble that runs west into Lancashire. The girls would not be interested in a geology lecture but just in enjoying the afternoon.

I opened my satchel and took out the camera I had bought for Harriet. 'This is for you. You've seen how I use mine, and there are instructions. You can take a picture of each other, and of the waterfall, as long you don't go too close to the edge.'

'Oh thanks, Auntie Kate! And you'll go to Settle.'

'Yes.'

'I'll tell Beth you're enquiring there, about Martin. And if you do enquire, then I won't be a liar.'

'All right, just be careful. Now let me see you eat and drink something before I go, and aren't you glad you put on your coat?'

'I'm not cold.'

The two of them sat down. When I had watched Harriet make a sandwich with a slice of chicken and take a few sips of cold tea, I went back to the path. I turned and waved, and then the girls were out of sight.

It was as I drove along the road from Stainforth to Settle that my confidence suddenly fled. What if I had a crash on the way back and the girls became lost trying to find their way to the village? What if some marauding lunatic who had done away with young Martin lay in wait to murder his sister and her new friend? The murderer of Langcliffe Parish who had lain low for a decade now prepared to strike again. How would I explain to Mary Jane if Harriet went tumbling to her death in this supposedly idyllic spot? I should have known better than to leave them.

Too late. The die was cast.

Nine

Harriet loved the sound of the rushing water. Here at Catrigg Force she felt cut off from the world. They had left behind what didn't matter so much. Here was a magic grotto, a secret place where if you listened carefully you might hear a message murmured by the waterfall, blown through clouds and leaves. Who might whistle to her on the wind from another place, another time?

As well as cheese sandwiches, Harriet had packed bread cakes, already buttered, and passed one to Beth. 'There's sliced chicken in the wax paper.'

She told Beth that Auntie Kate had gone to Settle and would enquire about Martin while she was there.

Beth opened her bread cake and made a sandwich with a slice of chicken. This was a treat. A big treat. She wanted Martin here, and her mam who never would be, and her dad who sometime might be.

'Is your auntie really a detective?' Beth bit into her sandwich.

Harriet wished she hadn't told her. She must remember to be more careful.

'Yes. She finds people.' Just in time, Harriet stopped herself from adding 'alive or dead'.

'How do you become a detective?'

Perhaps Beth was more curious than Harriet gave her credit for.

'Oh it's a bit complicated. You have to learn to do it. You have to ask questions, stand up to bullies.' She decided not to mention the assistant who carried handcuffs.

'What kind of questions?'

'It's to do with being logical.' Harriet studied her sandwich. 'There are right ways of going about everything. For instance, if you butter a piece of bread in the middle that leaves the crust dry. If you butter the bread near the crust, the middle takes care of itself.'

'Who buttered this bread cake?'

'I did.'

'You missed the edge.'

'That just proves what I say is true.'

The light changed as moving clouds shifted shadows. Stripes of sunshine and shade made a dappled pattern on Beth's arm. 'So these questions, if we ask them, you and me, who are we supposed to question? What if they say shut up, mind your own business?'

Harriet knew that people were quite likely to say just that, and worse. 'Whatever anyone says, a detective has to persist. "Little pigs should be seen and not heard," they might say that.'

'They better not say that to me because I'm grown up and go to work.'

Harriet unwrapped the currant cake. 'About the questions, you go by Rudyard Kipling.' She put the cake between them.

'What does Rudyard Kipling have to do with it?'

Slice of cake in hand, Harriet stood. She took a deep breath and began to recite. 'I have six honest serving men. They taught me all I knew. Their names are What and Why and When and How and Where and Who. Those are the questions. The rest of the rhyme isn't important.'

'Where what, who what, why what?' Beth asked.

'Good afternoon, young ladies!'

The deep voice startled Harriet into dropping her slice of currant cake. They had been so absorbed as not to hear the man who now stood so close that his shadow fell across Beth.

Both girls stared. He was weather-beaten, the colour of an acorn. He wore corduroy trousers, a striped shirt and a belted plaid like a Highlander.

'Did I startle thee?'

'Aye, you did.' Beth looked up at him. 'How did you know we were here?'

He took a child's telescope from his pocket. 'Best tanner I ever spent. I see when a sheep's in trouble. I see when there's strangers roundabout.' He offered the telescope to Beth. 'Take a look-see.'

His hands were swollen and full of little marks, not like real hands. Beth had seen these hands before.

Beth took the telescope. 'It was you. You were the one took my brother away on a cart when we came to Langcliffe.'

'I did. And now you're seeking him. I know you're Beth because he talked about you. I'm Gabriel, Gabriel Cherry.'

Beth put the telescope to her eye and looked across the stretch of rock and the torrent that raged between here and the other side of the waterfall. She looked all along the opposite bank. 'Have you seen Martin? Do you know where he is?' She handed the telescope to Harriet.

The man scratched his ear. 'Not since yesterday when he cracked old Gouthwaite's leg.'

Harriet did not look through the spy glass Beth had handed her. She wanted to be alert, and watch this fellow. There was no knowing who you could trust. She could outrun him if it came to that. She glared at Beth, trying to tell her to stand up and be ready to flee, but Beth seemed not to cotton on that this man might pose a threat. Harriet could see Beth's brain working as she thought what questions to ask.

Beth did not ask a question but said, 'Martin didn't come into the village last weekend, all last week or yesterday which was May Day, when everybody came.'

The man bobbed down on his haunches, close to Beth. 'A week's a long time when you're young. But he's a canny lad. He can stick up for himself.'

'It's been a fortnight, and he's little.'

'He's wiry, quick enough to trip up a big 'un, and that's what he did.'

'How do you mean?'

'I spied what went on. Your lad was walking along the lane. Up comes Farmer Gouthwaite waving his arms, shouting the odds like he's auctioning off a herd of Ayrshires. Farmer Gouthwaite speaks. Lad speaks. Farmer Gouthwaite has a stick and lays into him summat cruel.'

Beth let out a small yell.

'Nay lass, fret not. Lad tries to fight back but Farmer Gouthwaite has a bit of weight in his arm. Knocks him down. Lad goes for Gouthwaite's ankle, heaves it, sends him flying. Gouthwaite doesn't move. Lad stands and looks, comes a bit closer, bobs down, and I'm saying to meself, Don't be tricked lad, take to your heels. But Gouthwaite still doesn't move. Then the lad runs.'

'Towards the village?'

'No. Across country. He could've ended up here, that's my guess. See yon, where a fire was lit?' He pointed across to the other bank.

Perhaps he was not an enemy, but you never could tell. Harriet relented. She looked through the telescope at where the man pointed. She saw a ring of stones on the opposite bank where someone had lit a fire.

When the man knew both girls had seen the remains of the fire, he said, 'See this is how I reckon. Lad thought he'd killed the old beggar, that's why he ran off. Where would you camp out if needs be?' He did not wait for an answer. 'Where there's water and shelter.'

'That fire could have been lit ages ago.' Harriet was still not entirely sure about this Gabriel Cherry. What kind of name was that any road? He could be spinning a yarn. Some folk reckon to know everything under the sun, to make themselves important.

'That ring of ash wasn't there last time I looked, which was Friday. I come by this way because the trees hide my view. See down there?' He pointed to where water was still, a great calm pool beyond the waterfall. 'We wash the sheep there, so they remember this spot. They sometimes come here. In lambing time, you have to know all the places to look for 'em.'

'But he didn't kill the farmer.' Harriet picked up the currant cake she had dropped and took a good bite.

'He wasn't to know that. He wasn't to know that Gouthwaite had to drag hisself along the ground. I went to help the old so-and-so. I set his leg for him' The man looked into the picnic basket.

Harriet cautiously offered him a cheese sandwich.

He thanked her.

The girls watched him, as if this strange man might have a different way of eating to other people.

He savoured his mouthful. 'This cheese comes from Murgatroyds' farm. You made a good choice.' He sat down. For several minutes they all watched the water and listened, as if under the spell of some powerful hypnotist.

As he ate, he turned to Beth. 'He's a good little worker, thy brother, even though he's an incomer. He limed the old pasture off his own bat. I saw him do it.'

Beth pushed back a strand of hair. 'Then why didn't that man, Farmer Gouthwaite, let him have May Day afternoon off?'

Gabriel shrugged. 'Gouthwaite's a disagreeable old beggar. You wouldn't mind but him and her are incomers themselves. Allus hardest on whoever comes after.'

Trying to retrieve her exalted position as niece of the detective, Harriet asked where else Martin might have gone into hiding. What would be the best places to look?

There were too many places, Gabriel told her, and this time of year a handy lad turning up on a farm and offering his services would be bound to find himself engaged to help with the lambing.

He narrowed his eyes and looked from one to the other. 'When I saw thee from a distance I thought at first one of you was someone else. I wanted to see thee safe.'

Beth frowned. 'I need to find Martin. If you spied us, you can spy him can't you?'

'I'll keep a lookout.'

'If you see him, tell him to come to Mrs Holroyd's opposite the washing green. Or he could come and find me at the mill on my dinner break at twelve. I'm a doffer there, half past seven in't morning till half five. When we have us dinner break, I sit outside.'

He nodded. 'Aye.'

Not to be outdone, Harriet joined in. 'If you see him during the day, tell him to come to Lilac Cottage and let himself in by the back gate. I'll leave some grub in the shed in case we're not in.'

'Will you look for him?' Beth asked.

'I can't go searching when there's work to be done but if I see him, I'll catch him up.' He adjusted the faded plaid cloak on his shoulder. 'Pity the plaid's gone out of fashion. He could have done with an item like this to cover himself at night.'

Harriet looked at Beth and saw that it hurt her to think of Martin out in the open. Cold. Hungry. She wished the man had not reminded them that Martin might be in a poor way. To stop Beth dwelling on the thought, Harriet said, 'Is that why you wear it? To cover yourself at night?'

He smiled, showing white, even teeth. 'Many a Dalesman wore the plaid once upon a time. Not now.' He fingered his cloak. 'The colour's all gone. Dull as dishwater now.'

He sighed and walked away, as quietly as he had come.

When he had gone, Harriet closed the picnic basket. 'Martin thought he'd killed the farmer, so he ran away.'

'Why didn't he come to me?'

'He didn't want to bring you trouble.'

'That might explain it. But it leaves me worried. If he thinks he's a murderer, a fugitive, fleeing from justice, he could turn desperate. We had a story like that read to us at school.'

'He might not have gone far. We could leave messages on trees or something.'

Beth pulled up a stalk of grass, peeled off the outer layer and put the stalk in her mouth. 'He could've gone far. He could've gone a long way off. And what's he eating?'

'He'll find eggs and things. But why do you think he might've gone far?'

'What if he jumped on a train? He could be anywhere.'

'He wouldn't go without telling you, would he?'

'I'm not sure. You see, my dad is one for taking off. It's what he's always done. We had a farm, a small farm. For months at a time, Dad would do everything right, and then he'd take it into his head to go off. We didn't know when he'd come home. He left Mam and us to get on with things.'

'Where did he go?'

'He went wherever the yen took him. His other work is as a travelling slaughterman. He kills pigs and castrates beasts. He likes to travel about, oh all over the place, a little pack on his back and his knives on a belt at his waist. Then he'll come back and just act as if he's never been away.' She pulled at another blade of grass. 'That letter to Mam that was in the bag your auntie found, did you read it?'

'No!' Harriet was indignant. 'One mustn't read other people's letters.'

'Well I had to read it, because by the time it came, Mam

111

had died. I showed the letter to Mr Herbert who owned our farm. I said Dad would soon be back, and not to turn us off. He was very nice about it, but said he had to terminate the lease and put in new tenants. He was sorry, but claimed it was the best thing, because of me and Martin being old enough for work. We should start again in a new place. When Dad did decide to come home, Mr Herbert would tell him where we were, and make sure he came to see us. Mam was buried in a guinea grave because Mr Herbert was very fond of her, so at least her name will be on the stone. We were brought over here on a cart by the blacksmith. He has a grand horse called Pluto. Everyone was kind. He said it wasn't so far from Pendleton to Langcliffe Parish, only they had a different colour rose over this way, the white rose of Yorkshire, and not the red. I didn't mind coming here because Dad came here once to do some work for the farmers.'

'Did your dad always tell you where he'd been?'

'No, but I remember Langcliffe only because he was upset about it. He lost a good knife here. I heard him telling Mam.'

'Well then he'll know his way.'

'He will, but I'm wondering if Dad and Martin are peas in a pod. Martin enjoyed the journey over here on the cart. Is he going to turn out like Dad, a bolting horse, always making off? I'll feel so lonely if it's just to be me.'

'If Martin was going to be a bolter, he wouldn't have been so determined to defy Farmer Gouthwaite and set off for the village to see you yesterday – only yesterday.'

Harriet's words did the trick. Beth looked a little happier. But Harriet thought of the landscape roundabout them:

112

quarries, old mine shafts, disused kilns, deep caves and places where a boy might hide, and might lose himself in darkness, in death.

She stood a little too close to the edge of the jagged limestone rocks and looked into the raging torrent below. Something bad could happen so very easily.

Beth began to pack up the picnic hamper. She fastened the straps and then came to stand beside Harriet, too close to the edge.

'If that was his fire, how did he come to be on the other side of this ravine, and how could we find our way across?' Beth asked.

'I don't know.'

'If Gabriel Cherry is right and Martin was over there, he might come back to this spot. I want to leave him a message.' She glanced right and left, at the torrent of water, at the still pool. 'Do you think I could jump it?'

'No. And where the sheep were dipped, it's too steep to climb down from here. There'll be another way round.'

'I suppose so.'

'Martin will turn up. And so will your dad, once he knows where you are.' Harriet did not sound convincing even to herself, but Beth did not notice.

'I hope so.'

'Why wouldn't he?'

Beth sighed. 'I wish they'd sent us to Settle instead. Anywhere but Langcliffe.'

'Why?'

'I don't think I'm supposed to say. But it was a long time ago. I'd only just started school. I heard Mam and Dad talking, like I told you, about the knife. He said he'd never

113

come back this way.' She picked up a pebble and threw it into the water below.

'Didn't he like it here?'

'He said something bad happened and he had to come home without his knife, but worse than that.'

'Couldn't he afford a new knife?'

'It wasn't just to do with the knife. It was something to do with murder.'

Ten

It is a short drive along the road from Stainforth to Settle but long enough for uneasiness to set in. It makes no difference how many times I have witnessed death. Something like a shroud descends. Movements and thoughts become detached, as if someone else is taking charge. Always, there is that sharp sense of loss. The present brings back the past, as if then, that other time, other place, other loss, was here and now, and tomorrow and tomorrow. Yet more than reminders of the past, I felt on edge, that sensation of something way out of kilter. It should not be me reporting the sudden death of Farmer Murgatroyd. I did not know the man, the family. I had not even asked his Christian name. Though there was no telephone at Catrigg Farm, Mrs Murgatroyd must have some idea where the men were working. One of the farm workers ought to have gone for the doctor. How long had she let her husband lie there in the last imitation of slumber?

Is it something in me, I asked myself, some part of me that seeks to be death's handmaid? Some deeply ingrained feeling that it is up to me, believing myself to be the last one standing, to take on responsibility and set in motion what comes next.

I hoped that Harriet and her new friend were enjoying their picnic by the waterfall, soothed by the timeless music of its careless rush. I love fountains and waterfalls and wanted nothing more than to be sitting there with them.

Poor Mrs Murgatroyd. Her life would never be the same again. My shoulders tensed at the thought of her terrible experience, waking to find her husband lying dead beside her. Little wonder she could not find the words to tell her daughter when Jennifer came home from church in Langcliffe, full of news about her stay with the future in-laws and the pleasure of hearing her marriage banns read out to the congregation.

I looked up at the high white rock, Castlebergh, that towers over Settle, as if guarding the market town from harm. When doing my research with the intention of providing an educational holiday for Harriet, I learned that for centuries this rock was a source of limestone, quarried and burned in a kiln at the base of the rock. Once, long ago, the townspeople had the lime burner presented at the court of the lord of the manor, expressing their fears that if any more lime was dug out, the rock might fall and bury the town. This fear was sparked when loose stones tumbled into a garden. A panel of jurors met to calculate risk. How many had a financial interest in the quarry, that would have been my question. After much deliberation, the jurors reached the conclusion that the rock presented no threat to the town. If it collapsed, it would fall the other way, the townspeople were told. They and their dwellings and businesses would be safe. I wouldn't have believed a word.

I could understand the inhabitants' fears. We none of us know when our world may come tumbling down.

Who, what and why do we decide to believe? Did I believe that Mrs Murgatroyd had not realised her husband was dead? A sudden feeling of suspicion began to grow. If Mr Murgatroyd had been poisoned, delaying telling of his death might allow the poison to disperse in his body. Mrs Murgatroyd could have lied to the farm workers when they reported for work, saying what she had later told Jennifer: he was unwell. When I, a stranger, knocked on her door, she became alarmed. It would be viewed suspiciously if she went on pretending everything was all right. Perhaps Murgatroyd's death on the day his daughter's marriage banns were read in church was a cruel coincidence. Yet he was not in favour of the marriage, Mrs Trevelyan had told me. When I spoke to Jennifer, she was disappointed that her parents were not in church. Now I thought back to the conversation. Her regret may have been tinged with relief. Her father might have been unable to conceal his opposition, appeared grumpy, or made an objection.

A few years ago, I would not have thought like this, but now suspicion came all too easily.

I knew where in Settle to look for Lucian. He usually ate Sunday dinner with old Dr McKinley, who had his house and practice on Duke Street.

I drove slowly, squinting at nameplates until I saw a likely one and stopped the car. Dr McKinley's was a solid, well-polished brass plate, bearing his name and qualifications. Dr L Simonson's name had been newly etched below. So the partnership was complete, and Lucian's succession secured.

I pressed the bell.

After a few moments, the door was opened by a small, plump woman who wore a pinafore in an abstract pattern, a white tea cloth tucked into its pocket.

'Yes?' She looked me up and down cautiously, as someone not recognised but who might be counted on to pay a fee.

'I'm sorry to disturb you, but I'm looking for . . .' I could ask for McKinley, that would be the polite thing. After all, he was the man who had practised here for fifty-odd years and would likely know the Murgatroyds. But Lucian had told me that Dr McKinley had grown old and slow, and liked his naps. I compromised. 'Either Dr McKinley, or Dr Simonson.'

She hesitated. Was she, too, thinking that Dr McKinley must be informed about this stranger who had rung the doctors' bell at such an inconvenient time on Sunday afternoon? Lucian had told me her name: Mrs Pontefract – a trusted employee, in post here for several decades.

'Mrs Pontefract, I'm Mrs Shackleton, a friend of Dr Simonson's. My call concerns a farmer who is up on the tops and if Dr Simonson has his motorbike . . .'

Her look suddenly brimmed with understanding and perhaps approval. 'Dr McKinley is not presently available. You'll find Dr Simonson in the Town Hall, attending to photographs for the exhibition that's coming up.'

'Yes, he did mention that yesterday. Thank you. I'll go there, and not disturb Dr McKinley.'

'Come straight back if you don't find him.'

'I will.'

'I don't know where in the Town Hall they are, but you'll find them.'

Thoughts of the Settle Photographic Society Open Exhibition had slipped my mind. It is a very active group and Lucian enjoys the meetings and discussions. They sometimes go on photographic outings to particular spots. Lucian has photographed caves and captured decay – the crumbling old stone shelters that are dotted about on the tops, the skull of a ram, a dead raven. He had persuaded me to enter a few photographs for display. Two of my pictures had been accepted.

I walked to the imposing Town Hall. The architect must have fallen in love with his own design. On either side of the frontage were arched windows below and oblong above, the roof rising to a sharp point. Between these two sides was a curving middle section topped by a tiny turret.

The first door was locked. Being Sunday, perhaps I would have to walk around the building for a tradesman's entrance. But the second door opened. From the entrance hallway, I could hear a murmur of voices. The sound came from beyond a door on my right. The top half was frosted glass and I could not see through so pushed it fully open and stepped inside.

It was a large room with a trestle table, a few feet from the door, full of framed photographs ready to be hung. Some of the photographs were already hung, with a few taking pride of place on easels.

At the table in front of me, a woman was speaking, or rather announcing. 'A distant figure in a landscape is surely landscape, not figure?'

No one answered. She answered herself. 'Landscape then.'

The voice belonged to a voluptuous woman in her late

twenties, dressed in flowing red and purple, a green scarf tied in a band around her bobbed hair. The much younger man beside her wore dark trousers and a velvet jacket with a pink carnation in his buttonhole. I had stumbled upon the cream of Settle's *avant-garde*.

The young man sniffed and drew a handkerchief from his pocket to stifle a sneeze. Perhaps he was allergic to his own carnation. 'I don't agree, Miss Nettleton. Should we not display by photographer, rather than theme?'

'No, no . . . Variety would be sacrificed.' She caught sight of me.

I introduced myself and explained that I was looking for Dr Simonson.

'Welcome to the fold, Mrs Shackleton. Figures! We are in the process of sorting the exhibits. I shall be hanging you myself. Mabel Nettleton.'

Odd, but when Lucian had mentioned the newest member, Miss Nettleton, I imagined a stout middle-aged spinster with a lorgnette. What had he said to make me create that picture?

'How do you do, Miss Nettleton. I'm not here to look at the photographs just now – I shall enjoy doing that when the display is complete. I need to speak with Dr Simonson.'

She raised a superbly plucked eyebrow. As if I had not spoken, she set two framed photographs in the centre of the table, pushing others aside. 'These two are yours, Mrs Shackleton.'

My photographs looked strangely out of place lying on this table, to be handled and assessed. There was my young neighbour, Thomas Tetley, in Batswing Wood, hanging precariously from the branch of an oak. The other image brought back a sharp emotion: Lizzie the weaver, holding her piece of fine woven cloth as she stood in the doorway of her cottage in Bridgestead.

Miss Nettleton held the pictures at arms' length in graceful, well-manicured hands. 'I admire your portraits, but I could wish you had more of doorways. The human figure in itself does not furnish a theme.'

The velvet jacketed youth cupped his chin. 'D'you know, I'm not sure about that.'

Being disinclined to enter a discussion on aesthetics, I asked again, 'Is Dr Simonson here?'

'Ah, Mrs Shackleton!' Lucian's voice bellowed from the other end of the room as he caught sight of me. The click-clack of his walking stick marked his steps as he crossed the parquet floor. 'You've met Miss Nettleton and Mr Roberts. Now come and say hello to our chairman.'

We met in the middle of the room. 'Lucian, I need a private word. Urgently.'

'What's the matter? Is it Harriet unwell? Where is she?'

'Harriet is grand. I left her having a picnic with her new-found friend but . . . '

Lucian glanced over my shoulder. 'Here he is again, your friend and mine, Mr Wigglesworth. He's photographic society chairman, Kate, and he particularly admired your photographs.'

Mr Wigglesworth trotted towards us eagerly. My information about the farmer's death was for Lucian's ears, but before I had time to speak, Mr Wigglesworth was upon us, eyeing me in a way that made me guess there was something else he would like to tell me about Freda and the trial.

'Mrs Shackleton, what a pleasure to see you again. It was

remiss of me yesterday not to compliment you on your contributions to our show. I do very much admire your photographs.'

'Thank you. I'm pleased to be included.'

'Not at all. Our modest society takes pride in encouraging talented outsiders. Did you have a restful night at Lilac Cottage?'

The pat question required a standard answer. I lied, of course. My night had been anything but restful thanks to the information he had delivered in the shoebox.

'Come and see Mr Wigglesworth's photographs,' Lucian said, leading me away. 'He specialises in trains and houses.'

'Smoke gets in your eyes is what I prefer to call them,' Mr Wigglesworth corrected. He gave a nervous choking sort of laugh, as if embarrassed by his own turn of phrase. 'What I like most particularly is the challenge of capturing smoke from chimneys.' He hung back modestly as Lucian drew me towards Wigglesworth's prints.

Needing to speak to Lucian privately, I hoped we were out of earshot. 'I'm sorry to break up the party, Lucian, but I want to be quick. I've left Harriet and a young friend at Catrigg Force with a picnic. I'm here because Farmer Murgatroyd of Catrigg Farm died during the night. I spoke to Dr McKinley's housekeeper and she directed me here. Mrs Murgatroyd is in a state of shock and she had told no one until I arrived.'

For a moment, I thought Lucian would ask me was I sure, but he said, 'Did you see Mr Murgatroyd?'

'I did and I can assure you that he is quite dead.'

'Right. My motorbike's in McKinley's yard.' He straightened his tie. 'What were you doing at the farm?'

'It's a long story. I was helping Harriet's friend, a girl from the mill, look for her brother.'

He nodded. 'I see. I'm surprised to hear about Murgatroyd. McKinley gave me chapter and verse on all the unprofitable families. Adult Murgatroyds don't take poorly and the children let the side down only very occasionally. Murgatroyd's not that old I don't think.'

'I'd say he's in his mid-forties. Mr Murgatroyd complained of feeling unwell last night but his wife thought it was nothing serious.'

'I'm so sorry, Kate. Not a good start to your holiday.' He touched my arm. 'Thanks for coming. I'll call on you later.' He paused for a moment. 'I'll need to inform the coroner's officer. As far as I'm aware Murgatroyd hasn't seen a doctor in years. I won't be able to issue a death certificate.'

'Wait on, there's one other thing. Where do I find the police station?'

He frowned. 'Why do you want the police station?'

'To report a missing boy.'

'There's a constable in Langcliffe, and a sergeant here in Settle. The sergeant is coroner's officer so if you're going there, do please mention Mr Murgatroyd's death.'

'I will.'

'This boy, when was he last seen?'

'Yesterday.'

'That's nothing, Kate. Boys will be boys. He'll probably take an extra holiday for May Day. It's an old tradition. Workers treat the following Monday as a saint's day. Time to worry is if he doesn't show up for work on Tuesday morning, after St Monday.'

'You could be right, but I feel I ought to report him missing, if only for his sister's sake.'

'The station isn't far.' He glanced at Mr Wigglesworth. 'Wiggy will show you. Tell the sergeant I'll call at the station after I've visited the farmhouse, would you?' He gave me a rueful smile. 'Now you know what a doctor's Sunday can turn out like. Hurry back to Catrigg Force. Enjoy your picnic.'

With that, he was on his way, pausing only to say to Mr Wigglesworth, 'Mrs Shackleton admires your smoky photographs but she needs a favour.'

I watched Lucian go. He took his leave of glamorous Miss Nettleton and the young man in the velvet jacket. Miss Nettleton tried to detain him but he hurried away.

As Mr Wigglesworth made his way across, I glanced at his pictures of houses with smoking chimneys, and trains belching steam. From a vantage point on the viaduct, he had captured the Settle to Carlisle train as it bellowed out a great plume of smoke, gigantic enough to do battle with the clouds.

He had achieved a fine nuance in the shades of soot-black smoke, white steam and grey wisps in the air.

In a moment, he was standing beside me. 'Don't bother with my snaps if you have something better to do. How might I be of service?'

'Would you show me the way to the police station?'

'Of course. Nothing serious, I hope?'

He deftly ensured that we were unmolested by Miss Nettleton and Mr Roberts as we made our escape from the exhibition room.

It suddenly seemed over-cautious not to confide in him.

A few years ago, he would have been the man people sent for in case of illness or death.

As we walked back along Duke Street, I told him about Mr Murgatroyd, and about Martin Young. He listened carefully, nodding, lengthening his stride when he sensed I was in a hurry. We turned right.

He paused when we we reached the police station, pointing out a long, steep row of steps with a wooden rail beside them. 'That is the courtroom. It adjoins the police station. This is where it all began, with the inquest into the death of Rufus Holroyd, and the magistrates' committal proceedings. I don't suppose you have looked at Freda's papers on the case?'

'I looked through them last night.'

'Thank you. I didn't dare hope that you might take an interest.'

We looked at each other, and there was no need to speak. In that moment, I knew that he would never rest until he was able to vindicate his friend, Freda. After so many years, that might prove impossible. But if she was right, then the murderer of Rufus Holroyd was still at large.

Eleven

Mr Wigglesworth and I stepped into the police station yard.

'I'll wait here for you, Mrs Shackleton.'

'Thank you.'

There was no one at the counter. I tapped the small bell, and waited.

A woman in a dark green skirt and cream blouse with a white Peter Pan collar came to the desk. Her brown hair lay in a wing across a high forehead. She wore a neutral expression which I wondered had she cultivated for just this purpose. 'May I help you?'

'I need to speak to Sergeant Dobson please.'

'He will be back in an hour. I'm Mrs Dobson, and you are?'

Clever woman. Find out who has come to call on the police before that person changes her mind and scarpers.

'Mrs Catherine Shackleton. I'm visiting Langcliffe, staying at Lilac Cottage.'

Not wishing to wait an hour for the sergeant's return, I explained about Mr Murgatroyd's death and that I had informed Dr Simonson.

'Goodness what a shock. That is very public-spirited of you, Mrs Shackleton, and you here on holiday.' She wrote details in a log book. 'Is there anyone with Mrs Murgatroyd?'

'Her daughter, Jennifer. I looked out for one of the farm-workers but there was no one in sight.'

'That time of year.'

'Jennifer was only just back, after being in church for her marriage banns. She had been staying with her future in-laws in Settle.'

Mrs Dobson sighed. 'Poor girl. I know the Pickersgills.' She looked at the clock on the mantelpiece. 'I'm sorry to ask you this, but I suppose there is no doubt that Mr Murgatroyd is dead?'

'None. I saw him myself. I nursed in the VAD.'

'Thank you. Leave this with me. I'm sure my husband will want to make the farm his first call when I've told him. It's likely Mrs Murgatroyd will want her cousin to know, and the Pickersgills too.'

She was already mentally preparing herself to break bad news to neighbours. There would be so many people to inform, family members who lived at a distance and who later today, or tomorrow, would have a police officer knocking on the door.

'There is one other thing, Mrs Dobson.'

'Yes?'

'A sister and brother came to Langcliffe a little while ago for work, Beth and Martin Young. She works in the mill and lodges with Mrs Holroyd. He is thirteen and works for Mr Gouthwaite at Raistrick Farm. Martin has gone missing and his sister is worried. He was not on the farm when we went to look for him this morning.'

127

She frowned as from close by a girl gave an indignant yell. Mrs Dobson had brought her children to the station.

'When was the boy last seen?' She jotted down his name and 'missing from Raistrick Farm'.

'Yesterday morning.'

'It's a little early to be concerned, Mrs Shackleton.' She spoke reassuringly. 'The May Day weekend turns some young people giddy.'

'There was an altercation between Martin and Farmer Gouthwaite. He set about the lad and the boy stuck up for himself.'

'Did he now? So did the lad assault Farmer Gouthwaite?'

'The other way around I would say.'

She began to write again. 'Try not to worry about the kid. He may have taken to his heels to avoid a thick ear.'

'But he would have tried to see his sister.'

'He'll have his pride, young as he is. He may have gone off for work elsewhere. He'll no doubt come round boasting to his sister when he's found another place, or he'll be back to the Gouthwaites with his tail between his legs.'

'He's only thirteen, Mrs Dobson.'

She tapped the ledger with her pencil. 'Well you see I've made a note of all you've said. His sister should have made her first call to the constable in Langcliffe. And in my experience boys aren't always as keen to see a big sister as she is to see him.'

There was nothing more to add. From any reasonable point of view, the sudden death must take priority over the vagaries of a young lad who at this moment might be fishing in the Ribble or climbing a hill for the sake of the view.

I hoped Mrs Dobson was right and that, like Beth, I was worrying unnecessarily, which I sometimes do. Once you have expected a person to come home, as I had expected my husband Gerald to return from the war, and you never see that loved one again, there is a tendency always to fear the worst.

Outside, Mr Wigglesworth was waiting for me.

'All satisfactory?'

'As satisfactory as may be.'

'Good. Then allow me to escort you back to your car.'

We walked in companionable silence, Mr Wigglesworth politely ensuring he kept to the outside of the pavement. I don't know where the question came from or why I voiced it.

'Mr Wigglesworth, did you start photographing smoke when Lucian's Aunt Freda took ill?'

'Why bless you no.' He laughed his particular laugh, a strange choked sound that could be mistaken for the start of a nasty cough. 'Freda had been ill some time, but I suppose you have hit a nail on its head. I did start photographing smoke one day while visiting her, the smoke from her own chimney. Another time I photographed from her window, while she was dozing, smoke from the chimney of the opposite house.'

'The one that had been the White Hart?'

'The very same. Smoke is such a choker, so intangible, it's there and it's gone.'

'I suppose that's why it's beloved in pantomime for genies and for Neptune, smoke and mirrors. I only glanced at your photographs, but I could see that you capture it well.'

'I capture something, but not it, not the mystery of it.'

'May I ask you something?'

This time the nervous laugh did not wait until he had finished speaking but came first. 'Ask away.'

'Did you believe, like Freda, that Joseph Flaherty was not guilty of Rufus Holroyd's murder?'

He hesitated. 'I am thinking how best to say this. I trusted Freda Simonson's judgement, her truthfulness and her powers of observation. If she said there was a third man, then there was a third man.'

'But she was not believed.'

'The prosecutor raised questions about her eyesight and the distance between the house and the tavern.'

'Who else believed her?'

'Flaherty's priest must have believed her. He vouched for his parishioner, gave him a good character and stood by him to the end. There's much to be said for having faith.'

'And yet he was found guilty.'

'The counsel for the prosecution was the better man, a more powerful advocate than the counsel for the defence. He persuaded the jury. It was hard to take in the judge's summing up. It came as such a shock, you see, having expected – or at least hoped – for something different. When we read it together later, we were shocked. It made such chilling reading.'

I wondered had he noticed the letters that Freda had written each year to Joseph Flaherty. I felt sure he had, but did not like to mention them. This was not the time or the place. We had reached my car, which I had left parked outside Dr McKinley's house. I thanked Mr Wigglesworth for walking with me.

He raised his hat. 'I was very fond of Freda. We relied on each other a great deal. I'm sorry you did not meet her.'

'So am I.'

'Mrs Shackleton, how long will you stay in Langcliffe?'

'Oh, about two weeks.'

'Would you visit me in my pharmacy? I'm just along from here – opposite the Market Place.'

'Yes, I'd like that.'

'Good, good. I could speak more freely there. It would be difficult for me to come into Freda's house and sit drinking tea, expecting her to appear and make one of her wry remarks. And you are curious about . . . well, the Langcliffe murder, and perhaps . . . I don't know.'

'I admit I am curious.'

'Bring your niece with you. You and I can talk. My assistant will amuse her, let her weigh out poisons, children like that sort of thing. Call any day. I am always there.' He watched me get into the car. 'Always there,' he repeated as I started the engine. As I drove away, he laughed. It was the saddest sound I have ever heard.

Mr Wigglesworth had something else on his mind as well as the murder, something he could not bring himself to hint of, but what?

Twelve

It was a relief to find Harriet and Beth safely where I had left them.

They had saved me a cheese sandwich, a slice of currant cake and half a bottle of cold tea. I was so hungry that it felt like a banquet. As I ate, they told me about meeting Gabriel Cherry. They spoke together.

'He'll keep an eye out for Martin.'

'He works on the same farm.'

'That's good news.'

'What happened in Settle?' Beth asked. 'Has anyone seen him?'

'No, but it looks very hopeful. The police sergeant's wife made a good point. She said that Martin wouldn't want to upset you by telling you about leaving his job. There are lots of farms about and at this time of year they all need extra help. The minute he is settled and happy again, he'll send word, just you wait and see. Dr Simonson says the same thing. It's not unusual for a lad to do a bit of wandering. I'm sure he'll turn up soon.'

'Don't report him missing to the Langcliffe constable, will you?'

'Why not?'

'They'll send him back to that farm.'

'No one will send him back. Dr Simonson and I will see to that.'

I had convinced the girls, but deep down did not believe my own words. Was I being foolish or pessimistic in expecting an upsetting outcome? I wanted to imagine the boy fishing, climbing, walking by the river, tossing stones, but the image of a bruised lad hurt and alone came suddenly and unexpectedly. I tried to blot out the image.

Beth went back to her lodgings, keen to tell her friend Madge about her adventures. When Harriet and I were alone again in the cottage, I insisted that she sit in the best chair in the parlour and rest. Parlours are too often reserved for special occasions and I see no point in having them at all if the main use is for funeral teas and visiting clergymen.

'Are you any good at tapestry, Harriet? There's an unfinished country scene here.'

'No! I hate tapestry, and I don't like that picture.'

'Oh, all right, just a thought.'

'I have some information about our murder investigation.' She looked very pleased with herself and I did not want to burst her bubble.

'What information?'

'Oh!' She suddenly deflated without any help from me. 'Now I don't know if I should say.'

'Try me.'

'It might be upsetting for Beth.'

'I don't see how. The murder was ten years ago, so how could there be a connection with Beth?'

'Her father goes round the country when it's time to kill pigs. He once came to Langcliffe and he lost his knife – or that's what she said, and something about a murder.'

'She would have been five years old.'

'But it's a coincidence, isn't it?'

'Where is he now, Mr Young?'

'She doesn't know. He went off, doing his rounds, whatever he does. What if he's a murderer?'

'It's unlikely. He would have no motive for killing the innkeeper and I shouldn't think he would dress in a long dark coat and pulled-down hat. People wear what suits their trade and that doesn't sound like the uniform of a travelling slaughter-man.'

'No it doesn't. He'd have worn trousers tucked in his boots and a jacket or jerkin.'

'If Beth's father is one of those men who spends more time away than at home, a child is bound to take little bits of information and embroider stories.'

'Oh she doesn't think he's a murderer.'

'And we have no reason to suppose he is. Now you rest. Shut your eyes for half an hour while I work out what to have for supper. It's been a long day.'

The tap on the door startled me. It was long after ten o'clock. Harriet had gone to bed, disappointed that there had been no word of Martin.

After looking through the window and spotting Lucian, who gave a tentative smile, I went to the door to let him in.

'Sorry, Kate. It's late but . . . '

'Come in!'

He stepped inside, taking off his leather motorcycle helmet. 'I saw Mr Murgatroyd off to the hospital for an autopsy and then had a case of pneumonia in Giggleswick. Just wanted to check that you were all safe and sound.'

'Well I'm glad you're here. Have you eaten?'

'Not since midday at McKinley's.'

We walked through to the kitchen. 'I thought you might call. I've saved you ham and potatoes. How is Mrs Murgatroyd?'

He took off his jacket, went to the sink and rolled up his sleeves to wash his hands. 'She's over the initial shock. The daughter's fiancé and in-laws arrived just as I was leaving. One of their farm workers went into Settle to fetch his brother out of retirement to lend a hand.'

I put the food on the table. 'It's good that they will have someone to help in a practical way.'

'Folk will rally round. There are plenty of men who gave up the land, feeling old and tired, and within a matter of months they are back on form and climbing the walls for want of work.' He dried his hands. 'I was half tempted to offer my services.'

'You've worked on a farm?'

'Growing up here every lad did, and the girls too. There's not much I can't turn my hand to.'

'Hidden talents.'

'I enjoy it. I've put my name down for one of the Langcliffe allotments, though I'll have to wait for someone to die.' He sat down at the table. 'Do you garden?'

'I leave that to my housekeeper and a gardener.'

'How very Marie Antoinette of you.'

I had not thought of Lucian as a countryman, but of course he was, a countryman through and through, with his light tweed check suit, the waistcoat in a solid brown and – a concession to Sunday apparel – the brown brogues.

I sat down opposite him.

'What?' He spooned mustard onto his ham. 'What are you thinking?'

'Haven't you ever lived in a city?'

'Only when I was at medical school in Edinburgh, and even then I came back here during the vacations. Best thing that happened to me was coming to Langcliffe. That's why I'd like to make it my home again. We have an excellent school in the village.'

He looked at me quite pointedly as he made this round-about attempt to open a discussion about having children. Feeling a little mean, I parried his well-intentioned efforts. I was happy to spend more time with Lucian, and get to know him better, but it was too soon to let him turn this fortnight's convalescence for Harriet into an intense notching up of our growing friendship, or courtship.

'So it was village school science that turned you into a doctor?'

'Oddly enough, my vocation came in a rather chilly way when I was eleven years old. I'd been out swimming in very cold water, and knew how easy it was to go into cramp, and how sometimes there is such a narrow margin between life and death.'

'That was very thoughtful, for an eleven-year-old.'

'I suppose it was.'

We chatted about his school for a little while. When he had finished eating, he carried his plate to the sink.

'So tell me, Lucian, what will happen now regarding Mr Murgatroyd?'

He sighed. 'Of course I couldn't grant a death certificate, that's why we need the autopsy. Neither Dr McKinley nor I attended him and can't say how he died. There'll be an inquest. Being an agricultural district, we have to rule out any cause of death connected with livestock.'

'Are there any indications of that?'

'I prefer not to speculate. Mrs Murgatroyd was casting about for causes.'

I was tempted to ask whether Mrs Murgatroyd's administrations of morphia and laudanum may have done more harm than good, but I expect she had told him exactly what she told me.

'Had he done anything particularly strenuous that day?'

'Nothing more than usual. He had been out checking the stock, topping up feed, shifting milk churns, all those jobs that are routine on the farm.'

'A death in the spring is so very sad.'

He gave a rueful smile. 'I won't stay much longer but let's take a short stroll around the village. I've spent too long on that motorbike today. You can tell me what you and Harriet have planned for next week.'

'Not much so far.' We walked along the hall. 'Victoria Trevelyan has asked us to lunch tomorrow.' I did not tell him this planned visit was connected with some as yet unspecified investigative task.

'That's nice. Harriet will meet Susannah, if she hasn't already.'

'Neither of us has met Susannah. She seems a most elusive girl.'

'She's shy, a bit of a bookworm. And for some reason Bertie keeps her on a short leash.'

We stepped out onto the path and through the gate. It was a mild night. The moon shone bright and clear. Arm in arm, we crossed the street.

Suddenly I felt a chill, a shiver.

'Do you want my jacket?' Lucian asked.

'No.'

'I'll go back for your cardigan.'

'I wasn't cold. Someone just walked over my grave.'

'Not like you to be so edgy.'

The feeling of chill and dread had gone, as quickly as it came. I looked back to where we had stood. 'Do other people feel the atmosphere of that spot?'

'That spot?'

'You know what I'm asking, Lucian. The place where the innkeeper was stabbed?'

He followed my gaze, looking at the pavement. 'If they do, no one mentions it.'

The feeling of unease passed as Lucian pointed out houses where his childhood friends had lived and the allotments where he hoped one day to grow flowers and vegetables.

When we returned, the parlour fire was nothing more than dying embers. Lucian lit the gas mantle that created shadows in the corners of the room.

I poured two glasses of sherry from Freda's decanter on the sideboard. 'Let's raise a glass to Aunt Freda.'

We touched glasses. As we sat side by side on the sofa, I knew he expected some romantic moment, but I told him about Freda's archive of the trial that Mr Wigglesworth had given me, and about the judge's summing up, carefully typed by Freda.

'I wish Wigglesworth hadn't burdened you with all that.'

'I'm glad he did. She wanted me to know. Your aunt kept everything in such a methodical fashion, Lucian. She would have made a good court reporter.'

'Yes. She was a very well-organised person, not given to flights of fancy. She worked in an office as a young woman, quite adventurous for her day, and very proud of her shorthand.' He smiled. 'She'd leave a few shorthand notes around Christmastime when she planned a surprise for me. I'd see these neat outlines on the back of an envelope and try to decipher them. I asked her to teach me, and she did, a few outlines and phrases. I used them when I was a medical student. Funny how you remember so clearly what you learned when young.'

'What was she like?'

'She was just my Aunt Freda. Kind, amusing, hospitable to me and my grubby little friends. We were a very mixed bunch at our school, with Bertie Trevelyan from Threlfall Hall, kids from the farms, those whose mothers worked in the mill or whose fathers worked at Hoffman Kiln. I'd often bring some hungry child back with me after school. It must have been a trial occasionally, or a struggle at the very least. If it was a well-off child she would be very blunt. "Shouldn't you be off home for your tea?" But if it was one of the poorer children, she'd make whatever we had stretch, and we'd sit down together.'

'I wish I'd known her.'

'She liked the sound of you. She was intrigued to hear about a lady detective.'

'Is that what I am?'

'So much more than that, Kate. I think you know that, and she sensed it too. She asked me, "Do you think she'll like Langcliffe?" I said you would. Was I right?'

We sat in silence for a few moments. 'Lucian, I have a feeling that her real question was would I be able to clear Joseph Flaherty's name.'

He put his arm around me. 'Surely not. That business was so long ago and it's too late now.'

'Tell me honestly, might she, after all this time, have been hoping for a reversal of judgement for Flaherty, some appeal to a greater authority perhaps?'

'I don't know that she would have hoped for that. The establishment is somewhat unbending in these matters and I think we are not yet able to look back and admit all the mistakes that have been made since our century began.'

'At least she wouldn't have been disappointed in you, Lucian. She must have been very proud of you.'

'She was, and quite rightly because of her encouragement in all my endeavours. There'll be a scrapbook somewhere. I collected specimens of flowers and plants. We dried them together. She typed their names and I cut the strips of paper and pasted them in the book.'

'She must have been delighted when you decided to study medicine.'

'Ecstatic! Some ancestor of ours had been a physician. She had this theory that I had inherited his aptitude and that my vocation was meant to be.'

'Did you tell her that your vocation really came about when you went swimming in icy water?'

He frowned and then remembered the account he had

given me of realising that in bitterly cold water the margin between life and death can be so very narrow.

'Certainly not! What child tells their parent or guardian something that will make their hair stand on end and consider forbidding activities that they previously knew nothing of?'

'I'm trying to understand what she was really like. The accused man was Irish. Did she have political sympathies for Home Rule?'

'We never discussed Irish politics, but I doubt it very much. She had no great truck with politics and politicians, particularly of the radical slant. She was very traditional. We kept Empire Day in fine style. She hadn't a good word to say about Ramsay MacDonald and Keir Hardie. When I came home from Edinburgh with new ideas, she went very quiet.'

'The prosecution barrister didn't dare cast doubt on her integrity, but according to the judge's summing up he did suggest that she had grown short-sighted.'

'She wore spectacles only for reading. Of course we don't know whether her eyesight had deteriorated. It's quite likely.'

I stood and went to the window. 'The prosecution made much of the fact that the moon was in its last quarter and the night was cloudy.'

Lucian stood up and came to stand beside me. He put his arm around my waist. 'How strange. It must have been a night just like tonight.'

A crescent moon was sandwiched between clouds. For a moment we stood in silence, looking at the sky, and at the stars.

'I want to do a test, Lucian.'

'What?'

I freed myself from his embrace and went to the table, picking up a candlestick. 'I'll light my way upstairs. Will you go across and stand in the spot that gave me the shivers? I'll be at the bedroom window and will look across.'

'Is this necessary?'

I took a taper from the shelf and lit the candle. 'I want to know.'

'But you're two decades younger than she. Your eyesight is bound to be sharper, and what will it tell us?'

'Let us at least try to think ourselves back to that night, if only to acknowledge her experience. Humour me, please.'

He sighed. 'You're right. I owe it to Aunt Freda. I wasn't here when she needed me and I'll always regret that.'

We walked together into the hall. He opened the door and went out, closing it gently behind him.

I climbed the stairs, as Aunt Freda must have done that fateful night, and every night of her life. Opening the bedroom door, I trod softly to the window and looked across to what had been the alehouse.

Lucian had already reached the spot. The bracket lamp lit his familiar figure as he stood near the house wall. He took a few steps, this way and that. Tonight, Sunday, was quiet. On the Saturday of the murder, the place would have been busy. There may have been someone else going into the bar, coming out, turning away too quickly to have seen the murder. It was quite possible there were other witnesses who had not come forward, not wanting to be summoned to court and have the trouble of giving evidence and losing a day's pay.

Lucian now stood stock still. On the night in question, there would have been extra light from a high window that was now dark. After all, what attracted men to these places as much as the ale was warmth, light and comfort. A light from within may have created a shadow as the lamp now did. Was Aunt Freda standing here long, or did she merely glimpse something that might have been? She was so convinced. Yet back in that time of war, we all saw shadows that turned into someone familiar, someone we hoped to see.

It was not possible to recreate what she saw. As on so many other occasions in my life, I could be sure of nothing.

I waved to Lucian. He did not see my wave. I raised the candle up and down, to signal my test was over.

Shortly after that, we said our goodnights. I walked with him to the gate.

He turned back. 'Kate, don't take this the wrong way, but how is it that you have time for this . . . this investigation, but not for discussing . . . well, not for talking about us?'

'Lucian, what's your hurry? We've been here a day and half!'

'Well, precisely, and you're in the throes of an investigation. I'm sorry, but that's how it seems.'

He had put me on the defensive. 'I thought this couple of weeks would let us get to know each other a little better.'

'I want that, too.'

'Well then, have I complained that you've visited patients and organised a post mortem?'

'That's different.'

'How different?'

'I didn't ask you to come with me and make notes, or cross the street and pretend to be a . . . a murderer by gaslight or play the role of Pneumonia.'

'You made a very good murderer.'

He laughed. 'Is this our first falling out?'

'I think it is.'

He fastened his motorcycle helmet. 'Then I hope it's the first of many because no matter what you say, I know you well enough to hope we'll spend the rest of our lives together.'

Thirteen

Monday morning broke fine and clear. Harriet and I lounged over breakfast in our nightgowns. When she had dressed in her cotton summer frock and cardigan, Harriet went into the garden. I watched her through the window as she opened the shed door. She went inside and was in there rather a long time. A bit old for making a den, I thought, but perhaps she wanted to play at being a young child again. When she came out, she opened the back gate and looked about.

By the time I had washed the breakfast dishes, she was playing two-ball against the side of the house, the tennis balls slap-slapping against the wall.

The kitchen clock said quarter past nine.

Mrs Trevelyan had invited us for lunch. Whatever she had on her mind, it would not be what filled my thoughts: the innocence or guilt of Joseph James Flaherty and Freda Simonson's distress about the case.

That was something I could discuss with Bradley Wigglesworth who wanted to talk to me about Freda. Given the strength of his and Freda's friendship, a chat with Mr

Wigglesworth might be a prolonged event. A person with whom an interview might be brief and informative was Father Hartley, the parish priest of the Catholic Church in Settle that Flaherty had attended. I listened to the regular thump of Harriet's tennis balls against the wall and wondered would it be fair to drag her along. Certainly I did not want to leave her behind. We could be there and back in no time.

I opened the door and interrupted Harriet's game. 'Do you fancy a ride to Settle?'

She did.

I popped upstairs and put on my jersey Chanel cardigan suit with a silk blouse. It is in a tan colour that I am very fond of, although I had not brought my usual matching Louis heel shoes and made do with black patent.

Harriet was ready to go. 'Is this part of our search for Beth's brother? Because if it is, I asked Gabriel Cherry to tell Martin he could hide in our shed if he comes when we're not here.'

'Oh, so that was what you were doing in the shed.'

'Is that all right?'

'Of course. But our visit to Settle isn't about that.'

'So it's the case of the long-ago murder?'

'Yes. I would feel guilty about staying in Miss Simonson's house and not at least trying to find out a little more, as if I owe it to her somehow.'

'Do you mean we're under obligation because we're not paying rent?'

'Not that kind of obligation, the do-as-you-would-be-done-by kind. Like picking up a ball that someone didn't mean to drop. I only hope I won't be wasting the clergyman's time.'

Harriet handed me my satchel. 'Why would you be?'

'Just a feeling. Look, we don't have to go. If you prefer to stay in the garden and play ball until it's time to go to the Trevelyans, that's all right. This business has waited ten years.'

'Then it's waited long enough, Auntie. If we don't look into it, who will?'

On the way into Settle, Harriet asked me what Freda Simonson was like. 'I know you and Dr Simonson looked at the albums and scrapbooks because you left them on the sideboard. What did he say about her?'

'That she was ahead of her time, one of the first women to work in an office, and she promoted rational dress, part of that movement.'

'What's that when it's at home?'

'An attempt to show that some clothing for women was restrictive.'

'Do you mean like a liberty bodice?'

'More to do with long skirts and bustles.'

'She wore long skirts. I saw her photograph and I saw the skirts in your wardrobe.'

'She had a divided skirt, too, for riding a bicycle.'

'That explains why there are two bicycles in the shed.'

As we arrived in Settle, I wondered how to explain my interest in the trial for murder of Joseph James Flaherty. From what I had learned about the Catholic Church, I knew that the people who trotted up to knock on a priest's door would usually be there to have prayers or a mass said for the sick or the dead, to request a visit to the dying, or to arrange marriage or baptism. It must be rare indeed for someone to come asking about a parishioner convicted and hanged for a foul murder.

The priest had stood as a character witness for his parishioner and would be unlikely to retract or reinforce his statement for my benefit.

It was a steep drive up the cobbled street along an old cart road. The motor chugged valiantly. I stopped outside St Mary and St Michael's, hoping the car would not go rolling back down the hill.

'Will you come in and see the priest with me? There should be somewhere you can wait while I talk to him.'

'No, you go. I'll sit in the car.'

'Well then it would be better to wait in the church.'

'Do I have to?'

'Someone might come and drive off with you. Then what would I tell your mother?'

She pulled a face, but climbed out. 'Oh all right, but some churches are spooky. If it's spooky I'll walk about till you come back.'

After leaving Harriet safely in the church, I rang the doorbell of the presbytery and waited.

A housekeeper opened the door. Having my own housekeeper has taught me never to underestimate the importance of such women. This one was in her early forties, her pale skin finely lined, her eyes hazel triangles pointing to thick brows. A neat curtain of black and grey hair swept her brow under the print turban. She waited for me to state my business. I decided against producing a card. Let her think of me as a potential convert if that might gain me a speedy interview.

'Good morning. I'd like to speak with the parish priest if I may.'

'Who shall I say is calling?'

'My name is Mrs Shackleton. He doesn't know me.'

She hesitated for several seconds and in those seconds gave the impression of taking in every inch of me, including parts not usually discerned by the naked eye. She knew I was not of their persuasion. How? I did not know, and perhaps she could not have put it into words either.

She did not ask me to step inside but did me the courtesy of leaving the door open.

Her soft-soled shoes making no sound, she disappeared along the tiled hallway.

A few moments later, she reappeared. 'Come through, Mrs Shackleton.'

I entered the vestibule. On my right, a small metal crucifix hung on a nail, a little water filling the font at its base.

When she reached the far end of the hall, she tapped on an open door. 'Your visitor, Father.'

A burly man, about sixty years old, rose to greet me. He was at a desk that faced the wall. A window looked onto the back garden.

Setting down his pen on a glass pen rest, he indicated a chair by the window. 'Please. Take a seat. I'm Father Hartley. What can I do for you?'

I guessed from the sheaf of papers that he had been writing a sermon. Perhaps he liked to do that on a Monday morning and cross it off his list. As I sat down, he turned his chair to face me.

'Thank you for seeing me.' My mission seemed suddenly

149

absurd. What was to be gained by investigating a long-ago matter when so much in the here and now gave cause for concern? 'I am staying in Langcliffe, in the house that belonged to the late Miss Freda Simonson.'

'Ah.' He recognised the name. 'I heard that the good lady had died.'

'I am a friend of her nephew. He kindly let me have use of the property, which is still full of his aunt's belongings, and some of her history.'

'Then I have an inkling of what brought you to me.'

'She kept papers concerning the court case of one of your parishioners. She never ceased to regret that she was unable to convince the jury of Mr Flaherty's innocence. The note she left with her papers indicated to me that she would be sorry if the matter were forgotten.'

He sighed. 'A dreadful case. Miss Simonson was staunch to the end and that mattered to the poor boy. She wrote to his mother, you know.'

'I didn't know, but it fits with everything I have learned about her.'

'One of his workmates came to me for the mother's address. They are a Dublin family.'

'You gave a character reference for Mr Flaherty.'

'He was one of my flock, a regular attender at the eleven o'clock mass.'

'Eleven o'clock?'

He smiled. 'It's the mass for stay-abeds and for men who drink late on a Saturday. A High Mass, so their penance for drinking too much is that they must sit through several loud hymns and the full-blast organ playing of a man who never touches a drop. Some of the congregation will already have had their bacon, black pudding, sausage and eggs to fortify them, but not all.'

'And which was Mr Flaherty?'

'He was a communicant and so would have eaten and drunk nothing from the previous midnight. I expect he had his breakfast at half past noon and his dinner at four. But you are not here to enquire about the poor soul's Sunday eating habits.'

'No. I want to know if by the end of the trial you stood by the character reference you gave at the beginning.'

'I did and I do.'

'Did you see him in his last hours?'

'I was permitted to visit him in prison.'

There was a long pause. Father Hartley must have heard the man's last confession. He would know whether at the very end Joseph James Flaherty changed his story. He waited for me to phrase a question in a way that might make it possible for him to answer.

'You say Miss Simonson wrote to Mrs Flaherty with condolences. I wonder if you also wrote to Mr Flaherty's mother?'

'I did, sending a note to their parish priest who went to comfort the poor woman and the grieving family.'

'May I ask what you said regarding his guilt or innocence?'

'It was one of the most difficult letters – no, the most difficult letter – I have ever written.' He stood up and went to a filing cabinet, took the key from a jug on top, unlocked the cabinet and opened a drawer. He rummaged through files and produced a manila folder. Turning his back to me, he placed the folder on the desk. From it he produced a flimsy piece of paper, and then resumed his seat.

'You will recall, if you are old enough, Mrs Shackleton, that in April 1916 there was an attack on the post office in Dublin.'

'The Easter Rising.'

'That always seems to me a most unfortunate name for the event, verging on blasphemous.'

'I'm sorry.'

'Don't be. The nomenclature is used in the best circles.' He glanced at the paper. 'This is what I did *not* write to Mrs Flaherty because I thought better of it. I didn't want to risk inflaming a volatile situation. By the time I wrote, the Black and Tans were doing their worst over there.' He read from his letter. '"Your son Joseph was as much a martyr as any of those who took up arms at Easter, but without their guilt."' He looked up. 'If there had not been what everyone now calls the Easter Rising, and if the defence counsel had been as good as King's Counsel, Joseph would not have gone to the gallows. He did not break the sixth commandment.'

I knew it, but now the truth was confirmed.

The priest returned the unsent letter to its folder. 'But what can be done other than to say masses for his soul? No one would re-open the case.'

'I could try and find out who did murder Mr Holroyd.'

He frowned.

I explained. 'I work as a private investigator.'

He sighed. This was more than he wanted to know. 'It troubles me still, Mrs Shackleton. I dare say Miss Simonson's peace of mind was shattered because of the injustice. None of us understand the ways of the Almighty. Perhaps what happened saved Joseph from a worse fate, though I cannot imagine what that might be. Conscription may have been about to catch up with him. Workers from the kiln did not stay untouched by the war. I can hear him now. He was stoical after his conviction. I think part of him did not accept the inevitable would happen and that he hoped for a reprieve until the very last moment. We believe in miracles, you see, but there was no miracle for Joe Flaherty.'

'What were his words? You said he was stoical.'

He opened his hands in an expansive gesture. 'He was an Irishman, so full of words, but at the end, he'd almost run out. He said, "Tell the mammy . . . Oh you'll know what to say, Father. Tell her I send her a smile and a chuck of the cheek."'

A tightness gripped my chest. So many young men had no opportunity for goodbyes, including my own husband. Wartime was the excuse for that, but here was a situation quite different – a man who should have been safe. He had worked hard, crossed the sea to find employment, sent money home to his mother. If he was innocent, hanging him was as foul a deed as the stabbing of Rufus Holroyd.

The priest continued. 'Something else he said in the cell, I forget the exact words, but he thought the truth would come out and he would be vindicated.'

So this then was the reason for fate bringing me to Langcliffe. I felt the same kind of shiver as when I had stood on the spot where Mr Holroyd's life ebbed away.

That was the end of my interview. I rose and thanked the priest. 'I'll leave you to your sermon.'

He gave a small rueful smile. 'I am to declare from the pulpit that the General Strike is a sin.'

He rang a bell. 'Goodbye, Mrs Shackleton. I will remember you in my prayers.'

On the instant, his housekeeper popped her turbaned head around the door.

The housekeeper walked me to the end of the hall. Pausing with her hand on the doorknob, she gave me a knowing look. 'Sure the only thing to do for the poor fellow now is to offer a mass for the repose of his soul. That'd be five shillings. Of course there is always participation in the perpetual masses of the Capuchin Fathers, which costs a little more but comes with a fine certificate suitable for framing.'

I went back into the church where I had left Harriet. She was contemplating the altar and a fine array of candles whose flames had increased in number since I left her there.

'Has someone been lighting candles?'

'I lit them. They look nice, don't you think?'

'They do. They give off a splendid flicker.'

'I lit twelve. It says a penny each.'

'And did you have a shilling?'

'No but I lit one for every three minutes you were gone.'

'Why?'

'Just to do it. I'm good at time you know. First I count it, and then I know it. And I just thought, wouldn't it be odd if Dad was entirely wrong and there is a heaven and a little stained-glass window for him to peep through and see me lighting candles. He'd laugh. He'd say, Don't waste good money.'

I took two sixpences from my purse. 'Here. Put this in the slot.'

The sound of the coins falling into the box broke the silence. 'I'll call it a baker's dozen.' She lit another candle. 'Unlucky thirteen. This is my own money, Dad, if you're listening.' She dropped in a penny that made more of a clatter than the sixpences.

'Leave a few candles for someone else.'

Shuffling footsteps came from the back of the church. 'Come on,' I whispered. 'Let's go out into the world and find a teashop.'

We left the church. 'I've been inside long enough, Auntie. I want to be outside, by the river.'

'All right, as you like. You've been very patient.'

In a bakery, I bought her a vanilla slice. She lost weight in hospital and it wouldn't hurt for her to put on a few pounds. I would have liked a hot drink but settled for half-penny drinks from the baker's assistant. It was a very sweet drink, suspiciously pink. Harriet finished first. I finished mine, not wanting to insult the concoction's creator. We handed back the glasses.

On the river bank, Harriet almost polished off her vanilla slice before gaining the attention of a group of mallards.

'Are you going to tell me what the priest said?'

'Joseph Flaherty was innocent.'

'Do you think it will be hard to prove?'

'Very hard.'

'Can we do it?'

'I don't know.'

She scattered crumbs from her skirt. 'You said it's not done to read other people's letters. You didn't say anything about not reading what someone keeps in a shoe box.'

'You looked at Aunt Freda's papers?'

'I'm your assistant, aren't I?'

'Didn't it upset you?'

'Are you afraid I'll have bad dreams?'

'Yes.'

She thought for a moment. 'It was such a long time ago, and it's all over now.'

Ten years is an impossibly long time for a fourteen-year-old, almost a lifetime. It felt wrong to have involved her, but she seemed oddly cheerful about it.

'I'm sorry, Harriet. Our holiday wasn't meant to be like this. If you like, we could go somewhere else.'

'Where?'

'The seaside, or up to the Lake District.'

'How, when there's a rail strike and petrol shortage? Didn't you read the newspaper banners as we came here?'

'Yes I did.'

'It's all right. I don't mind that we're investigating.' She sounded pleased. 'I'd rather we did that.'

'Than what?'

'Well, my aunt Barbara May teaches me to knit. Grandma showed me tatting. If you'd insisted I have a go at that awful old tapestry, I'd have screamed. But investigating suits me.'

'So we're a team, Harriet.'

'I hope I haven't gone wrong already.'

'How do you mean?'

'Martin might think the shed is a trap. I mean, if you think about the word detective, all you need do is change one letter and it becomes defective. Odd, isn't it, how one tiny letter can change something?'

'Yes, I suppose so.'

'Is murder the worst thing in the world would you say?'

'It's a terrible thing, for the person who can never come back, for their family, and for the one who did the murder, and

156

their family. There's no undoing, there's no putting right.'

She was thinking about her father. I should not have left her in the church to brood and count time and look at flickering candles and the filtered light from stained-glass windows. In that way she has of jumping from one subject to another, so that the logic is not straight away apparent, she said, 'Do you believe my dad would have been pleased about the big strike, the miners' strike?'

'Yes. He would. He would have hoped for changes, perhaps even a revolution.'

'What kind of revolution? Like the French Revolution where they chopped off heads?'

'No, but a time when everything alters, and new ideas take over and different people run things.'

'Who?'

'It depends who comes out on top.'

'Mam doesn't talk about my dad, not ever.'

'But she hasn't forgotten him.'

'No.'

'Does Austin remember?'

'Oh yes, but he doesn't understand. He has bad dreams. He wets the bed.'

'Still?'

'Yes, and he can't read.'

'Do you mean he doesn't like to read?'

'No, it's not that. He looks at a page and it makes no sense and I think it's because nothing makes sense. He lives in a confusion.'

'I'll talk to your mam about him.'

'I wish you would. She didn't know he couldn't read till I told her.'

'Come on. We'd better go back to Langcliffe or we'll be late for lunch. Mrs Trevelyan expects us.'

Even though Harriet was now officially my assistant, I would not tell her that Mrs Trevelyan wanted me to take on an assignment. I had a feeling that it could involve something that might corrupt a budding detective of tender years.

Fourteen

By the time we arrived back in Langcliffe after visiting Father Hartley, I was glad that we were to lunch with Mrs Trevelyan, even if her main purpose in inviting me was to impart a sorry tale about finding herself in a difficult situation.

I had hoped our trunk would have arrived and was sorry to see that it had not. There was supposed to be a skeleton service on the railways.

I changed into a day dress and switched gloves and hat. Harriet kept on her print frock. She did not want to go.

'Auntie, Mrs Trevelyan invited you. Can't I stay here, in case Martin comes?'

'I'd like you to meet Susannah Trevelyan. She's your age.'

She pulled a face. 'Do I have to? She doesn't seem to want to meet me.'

'It's not done to make an engagement and break it.'

'I didn't make the engagement.'

'Give Susannah a chance. Perhaps you'll make friends.'

'What if she's a terrible snob, or spends all her time parading her belongings and showing off?'

'Don't make up your mind before you've met the girl. She may be lonely, with no girls of her own age to play with.'

'There are plenty of girls her age. We saw them on Saturday, soppy articles in white frocks. She didn't stay to talk to anyone, including us.'

'Perhaps she doesn't like soppy girls in white frocks, or she may be shy and need someone to make the first move.'

'Why doesn't she go to that school with the rest of them? Dr Simonson said she has a governess.'

'I don't know, but come on. At least try. We won't need to see them again if we don't want to. Bring your camera. You can take pictures. Take some of the village so your mam will see where you stayed. She'll like that.'

'You were going to show me how to do it properly. I think I did it wrong when we were by the waterfall.'

'You can't go wrong with that little camera.'

'Everyone who knows how to do things says you can't go wrong. I can.'

'Come on! Wash your hands and let's go.'

'My hair . . .'

'Looks just fine.'

As she washed her hands, I picked up the keys and locked the back door, as I would lock the front. It was not that I expected thieves, not in this generally law-abiding village, but I felt a duty to Aunt Freda to keep her belongings, particularly her papers, private.

Moments later, we were outside.

'Take a photograph now, Harriet. Your mam would like to see Lilac Cottage.'

'Oh, all right!' She spoke cheerily – anything to delay the visit to Susannah Trevelyan.

I had some sympathy. It can be difficult for a child to be under orders to make friends, as I well remember from my own childhood. 'Take out your camera then.' I had bought her the latest Butchers watch pocket carbine, very good for outdoor pictures, taking daylight loading roll films and with a simple high-speed shutter. 'Light is the main thing. When you take a picture, you are drawing with light. That's the meaning of photography. Where is the sun now?'

She turned and looked at the sky. 'It's there, but there are clouds.'

'Clouds sometimes soften the light without obscuring it. There's enough light for you to take a good photograph. Position yourself so that you can see the whole of Aunt Freda's house.'

'It's the doctor's house now isn't it?'

'Yes. I was just thinking of the person who lived here longest.'

'Stand by the gate, Auntie Kate.'

'No!'

'Why not?'

'Because it will look as if I'm laying claim to the place.'

She gave a sly smile. 'And aren't you? Isn't that why Dr Simonson invited us here, hoping you'll approve?'

'Don't be cheeky. Just look through the view finder. Try to make sure you capture the whole house evenly, and then click the shutter.'

She did so. 'Is that it?'

'That's it. Well done. Now let's go see Mrs Trevelyan and Susannah.'

'I just need to go to the post office. I have to send a post-card home.'

'Go there with Susannah. It will give you something to do. We need to be there at noon.'

Threlfall Hall was the grandest house in the village, sur-rounded by a high wall and tall gates. A gardener with rickety legs and lop-sided walk saw us approaching and came to open the gate, doffing his cap in greeting. Harriet gave him a cautious smile. When we were a few yards along the gravel path, she said, 'How can you tell whether a person is being polite or subservient?'

'Where do you get thoughts like that from? Why shouldn't he be polite?'

'My dad said there is a difference between touching your cap and doffing it. I thought he was doffing.'

'Well he may have been, to show us respect as strangers.'

'If he doffs too much, he's subservient.'

I had always known that Harriet would have to live with the dreadful experience of finding her father dead. But I had not guessed that the chip her father carried on his shoulder about the injustices of the world would be so readily taken up by Harriet. That must be part of the reason she hesitated to make friends with Susannah, the 'posh' girl. I refrained from giving my lecture about not judging people hastily. She had heard it all before.

Mrs Trevelyan received us in the drawing room. She was wearing a pretty floral morning dress, fine stockings and cream shoes. Susannah sat in the window seat, reading a book. Why did I have the feeling that she might be just as reluctant to make friends with Harriet as Harriet with her?

'Well, isn't this nice,' Mrs Trevelyan said, by way of putting us at our ease. 'Susannah, come and say hello to our guests.'

Susannah hadn't noticed us. She looked up from her book, blankly, as if trying to fit us into whatever story she had just been reading. She closed her book, but kept a finger in the page. 'Hello.'

The girls were introduced and looked at each other cautiously.

'It's such a fine day that you and Harriet should speak to cook about giving you a picnic lunch in the garden. That would be nice wouldn't it? Cook has made one of her special cakes and there's dandelion and burdock.'

'Could it be bacon sandwiches?'

'Well no, and Susannah, it would be a good idea to put your book away now.'

Susannah placed a bookmark in her page but did not put the book down. 'But could it be bacon sandwiches?' The girl was bargaining. She would not be out of place on a strike committee.

A rangy, olive-skinned girl, she had a languorous way of moving, or rather not moving as she held her book with great care.

I could see that Harriet, who also likes bacon sandwiches, was ready to put in her two pennyworth. I glared at her.

'Oh very well, run along and tell cook, and take Harriet with you and show her the grounds.'

Susannah put down her book. 'I don't suppose you'll be interested in seeing the grounds?'

'I don't know. Depends what's there.'

When they had left the room, Mrs Trevelyan said, 'I'm

so sorry, Mrs Shackleton. Susannah can be an awkward child.'

'Then perhaps they will get on, or at least understand each other if they don't.'

Bertie Trevelyan must have been alerted to our arrival because he tapped gently on the door and popped his head round. 'Am I interrupting, ladies?'

'No darling, come in. You're just in time to pour as a drink.'

'Lovely to see you here, Mrs Shackleton. Sherry?'

'Yes please.'

He poured our drinks. Bertie strikes me as a most amiable man, not at all good-looking in a conventional way, with his high thin forehead and sharp nose, but with a charming manner. He presented the sherry and asked how Harriet and I were enjoying our stay, offering far too many suggestions for places we should visit.

I told him about our picnic at Catrigg Force. Since neither of the Trevelyans mentioned the unfortunate Farmer Murgatroyd, neither did I. They were determined to keep the tone light and jovial.

'I'm so glad you are friends with Dr Simonson, Mrs Shackleton. He is a fine doctor and I have reason to be grateful to him.'

'I believe he treated your boys?'

'And Susannah. But more than that, he saved my life when we were boys.'

'Oh?'

'We were at the village school here together. As boys do, we went swimming somewhere we shouldn't, remote, dangerous and of course very chilly. I developed cramp and went underwater twice. Lucian saved my life. No one had ever taught him, but he'd read how to do it in *Mee's Encyclopaedia*.'

His wife looked at him, surprised. 'Darling, you never told me that.'

'He wouldn't want me to, and please don't let on, Mrs Shackleton, but I thought you would like to know the kind of man he is – if that's not too presumptuous of me. Modest, clever, keeps his wits about him.'

This was the incident that Lucian had omitted to describe when telling me about his sudden realisation that he would be a doctor and save lives. The story impressed me deeply. Often it is not what someone reveals that tells much about them, but what they withhold. My already-high regard for Lucian went up a notch or two.

When Harriet and Susannah came into the room, it was clear that they had become friends.

'Harriet has a camera,' Susannah told her parents. 'She's going to show me how to take photographs. I'll be her first subject.'

Bertie nodded his approval. 'Good, good.' He made a fuss of Harriet, admired her camera and told her where in the garden would be a good spot – by the summerhouse, or the fountain. He excused himself, regretting not joining us for lunch, but he would be meeting with his land agent in Settle.

When Mrs Trevelyan and I were alone, we chatted inconsequentially until a young maid dressed in black with a bright white apron came to tell us that lunch was served.

I assumed that Mrs Trevelyan had despatched Susannah and Harriet so that she could confide her troubles, but she

showed no sign of raising the matter she had mentioned yesterday. We talked about the girls, and the village and other
topics for so long that I began to think her request for my
professional help had been forgotten, or she had changed her
mind. She offered another topic of conversation.

'I would like you to ride with me, if you feel you can
leave Harriet with Susannah. There's a lovely wood I'd like
you to see, and afterwards you'll be able to take Harriet
there, if you like it. Susannah is a very steady girl and there
is nothing that will bring them to harm. She is more likely
to lend Harriet a book and ignore her than lead her into
trouble or danger.'

I wished I could say the same about Harriet, who might
take off on some quest to find the missing boy.

'Riding would be very pleasant but my trunk hasn't
arrived.' I did not say that when it did arrive, there would
be no riding outfit packed.

'Oh, don't worry about that. If you don't mind sorting
through what we have upstairs, we can soon fit you out,
including boots. That's an advantage of a large house. We
never throw anything away. Everything is cleaned and
mothballed.' She glanced at my feet. 'We'll have your size,
I'm sure.'

'Then I'll be glad to go riding. But let me speak to Harriet
first. I don't want her to think I've abandoned her.'

'Of course, and you'll like my grey mare, Miss Shady. I
don't ride her so much since Bertie bought me the bay.'

I found the girls by the summerhouse. Harriet seemed suspiciously eager for me to enjoy my ride. I suppressed my
regret about having mentioned the nearby caves to Harriet,
and my anxiety about the need to return my sister's daughter

in one piece. Caves would make a good hiding place for a boy and sooner or later Harriet would think of that.

'Be very careful,' I said quietly.

She gave me a look of wide-eyed surprise. 'Of course we'll be careful, Auntie, and we've taken some good photographs of each other.'

After Mrs Trevelyan and I had on our riding outfits and had mounted the horses, Harriet and Susannah came to see us off at the gate.

'Where will you ride to?' Susannah asked, with a studied innocence.

'To Borrins Wood, darling.'

If Victoria Trevelyan sensed her daughter was up to something, she showed no sign. Nor, as we rode, did she broach the subject that troubled her and that required my attention.

I took the opportunity of her silence to ask about the murder of Mr Holroyd.

'Dreadful business,' she sighed. 'We were in London at the time of course. Bertie was kept busy with war work and I was doing my dutiful bit.'

'You didn't come back for the trial then?'

'Goodness, no. It was all dealt with so quickly. An open and shut case. The murderer really was caught red-handed. Bertie gave orders for the White Hart to be closed straight away. It was the right thing to do, though there was some grumbling at the time.'

'It's your property then?'

'Yes, much of the village is. We allowed out-sales to continue once a new tenant was found but it will never again be used as a public beer house.'

'Was it really such an open and shut case? Miss Simonson gave evidence for the defence.'

'Did she? I don't know that I was aware of that. She was such a nice woman, not that I knew her very well. The perpetrator was a Fenian, hell-bent on trouble when England was at her most vulnerable. He considered himself at war with us. Bertie blamed the Easter Rising in Dublin. The man probably regarded his compatriots' futile attempts to overthrow the British as a signal for the start of their revolution.'

It puzzled me that she could think the killing of an innkeeper in Langcliffe might contribute to a revolution in Ireland but I decided not to press her on the matter.

A mass of delicate bluebells carpeted Borrins Wood, and their intoxicating scent made me feel lighter, younger, as our horses trotted along the path.

We dismounted at a spot where the animals could graze and drink at the stream. Mrs Trevelyan spread a blanket and invited me to sit beside her.

'You must think I'm mad, bringing you here, when I asked for your help in a professional capacity.'

'I did wonder.'

'I used to come here a lot, before the war.' She picked a bluebell and held it to her nostrils. 'Such a long time ago. It's a romantic spot, don't you think?'

She was hinting at something and I would have preferred her to come out with it. 'It's a beautiful spot. I always wish bluebells lasted longer. No sooner have they turned you dizzy with their scent and their beauty than they are gone.'

'True. Is there anywhere more beautiful than England in May?'

'I can't imagine there is.'

Mrs Trevelyan gave me a sharp look, as if she suspected I had guessed something of her story, though I had not. I waited.

Somewhere nearby a woodpecker tapped.

She stretched out her legs and looked at her toes that pointed to the sky. 'I loved it here. We loved it here.'

Who, I wondered, sparked such a bittersweet memory?

'There is a man who has something that belongs to me. His name is Gabriel Cherry.'

Gabriel Cherry. There could not be two people of that name roundabout. I had now heard about him from several different quarters. He was the man who had set Gouthwaite's broken leg. Freda had mentioned him in her writings as having visited her and been given books. When I had left Harriet and Beth by Catrigg Force, Cherry had come to talk to them. The man was everywhere. I did not mention my knowledge of him to Mrs Trevelyan and did not need to. She had begun her story.

'He works for the Gouthwaites at Raistrick Farm.' She did not look at me but gazed into the wood. 'I used to come here on days like this, and so did he. He knows all the birds, he can imitate their songs. When you see him now, it will be hard for you to imagine what he was like before he went away to war. He was handsome, full of life and ideas, such a love of the country, such knowledge.'

I began to see where her conversation was leading, but let her go on speaking, wondering whether she needed encouragement, but unsure what words to use.

'Bertie and I, we rub along well enough now but at that time things were difficult between us. I'll say no more than that he was away a great deal. We had two boys so I had done my duty. The thing is that I wrote letters to Gabriel. I want them back.'

This then was to be my part in the matter. I waited.

'We had several spots where we left our letters. One of the spots was over there, in the hollow of that tree.' She stood and went to the tree, pointing to a hollow, high on the trunk. When she put her hand inside, she felt something, and froze before withdrawing a small posy. Three bluebells had been wound with a blade of grass. She stared. 'Did he know I might come here?' She took out her handkerchief and wiped her nose.

I wondered whether there were many places they had left their notes for each other, and whether Gabriel Cherry had put posies in all of them. I hoped not. That would strike me as worryingly extreme. The other possibility was that more recent lovers resorted to the same hidey holes. This was spring after all.

The same thought must have occurred to her. She put the posy back in the hollow of the tree trunk.

'I need my letters back. I asked Gabriel once before. He said they were safe and that he wanted to keep them for his old age but I have heard that things have changed for him. He is seeing someone else.'

'Could you ask him again? If you are right and his life is changed, he ought to react differently. I'll come with you if you want me to.'

'I can't humiliate myself again, and we all know how dangerous a woman's letters can be. I trusted him, but I fear they have fallen into the wrong hands and he doesn't know.'

'Whose hands?'

'Selina Gouthwaite's. She came to the May Day celebrations. You won't have met her.'

'As it happens, I have, when I was helping Beth Young look for her brother. Mrs Gouthwaite was delivering a calf in the barn.' Her image came back to me, dishevelled, with an air of dull hopelessness. She did not strike me as having enough initiative to steal letters.

'She appeared on Saturday morning. Has a knack for making herself inconspicuous. She was trying to blackmail me. She did not say in so many words that she had the letters, but I know so.'

'Did she ask for money?'

'Not money, no. She wants me to influence Bertie, so that she and her husband can stay on the farm. Bertie refuses to renew their lease. The Gouthwaites are slipshod farmers, cut corners. They neglect their livestock and the land. Their farm, Raistrick Farm, and Catrigg Farm, which is tenanted by the Murgatroyds, are less than two miles apart. It was never viable to have two farms in such close proximity. It makes sense to bring the land under a single stewardship.'

'The Murgatroyds?'

'Yes.'

'But now that Mr Murgatroyd is dead . . .'

'Of course you heard about that through Dr Simonson. But Bill Murgatroyd's death will make no difference. The Gouthwaites are not good stewards. Bertie has had enough of them. I don't blame him. He has cajoled, taken a stern approach, made it clear they must improve and nothing helps. He won't renew their lease. He placed that boy from Pendleton with them who was no doubt mistreated and now has run off. Bertie feels responsible. He says he should have

171

known that Gouthwaite was a bully. Other boys have cleared off in the past.'

I felt a sudden chill. Run off, or something more sinister?

She continued. 'There was no mistaking Selina Gouthwaite's hints. She has my letters.' Mrs Trevelyan grimaced. 'I can't bear the thought of that woman's paws on my correspondence.'

'Does Gabriel Cherry know she has them?'

'I think not. That is where my hope lies. I daren't approach Gabriel, given how touchy he was when I asked him before, and that he might misunderstand me. That is why I am asking for your help. Will you see him on my behalf, ask him to retrieve the letters from her and return them to me, or destroy them?' She waited. When I did not answer straight away, she said, 'Naturally I would reimburse you at your usual professional rate.'

'But how might I succeed where you failed? There is also Harriet for me to consider. This is meant to be her convalescence and I am responsible for her.'

'It won't take long to ask him will it? We could try now, if you are willing.'

'All right. If I can help, I will.'

'Thank you.' Her voice was a whisper.

We sat in silence for a few moments, watching a bee as it buzzed towards a bluebell. 'How would you begin?' she asked.

'I am just thinking about that. It's known that I am concerned about Martin Young going missing. That would give me a reason for speaking to Gabriel Cherry. I can quite legitimately ask about Martin and then bring up the delicate matter of your letters.'

'Oh yes. How clever. He'll be courteous. He is a good man. It's a mystery to me that he has put up with the Gouthwaites for so long. He went to that farm as a boy, and so knew little else. My mother-in-law made sure he was educated at the village school. He stayed on when the Gouthwaites arrived and took over the lease. I thought that after the war he would try his luck elsewhere, but he came back. Came back to what he knows, perhaps came back to me, but it was over.'

I did not relish the task of asking this estimable farm labourer for love letters, no matter how many bird calls he could whistle or books he had read.

A squirrel scuttled up a nearby tree, watched by a thrush. I gazed at the bluebells for inspiration. None came. 'Very well, I'll try. I'll go now.'

She sighed. Her body suddenly became very slack as if a weight had been lifted. 'Thank you.'

'I'm not sure how I'll find him.'

'I'll come with you part of the way before I peel off for Catrigg Farm to pay my condolences to Mrs Murgatroyd. We'll pick a spot where we'll wait for each other on the way back.'

'That doesn't answer how I will find Mr Cherry.'

'I will find him, and point him out. Strange, but I could always find him, as if some magnetic force existed between us.'

That sounded to me rather like Beth's casting of spells to bring Martin to her, and that hadn't worked.

Victoria Trevelyan looked so very sad, as if her world depended on the outcome of my mission, which perhaps it did. I thought of charming Bertie Trevelyan and imagined

173

what it would be like for him if Selina Gouthwaite burst in with Victoria's love letters.

My attempt to retrieve the letters would be as much for Bertie as for Victoria.

Fifteen

Harriet and Susannah left Threlfall Hall by the side gate, taking their bacon sandwiches with them. She was a strange creature, more like a Spanish person than an English girl, dark and slender, but with pale blue eyes.

Susannah swung her small round leather bag on its long strap. 'I've silver thrupenny bits in here.'

'I have holiday money.'

'Well then, we better go to the shop.'

First they went to the post office where Harriet purchased a stamp for her postcard home. She was surprised that Susannah hung back, refusing to be drawn into conversation by the postmistress's assistant.

'I don't mix,' she said, by way of explanation when they left the shop.

'Why not?'

'I just don't.'

Next they went to a confectionery shop where Susannah bought two ha'penny drinks and bars of Fry's Five Boys chocolate. Harriet bought strips of liquorice and cones of pear drops. The pair of them stood outside the shop, sipping at their drinks. Harriet had to trust Susannah because there was no choice. She could not break her word to Beth that she would go on searching for Martin. Beth wouldn't be home from the mill until six o'clock and by then her brother could be miles away. 'Can you keep a secret?'

Susannah's drink went down the wrong way. She coughed and turned away, coughing some more. 'I am one big secret, so yes.'

'What do you mean? How can a person be a secret?'

'Take no notice of me, Harriet. It's just something I think about now and then.'

'That's very odd.'

'Lots of things are odd. If you don't know that by now, what do you know?'

'What in particular is odd?' Harriet's dad had always said a person must be precise and look at the details or it was not possible to make a good argument. From Auntie Kate, she knew about the importance of the right questions.

'I don't go to school, am taught by a nice French woman who keeps having to rush back to France to be inspected by prospective husbands, and I live behind a high wall. Don't you think living behind a high wall is odd?'

'Not if it's like *The Secret Garden*.'

'Have you read *The Secret Garden*?'

'Not properly. We were having it read to us at school when I caught diphtheria. I'm not infectious in case you were wondering.'

'I'll lend it to you. You've seen our garden and it's not in the least like the secret garden in the story and there's no Dickon. If there was, I wouldn't mind. I didn't show you the summerhouse but I will. I find books there, wrapped in brown paper and I know they're for me. Don't tell anyone.'

'I don't know anyone to tell.'

'Not anyone, not even your auntie.'

'All right.'

Harriet finished her drink. 'I'd like to borrow *The Secret Garden*. I have a book in my auntie's trunk that's supposed to be coming by rail but it's not going to arrive now is it?'

'Why not?'

'There's a rail strike.'

'I don't hear about things like that, not unless I snaffle Father's newspaper. It's good you came today or I wouldn't have escaped. I don't come out much. Walled gardens are one thing. High walls all around and big locked gates, that's different. Sometimes I pretend I am the prisoner of Zenda and will break out.'

'I don't know any prisoner of Zenda.'

'Neither do I, but that doesn't stop me feeling like her. There's a book about her and I want to read it.' Susannah tipped her glass for the last drop. 'I don't usually have drinks from this shop, or any shop.'

They went inside and returned the glasses.

A sudden whoop and cry came from the school yard. Children had been let out into the playground.

Susannah increased her pace, hurrying to leave the school behind her. 'Come on. I don't want to be ogled. If we're going to the caves we better go.'

'Why don't you go to that school?' Harriet asked as they took a path out of the village.

'I don't know. My brothers went there but that was different. Apparently.'

'When will your governess come back?'

'Who knows?' Susannah shrugged. 'She's gone home to Lille on some family business. They've probably scraped up someone for her to marry. She's poor, you see.'

'If she's poor, who pays her fare?'

'I do but don't tell anyone. My grandmother gave me secret money because she said my father won't, or at least he might not. I'm in my grandmother's will.' They walked in silence up the track towards the caves. Once away from the village, they found a sheltered spot by the dry stone wall and sat down in one of the few places where there was no sheep dung.

Susannah handed Harriet a bacon sandwich. 'You asked me before if I could keep a secret. I've told you a few things about myself so you know we have to trust each other. What is the secret?'

Harriet dabbed at her lips with her hanky. 'There's a reason I want to see the caves.'

'What reason?'

She told Susannah about Martin Young, and how he had run away from Raistrick Farm and that a Mr Cherry was helping to search for him.

'Then I expect he'll find him.' She frowned. 'What makes you think this boy will be hiding in a cave?'

'Because that would be a good place to hide.'

'Won't Gabriel Cherry look in the caves?'

'Do you know him?'

'Why should I?'

'You know his Christian name.'

Susannah looked a little guarded and hesitated before answering. 'My father owns the farm Mr Cherry works on so why wouldn't I know his full name?'

'He might not look in the caves. He's busy looking after sheep and lambs so he'll only look where there are sheep and lambs and they won't go in caves, will they?'

'I can't answer for stupid sheep, but we won't go in caves. You're my guest and I live here so it's up to me to see that you don't go into darksome caves and never be seen again, or break your ankle clambering into one. They're slippery.'

'Then why come with me, if you don't want to go in?'

'Because we can call out. He'll know we're not the constable, or Farmer Gouthwaite.'

This made sense to Harriet. Perhaps Susannah had more about her than she first thought. 'All right. When we get to the caves, we'll peer in, and call his name.'

'That will be best, because remember what happened to Injun Joe in *The Adventures of Tom Sawyer*.'

'What happened?'

'He went too far into a cave and perished in the bowels of the earth.'

It was mid-afternoon when Harriet and Susannah walked back to the village, footsore and weary. If Martin Young had entered one of these caves then he had gone so far in as to never be seen again. They had finished the liquorice, and grown sick of pear drops.

Harriet pondered the difficulty. Perhaps Martin had not gone into a cave, especially if he knew what happened to Injun Joe in *Tom Sawyer*.

As if she knew what Harriet was thinking, Susannah said, 'Injun Joe was a bad lot. Not everyone who goes in a cave dies. Tom Sawyer and Huckleberry Finn found a hoard of gold.'

'I wish you'd said that before.'

'I didn't want you to go in too far. We're only just friends and it would be a shame to go back without you.'

Harriet told herself she was not downhearted. It would have been wonderful to find Martin and take him to the mill as work ended for the day, to see the surprise and pleasure on Beth's face. But at least she would be able to say that they had searched.

Auntie Kate had left the cottage door key under a plant pot. Harriet led Susannah inside and through to the back garden. They tried tying one end of the rope to the drainpipe and Harriet twining, but it didn't work. Skipping was too babyish anyway. They took it in turns to play two-ball against the wall, unders and overs until one of them was out. Harriet taught Susannah some rhymes, surprised that she knew so few. They liked the alphabet one for playing ball, doing unders for the rhyme and overs for the names of people, places and goods.

'A my name is Ann, my husband's name is Arthur, we come from America and we sell apples. B my name is Beth, my husband's name is Billy, we come from Borneo and we sell beads. C my name is . . . '

Harriet had reached M and was chanting, 'M my name is Madge, my husband's name is Martin, we come from Manchester and we sell . . ...' when the shed door opened. She stopped.

Both girls turned to see a boy of about their own age with unkempt black hair, an anxious face and scruffy clothes. He rubbed sleep from his eyes.

Harriet took pride in the fact that she hadn't dropped the tennis balls, in spite of her surprise. 'Hello, Martin. I wondered when you would come.'

He looked about cautiously. 'Was it you who left the cake?'

She nodded.

'You should've put it in a tin. I had to tussle a mouse for it.'

'I'm glad you appreciated it.'

'Where's our Beth?'

'She's at work. You've missed her dinner hour.'

'I could murder a drink of water.'

'There's dandelion and burdock.'

He stretched and yawned. 'Go on then, if you don't mind.'

Harriet went inside.

Susannah looked at Martin. 'How did you know where to come?'

'Mr Cherry saw me and called out.'

'Why did you run away?'

'Because I thought I'd killed my boss but Mr Cherry said I only fractured his knee. Any road, I couldn't go back.'

'We only looked in two caves. Harriet doesn't know about the others. I saved you a bacon sandwich but when we didn't find you I ate it.'

'Ta very much.'

Harriet came out carrying a glass of dandelion and burdock and a plate with buttered bread and a hunk of cheese.

Martin sat on the grass, eating and drinking. Susannah gave him a bar of chocolate. 'It's a bit melted.'

'I don't mind.'

When he had finished eating, Harriet said, 'Beth will be right glad you're safe and sound.'

'Aye, I knew she'd be worried. Will she come here? I

don't want to be seen and charged with breaking old Gouthwaite's leg.'

Harriet snorted. 'He broke it himself.'

'I would have run off anyway, after everything. And I can't stop round here now.'

'I don't see why not, if you can find other work. Your Beth said you could. There's lime kilns. There's the railway. There's all sorts a lad could do.'

'I want to go back to Pendleton. There's work for me there.' He wet his finger and went round the crumbs on his plate.

Harriet thought she had not given him enough to eat. 'Why did you come to Langcliffe if you want to go back to Pendleton?'

'Because there was work for Beth in't mill.'

'Didn't you like farming?' Susannah, sitting on the bench, stretched her legs and looked at her feet. 'I would, if I were a boy.'

'I liked it well enough, but I'm not stopping here.'

Susannah's hair had fallen in front of her eyes. She parted it so as to look at Martin. 'There's other farms. The Murgatroyds.'

'Excuse my rudeness, girls, but they all piss in the same pot. Mr Murgatroyd might be better at looking after his cattle, the sheep and the walls, but they're cut from't same cloth.'

It gave Harriet an odd feeling to realise that neither Susannah nor Martin knew Mr Murgatroyd was dead. She couldn't tell them, didn't know how to say it.

Susannah spoke quietly. 'I think you're wrong, Martin. People like the Murgatroyds.'

'I don't care. They're friends them two, Mr Gouthwaite and Mr Murgatroyd. They drink together.'

Harriet was feeling left out of the conversation. 'I didn't see any pubs up there. Where do they drink?'

'Old Gouthwaite makes his own booze.' He yawned again.

Harriet thought what to do next. 'You can't go wandering about the countryside half-starved and hardly able to keep your eyes open.'

'Who says I can't? Anyway, I'm not stopping. After I've seen our Beth, I'll walk back to Pendleton. All I have to do is follow the river.'

Harriet could see from the way that Susannah gave little glances out of the corner of her eye that she liked him. He probably reminded her of Dickon in *The Secret Garden*. She would think it a good idea to take him home. So Harriet got in first.

'You can sleep in our shed, or I could ask my auntie if you can stop here. There's a loft.'

'What if your auntie says no?'

'She wouldn't.'

Susannah consulted her watch. 'This is what I think must happen. Harriet will meet your sister when the mill workers come out. She will fetch her here. You and she will have a good chat about everything but you needn't make any plans yet. Then, you come back with me to the hall. We have masses of rooms that no one ever goes in from one year to the next. You can stay there. I'll bring you food until you decide what to do.'

'I've already decided.'

'You'd like our garden. The gardener is old. He'd be glad of some help.'

I was right, Harriet thought. Martin didn't answer. He just sat there, looking unhappy and sulky.

Harriet went inside. There was a bit of currant cake left. He could have that.

Susannah leaned forward. 'Martin.'

'What?'

She hesitated. 'Did Gabriel Cherry ever give you books?'

'No. Why?'

'Oh nothing. It's just . . . you won't tell?'

'I'm off back to Pendleton. Who would I tell?'

'I think he brings me books and leaves them in the summerhouse. Twice I saw him talking to the gardener and on those days, there were books for me.'

'He might do that. He's the only one up there who's any good. Why don't you ask him?'

'Because I'm not supposed to know.'

Sixteen

As it turned out, Mrs Trevelyan did not need to call on the powers of magnetic force in her search for Gabriel Cherry. When we reached the entrance to Catrigg Farm, where she intended to pay condolences to Mrs Murgatroyd, she took a pair of field glasses from her saddlebag and scanned the land as if it were an enormous prairie instead of patchwork fields divided by stone walls and overlooked by hills. Her small purr of satisfaction, or triumph, told me that she had spotted her man.

'There he is.' She held onto the field glasses, gazing at the loved object, speaking of him as though it might be necessary for me to pick him out of a line-up of heroes and villains. 'He is brown as a bright horse chestnut. His hair is almost black until you see it on a bright day and then there is a coppery glow, as if stroked by the sun. Did I tell you he can imitate every bird?'

'You did.'

'He is turning out the cows. Have you ever seen a man so lithe and graceful?' She handed me the binoculars and pointed. 'His dog is with him. Nipper.'

I looked in the direction she indicated. The figure of a tall man came into focus. He was standing still as an oak near a small herd of dejected-looking cows. A little dog, as motionless as its master, stood by his ankles.

When I handed back the field glasses, Mrs Trevelyan pulled on her reins and turned her horse to enter Catrigg Farm. 'Please don't take no for an answer, Mrs Shackleton. He must give me back my letters. I don't know whether that Gouthwaite woman has taken them or simply discovered their hiding place. Either way, she poses a terrible threat to me.'

Feeling less than confident, I urged on Miss Shady. The mare tossed her head and trotted up the lane. From the field on my right, a lamb separated from its ewe gave a cry of complaint. 'Go find her,' I called to the lamb. 'Don't just bleat about it.'

No casual conversation gambit came to mind as I drew closer to the man I sought. My mission seemed unreal in this atmosphere of pastoral tranquillity. We were close now, but a wall separated us. I could see no way through or over. He paid no attention to me but began to walk away. We were on parallel tracks. If he turned off, he and his dog would be off before I had time to speak to him.

Fortunately, around the next bend was a gate. I dismounted. A great deal of frayed rope had been wound somewhat drunkenly around the gatepost to hold it shut. I tugged and tussled at the rope until I freed the gate which straight away dipped because it had been held in place by the rope. It was heavy and difficult to close but I did not want to be responsible for letting cows escape. The dog barked. The man stopped in his tracks. All around the gate was muddy. Not wanting to leave the horse here, or lead her across the field, I re-mounted and rode towards him.

He was not quite the golden boy Mrs Trevelyan had painted. His face deeply lined from exposure to the elements; hair turning grey. The little dog beside him was thin with old age, skull sharp as a knife blade, eyes rheumy as he looked up. But Mrs Trevelyan was right in one respect. The man moved with a certain grace, and there was kindness in his lived-in, wearied face. The dog, eager to impress upon his master that this stranger needed attention, stood on his hind legs, front paws on the man's calves. The man leaned down and patted the dog, shushing him. That was when I saw his hands. They were stretcher-bearer's hands, full of so many tiny scars that they would never be properly healed and would always cause him pain. Stretcher bearers had the worst job. They did not charge out of a trench with a surge of emotion, camaraderie and blind determination. They held back until the first of the fallen needed them and then calmly and bravely stepped out to gather in the wounded, slipping, sliding, unable to wear gloves or they would not hold onto their stretchers.

'Mr Cherry?'

'That's me.'

'My name is Mrs Shackleton, Kate Shackleton. I'm staying in the village.'

'I hope you find it to your liking.'

'I'm here with my niece who is recuperating from an illness.'

'You picked a fine spot.'

'Yes, and I have friends in the area.'

'Ah.'

It would have been easier if we could sit somewhere and

talk. Looking down at him from the horse, I was conscious that we had trampled the grass, that the field was full of dung. I could not bring myself to broach the subject of letters. Yet I must say something.

'Dr Simonson has kindly let us stay in the house that was his aunt's.'

'Very nice for you, madam.'

'And you met my niece Harriet on Sunday and you were kind to her. She is of an age with Susannah . . .'

Something in the way he shifted his weight and the slightest flicker in his eyes made me glad I had not said Susannah Trevelyan. The image of Susannah, with her golden brown looks and pale blue eyes stopped my train of thought and made it even more difficult to continue. He and Susannah had the same colouring, their eyes the same shade of blue. I recalled Lucian saying something to the effect that Mr Trevelyan did not like Susannah to be out and about too much. Was it because he did not want her natural father to see her, or because villagers might gossip? Perhaps he cherished the forlorn hope that she would grow to look more like her fair, plump mother than her farm labourer father.

Gabriel Cherry did not help me by offering a comment or asking what I wanted.

'Is there somewhere we might have a private word, Mr Cherry?'

'Is it Susannah? Is something wrong?'

'No. She is with my niece. I'm hoping they will make friends.'

'Does it look likely?'

'I don't know. Susannah had her head in a book when we arrived and took some persuading to put it down.'

He gave the smallest smile.

I had found a way to slide under his guard. 'Susannah angled for bacon sandwiches for the pair of them for lunch. I expect they will have gone out wandering. Harriet has set herself the business of finding a boy called Martin who went missing from your farm.'

'It's not my farm.'

'No, but you know what I mean. I had hoped you may have seen him. Mr Trevelyan placed Martin Young with Mr Gouthwaite to work as an apprentice.'

'If you want to call it that. I told your niece and her friend I would look out for him. He's safe, and probably with them now.'

'He was mistreated by Gouthwaite.'

'I was on that farm as a lad. I put up with the same and worse.'

'It sounds as if you excuse Gouthwaite his brutality.' This was not what I should be saying. I would put his back up before we started on the business of letters. He repeated my words as a question.

'Abner Gouthwaite has a rage in him, and so does she, a deep rage.'

'What will you do when the farm changes hands?'

He shrugged. 'I don't know what will happen now with Bill Murgatroyd dead. It's all in the air now.'

'So might the Gouthwaites stay on?'

'Nay. Trevelyan gave them chances. They didn't know how to take them, and didn't see the consequences. It'll be up to Mr Trevelyan and Mrs Murgatroyd. Bill Murgatroyd asked me to stay on and I said yes.' The dog looked up at him, as if asking to be included in the conversation.

'Nipper's too old to go on the tramp.' Hearing his name, Nipper thumped his thin tail on the ground.

That made me smile. I was still not ready to ask about the letters.

'You were a stretcher bearer.'

'Yes.'

'I was with the VAD, nursing. We all had a most high regard for stretcher bearers.'

He gave a small laugh. 'Aye. Even them that jeered in the beginning ended up glad of us.'

He came closer, patted Miss Shady, and spoke softly. That was why he had not sent me packing. Mrs Trevelyan was clever. She had let me ride her grey mare knowing that he would recognise the horse.

'There's something else that I must ask you, Mr Cherry, and I'm sorry to do this if it is painful. Mrs Trevelyan asked me to be a go-between in a particular matter.'

He gazed past me, towards the horizon and the hills beyond. At first I thought he would not answer.

'I know what she wants.'

'She is afraid that her letters have fallen into the wrong hands.'

He frowned. 'There's no chance of that.'

Once more, the dog wagged his tail.

'Mrs Trevelyan . . .

'Her name is Victoria and my name is Gabriel. Isn't that how lovers from time immemorial are named? Tristan and Isolde, Romeo and Juliet, Dante and Beatrice. Oh don't look surprised. I read every night by lamplight, running the risk of setting the place on fire. Of course, Gabriel and Victoria doesn't have the same eternal ring as Antony and

Cleopatra. And why do you think the man's name allus comes first, when the woman has the final word?'

'She really does think her letters have fallen into the wrong hands.'

'What hands?'

'On May Day, Mrs Gouthwaite was in the village. She dropped a hint that sounded rather like blackmail.'

'Selina knows nothing.'

'Mrs Trevelyan believes the Gouthwaites don't want to leave the farm . . .'

'Of course they don't. They've done their best but their best was never good enough. They don't know best.'

'Mr Cherry, I'm a stranger here. Apart from Dr Simonson and Mrs Trevelyan, I know no one. Anything you or she say to me will be in confidence. If you're so sure the letters are safe, please make certain while I'm here.'

If I could see the letters, and have a little longer with the man, I may be able to persuade him to hand them over.

He hesitated and then nodded his head, indicating for me to follow him. He began to walk towards the gate.

I rode back across the field. He opened the gate, let me through and then tied it once more with the old rope.

He did not speak again until we reached the farmyard when he held the bridle and reached a hand to help me down. I took his hand which was calloused and roughened by splinters. He must soak his poor hands each night for relief. What would he apply? Sheep fat, I guessed. Lanolin.

He hooked the horse's reins over a post. 'I wish young Martin had stayed. He was a useful little fellow and there's a lot to be done.' Was there an apology for the state of the farm, I wondered, when he said, 'Gouthwaite isn't good at keeping men and now is out of action himself.'

We walked side by side towards an outbuilding. Close up, he smelled of hay and dried sweat. He led the horse towards a stable.

This stable, unlike the rest of the farm, was neatly arranged, with symmetrical bales of hay, and a series of hooks around the wall on which hung bridles, reins and items of equipment. From a stall, a horse whinnied. He went up and spoke to the creature, promising to take him to the meadow as soon as he was done.

A ladder led up to the roof space. I glanced at it. He followed my look, saying, 'That's where I bed down, if you want to know.'

'Oh? It's such a decent-sized farmhouse.'

'I prefer it out here.' He hesitated, and then added, 'I don't like to disturb anyone.'

There was something about his voice and his look as he spoke, that made me think he must sleep badly, haunted by nightmares, like so many men who had come back from war.

He gave a mocking wave of the hand in the direction of a bale of hay. 'I'm sorry this is all the seating I can offer.'

I sat down.

The old dog came and licked my hand and then sat beside me. I put a hand on its bony head.

Gabriel climbed the ladder to the top of the barn.

Within a few moments, he reappeared, his face hard with anger. 'Tell Victoria she has nothing to fear. I pitied Selina Gouthwaite. Now I loathe her.'

I did not need to ask, but it is better not to take anything for granted where love and loss are concerned. 'The letters are gone?'

'Yes, but if Selina could find my hiding place, I'll find hers. Failing that, I know far worse about the pair of them than they ever knew about me.'

'What? What do you know?'

He gave a small bow. 'Give my respects to Mrs Trevelyan, Nurse Shackleton. Leave it to me to retrieve the letters.'

There was nothing more to be said, but I said it anyway. 'Thank you, Corporal Cherry. I wait to hear from you.'

Seventeen

After parting company with Gabriel Cherry I rode back along Silverdale Road towards Goat Lane in the direction of the Murgatroyds' Farm. If Mrs Trevelyan was still there, we could ride back together and I would be able to tell her about my talk with Gabriel. As I drew nearer, I saw that her horse was not in the farmyard. Nor was there any sign of her on the lane ahead. Of course the horse could be in the stable. If she had already set off for home, a call by me at the farm might be a little awkward, so soon after Mr Murgatroyd's death. To heartlessly pass by, or to obtrusively call? I sometimes make decisions, not by choosing heads or tails but by pretending to choose heads or tails and then judging my own reaction when the coin lands. Am I glad, or sorry?

There being no coins in the borrowed riding habit, I made an instant decision, reined in the horse by the farmhouse gate, dismounted and tethered her to the gatepost.

Lucian had said neighbours would come to help, and here they were. A man tending pigs concentrated very deliberately on his task. A young chap lifted cheeses onto a cart.

All the curtains in the house were drawn tight shut. Jennifer answered my knock. She looked pale, drawn and somewhat dazed. I began to introduce myself again. She interrupted. 'Yes, I remember you. You're the lady with the car. Sorry, I've forgotten your name.'

'Shackleton.'

'Come in, Mrs Shackleton.' She was wearing the same dress as yesterday. It was crumpled and had a greasy stain on the bodice that might have been butter.

I stepped inside. On the kitchen table there were two pies, a stew pot and several cake tins. I had come empty-handed when others had brought food.

'I don't want to intrude, Miss Murgatroyd. I see you have had callers and have help in the yard. But if there is anything I can do . . .'

'My mother wanted to see you. She's fed up of everyone but she wanted to see you, to say thank you.'

'I should like to see her, but there's no need for thanks.'

'Let me see how she is. I tried to get her to rest in the parlour. Sit down, do.'

The kitchen was quiet and warm. The walls of the farmhouse were thick, and the windows closed, keeping out the noises from the yard. The only sound was the tick of a clock on the mantelpiece. The peat fire burned steadily.

The black lead kitchen range had been polished and the steel oven knob and hinges shone brightly. On the ceiling was a wooden clothes airer on a pulley. It held neatly straightened pillowcases and towels. On the wall to the right of the kitchen range was the cabinet I had noticed on Sunday, comprising three drawers at the base and open shelving above. This was where the tea caddy was kept, and above it the remedies Mrs Murgatroyd had used to treat her husband. The sheer numbers of brown, clear and blue bottles intrigued me. I took a closer look at these neatly labelled concoctions. Dr McKinley had been only partly right when he told Lucian that the older Murgatroyds never ailed. When they did, they knew how to treat themselves. There was arnica, belladonna, *nux.vom* and morphia. Between the bottles and jars were spaces I had not noticed before. Some items had been removed. That was not so unusual, perhaps Mrs Murgatroyd or Jennifer had needed to take something for shock, or nerves.

When I heard Jennifer returning, I moved to the hearth rug and looked into the fire, not wishing to be thought nosy.

'You can go in. Mam is awake.'

'Thank you.'

'Will you have a cup of tea?'

'Yes, if it will encourage your mother to join me.'

'Well it might.' She glanced at the table. 'I'll fetch something. Mrs Pickersgill, Derek's mother, has been very good but my mother sent her away. It made me feel so awkward and embarrassed.'

'It's a difficult time for you all.'

'Mam thinks she's losing me, and she's not. I'll only be in Settle for goodness' sake.'

'The wedding will go ahead as planned?'

She sighed. 'It's what Mam wants. We shouldn't, I know. People will talk.'

'Never mind anyone else. You must do what you think is right.' I wondered if she was pregnant. Everyone would wonder that now. 'I'll go in and see your mother.'

'Right. Tea coming up.'

I braced myself as I entered the parlour. This was always such a difficult time, between a death and a funeral. There would be little or nothing I could say that would not sound crass or trite.

The dim room was lit by a single shaft of light that came through a gap in the curtains, setting the heavy furniture in sharp relief and creating an unreal feeling, as of a stage set. A log fire burned in the hearth. The atmosphere in the room felt oppressive.

Mrs Murgatroyd lay propped on the sofa, staring ahead. On hearing me come in, she swung her legs round so that she was seated, looking up at me. Never sure of the right thing to do, I approached and took her hand.

When we had shaken hands, hers gave a small flutter. 'I shouldn't be this useless. But if I shift myself all I do is walk in circles and get in everyone's way.'

'How else could it be, after what's happened?' I sat down, without being asked. 'I see from the men in your yard and from the food on the kitchen table that people are rallying round. I'm sorry I haven't brought anything.'

'There's too much been brought, women fetching food, sending their sons to lend a hand, men finishing their own work and knowing what to do here without being asked. But what good is any of it? A farm is no use without a farmer. And he was going to take more land into care.'

Anything I said would sound ridiculous, yet she was waiting for me to speak. 'There is that.'

'Aye, that there is. We've two sons but they've married into bigger farms. Bill had talked to Gabriel Cherry and he was willing to come and work for us. There's nothing he doesn't know. Bill was right pleased about that.'

'Might that be a solution, a farm manager?'

She groaned. 'It's too soon.'

'Of course it is.'

'They've taken him to the hospital to find out what was the matter. I want him home. I don't know how long they want to keep him there. Do you know?'

'No I don't. Perhaps the doctor will call again.'

I wondered whether the autopsy had been completed.

'He should be here, with me. His shirt is ironed and waiting, and his black tie, and his best suit. Jennifer's Derek made himself useful for once. He polished the shoes.'

She would probably want to dress him herself. The autopsy would leave her husband scarred, and may be an unexpected blow for her. I wondered if he could be dressed for burial at the hospital. But I also wondered about the potions on her dresser.

She put her hand on her heart. 'He must have been dying when I put him to bed. He said to turn off the light. Well there was no light, only the shine from the base of the brass lamp, but he saw a circle of light around it, like a halo. Don't they say that the dying see a light and should follow the light, a white light, through a tunnel? I could have brought him back. Made him keep his eyes open, turned on the lamp, done something.'

'You weren't to know. He knew you were there and would always do what you could.'

'I blame myself for going to sleep, but he'd dropped off. I thought he'd been overdoing it and he'd be reet in the morning.'

She began to weep. 'I wanted him to give it all up an age ago. It was too much, running a farm without sons. My cousin's a feed merchant in Settle and he would have taken my mister into partnership, but no, there was nothing but the farm for him, morning, noon and night.'

'He must have had a lot on his mind, with the thoughts of taking over Raistrick Farm.'

'He was pleased to be expanding. He hated to see land go to the bad, and livestock not properly cared for.' She sighed. 'But it upset him, the thought of turning a man off the land.'

'Mr Gouthwaite?'

'Aye. Not that the Gouthwaites deserve sympathy. Farmers have to pull together, keeping up walls and gates and not turning the common areas into a squelch of mud when there's no need. Gouthwaite never pulled his weight and he couldn't keep his men. He left it all to Gabriel Cherry and there's only so much one man can do.'

'All the same, I expect your husband wanted to part on good terms.'

She gave a small bitter laugh. 'You have my man to rights and you never met him. That's just what he wanted. I told him not to make a fool of himself by trying to make peace with Gouthwaite.' She took out her hanky and wiped her nose. 'They're the only ones from ten miles around who haven't called or sent word.'

Jennifer came in bringing a tray of tea and slices of pie. She spoke with forced cheerfulness. 'Here you are Mam, Mrs Shackleton. I'll pour, eh?'

'Thank you, love.' When Jennifer had gone, Mrs Murgatroyd sipped her tea. 'I'll be lost without Jenny. I don't think I'll be carrying on here.'

'You'll have a lot to think about.'

'When he came home like that, I thought it was something he'd eaten.'

'Did anyone else take poorly?'

'No. We'd all had the same Sunday dinner at one o'clock. We had Yorkshire pudding and gravy, roast mutton with mint sauce, potatoes, swede, and then Yorkshire pudding with Golden Syrup and a pot of tea. What was it, Mrs Shackleton? What ailed him? Something isn't right.'

Something was not right, and she had put her finger on it. Nausea, dizziness, halos of light, and the fluttering of his heart that she mentioned yesterday. All signified poison. But that was up to the doctors and the coroner to find out.

I handed Mrs Murgatroyd a slice of currant pie. She took the pie from me with a mechanical gesture, and then stirred more sugar into her tea.

'If only we'd gone to Settle, to take up our Robbie's offer, we'd be off the farm and this might never have happened.'

When I had stayed just long enough and not too long, I took my leave of Mrs Murgatroyd and went back into the kitchen.

Jennifer was feeding the tiny lamb that I had seen on my previous visit. She looked up. 'It's a puzzle, Mrs Shackleton. I don't know what to make of it and I daren't tell Mam.'

'Tell her what?'

'Mrs Pickersgill, Derek's mother, she said the strangest thing, and I wasn't going to repeat it but it keeps going round and round in my head.'

'What did she say?'

'She said that if Dad took his own life, the insurance won't pay out.'

'What a ridiculous thing to say.'

'I know. I'm beginning to think I don't know her at all. There's a mean side to her. And we're supposed to live with them, me and Derek, until we find a place of our own. How can I if she thinks Dad poisoned himself?'

'What reason did she have for saying such a thing?'

'I can't remember properly. It made no sense. About Dad thinking he'd taken on too much and not able to face it without Mam behind him.'

'Why wouldn't she be behind him?'

'Because she once talked about moving into Settle, giving up farming. Her cousin, my Uncle Robbie, is a seed merchant and he's getting old, but it would never have happened. Just one of those things people talk about when they weary of going on about lambs and milking and harvests.'

'Mrs Pickersgill shouldn't have said that. Don't let it worry you.'

'No she shouldn't. Mr Pickersgill told her off about it.'

We chatted a while longer, and then I left.

As I rode away, a most unworthy thought struck me in relation to this good and grieving woman. Had she so wanted to be shot of the farm that she had poisoned her husband?

When I trotted Miss Shady back along the drive at Threlfall Hall, the elderly groom appeared, tweed cap in hand. He fixed me with his beady nutmeg eyes as he took the reins. His glance was curious. 'Mrs Trevelyan isn't over-fond of anyone but Susannah riding Shady.'

'Then I'm honoured.' I patted the horse's flank. 'She's a grand creature.'

'Mistress is waiting for you on the terrace.'

He led the horse away.

As I crossed the lawn, Mrs Trevelyan waved. She was seated at a wooden table under a covered way that had been added to the southwest facing wall. It spoke of an abiding optimism that the weather would be clement and the Trevelyans and their guests able to dine *al fresco*. This day lived up to expectations.

She had changed from her riding outfit and wore a rose pink dress in linen with a squared neck. A finely knitted cardigan of cashmere and silk draped her shoulders. Her smooth plump cheeks were pink from riding. She looked far too young to have grown-up sons.

'The girls are off adventuring.' She tapped the ash from her cigarette in its long ebony holder, showing no sign of the concern she must be feeling about her love letters and my interview with Gabriel Cherry. 'It will do Susannah good to enjoy a little freedom.' The neatly attired maid stepped onto the terrace, ready to escort me upstairs to change. Mrs Trevelyan smiled. 'Tea will be here shortly.'

In the allotted dressing room, I changed quickly and with only one wrong turn found my way back to the terrace. The butler must have had spies dotted about the house because shortly after I sat down, the tea trays appeared with a very fine white china tea service, dainty tongue sandwiches and apple cake.

Mrs Trevelyan poured tea. There was the slightest movement at the corners of her mouth. 'It's not good news or you would have told me straight away.'

'I was with Gabriel when he went to the place in the barn where he kept your letters. They weren't there.'

She gulped. 'That woman is trying to blackmail me. I was right.'

'Gabriel feels certain he will find where she has put them. He said that if she was able to ferret out his hiding place, he will do the same.'

'I'm glad someone feels certain. Damn her! And how could he be so careless?'

'From what little I saw of Mrs Gouthwaite yesterday, she strikes me as being in a poor way mentally. I doubt she would have the nerve to carry out her threat.'

'It would do her no good. And I won't intercede with Bertie for the Gouthwaites to stay on their farm. That would be madness.'

'Try not to worry. Gabriel is an honourable man. It shook him to be told what Mrs Gouthwaite had done. He is confident of retrieving your letters.'

'I hope you're right.'

Wary of continuing one of those conversations that went round in circles, I changed the subject and we talked about the girls. I did a little fishing regarding the absent governess.

Mrs Trevelyan pushed away her teacup. 'I have a feeling we may lose the governess soon, which would be a shame. Bertie insists I keep Susannah on a short leash. That is why she is being educated at home rather than attending the village school, which he much preferred for the boys. It's a good thing that he is off on business or he would be asking where she is now.'

'Why is he opposed to the village school for her? Lucian said it has a very good reputation.'

'And so it does. He is afraid she will make unsuitable friendships.'

I guessed that Bertie worried that the child he had accepted as his daughter might run true to type, fall in love with a village boy and make an unsuitable marriage.

Mrs Trevelyan offered me more apple cake. I declined.

She sighed. 'Why do the wrong people die first? I wish Gouthwaite had suffered the heart attack instead of Bill Murgatroyd. That would have made everything so much simpler.'

This gave me the opening I needed. I wanted Lucian to know what Mrs Murgatroyd had told me about her husband's symptoms. I had no idea what kind of post mortem examination would be carried out. If Mrs Murgatroyd had accidentally poisoned her husband through over-enthusiastic medication, that would be a disaster. It was not for me to judge or jump to conclusions, but simply to know the death was properly investigated.

'Have you heard any news of the post mortem? Are they saying it was a heart attack?'

'Well, no, but that's the most usual cause.'

'I suppose so.' I took a breath. 'Mrs Trevelyan, do you have a telephone here?'

'No, I'm sorry we don't. Bertie won't have one. He says we have enough interruptions in town without making ourselves entirely accessible here. They do have one at the post office.'

'I'd prefer not to go to the post office. If I write a note to Dr Simonson, do you have someone who might deliver it to the surgery in Settle?'

'Yes of course.'

'If Mrs Murgatroyd can be given some indication of when her husband's body will be brought home, she will feel a little less restless.'

She sent for notepaper, envelopes and pen and poured more tea as I wrote my note to Lucian. I should hate not to mention my suspicions regarding poisoning and create a situation where the unfortunate man's body had to be opened up twice. Lucian would no doubt see me as a terribly interfering sort of woman, but if he did not already have me down as such then it was time for him to be enlightened.

Dear Lucian

My main reason for writing is because Mr Murgatroyd is to be buried in his Sunday best. Will it be better to take the suit to the hospital, so that his widow does not have to see the post mortem scars?

I spoke to Mrs Murgatroyd this morning. I am sure she already told you that her husband complained of nausea, dizziness, fatigue, a fluttering sensation and seeing a halo of light around the base of a lamp. I mention this in case in her confusion after his death she failed to fully report his symptoms.

Kate

Of course he would know very well that my main reason for writing was the suspicion that Mr Murgatroyd had been poisoned.

I wrote Dr Lucian Simonson's name and Settle address on the envelope and the words Private and Urgent. That would set tongues wagging among the Threlfall Hall staff but there was nothing I could do about that.

Thinking it best to give some reason for my urgent note to Lucian, I told Mrs Trevelyan part of the truth – that it might be kind to have Mr Murgatroyd laid out at the hospital rather than taken home with his stitches on display.

Our lunch at an end, Mrs Trevelyan walked me to the gate.

'You'll let me know just as soon as you hear from Gabriel?'

'I will. Thank you for letting me ride your beautiful horse.'

'Gabriel recognised Miss Shady of course.'

'He did.'

She took a breath, ready to speak, more about the affair, I guessed. But she changed her mind.

'Susannah told the gardener she and Harriet would go as far as Lilac Cottage. Would you mind if Harriet sees her back to the gate? It's Bertie you see. He'll be back soon and be terribly worried about her being on the loose.'

It was an odd request, given that Susannah was the local girl and Harriet the stranger. I wondered whether Mrs Trevelyan thought that her husband was punishing Susannah because he could not openly admit his wife's infidelity.

I mentioned something that had slipped my mind until now. 'Dr Simonson asked me if I would enquire about who might want his aunt's clothing. Do you know of anyone in the village I might approach?'

She thought for a moment. 'It's very inconvenient to have a vicar without a wife who would know these things. He does have a housekeeper but she is rather unsavoury and would probably pass the lot to her sister for sale on a market stall. Ask Mrs Holroyd. She chairs the village women's committee and is always worthily knocking at the door for something or other.'

'Oh dear, I already made the mistake of asking Mrs

Holroyd. She gave me the impression that no one would want Miss Simonson's clothing because she was a witness for the defence in the murder trial.'

'How tiresome of her.'

'Don't worry about it. I'll think of something else.'

We parted and I walked back alongside the village green.

Walking back to Lilac Cottage felt slightly unreal. This seemingly friendly village had acquired a cold shoulder, and bared it. Lucian in his enthusiasm and love for the place had been protected from this different view by his kindly aunt and by inhabitants who remembered him as a boy and held him in affection and esteem.

An elderly woman tending a garden looked up as I walked by. I wished her good afternoon but hurried on, asking myself, Were you a person who cut Miss Simonson dead? Did you feel the same as Mrs Holroyd? Surely Aunt Freda must have had some friend who stood by her?

As I reached the cottage gate, someone called to me.

I turned to see a young woman of about twenty, neatly dressed in black skirt, white blouse and dark waistcoat, her hair centre-parted and looped over her ears giving her the look of someone much older. She walked towards me but did not speak again until we were within a couple of feet of each other.

'I'm looking for Mrs Shackleton.'

'Yes, that's me.'

'I'm Monica from the post office. Someone has telephoned for you and will ring again shortly, a Mr Sykes.'

'Thank you. How "shortly" will he ring again?'

'I said it would not take me long to come and find you. He'll place the call again in ten minutes.'

'Then I'd better come with you.'

As we walked together, I went through a dozen possibilities of what may be wrong. Something had happened to my mother or father. Mrs Sugden had taken ill. Sykes had been approached to accept a sensitive case and needed to consult.

Back in the post office, Monica went behind the counter. The postmistress greeted me politely. I wondered what Sykes had said to make them both so eager that I should interrupt their working day to take a telephone call.

I waited what seemed an age for the telephone to ring.

When it did ring, it made me jump.

The postmistress answered and then called me behind the counter.

She and her assistant, almost too deliberately, showed no interest whatsoever in my call but could not help but overhear my side of the conversation.

'Mrs Shackleton, Sykes here, sorry to disturb you.'

'That's all right. What is it?'

'I retrieved your trunk from the railway station. You'll know that the train drivers are on strike.'

'Yes, of course.' I had read this in the hastily produced government newspaper.

'There is a skeleton staff but I'd rather not trust them with your luggage. If it's all the same to you, I'll bring it out there myself today.'

I made some neutral remark, to give me time to think.

My thoughts began to whirl. The first instinct was to say I would manage without extra luggage, but Mrs Trevelyan had hinted at supper, Lucian wanted me to meet Dr McKinley and of course there would be a funeral for Mr Murgatroyd.

Sykes took advantage of my pause. 'Your letter came by second post. I straight away looked into that old assizes matter you mentioned.'

I had forgotten that I had asked him to take a look at the records of Joseph James Flaherty's trial.

It would be good to have Sykes here, though I did not imagine he could have learned much more than I had gleaned from Aunt Freda's papers and my conversation with the priest. All I had to say was yes or no. He was offering, in spite of the petrol shortage, and so there must be something that mattered other than my extra clothes. He was solid, reliable and I could trust him. I might even ask him to try and interview Joseph Flaherty's friend. He would certainly make better progress with Mrs Holroyd than I had. Then there was the mysterious death of Mr Murgatroyd, and the disappearance of Martin Young.

'How is the work going?' I asked. The postmistress was listening. For all she knew I might be enquiring about having a garden wall built or the ceiling re-painted.

'Everything is complete and up to date. The insurance business won't come to court but the person in question has his marching orders. The missing dog is safely returned to the bosom of its family. It's as if the world has realised that Mrs Shackleton has left town.'

'I'm glad to hear everything is under control.'

'To tell the truth, I'd be glad of the diversion of bringing the trunk to you.'

Decisiveness seized me. 'Come tomorrow. If for any reason we are not at home, let yourself in.'

There was a brief pause. Either my answer was not what he had expected, or he noticed something in my tone of voice that told him of my unease. I needed to warn him we may be working. Without giving anything away to the post-mistress or her assistant, I found the words to give him a great big hint that I needed his help. 'You may want to spend a little time here. The landscape is most interesting and worthy of investigation.'

'Ah.' His response contained all the understanding I needed.

'Of course, only if family matters allow.'

I always felt slightly guilty about Rosie Sykes, especially when I dragged her husband away for any length of time.

'A change of scene will be most convenient.'

'Good. You have the address.'

'Mrs Sugden is waving it under my nose as we speak.'

'Say hello to her.'

'I will. Goodbye.'

'Goodbye.'

Only when I had hung up the receiver did I wonder where I would put Mr Sykes, and how to explain his pres-ence to Lucian.

Eighteen

Back at Lilac Cottage, I walked up the path and looked for the key under the plant pot. It was not there. Harriet must be back. Slowly, I walked through the hall and into the kitchen.

Through the window, I saw the tops of three young heads. Harriet and Susannah were seated on the garden bench. Sandwiched between them was a third head, dark, tousled and male.

I opened the kitchen door and said hello.

'Look who's turned up, Auntie! It's Martin, Beth's brother.'

The unkempt boy cast a suspicious glance in my direction as he politely came to his feet. The resemblance to Beth was clear. The fine tidemark on his neck showed that he had washed his face and hands. Harriet had probably seen to that, being used to bossing her brother. His clothes were filthy.

'Hello, Martin. I'm very glad you're here. We were all worried about you. Have you eaten?'

'I have now, thank you.'

All three were looking at me. Harriet spoke. 'Can Martin stay here for now?'

I hesitated, wondering what might be for the best.

Harriet pressed her request. 'By the time he's seen Beth, it'll be too late for him to go back to Pendleton, especially on his own.'

Susannah said shyly, 'If not it's all right, he can come home with me. We have plenty of rooms where no one ever goes and it could be a secret.'

Susannah made me smile. Bertie Trevelyan had gone to such lengths to prevent Susannah from mixing with her social inferiors. Now she was hoping to smuggle just such a one into their house.

'Well perhaps since Martin has landed here, he should stay for now. You can have the loft until we decide what to do, and I had better let the police know we've found you.'

Mistake. I should not have mentioned the police. His eyes under their long lashes filled with alarm. 'Are the bobbies looking for me?'

'Probably not. They may be keeping a look-out because I reported you missing to Settle police station.'

'I don't want to be sent back to the farm.'

'No one will send you back. Anyone who tries will have me to deal with. There is just one condition.'

He tilted his head. 'What?'

'I'm going to run a bath for you and while it's running, Harriet and Susannah will take you up to the loft where you'll find some of the clothes Dr Simonson had as a boy. Then you won't give your sister a fright. Pick out some trousers and a shirt that'll fit. While you're at it, look for a nightshirt and some socks. And take your boots off and leave them on the step.'

'I don't need a bath.'

'Yes you do. Go on, the three of you.'

We trooped upstairs, Martin meekly following the girls, with me at the rear to cut off his escape.

I turned on the geyser and began to fill the bath, glad that Aunt Freda had at least run to some modern conveniences other than the unused gas cooker. I placed a tablet of soap on the side of the bath and hung a fresh towel on the wooden rail.

There was much noise from upstairs as the three marched about the loft. When they laughed, I guessed they had come across items of clothing that they regarded as antique.

'Can he take whatever he wants?' Harriet called down.

'Anything that fits.'

When Martin shut himself in the bathroom, I asked the girls to buy a toothbrush and some more groceries. Buying groceries was not something I usually had much to do with. The thought of planning meals across a week had seemed a good idea when we set off on Saturday. Now, with my thoughts on Aunt Freda, the murder of Mr Holroyd, the innocent Joseph James Flaherty, and the puzzle of Mrs Trevelyan's missing letters, I could not quite bring myself to the point of knowing how to organise food for this evening, much less a week.

In the past, I had criticised my sister Mary Jane for giving Harriet too many jobs. Now I was in danger of doing the same.

Harriet solved the immediate difficulty by asking, 'What shall we have for tea?'

I tossed the question back to her. 'What do you fancy?'

'I noticed the butcher does a meat and potato pie and there's tinned peas in the pantry.'

'Perfect!' I gave her my change purse. Her ideas gave me inspiration. 'And buy some cakes, a curd tart if they have one, and an egg custard.'

'We'll leave a message for Beth to come.' Harriet picked up the shopping basket.

Poor little rich girl Susannah looked so pleased at the prospect of running an errand that I felt quite mean telling her that she was wanted at home, and that Harriet would walk her back.

Never have I seen dismay flood a girl so quickly. 'Well then I won't be able to say goodbye to Martin.'

'You'll see him again. He'll be here tomorrow.'

I watched them go.

Not long after, Martin came downstairs, pink and shining from his bath and looking much better, if self-conscious, in tweed britches, long socks and a twill shirt. In spite of sleeping rough for two nights, he looked perky.

The two of us were seated at the kitchen table. His hair was still a little damp from bathing.

'Was it very bad at the Gouthwaites, Martin?'

He nodded.

'Was he violent?' I knew the answer before I asked the question.

'Aye, and he was nuts with it. When I thought I'd done him in, part of me was glad.'

'What about Mrs Gouthwaite?'

'There's summat up with her. She doesn't speak. She cries a lot. I think he knocks her about.'

'Didn't anyone stick up for you? What about Gabriel Cherry?'

'He told old Gouthwaite to lay off me and he didn't hit me when Gabriel was there.'

So Gabriel Cherry had tried to protect the boy.

'It's unfortunate you were sent there. I'm sorry you had such a terrible time.'

'I'm not off back.'

'Of course not.'

'They'll try to send me back.'

'No one will try to send you back. It would have been better had you gone to Murgatroyds' farm.'

'He was all right to me, and Miss Murgatroyd was nice. I only once saw Mrs Murgatroyd. She gave me a boiled sweet.'

'Well perhaps you could make the change and go there. They could do with a good lad like you.'

'I don't want to go there, or anywhere round here. Besides, old Gouthwaite would see me. I broke his leg so he'd be out to get me.'

'He'd have a job on to catch you after you saw to his leg for him.'

This made him laugh, but not for long. 'I'm not off anywhere near there. He'd send his missis. She does his bidding. She clouted me a few times.'

'There are going to be changes. It's likely the Gouthwaites will leave the farm, and the area.'

'Good riddance. Who'll take over, Mr Murgatroyd?'

So he did not know. 'I'm not sure what will happen. You didn't hear about Mr Murgatroyd?'

'What about him?'

'Sadly, he died.' I should not be telling him this. He had gone through enough.

Martin stared at me in disbelief. 'He can't be dead. I only saw him on Saturday.'

'When on Saturday, what time?'

'Early evening.'

'Where did you see him?'

'Going in to the Gouthwaites' farm.'

'But you'd run off by then.'

He reddened.

'I didn't know whether I'd killed the old fella. I went back to look where he fell. There was marks in the mud where he'd been, so I didn't dream it, but he was gone. I thought someone would come looking for me, and I thought is he dead? There might be police and people searching. But I'm good at dodging about, hiding. I saw Mr Murgatroyd going in the house.'

'I don't suppose you know what time that was?'

'Well before dark, before suppertime. I waited by the pigsty, waiting for him to come out. I thought if Gouthwaite wasn't really dead, he'd come to the door with him. If he was dead, there'd be other people. There always is when someone dies, they come round like flies.'

So why had Murgatroyd visited Gouthwaite? Perhaps he had wanted to make his peace, to express his regret that the lease was not to be renewed.

'Did you speak to Mr Murgatroyd when he came out?'

'I thought about it. I nearly did. But when I saw him coming out, he wasn't walking straight, as if they'd had a drink together. When people drink together they get on don't they? I thought if Mr Gouthwaite wasn't dead, the pair of them must have been yattering about me, and how to catch me.'

The corners of his mouth turned down.

'It was unlikely to be about you, Martin. They had things to talk about concerning the future of the farms.'

It was after Harriet, Martin and I had finished our meat and potato pie that Harriet went to see who was at the front door.

Beth came into the kitchen like a whirlwind. 'Martin, where've you been? I was that worried.'

He shrugged. 'Here and there. There was no need to worry. I can look after meself.'

I stood up. 'I'll leave you two to talk.'

It was as if she had not heard me. 'What you doing here? You know where I live. Come on, Martin. Mrs Holroyd wants to meet you and so does Madge who I share a room with. You'll like them. Mrs Holroyd's just putting tea on the table. Only thing is you can't stay there.'

'I've eaten.'

She dragged Martin to his feet and then turned to me. 'He'll have to come back here to sleep. Mrs Holroyd would put him up if she could.'

Martin protested. 'Someone'll see me and I'll be in bother.'

'No one'll see you . . .'

'They might. There was someone at the workhouse window staring and . . .'

She folded her arms across her chest and glared at him. 'I've a wage coming in. You're my brother. Anyone tries to interfere and they've me and my friend Madge to deal with.'

'I'm not being looked after by lassies.'

'Since when? Don't be a mardy.'

He stood his ground. 'I'm stopping here. Mrs Shackleton said I can.'

When she realised he would not budge, Beth reluctantly gave in. I left them in the kitchen to talk and found Harriet in the parlour, looking out of the window.

'I'm glad Martin has decided to stay here. You'll make sure no one takes him away?'

'I will.'

'I feel sorry for Beth that Martin's dead set on going back to Pendleton.'

'It's not so very far. They'll be able to visit on Sundays in the fine weather when the days are long.'

'I suppose so. Oh and did you see that letter that came for you?'

'No.'

She went into the hall. With the door open, I could hear voices from the kitchen. Beth had calmed down.

Harriet brought me the envelope. It looked official and was therefore quite unwelcome. The letter had the merit of brevity, to wit:

Madam,

By virtue of this my Order as one of His Majesty's Coroners for the County of Yorkshire you are hereby required to appear before me and the jury on Wednesday, 5 May at ten o'clock in the morning in the Court in the Parish of Giggleswick, and then and there to give evidence on His Majesty's behalf touching the death of William George Murgatroyd.

Dated the third day of May, 1926.
T J Beale,
Coroner

I don't know why I had not expected this summons. Given the twist of fate yesterday morning, it was I who told Mrs Murgatroyd that her husband was dead. As if she did not already know.

What gave me the shivers was the similarity between this coroner's letter and the one received by Freda Simonson just over ten years ago. The wording was almost identical and the signature the same. It was as if something was starting all over again, with the possibility for misunderstandings and faulty conclusions.

It was late. Harriet had long ago gone to bed with a copy of *The Secret Garden* borrowed from Susannah. Martin was ensconced in the jumble that was the loft.

I let the fire in the kitchen range die down and brought a shovelful of burning coals into the parlour where I continued to read and reread Aunt Freda's papers about the trial. By now, I felt I knew Freda Simonson. She was becoming so familiar to me that I half expected to see her walk into the room. Her gold-rimmed reading glasses were in the top drawer of her dressing table, alongside her face cream. She liked Pears' soap in the bathroom and carbolic in the kitchen. Her recipes were in a tin on the kitchen dresser, knitting patterns in the parlour corner cupboard with the tapestry bag that held balls of wool and knitting needles. She had lived simply and was a woman of many skills. The typed report of the judge's summing up was entirely without error. At commercial college, she would have earned full marks for this and had her typing displayed on the wall.

So absorbed was I that I forgot to hope that Lucian would call and tell me the results of the post mortem on Farmer Murgatroyd. The gentle tap on the door startled me. I expected Lucian to come in, but when the door did not open I went to see, taking the precaution of returning the papers to the cupboard.

At first, in the dim light, I did not recognise the tall figure, not until he spoke and apologised for disturbing me so late. It was Gabriel Cherry. He dangled a pair of rabbits in one hand, and a lantern in the other. Under his arm was a parcel, wrapped in newspaper.

'Come in.'

He hesitated, and then held out the rabbits. 'I brought you these, as well as what you were after for Victoria.'

I am not an entirely squeamish person – what former nurse could be? – but there is something about furry dead creatures that makes me queasy.

'Why don't you step inside, and I'll show you the pantry. There'll be a hook there.'

'If I'm not disturbing you.'

'You're not disturbing me. Do come in.'

He hesitated for a moment before extinguishing his lantern, setting it on the doorstep and following me through the hall into the kitchen.

'I'm sorry to call so late.'

'That's all right.'

The kitchen was gently lit by the low fire and the gaslight. I opened the pantry door and stepped aside, but not quickly enough to prevent a black furry rabbit brushing against my

220

arm. They are too similar to cats, especially the black ones. It made me think of my cat, Sookie, who has that same glossy black coat. That's why I don't like them.

When he had hung his offering on the hook behind the door, I closed it firmly. 'Come through, Mr Cherry.'

'Well all right. There was something I wanted to ask you.'

I led him into the parlour and waved at the chair. 'Please sit down. I'll be with you in just a moment.'

If I offered him refreshment, he would refuse. I had put a plate ready for Lucian with pork pie, cheese, pickles and bread. The kettle was off the boil and Aunt Freda's sherry did not seem appropriate. Fortunately, I travel with emergency brandy, and poured him a glass.

I brought in the tray.

Gabriel was looking into the fire and turned as I entered. 'Oh there was no need.'

'You've come a long way.'

'How did you know I'd come?'

I smiled. 'I didn't. But this is here anyway so please, tuck in.'

'Much appreciated. I didn't eat much today as it turned out.' First, he removed the newspaper from the parcel that he had carried under his arm. He screwed the newspaper into a tight ball and put it in the coal scuttle. It had covered a biscuit barrel in antique brass, about ten inches high and four or five inches wide. Inside was a removable glass jar, etched with a delicate pattern of bows and ovals. It contained letters, still in envelopes, bent to fit the shape of the jar. 'I kept them in here in case of rain or damp.' The biscuit barrel was battered and discoloured. He noticed me

221

looking at it. 'I buried it while I was away, and dug it up when I came back. But it was all over by then.' He placed the biscuit barrel on the hearth rug between us. 'They are all here, her letters.'

'Thank you. Was it difficult to find them?'

'No. Selina Gouthwaite does not know I found her hidey hole. I never go in the house these days, haven't since I came back from the war, but I know every nook and cranny from being a boy – all the secret places. I went in while she was in the cowshed and he was sleeping. They are such a pair.'

'Why did you come back there after the war?'

He shrugged. 'I didn't, not straight away. My mind had turned mercifully blank for a little while. My body knew the way back to the Parish of Langcliffe and that was where my legs brought me. I felt as if someone else had come back, someone I was watching, and me or the watcher was telling me what a fool I was to come back. But I didn't know what else to do. And they welcomed me with open arms.'

'And you stayed.'

'There was a great separateness from everything that had gone on before. Nothing was the same again.' He looked at the letters, and I knew he included Victoria Trevelyan among what was never the same. 'I keep to myself, don't go in the house. I just get on with what I can, tending the stock, keeping the farm in good heart which is a losing battle. Having my spot in the barn was luxury after the show over there. I didn't want for much else.'

'And now?'

'Another ending.' He touched the biscuit barrel with his toe. 'I don't suppose you need this. I have another use for

222

it.' He took the letters from the glass jar and handed them to me.

We sat quietly while he ate. At last, between mouthfuls, he said, 'Did the lad find his way here?'

'He did. It was you who sent him?'

'I brought him. He was scared. Two nights is long enough for any kid to camp out without a blanket.'

'He's upstairs, sleeping. His sister was greatly relieved to see him again.'

He smiled for the first time. 'There'll be a place for him at Murgatroyd's if he's inclined. Mr Trevelyan went to see Mrs Murgatroyd. They called me in and asked would I be foreman on Catrigg Farm. Take the livestock in hand.'

'And you agreed?'

'I did. I'm to have a cottage that's been standing empty since the shepherd's wife died and he went to live with his sister.'

He said this in the most neutral of tones. Mr Trevelyan must be a man of great discrimination if he could separate the fact of his wife having had an affair and a child with this man and yet be confident enough to offer him a step up. Perhaps there was method in what seemed like Trevelyan's madness.

'I'm glad you'll have a roof over your head.'

'Aye, and when I look about this room and see the fire in the grate, see how cosy a place can be, I look forward to moving in. Nipper's getting too old to bide in a barn.'

'Where is Nipper?'

'I left him sleeping. It's too far for him, this walk in the dark. I'd end up carrying him.'

'You said there was something you wanted to ask me.'

He drained his glass. 'Being as you took on the job of go-between, when you give back the letters, please say I won't trouble Victoria again. It's all over and done.'

This surprised me. Surely 'it' was long over and done. 'Yes, I'll say that.'

'She may have heard that I'm courting a widow from Stainforth. And tell her there's no need to fear Selina Gouthwaite. I took the precaution of helping myself to summat of theirs and have hidden it where no one will look. But she'll know it's gone and might make some threat to me or Victoria.' He took a sealed brown envelope from his pocket. 'If something happens to me, open this.'

I wanted to refuse, because after all I was only here for another week or two and something untoward might happen after I left. I should have explained this, but that would look like a refusal.

He saw my hesitation.

'If something happens, it will be soon. This can't go on. It will come to a head.'

'You are mysterious, Mr Cherry.'

He smiled. 'A man of mystery, that's me. It's just this, just in case there is some threat to Victoria, or revenge against me, or my dog.'

I took the envelope and put it and the letters in my satchel. 'I'll find a safe place for this.'

He looked at the picture above the fireplace, a country scene done in watercolours. 'I remember that picture from when Miss Simonson fed me and another boy during the storm. She was kind. After school one day when it was snowing, teachers asked people in the village who could give children from the tops a bed for the night. She took two of us in, and always did if the weather turned bad.'

'She was a good woman, from all I've heard.'

'A kind lady, now that I see her from the distance of time. As a lad, I thought her fierce. She made us mind our Ps and Qs and stood no nonsense.'

He moved as if to go, yet seemed reluctant to leave the fireside. I gave him another tot of brandy. It would be cold outside now.

'I don't suppose you were here in 1916 when she witnessed a murder outside the White Hart?'

'No. I'd just gone back to the front after a spell in hospital. But I heard about it later.'

'What did you hear?'

'The landlord at the Craven Heifer told me. He had a lot of time for Rufus Holroyd.'

'Did he say whether he thought the Irishman was guilty or innocent?'

'He thought he was guilty. It upset him. He said a drinker stabbing a publican goes against the laws of nature.'

'Miss Simonson was a witness for the defence.'

'I didn't know that. Apart from the landlord filling me in on events, people had stopped talking about it. It was never mentioned on the farm.'

The farm. This brought me back to my other question.

'Mr Cherry, Martin told me something and it puzzles me. On Saturday, after the poor boy thought he'd killed Mr Gouthwaite, he hovered about the farm, to see if he really had killed him, or whether the man would come out, or a policeman appear.'

'When I'm foreman, I'll be happy to take young Martin under my wing. He's a good little worker.'

'At present he's reluctant to go anywhere near the farms.'

'I don't blame him. But the Gouthwaites will go. They have no choice.'

'Martin said he saw Mr Murgatroyd go into the Gouthwaites' farmhouse on Saturday evening.'

'I know nothing about that.'

'Does it seem likely, and that they would have had a drink together?'

He thought for a moment. 'Gouthwaite brews his own firewater. He drinks plenty of it too, that's half his trouble, but I can't see Bill Murgatroyd socialising with him.'

He stood. 'Can I get a light for my lamp?'

'Yes of course.'

He brought in his oil lamp, lifted the glass, took a taper from the mantelpiece and lit it. 'Only thing makes sense to me is that Mr Murgatroyd would have tried to part with Gouthwaite on good terms. That would be his way of doing things.'

I walked him to the door. 'Thank you for the rabbits.'

I watched him go, the light of the lamp becoming smaller. Back in the house, I remembered what Mrs Murgatroyd had said. She had not wanted her husband to make peace with the Gouthwaites. If he had done so without her knowledge, he may have kept that to himself.

I made sure that I locked and bolted the doors front and back before going to bed.

When I looked in first on Harriet and then on Martin, both were sleeping soundly.

Sleep did not come for me for the longest time. I had expected to hear from Lucian, and was surprised by my own disappointment. True, I had seen him only yesterday but so much had happened since then that it felt as though days had passed.

Perhaps it was the tumultuous events of the day, or the responsibility not just for Harriet but for Martin that jolted me into wakefulness in the early hours, thoughts swirling round my brain and my head aching. Why had Lucian not come? What were the results of the post mortem on Mr Murgatroyd? Perhaps my note had not reached Lucian in Settle. He may well have gone back to Embsay where he also had patients.

I decided to go downstairs, make a cup of cocoa and cut a slice of bread. Aunt Freda must have never suffered headaches because I could not remember seeing a bottle of aspirins.

Drawing my dressing gown tightly, I placed a pan of milk and water on a ring of the little-used gas cooker.

Having made my cup of cocoa, I thought a breath of fresh air would help. I unlocked the back door and went into the garden, breathing in the scent of stock.

Looking up to see the stars, I saw that the sky over the hills was red and full of sparks and smoke. Something was on fire.

My mouth felt suddenly dry and a pain gripped my chest. Where was the fire? I couldn't tell. I ran to the back gate and stepped out onto the lane, as if that might allow me to get my bearings. It didn't. Every house I could see was in darkness.

What did people do here when there was a fire in the middle of the night, in a village that prided itself on shunning the telephone? What should I do? I wished Lucian were here. No telephone. No fire brigade to call. There was a police house, but where?

I stumbled back into the house, through the kitchen, along the hall, clumsily struggling to draw back the bolt on the front door. The post office – they would know who to contact. It was so dark. A cloud hid the moon. I didn't feel confident that I could find my way to the post office in darkness.

I grabbed a coat from the hall stand, slid on a pair of galoshes and went outside. As I hurried along the path to the gate, I heard sounds, voices, saw the flash of a lantern.

People who knew the area would look at the sky and locate the fire.

Two men stood near the odd three-storey house, the workhouse. One of them saw me. 'It's all right, missis, alarm's been raised.'

I heard a motorbike start and, as my eyes adjusted to the gloom, saw a man climb into the sidecar. A lot of good that would do! What did he have with him, half a gallon of water? They sped off into the night.

A third man with a lamp walked quickly in the direction of Threlfall Hall.

Distance and direction are difficult to judge in a strange place, especially at night, but I guessed the fire must be north of Catrigg Force.

Why hadn't I questioned Gabriel more carefully when he told me his fears of reprisal for having taken something from Selina Gouthwaite? I thought of him and his dog Nipper sleeping in their barn, being overcome by smoke, and then by fire. What an idiot I was. A man gives me an envelope and says, 'just in case there is some threat to Victoria, or revenge against me, or my dog.' What do I do? Take it and ask him pointless questions about a murder that took place a decade ago and can't be undone. If he burned to death, it would be my fault for pushing him to retrieve the letters, for not understanding the implications.

In spite of my haziness about the lie of the land, fear gripped my bowels. With a terrible certainty, I knew that the blaze came from the barn where Gabriel slept with his horse and dog.

Nineteen

When I woke suddenly from a smoke-filled dream, it took me a few moments to recall the events of the early hours, being in the garden, looking at the red sky and knowing that there must be a fire somewhere.

Feeling sick with apprehension, I glanced at the clock as I slid from the bed. News of the fire would be all around the village soon enough.

Wanting to let Harriet and our guest Martin sleep for as long as they needed, I went to the bathroom and washed at the basin. The pipes creaked so loudly I thought the house must be in pain. I dressed, putting on Freda's divided skirt, and tiptoed down the stairs.

I need not have tried to be quiet. Martin was already up and dressed. He had cleaned the range, lit a fire, filled the kettle and was toasting a teacake. He looked slightly embarrassed to be interrupted.

'You make yourself at home, Martin. You've saved me a job I hate, making fires.'

This appreciation cheered him.

'I looked in the garden to see where you spread ashes and soot.'

He was as practical as Mrs Sugden, who spread ashes around the rose bushes and had tried soot for whitening her teeth. 'Have you been up long?'

'Yes. I saw our Beth before she left for work, walked to the mill with her. I told her I'm definitely going back to Pendleton.'

'Was she all right about it?'

'No, but I'm going anyway.'

'Are you sure you'll have somewhere to stay and work in Pendleton?'

'Yes, with the blacksmith. He said he'd set me on if things didn't work out for me here. And I'll be well away from them Gouthwaites.'

He looked rested. I was glad of that because the thought did cross my mind that he might be the arsonist, taking revenge against Abner Gouthwaite. But Martin was too clean and still smelled of carbolic soap. I declared him not guilty.

'When you went to see Beth, did anyone talk about a fire during the night, somewhere on the tops?'

He shook his head. 'Nobody mentioned it. Whereabouts?'

'That's what I can't work out. I saw sparks in the sky.'

He finished toasting the first teacake. I buttered it and took it to Harriet, with a cup of tea. She was awake, bleary-eyed, and propped herself on her elbow. 'Is Martin up?'

'Yes, and dressed, but don't you rush. Stay in bed as long as you want.'

She sat up. 'Nah. I won't be long. I don't want to miss anything.'

I didn't tell her about the fire, but left her to eat her teacake in peace.

Downstairs, Martin toasted two more, and we each had one.

That was it. There was no bread in the crock, no cheese in the dish, not a drop of milk in the jug and a single egg in the basket. Sunday's half leg of ham was a clean bone. I could imagine my sister questioning Harriet when she went home. 'How did your Auntie Kate look after you? What did she feed you?' Mary Jane was of the opinion that I was sadly lacking in the skills and arts of domesticity. Well there would be no question of not taking care of Harriet. I would go out very soon and shop. For what, I had not quite decided.

It was quite likely that Mrs Holroyd had given Lucian the impression someone would come into Lilac Cottage and 'do' for us. She would be laughing up her sleeve, having met and disliked me, at the thought that I would have to shift for myself.

Martin went into the garden.

I opened the door. 'Martin, I know you are anxious to go home but don't run off will you? Someone will take you, to make sure you're all right.'

'Might it be you and Harriet?'

'Yes, or Dr Simonson. I don't have a lot of petrol but there's a friend coming today in another car and he may drive you back, depending on the petrol situation.'

Martin eyes widened. 'I've never been in a car.'

'There's always a first time.'

'Or Dr Simonson might lend me one of the bicycles you have in the shed.'

'Well just wait. You're safe here, and there's no great rush. It won't hurt you to have a bit of a holiday, unless you feel fed up being here.'

'Oh no.' He took a knife and a piece of wood from his pocket. 'I'm doing this. It's a surprise for Harriet and Susannah. I'm making each of them a little animal.' He began to whittle the wood.

'What kind of animal?'

'I'll see as I go along. I have a feeling Susannah's will be a tortoise and Harriet's a hare.'

'Who taught you?'

'My dad. I wanted him to carve my initial on the handle, but he did this.' He showed me a circular squiggle.

'What is it?'

'It represents the only part of a pig you can't eat.'

'Its tail?'

'Guess again.'

'You have me stumped.'

'Its squeal!'

When he laughed, he looked like a little boy without a care in the world. I left him to his carving, determined that he would go back to Pendleton if that was what he wanted.

I tore the blank stop press column from the newspaper and took a pencil from the jar to write a shopping list. My mind was not on groceries, but on the letter Gabriel Cherry had given me to be opened only if 'something happened'. I liked and felt an affinity with the man. When I thought of him, it was to see him in action as a stretcher bearer, that worst of tasks, picking up the wounded, often under fire, making agonising decisions that could determine whether a man lived or died. If anything had happened to him . . . I felt weak at the thought. I had to know.

Harriet came downstairs. She had washed, dressed and done her hair in a single neat plait. I wondered what had come over her to present herself so tidily first thing in the morning, and then I remembered Martin.

She looked at him through the window. 'I hope he'll stay a bit longer.'

'I think he will.' I picked up the basket. 'I'm going to do some shopping.'

'Do you want me to come?'

'No. Stay and keep Martin company.'

I opened the front door at the right moment. The milk-man's horse and cart was next door. I went for the jug and took it to the gate. He poured a gill for me. 'Did you hear any news of the fire on the tops?' I asked.

'I did, missis. It was a barn on the Gouthwaite farm, burned to the ground.'

My worst fear. With great effort, I managed to sound calm. 'Was anyone hurt?'

'There'd be no one in there, would there? Unless some tramp bedded down and had a smoke.'

Was he speaking from knowledge, or guesswork? 'Do you get your milk from up that way?'

'Oh no. This milk's from Hope Hill Farm here in the village.'

'Thank you.'

My hands were shaking as I took the jug through to the kitchen. A barn on the Gouthwaite farm, the barn occupied by Gabriel Cherry, his dog, his horse and his nightmares.

The one place I would learn about the fire was Threlfall Hall, but I had to buy food, make sure that Harriet kept up her strength and that our guest didn't go hungry.

At the butcher's I bought liver, sausages and black pudding; I shopped at the baker's, the grocer's and the greengrocer's. Everyone had heard about the fire. No one yet knew whether there were casualties, but that did not mean there were none.

When I went back to the cottage, Harriet and Martin were playing cricket in the garden.

'Is it all right if I call for Susannah?' she asked. 'It's best if the bowler doesn't have to field.'

'Yes of course, and will you three be all right if I stay and chat for an hour or two to Mrs Trevelyan?'

She would. In fact, she seemed pleased to be left in charge.

I had carried Victoria Trevelyan's love letters to her in a tapestry needlework bag.

We sat on either side of the fire in her private sitting room. She nursed the letters in her lap, the envelopes having kept their curved shape from being so long in the biscuit barrel. Mrs Trevelyan was not yet dressed. She wore a tangerine-coloured silk dressing gown trimmed with exquisite lace.

She sniffed an envelope. 'I used to dab my letters with scent, ashes of roses.' She breathed in deeply. 'Even paper has a memory for romance.' She glanced again at the letters, and hesitated before committing them to the flames. 'Should I?'

I did not answer. It was a choice only she could make.

235

'How did he seem when he brought the letters to you?'

'He was quite calm.'

'Was he loath to part with them?'

I hadn't really thought about that, but now that I did it struck me that his emotion had been relief. Was it relief at having rescued the incriminating letters from Mrs Gouthwaite, or of being shot of the whole business of that long-ago affair? If I had to guess, I would say the latter.

'Once he knew they had fallen into the wrong hands I believe he saw that it was best to do as you asked. He said he wouldn't trouble you further.' Out of kindness, I slightly rephrased his words. 'He realises it is all over between you.'

'Long over.' She lowered her head. 'I should do it. I should burn them.'

She waited a moment longer, perhaps to see whether I would contradict her, or she might contradict herself.

'He said to mention that he is courting a widow from Stainforth.'

A stillness came over her. She held her breath and stared into the fire. When she took her next breath, something in her had changed.

'The barmaid from the Craven Heifer?'

'He didn't say.'

'My young maid keeps me informed of village gossip. I didn't know it was as serious as courting, but I don't begrudge him. I know I'll be the love of his life.'

Slowly she dropped the first letter into the fire, and the next, and the next. The flames shot up. Specks of soot in the fireback sparked blue and orange.

'You need to poke the paper into the coals or you'll set the chimney ablaze.'

She picked up the poker awkwardly, possibly for the first time in her life.

When the job was done, I asked the question that had been gnawing away. 'The fire last night, did you hear anything about it?'

'My maid mentioned it, but she was a little vague.'

'It was a barn on Raistrick Farm. She didn't say which barn, or whether anyone was hurt?'

I did not tell her that Gabriel made it his habit to sleep in a barn. Perhaps she did not know, because she showed no particular interest, except to say, 'It's one thing after another round here.'

'Might you enquire from Bertie whether there were casualties?'

She suddenly remembered her position as the landowner's wife. 'Of course! You're absolutely right. Here's me thinking only about the past. I'll find out immediately. I do know he was called out because of it, during the night.'

She moved to ring the bell and thought better of it. Anyone who came in would see the letters burning. She dropped the remaining letters into the fire and handed me the poker. 'I'll ask him.'

Harriet and Susannah bumped into her as she was leaving the room. They had been hatching some plan. It was left to Susannah to speak. 'Mother, is it all right if Harriet and I go to her house and play draughts?'

'Well you could play draughts here.'

'I know but it makes a change for me. I never have a friend to be with and I'm always here.'

I smiled at them, glad of an opportunity to make an exit. 'Give me a few minutes and I'll come with you.'

It is a good thing that I am not sensitive. The failure of the girls to hide their disappointment would have cut me to the quick.

'It's all right, Auntie. We don't mind being on our own.'

Mrs Trevelyan and I exchanged a look. They were almost grown up. They wanted some independence. Mrs Trevelyan said, 'Off you go, but come back for lunch.'

'It's all right,' Harriet said. 'We have lunch planned.' That was a very suitable answer to give and Harriet kept a straight face.

'Then be back for tea, Susannah.'

Off they went.

I waited, while Mrs Trevelyan went to enquire about last night's blaze, looking at the ashes of love letters in the grate, wondering whether somewhere in this house was a bundle of notes from Gabriel Cherry to Victoria Trevelyan, and if so how well-hidden they might be.

When Mrs Trevelyan returned, she said, 'Bertie's up on the tops now, assessing the damage. They're raking through the ashes to see what was lost.'

Had a life been lost, I wondered.

Her mouth opened. She turned a little pale. 'What, what are you thinking, what?'

'I was just wondering . . . '

'Gabriel. You think Gabriel . . . '

'No, of course not. But . . . '

'What?'

'He sleeps in one of the barns. But you must know that.'

'No. I didn't know he slept in a barn, why would he?'

'By choice. It was that or share a house with the Gouthwaites.'

'So, are you saying he caused the fire with a cigarette?'

'Let me take Miss Shady. I'm wearing the right sort of skirt so don't need a riding habit.'

'I should come with you.'

'Think about it, Victoria.' It was the first time I had used her Christian name. 'Your husband is there. Isn't it better if I go?'

'What reason would you have for riding there, except as my emissary?'

'I am not an emissary. I saw the fire in the early hours and went out to raise the alarm. Naturally I am concerned.'

'You're right, of course. You are staying in Dr Simonson's house and may be a neighbour, soon.'

She went to her bureau and opened the drawer. I saw that she was taking out a cheque book. 'I want to compensate you for your assistance. Please don't write out an account. I have had enough of pieces of paper.'

For once I broke my rule and refused payment. 'No, Victoria. Your daughter and my niece are friends.'

'And we are too, I hope, and may become much better acquainted if you and Lucian . . . Well, I hope we will stay friends, and neighbours.'

Part of me would love to think of sharing a house, a life, with Lucian. From our first meeting he had never been anything other than kind, thoughtful and amusing. He was keen to marry and settle down, and sometimes I dreamed of that myself, and of having a child, children. I pushed those thoughts aside as I went to the stable to seek out the grey mare.

Miss Shady knew her way to the two hill farms. She slowed as we neared Catrigg Farm. I urged her on to Raistrick

Farm. As we drew closer, the mare tossed her head, nostrils flaring, disliking the acrid smell of smoke and ashes as much as I did. Miss Shady was on edge, perhaps picking up on my nervousness as well as sniffing the unwelcome stench of dying embers.

Two men stood near what was left of the barn. It was the barn where Gabriel had slept and kept his secrets.

As I grew closer, a wave of relief spread over me. One man, old and bent, the other tall with black hair turning grey and a plaid cloak draped over his shoulder. They had herded half a dozen sad-looking cows. They animals stood nearby, hooves deep in mud, watched by Gabriel's little dog with rapt attention. Nipper knew that he alone prevented a mad stampede.

The old man tipped his cap to me as he urged the cows towards the farmyard gate. Nipper trotted beside them.

I dismounted.

Miss Shady, disliking the reek of smoke, refused to go further, but she did not need to.

Gabriel Cherry walked across, running his fingers through his hair. 'It's all but out.'

'What happened?'

He shrugged. 'Well, it didn't light itself.'

'Were you inside?'

'No. I've you to thank for that, Mrs Shackleton.'

'Me?'

'I told you last night that Mrs Murgatroyd offered me the shepherd's old cottage. It wasn't her first time of offering. When I spent that half hour in your parlour, well, in Miss Simonson's parlour, I thought why shouldn't I have a bit of comfort? Why be tied to the place you know best when there's another that invites you? When I came back after visiting you, I picked up my bits and pieces and Nipper, and moved us up to the cottage then and there.'

'What about your horse?'

'Him too. He's stabled at Catrigg Farm.'

'How did the fire start?'

He jerked a thumb towards the farmhouse. 'How do you think? I got the better of Selina Gouthwaite. That wouldn't do, would it?'

'Arson?'

'When I hammered on their door early hours, Gouthwaite was already blaming the lad, Martin. Gouthwaite wants to believe that. Some people are quick to swallow their own lies.'

'I'm very glad you're safe.' I looked across at the farmhouse. It was tight shut, windows and doors. 'Did you tell Mr Trevelyan of your suspicions?'

'I told him I knew Martin was several miles away, with you. Mr Trevelyan's in with the pair of them now. Gouthwaite can't come out. She won't come out.' He shrugged. 'They're past help. They always were. We're moving their livestock along to Catrigg Farm. No reason for the beasts to suffer.'

'What's to become of them, and all of this?' I looked around the farm, more ramshackle than ever in the wake of the fire.

He shrugged. 'Happen the Gouthwaites will go back where they came from.'

We stood in silence for a few moments. 'Mr Cherry, you entrusted me with a letter because you feared there would be some reprisal against you. Well that has happened.'

'I can barely credit it, the sense of Selina burning her own barn.'

'It's not her barn any more, and people aren't always logical. We who came through the war know that.'

'True.'

'I don't want to seem melodramatic, but Freda Simonson wanted me to find out who really did murder Rufus Holroyd. The only way I have any possibility of doing that is discovering what secrets people have, grudges, jealousies, fears. I'm good at keeping secrets, Mr Cherry. Will you give me permission to open that letter you entrusted to me?'

He hesitated.

I pushed the advantage of his hesitation. 'Had you not gone to the empty cottage last night, I would be opening the letter now.'

A call from the old man caught his attention. The gate was open, the cows beginning to move. Nipper had followed the cows into the lane, now he ran back to Gabriel, gave a small yelp and turned, ready to go back to the cows.

Gabriel moved to leave. 'Open it if you must, Mrs Shackleton. But if you act on the information, it had better be at night.'

Before I had time to ask what he meant, he strode off.

I remounted.

Gabriel waited, and closed the gate behind me.

I was a hundred yards or so along the lane when Mr Trevelyan, riding a chestnut stallion, caught up with me. We exchanged a greeting.

'Are you and Harriet enjoying your stay, Mrs Shackleton?'

'Yes, thank you. Mrs Trevelyan has been very kind. As you see, I'm entrusted with Miss Shady for my morning ride.'

We chatted about horses and although I am not very knowledgeable I scraped together a few pertinent questions about his stables, and about a racehorse he had acquired. Conversation eventually turned to the fire. He had heard that I rose during the night and went out to raise the alarm.

'Is that why you rode up this way this morning, to see the damage?'

I shot him a quick glance, to try and guess what he knew, but his expression gave nothing away. 'Having seen the sparks in the sky last night and driven this way yesterday, I wanted to see for myself.'

He chuckled. 'Occupational hazard for you, I suppose. Your reputation goes before you, you know, that business at Bolton Abbey.'

'Ah yes.'

'I know a chap who works for an insurance company. He would do exactly the same, whether his company held the policy or not. He would want to investigate.'

'I'm relieved there was no loss of life.'

'So am I.'

'Do you have an idea of the cause, Mr Trevelyan?'

He frowned. 'You may have heard that I am not renewing Abner Gouthwaite's lease?'

'Yes, I did hear.'

'Fire-raising is treated very seriously by the magistrates, but one has to have evidence, and I do not have evidence. I came up here to send them packing this very day. Ended up relenting and telling Gouthwaite they could stay until his leg is on the mend.'

'That is good of you.'

'I don't need that house yet. They may as well stay on for the present.' He sighed. 'Murgatroyd's death is a terrible blow. Fortunately for all concerned, Gabriel Cherry is a good all-rounder. He's been on these hill farms since he was a boy. I was unsure what the war might do to him, but I do believe it has sent his roots deeper into the land. He will doubtless acquit himself very well.'

He nodded to himself, as if until that moment he had not entirely decided about Gabriel Cherry.

Was that all he concerned himself with, I wondered. Something in his enigmatic expression made me believe he knew all there was to know about his wife's affair, that Gabriel Cherry was Susannah's father, and that the relationship between Gabriel and Victoria was well and truly over.

I wanted to give some words of praise about Gabriel, and how he had found Martin Young and sent him to Lilac Cottage. But he knew that too.

'Thank you for taking care of the lad from Pendleton, Mrs Shackleton.'

'He's no trouble. He's a helpful boy and he feels sure the blacksmith in Pendleton will take him on. He wants to go home.'

'Won't he mind being parted from his sister?'

'I think not. She's well settled and he has made up his mind, young as he is.'

'I'll make an enquiry. Make sure the blacksmith wants him.'

We talked of other things, the hospital in Skipton, the need for a doctor in Langcliffe, and the excellence of the Village Institute.

But I could not help thinking about Gabriel, and how close he had come to death. He was safe for now, but for how much longer?

The Gouthwaites were a brooding malignant force and their reign was not yet over.

Twenty

When Mr Trevelyan and I returned to the stables, Victoria was preparing to go riding, but clearly hovering, waiting for my return. As I dismounted, her husband exchanged a few words with her, giving her arm an absent-minded pat. 'No loss of life, dear, nothing to fret over. Won't happen again, now that I've marked a certain person's card.'

'Have the Gouthwaites gone?' she asked.

'Not yet but they won't dare put a foot wrong until they take their final leave, not now I've spoken to them.'

'Bertie, how did the fire start?'

'The constable is investigating, dear. Difficult, you know.' He turned and wished me good day.

When he had gone, she said, 'He lets people off too easily.'

It was just as well for her that he did. 'He's a kind man, Victoria.'

'Yes. Kind.' She mounted her horse. 'Is Gabriel safe?'

'He moved into the vacant cottage. The move saved his life.'

*

When I arrived back at Lilac Cottage I saw Lucian's motor parked outside. Harriet came to meet me. 'Where did you get to, Auntie? Dr Simonson has come to take us to lunch. We might go to Pendleton because Martin wants to go home.'

'Where are they?'

'In the garden.' She walked into the hall. 'Susannah didn't stay long. Her governess arrived back and she's keen to see her.'

'That's good. Perhaps she'll let you sit in on some of their drawing lessons, or French.'

Lucian was batting in the garden. Martin bowled. Lucian hit the ball, sending it over the garden gate.

I went into the garden, conscious of what I was wearing and wondering if he recognised his aunt's skirt. If he did, he said nothing. He kissed me on the cheek. 'Just in time. I've persuaded these young people not to bring a charge of neglect against you.'

'What about your neglect of me?'

'You'd have cause to complain if I were here all the time.'

'What's this about going out?'

'I want to stand you lunch. It's just the day for a ride in the country.'

Martin came back with the ball. He set it down and tucked his thumbs into his trouser pockets. He rocked a little back and forth on his heels as if wanting to be off and running. 'Might you take me back to Pendleton, sir?'

Lucian looked at me, waiting to hear what I had to say.

'Let's not be hasty, Martin. You've had a bad experience. Stay here just a little longer.'

I wanted to be sure he would find a place in his own village. After all, there may have been a very good reason why he and Beth were sent packing and I preferred to wait until Bertie Trevelyan had made his enquiries.

Lucian frowned. For some reason he seemed to want shot of the boy. 'Martin was telling me about the Pendleton blacksmith.' He looked at Martin who took up the story eagerly.

'He said I could come to him and his wife anytime. I helped him, see, and his son didn't come back from the war. They'd be glad to see me. And it's where my dad will come back when he's finished his travels.'

'Martin! We've talked about this. You're not a prisoner. You'll go back very soon when one of us can take you.'

Lucian nodded. 'Go take another look round upstairs and see if there's any more clothes of mine that fit you. There's a valise there too, you could put them in that. Then you'll be packed and ready to go as soon as we can arrange it.'

For a moment the boy stood with a surprised look on his face, as if someone had given him a great big unexpected present. Harriet took his hand. 'Come on, you don't need telling twice.'

When they had gone upstairs, Lucian said, 'He and Harriet told me what happened. The lad's had a bad time at Raistrick farm. If we drive him to Pendleton we can see for ourselves whether there's a place for him. If he's big enough and old enough to be sent out to earn his living, he should have some say in the matter.'

We sat down on the garden bench. 'Bertie Trevelyan is going to contact his friend in Pendleton and make enquiries,' I told him.

'Oh that's all right then. I thought if Martin left, it would be one less thing for you to worry about.'

'I'm not worried! But I am curious about the post mortem on Mr Murgatroyd. Can you tell me about it, or do I have to wait for the inquest tomorrow?'

'You'll know soon enough. The autopsy was undertaken as a matter of urgency. You can't be too careful in an agricultural district.' Although the walls surrounding the garden were high, he lowered his voice. 'There was a full analysis of blood, stomach contents, and what had been absorbed in the gut and stools.'

'And?'

He hesitated, reluctant to say more, or thinking how best to phrase the findings. 'There were sufficiently high traces of potassium to cause concern.'

'Meaning?'

'Meaning that he was poisoned.'

It was one thing to have suspected this, and quite another to have it confirmed. Everyone would expect an anodyne cause of death, heart attack, some undiagnosed condition, a sudden rush of blood to the brain. Now the tenor of life in the Parish of Langcliffe would once more suffer a jolt. Farmer Murgatroyd had been murdered. In one of those sudden mad insights, I could understand why people lied, smoothed over, pretended something had not happened when the evidence told another story. There had been the likelihood that Jennifer Murgatroyd's wedding might have proceeded quietly after a natural death. But what would happen now was difficult to guess. My thoughts turned to that shelf of home remedies in Mrs Murgatroyd's kitchen. Just the right measure of a potion might do a great deal of good. The wrong measure could kill.

'Was it possible to identify the poison?'

'It's likely to have been digoxin.'

'A heart remedy?'

'Yes.'

'Was he taking medication for a heart defect?'

'No and neither was anyone else in the household. Sergeant Dobson tells me there are foxgloves planted in the garden but it would take a barrow load of the leaves to kill him.'

'Could the poisoning have been gradual?'

'The indication is of a massive dose.'

'What had Mr Murgatroyd eaten or drunk?'

'A Sunday dinner with mutton and two veg, a corned beef sandwich with mustard, and something alcoholic.'

'Mrs Murgatroyd said that his last meal was the Sunday roast.'

'Perhaps he was peckish and made himself a sandwich.'

'Not when he was out on the farm all afternoon and she was at home.'

'What are you suggesting?'

'Someone must have made him that sandwich and given him a drink, either his wife or Abner or Selina Gouthwaite.'

'The Gouthwaites?'

It felt unfair to bring in Martin. He was too young and had been through enough, but the interests of truth and justice left no choice. 'Mr Murgatroyd was seen coming from Gouthwaite's farm on Saturday evening.'

Lucian's eyes widened. 'By whom?'

'Martin. He saw Bill Murgatroyd go into the farmhouse and come out rather unsteady on his feet.'

Lucian let out a whistle of surprise. 'I'd better take the

lad into Settle police station. Sergeant Dobson needs to hear this in advance of the inquest.'

'Yes, another reason why he can't go dashing back to Pendleton just yet.'

On the stairs there was laughter and the thump of footsteps.

'Martin has packed!' Harriet came into the room, followed by Martin. 'Do you want to see what he's taking, Dr Simonson?'

'Er, yes. I'd better.'

Martin presented his suitcase for inspection.

I caught Harriet's eye and led her into the parlour, to give Lucian the opportunity to prepare Martin for the fact that he would need to give a statement to Sergeant Dobson, the coroner's officer.

The four of us lunched in Giggleswick in a small café that suited us very well. Martin and Harriet chose egg and chips. Lucian and I followed suit. I did not know what Lucian had said to Martin about the need for him to give evidence at the inquest, but it had done the trick.

With Lucian, Martin had almost willingly entered the police station at Settle to give the sergeant the information he had so casually passed to me – that he had seen Mr Murgatroyd leaving the Gouthwaites's farm appearing unsteady on his feet. I only hoped it would be possible to let Martin leave the court as soon as he had given evidence and that it would not be too harrowing for him.

In the café, Martin sat tall, paying his food a good deal of thoughtful attention. I gave Lucian a little smile of appreciation. He grinned.

Thinking about eventually being able to take Martin

home brought to mind the rail strike and petrol shortage, and I remembered to tell Harriet the good news.

'We'll have a change of clothes soon. Mr Sykes is bringing our trunk across.'

'I thought it was coming on the train.'

'It would have been, if not for the strike.'

Harriet dug a spoon into her treacle pudding and custard. 'I'm glad the railway workers are showing solidarity.'

'Yes.'

'Do you know if there is a strike fund, Auntie? I'd like to put my sixpence in.'

'I'll try and find out.'

Lucian and Martin glanced at her in surprise, but she did not notice. I suppose it was unusual for a girl of her age to be on the side of the revolution, but she had her poor dead father to thank for that.

Only Lucian had not ordered pudding, not having a sweet tooth. He took a drink of tea. 'Sykes must have good contacts if he has no difficulty finding petrol to come to Langcliffe and back.'

After our meal, we went for a walk to Tarn Brow. Martin and Harriet strode ahead. Lucian and I walked arm in arm. He never talked about his gammy leg except to be amused by it and thankful for the fact that he still had two legs. I wondered how much it pained him and what difficulties it caused. I asked him.

'Oh it helps to give it a good swing about, as long as I have my stick. You'd be surprised how far I can walk when I put my mind to it. Uphill, too. Downhill isn't so clever but I can do it.'

When we reached the tarn, Harriet and Martin took off

their shoes and socks and paddled. Lucian had brought a rug and spread it on the ground, playing Walter Raleigh, giving a mock bow. We sat down.

'So how do you like the Parishes of Langcliffe and Giggleswick, Kate?'

'Very much. Listen to that silence.'

'So quiet that it hums.' He took out a cigar. 'Too much fresh air doesn't do me any good.' He lit his cigar. 'Could the joint attractions of Langcliffe and Giggleswick parishes and me tempt you into taking a big step?'

'That's a rather unconventional way of popping the question.'

'Then which knee do you want me to go down on?'

'Neither as I'm not sure I could help you up.'

He smiled. 'I'd like you to be sure. I don't want to hurry you and hear a no.'

'You haven't asked me anything yet.'

'You told me not to rush you and I won't.'

We sat quietly for a while, watching a hen harrier dip over the tarn.

Harriet had taken out her camera and was showing it to Martin. He took it from her and looked through it. The pair of them sat very still, watching a flock of ducks.

'But did you give any thought to whether Lilac Cottage parlour might make a good consulting space, or whether I'd need to expand into next door?'

'I did as it happens.'

'Oh, thank you! What did you come up with?'

I did not say that I had thought up this plan during my restless night in a desperate attempt to send myself to sleep when counting sheep did not work.

'Get rid of the sideboard and replace it with a desk. Find yourself a suitable chair. An existing chair would do for the patient. Banish all those ornaments to a jumble sale if you can be hard-hearted about it. Use a screen at the other end of the room, which you could remove, and still have a parlour when you want it. There's plenty of room in the kitchen for the medicines you can't keep in the corner cupboard. Have that bed taken out of the alcove. It's old-fashioned to have a bed in the kitchen.'

'What a good idea. That would allow me to set up fairly quickly and think about taking over the adjacent cottage once I'm more established.'

'Mr Sykes could help you move the sideboard.'

'Sykes? How long is he planning to stay? I thought he was just bringing your trunk.'

'There's a bit more to it than that.'

'Oh?'

'I asked him to see what he could find out about the murder case that so upset your aunt.'

'Why?'

'The trial was Leeds Assizes. He has a lot of connections.'

'I mean why are you looking into it?'

'Your aunt wanted me to.'

'This is Wiggy's doing, don't tell me it's not.'

'Partly. He brought me her papers. She mentioned me, Lucian. She hoped I would do something about it.'

'You can't, not after all this time. Wiggy had no business interfering.'

'She had it in mind that I would find the truth.'

'That's ridiculous.'

'You see if she was right and Flaherty was innocent, the

one way to prove that would be to find who really did kill Mr Holroyd.'

'I respect that Aunt Freda was convinced of Flaherty's innocence, but the police don't want to hang the wrong man. No one does. She didn't want me to do anything about it because . . .'

'Because you're a doctor, and your business is medicine. You had told her about me.'

'I wish I hadn't.'

'But you did, and so what I'm saying does make sense.'

'Because of who you are, you would see it that way. There is no other way for you to see it, except to want to find out the truth.' He put his arm around me. 'That's part of your appeal, Kate. I wouldn't want to stop you doing what you do best, only I suppose it doesn't entirely fit with what I do.'

'It's possible it might fit very well in a place like Langcliffe.'

'What do you mean by that?'

'I've only been here a few days and we're to attend an inquest tomorrow that could result in a murder trial.'

At that moment, Harriet and Martin looked in our direction. She waved.

'I want to protect them, Lucian. Harriet has had her fill of the dark side of life, and so has he. She wants to be my assistant, and she's a very good little helper, but I need Sykes. I hope he'll be able to do a little digging.'

'What kind of protection do you mean? If you don't feel safe here, we can go to Embsay, all of us.'

'I've asked Mr Sykes to stay. I want him to help reinvestigate the murder of Mr Holroyd. I've done what I can.'

'Which is?'

'I'm not going into details, not yet.'

'You are here for just two weeks and you are not able to leave off your sleuthing.'

'You were the one who started me off, and don't deny it.'

'Me? How?'

'Because you invited me here. You asked me to come to the place where your aunt witnessed a murder, and it turns out to have been her intention that I investigate.'

There was a slight frostiness when Lucian dropped us off at the door of Lilac Cottage.

Harriet and Martin went inside. Lucian sat glued to his driver's seat.

'Will you come in?' I asked.

'No. I'd better get back. Patients are no respecter of a doctor's day off and I don't want McKinley to overdo it. He hasn't been well lately. In any case, I'll leave you to your visitor. I suppose assistant detective Sykes will be arriving shortly.'

'I was hoping you might be here, and suggest somewhere he could stay.'

'He's not staying here then?'

'Of course not.'

I knew Sykes irritated Lucian, but I had not suspected he could be jealous or think there might be something between us. That was ridiculous.

Lucian looked relieved. 'He could do worse than the Craven Heifer in Stainforth. It's not a hotel but they have one or two rooms that they let out occasionally.'

'Right, I'll tell him.'

'I'll see you and Martin at the inquest tomorrow. Shall I pick you up?'

'No need.'

'I expect Sykes will drive you.'

'And I expect we'll walk. It's no distance and Mr Sykes is bound to be low on petrol.'

'Right then, till tomorrow!'

Feeling utterly miserable, I watched him drive away. We both had such high hopes of this time we would spend together, and with Harriet, trying out what it might feel like to be a family. Was it me? Was it him? Harriet was the only one emerging with credit, being helpful, tactful, with her endearing wish to be a detective.

It must be me. He was a nice, sweet, reasonable man. Look at the way he reassured Martin and made the lad feel good about himself.

Fate conspired to make life difficult. All I could hope for just now was a better day tomorrow, the day of the inquest.

I looked up at the speeding clouds. I could blame the planets. Perhaps the fault was not in ourselves but in our stars.

Twenty-One

Lucian waved as he drove away. As soon as I opened the front door, I smelled baking. I walked through the hall into the kitchen.

There was Mrs Sugden, sitting in the Windsor chair, knitting and holding court as Harriet told her where we had been, and introduced Martin.

'Mrs Sugden, what are you doing here?'

'That's a fine greeting.' She looked up from her knitting. 'I wonder how long you would have let them rabbits hang. They belong in a pie, not behind the pantry door.'

'I expected Mr Sykes.'

'He's here. What a journey we had. I'd no idea how far flung you were.'

'Well I'm pleased to see you. It's a surprise, that's all. Where is Mr Sykes?'

'Doing what he calls his reconnoitre round the village. Oh and he's taken your trunk upstairs.'

'And where's his motor?'

'Mr Mysterious chooses to leave it round the back. As if in a village the size of a postage stamp folk won't notice an additional car no matter where he puts it. They'll all take a gander, discuss where he scratched the black paint and it shows through blue.'

'Who's Mr Sykes?' Martin asked.

'He works with my auntie,' Harriet said. 'Come on, Martin, let's go out and see if we can find him.'

When the door closed behind them, Mrs Sugden paused in her knitting. 'I see it didn't take you long to pick up a waif.'

'Things haven't worked out as I thought they might.'

'Well I'm here now, and I'll stay a couple of days. That cat doesn't take up all my time and young Thomas Tetley comes in to feed her and let her in and out. She'll survive. I'm not sure you will.'

'This was to be a holiday for you as well as me.'

'How is it a holiday for you when you're shopping and cooking? For me staying here will be a change of scene.' She clicked her needles, a new row. 'Unless you have someone else looking after you?'

'No.'

'Good. I'll have that bed in the alcove. I always thought it a good idea to have a bed in a kitchen corner and make use of the warmth.'

'I'm glad you're staying. One or two things have cropped up.'

Without a pause from her knitting, Mrs Sugden looked up. 'Mr Sykes hinted as much from what you said. He didn't want me to come, you know, but I had this sixth sense that you might appreciate my help.'

It suddenly occurred to me that she was absolutely right. If anyone could make sure Harriet was properly fed, it was Mrs Sugden. What's more, if anyone could cajole Mrs Holroyd into talking, it would be Mrs Sugden. The women had a lot in common, both being practical, down to earth and knowing the value of sixpence. Mrs Holroyd had taken against me, probably thinking me a cut above.

We chatted about how things were at home, and what needed doing here. I told her about Mr Wigglesworth and his request.

'You see, Lucian's Aunt Freda left me something of a tragic puzzle.' I told her about the murder, the trial, and Aunt Freda's conviction that the wrong man was hanged. 'And if anyone knows whether Rufus Holroyd, the murdered innkeeper, had enemies, it would be his widow. She won't talk to me. I rubbed her up the wrong way.'

'That's a turn up for the books.' Mrs Sugden reached the end of a sleeve, examined her work and then folded it around the needles. 'What's she like, this Mrs Holroyd?'

I described her, adding that she took in lodgers and had the house on New Street opposite the washing green. 'But don't call them lodgers. According to Lucian, she likes to call them paying guests.'

'From what you say, it sounds as if she has made a nice little niche for herself. Perhaps I could ask her advice about who are the reliable tradesmen.'

'If she knows you are my housekeeper, she may be reluctant to have anything to do with you.'

Mrs Sugden gave a mysterious smile. 'Not if I explain how difficult my life is working with you, and how I envy a woman like her who has her independence.'

'Mrs Sugden, you are a genius.'

She nodded agreement.

'If she's taken against you, she'll be willing to believe me, and be very anxious to hear my complaints.'

'Then do it. Say whatever you like. Tell her I throw plates and deduct the cost from your wages, anything at all to make her talk.'

'What do you want to know?'

'If Aunt Freda was right and the wrong man was found guilty, I want to know if there are any other men in this village who would have wished her husband harm.'

Mrs Sugden let out a sharp breath. 'And here's me thinking the worst thing about this village was that the butcher sells so many pies. I expected women in Langcliffe to be quite capable of doing their own baking.'

'Some of them work in the mill. So I suppose they like to have something convenient.'

'I'd better know a bit more about this murder.'

I told Mrs Sugden about Aunt Freda's evidence for the defence. I also, by the by, told her about calling at Murgatroyds' farm on Sunday, and the suspicious death of Mr Murgatroyd.

'What kind of place have you fetched up in? I said you should have gone to Whitby. No wonder that doctor wants to marry you. He won't feel at peace until the Langcliffe murderers have been caught and seen to. Which one are we looking into?'

'It has to be the death in 1916.'

'Why, if there's some poisoner abroad now?'

'Because I don't know enough about that yet. There'll be an inquest tomorrow and I'm hoping that the coroner will find the truth.'

'And what progress have you made on this wartime murder?'

'I've spoken to the priest who confirmed what I thought, that Flaherty was innocent.'

'Well he would say that wouldn't he? Left footers are bound to stick together.'

'Perhaps. But if you had been there, I think you would have believed him too. Aunt Freda's good friend, Bradley Wigglesworth, brought me Aunt Freda's papers and wants to talk to me.'

'What are we hoping to do? We can't bring the hanged man back.'

'I know. But it was Aunt Freda's dying wish that we try to clear his name.'

I described my meeting with Mrs Holroyd at the village institute on May Day and how she had resented Aunt Freda's involvement in the trial, believing that it prolonged her own agony.

Mrs Sugden listened carefully. 'I think I have the woman's measure. I'll see what I can find out.'

'Oh and you might want to say that Mrs Trevelyan or the vicar recommended you to talk to her, or she may smell a rat.'

'Hey up!' It was Sykes. 'Do I catch a whiff of rabbit pie?'

I smiled at them both. Their arrival gave me an inkling of what it must have been like at the relief of Mafeking. I was no longer investigating alone.

Mrs Sugden took off her pinafore. She pointed to the clock. 'Can somebody keep an eye on that pie, and take it out in ten minutes without severely burning their hands?'

'Where are you going?' Sykes asked.

'To call on a neighbour. Is Harriet about?'

Sykes nodded towards the front of the house. 'She and Martin are sitting on the garden wall.'

'Then she can show me the way.'

When Mrs Sugden had gone, I talked to Sykes about where he might stay. He liked the sound of the Craven Heifer and would cycle there. 'It's a devil of a do about the petrol supply just now, what with the strike and not knowing how long it will last. I've brought enough for the return journey to Leeds and I've stashed it in the cellar here for safe keeping.' He took an envelope from his pocket. It was my note to him about the trial of Joseph Flaherty at Leeds Assizes in 1916.

'Do you want to see what I found?'

'Yes I do. And if we go in the parlour, I'll show you Aunt Freda's box of cuttings and her papers.'

He followed me into the front room.

Sykes reads very quickly, particularly any notes to do with crime. He seems to absorb the words through his fingertips as he handles a page. 'She was a thorough woman, your doctor's Aunt Freda. Have you read all this?'

'Yes of course.'

'Then there's not a great deal I can add. The prosecutor made much of Flaherty being a hot-headed Irishman and the judge very fairly plays that down in his summing up, but it's there all the same, and quite rightly.'

'Why do you say quite rightly?'

'Mrs Shackleton, the man was guilty. He had the knife in his hand.'

'I don't think he was guilty. I believe Freda.'

He groaned. 'Well I might have expected that.'

'Mr Sykes, humour me. We were bound to take different points of view. But let us proceed on the presumption of innocence.'

'It's a bit late for that.'

'I know. But that is what I want to do. You said there is not a great deal you can add. What can you add?'

'Photographs, and it was a bit of a devil to get them.' He handed me a manila envelope. 'Are you sure you want to see them all?'

'Yes.'

The photographs showed the body of Rufus Holroyd; the blood-stained clothing of Joseph James Flaherty; the murder weapon, a knife as described by the judge, taken next to a ruler to show its length of nine inches. The handle was carved with a distinctive swirling pattern. There was the prisoner, too, a young man with dark hair, no expression in his eyes, a bruise to his cheek.

Sykes waited until I had examined the photographs. 'There's nothing to go on.'

'The village must be full of people who remember and are willing to talk.'

Sykes sniffed the air, and so did I. 'The pie!'

We both leaped to our feet.

Sykes reached the kitchen before me and opened the oven door. Mrs Sugden had ignored the gas cooker and used the oven on the range.

'Ow!' Sykes burned his fingers.

'Use the oven cloth, not a tea towel.'

He removed the pie and placed it on the table. 'Just in time. And she's done two.' He removed a second pie.

While Sykes ran his fingers under the tap to cool the

burn, I told him who I would like him to speak to regarding the murder of Rufus Holroyd.

'And do we know if this friend of Flaherty still works at the lime kilns?'

'I don't know. But it's worth a try.'

Mrs Sugden had decorated the top of the pie by placing extra pieces of pastry, making a pattern that resembled a wheel.

I stared at it. 'I've seen that pattern before.'

Sykes was still holding his finger under the cold water. 'Well you would. It's the thing to do isn't, put a little decoration on the top of a pie.'

'Not that pattern, the one on the knife handle, the murder weapon.'

He turned off the tap. 'I'm not with you.'

'Go see if Martin Young's knife is on the bench outside. He was out there earlier, whittling wood. Look at the squiggle and we'll compare it with the photograph you brought me of the knife that killed Mr Holroyd.'

I went back into the parlour and took out the photograph.

In a few moments, Sykes joined me, carrying Martin's penknife. 'It's the same all right.'

'I didn't think anything of it when Harriet said that Martin's father had been in Langcliffe and it was an unlucky place for him. He lost his set of knives here.' I put the photo down. 'What if he didn't lose them? What if he threw them away because he had used one to kill a man?'

Sykes stroked his chin. He did need a shave but that was not the purpose. He does that as a way of helping him think. 'Have you checked in with the village bobby?'

'No. I didn't see the need, since I'm on holiday. I

reported Martin missing at Settle police station because I happened to be there, telling Lucian about Mr Murgatroyd's death.'

'Mr Murgatroyd?'

'A farmer who was poisoned. The inquest is tomorrow.'

'I see. Well, you and I find ourselves in the right place at the right time, Mrs Shackleton.'

'We do indeed, Mr Sykes.'

'Right. I'll take myself off to the Craven Heifer and catch a bite to eat there. If it's not too late, I'll be back to let you know how I get on. And I have another idea up my sleeve.' He was looking pleased with himself and I knew better than to ask what this 'other idea' might be.

With the support of Sykes and Mrs Sugden, my chances of solving Aunt Freda's mystery had tripled. I wondered how Mrs Sugden was getting on with Widow Holroyd.

Twenty-Two

Mrs Sugden's confidence waned the moment she shut the gate of Lilac Cottage behind her. It was one thing to imagine conducting an interview under false pretences and quite another to face the flesh, blood and bile of the individual she needed to quiz. The difficulty lay in discovering how to squeeze the juice of old truths from Mrs Holroyd, widow of the murdered Rufus Holroyd, without arousing suspicion.

Harriet pointed out the house. Mrs Sugden thanked her but did not straight away knock on the door. She walked about the village with the concentration of a horse, blinkered against distraction, its nose deeply into the hay bag of possibilities. Mrs Sugden considered her approach, bearing in mind what she had learned from Mrs Shackleton and from Harriet's chatter as she had shown her the way.

What a pity today was Tuesday. Yesterday, she might have caught her prey in the act of bringing in washing from the line. That would have allowed her to broach some suitable topic in a casual manner. Knocking on the door would demand a bolder means of entry.

Mrs Sugden thought of the lame doctor and Mrs

Holroyd's high regard for him. She also knew that Mrs Holroyd relished the company of her young lodgers. The woman looked up to those who were her social superiors and knew how to treat those below her. She would be unlikely to welcome a lame duck but may be prepared to play Lady Bountiful and instructress to a woman in temporary distress, as long as it cost her nothing.

Yards from the house, Mrs Sugden's knee gave way in a most convincing manner. Agony infused her very being and contorted her handsome features. She struggled on until she reached the house with the thick cream net curtains before giving a cry of pain and supporting herself against Mrs Holroyd's wall, outstretching her painful leg.

She gave a loud groan, hoping the sound would not bring out an interfering neighbour. It took two minutes and another groan before the door opened.

Mrs Holroyd might have objected to the stranger's presence had Mrs Sugden not let out a stifled cry.

'Hello,' said the object of Mrs Sugden's curiosity in a sharp voice. 'What's the matter?'

Mrs Sugden, respectably dressed in light tweed with a brown brimmed hat and calfskin gloves, looked up at the tall, gaunt figure neatly attired in black skirt, grey cardigan and blue pinafore, her grey hair fiercely tamed under the dark net.

In a brave but pained voice, Mrs Sugden apologised profusely for intruding and trespass. 'My knee catches me out. If I can just hold my leg straight for a moment until it clicks . . .'

They both looked at Mrs Sugden's outstretched lisle-stockinged leg, or what little was exposed of it beneath the skirt that ended a respectable three inches above her ankle. Having ascertained this intruder was not a vagrant, Mrs Holroyd asked, 'Would you care for a glass of water?'

Mrs Sugden did not care for a glass of water. She cared to step inside and give this woman the third degree. 'Yes. A glass of water, thank you. Thank you so much. How kind. You are a good Christian woman.'

Mrs Holroyd went inside and very quickly came back with a glass of water.

As she did so, large drops of rain obligingly fell.

Mrs Sugden looked up helplessly at the clouds. 'The heavens have opened. This is the last straw.' Her voice threatened to give way. 'And here I am, such a nuisance, and not in the village five minutes before I must beg your indulgence. May I remain leaning on your wall a while longer?'

'You had better step inside, if you are able.' The merest hint of curiosity coloured the invitation.

Leaning on Mrs Holroyd's proffered arm, Mrs Sugden hobbled into the cottage, turning right into the neat kitchen where a small but cheerful fire burned in the gleaming range. Next to the highly polished brass fender was a rag rug in tasteful greys and reds. A pair of China dogs of indeterminate breed graced the mantelshelf where an ornamental clock with a green face held pride of place.

'Sit there,' Mrs Holroyd ordered, indicating a sturdy bentwood chair. Bringing a high stool and cushions, she helped Mrs Sugden raise her painful leg, saying, 'My poor dear mother had the same ailment. It can be a twisted cartilage or wear and tear.'

Mrs Sugden felt the slightest pang of guilt but suppressed

it with her usual efficiency. She was here to do a job. She looked around the room and could genuinely admire how well it was kept, the square table covered in a speckless oil cloth and condiments on a small tin tray decorated with daisies. In the corner, against the wall, was a curtained-off area – Mrs Holroyd's bed.

When Mrs Sugden complimented the woman on her fine and comfortable house, Mrs Holroyd tilted her head. Her eyes narrowed in suspicion. Too soon, Mrs Sugden told herself. She thinks I am a flatterer. Tread carefully.

'I am sorry if I appear forward. It is not my habit to trespass on the kindness of strangers, but this house reminds me so much of the one I had myself before I was widowed and had to go into service.'

'Indeed.'

'Yes. I should say who I am. My name is Olive Sugden. I am a housekeeper, which I suppose is why I admire a person who has her independence, as you so clearly do.'

'You have just arrived in the village, you say?'

'I have, and was familiarising myself with the area, looking for the shops and so on. My mistress has been here a few days and I had expected her holiday to be my all too brief respite from service, but I was sent for.' She sighed heavily, trying to indicate without words her animosity towards the mistress who could not do a hand's turn without her. She glanced up at the china dogs. 'But you are your own woman and I am guessing you are at no one's beck and call.'

Her companion softened very slightly. 'I am also a widow. Mrs Holroyd.'

'Mrs Holroyd! Then you are the very person I was

recommended to apply to, to be initiated into the mysteries of buying provisions in the Parish of Langcliffe.'

'Oh? Who recommended me?'

Mrs Sugden felt certain that if a situation called for a lie, that lie should be quick and extravagant. 'Mr Trevelyan recognised me as a stranger. He was kind enough to mention you as the most worthy and knowledgeable female in the village – I particularly remember his words, thinking them a little quaint and old-fashioned. I believe you were born and bred here.'

This was a lucky guess. Mrs Sugden had said the right thing. Having finished her ironing and set the pot on the hob for the evening meal, Mrs Holroyd settled herself to favour this stranger with a little history regarding her parentage, birth, chapel upbringing and artistic triumphs as a scholar at the village school as illustrated by the exercise book she produced from Standard III Nature Study class, coming up to date with the care she took of the young charges who were guests in this humble abode.

This was not what Mrs Sugden had in mind. She was here for information, and to prise that information quickly before she must admit to being in the employ of Mrs Shackleton.

'Your young charges are very fortunate, Mrs Holroyd, that you give them a roof over their heads and the benefit of your knowledge. Even I am turning a little philosophical under your influence. You see, it strikes me that some of us are born to widowhood – under an unlucky star. Others have widowhood thrust upon them by destiny so that they will have the time and opportunity to do some good in the world. You were a budding artist as a girl and a Samaritan now. I am not surprised yours was the name that sprang to Mr Trevelyan's lips.'

'Ah, thank you.'

Mrs Sugden felt the satisfaction of one who has picked up a great bunch of keys and found the right one from the jangle. A little flattery might raise suspicion. A great dollop would open her subject's heart, mind and mouth.

'Mr and Mrs Trevelyan know me well, and the unfortunate circumstances surrounding my widowhood.'

'The war?' Mrs Sugden suggested. She sighed. 'You may tell me, Mrs Holroyd. I never speak to a soul. My work keeps me busy, morning till night.'

'Not the war. That brought him home wounded in 1915.' Mrs Holroyd tilted her head to one side and gave Mrs Sugden an appraising look. 'You are a housekeeper, only just arrived in the village, with a mistress who keeps you busy.'

'Yes.'

Mrs Sugden saw where Mrs Holroyd was leading. 'You work for the woman who is staying at the doctor's house?'

'I do.' Mrs Sugden sighed out a breath of tragedy. The resigned tone of her voice conveyed more than any tirade against her employer could. 'And we never speak, above my taking her orders.'

'I thought she must be a petty tyrant, coming into the Village Institute, trying to quiz me about things that are not her business.'

'Oh, she is like that. But believe me, she hears not a word from me. Our arrangement is entirely business. I will not say how she treats me, but you do not know what a pleasure it is for me to be in the company of a lady with conversation. We widows have our sorrows, at least most of us do. I hope you and I can speak freely, Mrs Holroyd.'

'I am sure we can. Is she the devil to work for?'

'Beelzebub's dam could not be worse.'

'I thought as much. Sweet on the surface, but doesn't know how to conduct herself.'

'You have it in a nutshell.'

Mrs Holroyd pursed her lips and gave a sympathetic shake of the head. 'Then you must feel free to call on me while you are staying, and unburden yourself.'

'That is most kind. If she gives me a moment, I will call on you. Perhaps you might give me some tasks at the church or in the Village Institute, so that she will not suspect you have taken me under your wing.'

'I should think that could be arranged, your knee permitting.'

Mrs Sugden gave her leg a rub. 'Your fire helps. A little warmth, you know.'

'I expect you live in poor conditions while your mistress plays the lady.'

'I do not complain.'

'And she has her hooks into the doctor.'

'Perhaps he does not know her as well as I do. But you were telling me, you were a Methodist and I believe you are now Church of England.' Fearing to seem too knowledgeable, Mrs Sugden added quickly, 'According to Mr Trevelyan.'

'Yes. As a young woman I was courted by a fellow Methodist. We were to have married but he was called to the missions. I could not see it as my vocation to travel to South Africa with him as a missionary's wife.'

'That was highly principled of you. Some women would have gone for the sake of being wed.'

'Indeed. It was a long courtship, and my refusal meant that I was unmarried at the age of nine and twenty and resigned to spinsterhood. That was when I joined the Church of England.'

'And there you met Mr Holroyd.'

She smiled at the memory. 'Not exactly. He was a new-comer to this area from a hamlet called Eggleswick.'

'Eggleswick.' That sounded to Mrs Sugden like a made-up name.

'Yes Eggleswick, a village in remote Lawkerdale, which is even more remote than Dentdale and little known except to those who live there.'

'Just fancy! We never know what lies around the corner.'

Mrs Holroyd smiled at a happy memory. 'He did come from around a corner. I was in Settle, shopping, and had just come out of the bank. He bumped into me.' She laughed. 'All my packages went flying. He picked them up, insisted on helping me to carry them while I managed my bag. He walked me back to Langcliffe, and that was that as you might say.'

'How romantic.'

'Not at first. We became friends. He was a most gregari-ous man. He could not have been more different to Cedric, my former fiancé.'

'And you married. I am guessing he did not waste time in asking.'

Mrs Sugden wondered whether Mr Holroyd from the remote dale believed he had bumped into a woman of sub-stance when he saw her coming out of the bank.

'It was what you might call a whirlwind. He took over as licensee of the alehouse and carried me across that threshold before I had time to say nay, much less explain to him that the smell of ale made me want to vomit. I now advise my young guests that if they marry a man from a distant dale they will not know him to the bone as they might the lad who sat behind them in the classroom undoing the ribbons on their pigtails.'

'Oh but what a picture, being carried over the threshold.'

'Sideways. I'm rather tall you see and my feet caught the doorframe.'

'Still, carried is carried.'

'Yes. You were not? Carried I mean.'

'No. Sadly. Different circumstances.'

There were several more moments of chat, enquiry about Mrs Sugden's knee and a reviving glass of port wine before Mrs Holroyd confided the manner of her husband's tragic death.

'He was murdered, Mrs Sugden, after he ejected a Fenian who carried a knife.'

'How shocking. What a shadow that must cast over you.'

'I pray, and I make myself useful.'

'Did you attend the man's trial? Was there any indication of why he killed your husband?'

'He was a violent drunkard who took umbrage at being thrown out when he became objectionable. I attended as many days as I was able. Being the object of pity was trial in itself. His death was on the weekend of the special supper to welcome the new clergyman. We would both have attended.'

'How unfortunate.'

'Yes. We had a pig specially slaughtered for the occasion and donated the better part of it. Strange how everything becomes confused at a time like that, feelings of regret, and guilt.'

Was it her imagination, Mrs Sugden asked herself, or did Mrs Holroyd have greater regrets about missing the new clergyman's welcome supper than losing her husband?

'You had nothing to feel guilty about, Mrs Holroyd.'

'No, but that does not stop the feeling.'

Mrs Sugden's spirits rose at the possibility of an imminent confession. Mrs Holroyd had engaged the Irishman as an assassin because she hated the smell of ale but could not bear the scandal of leaving her husband. Or, she had engaged a man to kill a pig in order to impress the new clergyman. Perhaps the slaughterer had dropped some hint, or she saw evil and greed in his eyes to match her own. The possibility occurred to her that this man might do the dark deed, for a price. With her husband dead, she would be able to leave the hated alehouse, and collect the insurance money.

Give yourself away, you nasty woman. Say something to trip yourself up.

'What can possibly haunt you, Mrs Holroyd? In spite of any little drawbacks and the ultimate tragedy, your union sounds most romantic, and you stayed on in your own village. Mr Holroyd must have cared for you very deeply.'

Mrs Holroyd crossed her arms over her chest as if to warm her heart. 'Oh he did, but we had argued. He wanted me to put money into the business, strike out with bigger premises, perhaps in Settle or Skipton.'

'That was not what you wanted.'

'I am teetotal, Mrs Sugden, and had made sacrifice enough simply living in the White Hart, and being occasionally prevailed upon to keep order and ensure men drank in moderation.'

'You must have been fortunate to have money that could have gone into such a business, and prudent to ensure that it did not.'

He didn't know you had a house to sell, Mrs Sugden guessed, not giving voice to her thoughts. He understood it to be rented, and you flogged it without telling him.

Mrs Sugden risked a conspiratorial smile. 'A Yorkshire lass knows how to keep hold of her purse.'

Mrs Holroyd returned the smile.

'Family funds left me comfortably off. I had been advised by the bank to insure my husband's life, and the bank manager suggested railway shares.'

Mrs Sugden's admiration was genuine. Here was a woman whose head could not have been more tightly screwed on. Mrs Holroyd had pocketed the money from a house sale, lived in the rented White Hart, and turned herself into a tycoon. 'Most prudent and sensible.' Mrs Sugden allowed herself the briefest of fantasies about what she would do if three hundred pounds fell into her lap. 'Did Mr Holroyd guess how much you were worth?'

'I believe he did. When he knew how dead set I was against staying in the licensed trade, he began to look in the *Craven Herald* for other business opportunities and would leave the pages on the kitchen table, with certain advertisements heavily ringed.'

'He valued you, and your judgement.'

'You are right. And Rufus did not harbour resentments. Nor did he gossip. He drank very little himself. He encouraged others to tell him their troubles, and while he would seem to have something to say, he in fact said nothing. He knew a lot, as publicans do.'

'You must have known a lot too.'

'No! The customers kept quiet while I was within earshot. Because they knew I would not put up with any nonsense.' A shadow of annoyance crossed her face. 'Rufus knew things. He knew secrets. He had lost the sight of one eye during the war, but my goodness he missed nothing.'

'What did he know?'

She shook her head. 'He would never confide in me.'

'Then he did not believe that there should be no secrets between husband and wife.'

'He said some secrets were not his to tell.'

Blackmail, Mrs Sugden thought. The man knew things about his customers and extorted money to fund his move to the bustle of Settle or the bright lights of Skipton. That was why he died.

'Did you guess any of these secrets – not that I would expect you to reveal them.'

'No. I did not. He made it a point of honour not to talk about what he knew. If ever a man was capable of taking a secret to the grave, Rufus was that man.' She stood and opened a drawer, took out another exercise book. Mrs Sugden hoped there would not be more nature drawings to admire. 'He was a great one for aphorisms and would write them in a notebook.' She read aloud with great solemnity. '"You can tell more from what a man keeps to himself than what he says aloud."'

Mrs Sugden nodded sagely, as required.

'And this one, "Discretion is the better part of inn-keeping." There is a whole page, but I will give you just one more. "Mischiefs feed like beasts till they be fat and then they bleed." Is that not deep?'

'That is very deep.' Mrs Sugden wished she could make a note. She hoped she would remember these sayings that gave some indication of the character of Mr Holroyd and his way of conducting himself. Mrs Shackleton would be interested in that, the character of the victim.

They were at a point in the conversation when something more was expected of Mrs Sugden, and she knew it. The balance of conversation had tipped in that mysterious way. Mrs Holroyd was waiting, and she prompted.

'How are you liking Lilac Cottage?' Mrs Holroyd's voice remained deliberately neutral but with an underlying animosity as if the stones of that cottage had done her a bad turn.

'It has a chilly atmosphere,' Mrs Sugden said, aiming for hints of melancholy, or worse.

'Does your mistress, Mrs Shackleton, say anything about the events in Langcliffe ten years ago, about my husband's death?'

'Not to me. But I sense that she is intrigued by something. She calls herself an enquiry agent.' The words tasted sordid on Mrs Sugden's tongue. 'She feels entitled to meddle in all sorts of affairs but her meddlings are a closed book to me.'

'I am glad to hear it. I put a stop to her interfering questions regarding my late husband.'

'Never!' Mrs Sugden looked truly shocked. 'Even she would not stoop so low, surely?'

'Oh yes. You see Lilac Cottage was the home of Miss Simonson, the doctor's aunt. She insisted someone else other than the Irishman killed Rufus, even when the evidence was laid before her. One should not speak ill of the dead, but that woman brought blight to the village and I am not sorry she has gone. Now Dr Simonson, he is a different person altogether, a credit to the village and I hope he will stay.'

'A doctor in a village is a great asset.'

'And so should his wife be an asset. He is as different from his aunt as chalk to limestone. And speaking of aunts . . .'

'Yes?'

'I am guessing that the Harriet girl is not a niece to Mrs Shackleton?'

Mrs Sugden was genuinely puzzled, and it showed.

'Come, Mrs Sugden, you must see the close resemblance, more than a niece I think, and is it not odd that the girl's "mother" allows the aunt to take her away when she is at an age to be useful around the house? Unless there is a closer relationship, and if that were the case and the doctor knew, he would think very differently about the sweet-natured Mrs Shackleton.'

Mrs Sugden failed to dissemble. Her mouth dropped open. The woman thought that Harriet was Mrs Shackleton's love child.

'That thought never occurred to me,' she said somewhat lamely.

'Why would it occur to a good Christian woman like yourself? We know not how the other half lives, Mrs Sugden. I hope Dr Simonson will not make the mistake of marrying her. If there was something that could put a stop to it, the village would be much obliged. Anything you can divulge will not be traced back to you. Be assured of that.'

Mrs Sugden, aware that there might be something else she needed to know, agreed to bear these thoughts in mind. She flexed her leg. Her knee felt suddenly whole again. Her need to escape became paramount.

Twenty-Three

Jim Sykes's second reconnoitre around the village took him to the Langcliffe Men's Institute, a place where working men might improve themselves in languages, science and history. Its shelves also housed local directories. By examining these directories and the electoral roll, Sykes discovered that Matthew Walsh, Flaherty's former workmate and friend, now lived in Stainforth.

Jim Sykes cycled to Stainforth. Young Martin had done a good job on the old bicycle. The lad would make a fine blacksmith, or a mechanic. Sykes booked a room at the Craven Heifer and ordered supper.

It is a rule universally acknowledged that a stranger who arrives at a public house dressed in a good suit will be expected to stand a regular a drink. The regular Sykes hoped to meet was Matthew Walsh. At Flaherty's trial, he spoke for the defence. Walsh had lived in Langcliffe at that time. Now his house stood a stone's throw from the Craven Heifer. It would be a strange occurrence indeed if Mr Walsh did not put in an appearance for at least one pint at his local, especially if he still worked in the kilns, straining his sinews and sharpening his thirst.

Sykes took a guess that the man would frequent the tap room, and so stationed himself at the bar and fell into conversation with the landlord who came through to serve him. Naturally, they spoke on general matters as well as topics of the day. Sykes praised the brew. Did their beer come far? No, it was brewed locally. Were they much affected by the General Strike? Not very much so far. Coal, or the shortage of it, might soon become a worry. Folk were already out at night by the railway sidings with their shovels and buckets. They were up on the tops digging peat and charging top price. Would the men from the lime kiln be coming out in support or sympathy? That the landlord did not know. They might be laid off before they had time to make up their minds because without the railways there'd be nowhere for the lime to go.

This gave Sykes an opening to enquire further about the lime kilns and the workers and to hear that some of them lived hereabouts. How would they pay their rent if this strike went on, the landlord asked, not expecting an answer. What about the tick they had run up at the local shops? He needed to decide soon what sort of slate he might keep for regulars.

It was an hour before Sykes's quarry, witness for the defence at Joseph James Flaherty's trial, strolled through the door and up to the bar. His rosy face well washed, his hair combed of lime though a light dusting remained and he brought with him a bitter aroma of earth, charred coke and smoke. When he rested his arm on the counter to pick up the pint the landlord drew, he left a thin coating of dust on the solid wood. As he picked up his drink, he spilled the merest drop and turned the dust from his sleeve into something resembling sand washed by the tide.

'Nah then, Matt.' The landlord brought out a cloth and wiped the surface. 'Counter's had its wash for this week.'

Yes, thought Sykes. Got you. Matt had been a loyal friend to the convicted man. Sykes wanted to know whether ten years on he still believed his friend innocent and if so whether there were thoughts or ideas he had pondered in the time between. Perhaps he let into his mind the fleeting thought that Flaherty had indeed been guilty, or he may have held to his firm conviction and racked his brains wondering about the real culprit. Sykes would need to tread carefully. The information he sought might open up old wounds.

'What's new?' the landlord asked.

'Oh, the usual. The rich get rich, the poor get poorer, and pennies find their way into the publican's purse.'

'Pennies is right,' said the landlord. 'And we'll all be the poorer if this business drags on much longer.'

Sykes listened respectfully, inserting the odd comment, as the two men put the world to rights. Only when the landlord had gone down to the cellar to change a barrel did Sykes address the man directly.

'Landlord called you Matt. Now, squire, do you mind a question? Are you by any chance Matt Walsh?'

'I am. Who's asking?'

Sykes held out his hand. 'Jim Sykes. I'm from Leeds.'

That was giving nothing away. Unless the man lived a sheltered life he would recognise the accent.

'And what brings you into the country from the big city?'

Sykes let a pause build, as if reluctant to continue, and then said, 'It's delicate, or you might think it so.'

'Spit it out. Does it concern me?'

'It does.'

'I owe no one and I'm not expecting some distant relative to pop their clogs and leave me a fortune, though I wouldn't turn my back.'

Sykes was tempted to ask did he look like a solicitor's man but decided against it for two reasons. He might be accused of looking like a policeman, though he had not worn that uniform in half a decade. Besides, Matt Walsh was not a man who would like to beat round the bush.

'I'm interested in a tragic event from ten years ago.'

The man's drink was halfway to his mouth. He lowered the glass, his hand tightening around it. 'Why?'

'Because happen an innocent man went to the gallows.'

'Happen you're right. There's nowt to be done about that now. What's your interest?' He took a gulp of his pint.

Sykes thought, he's trying to work out whether I'm connected with Flaherty, or the murdered man. I don't look Irish. 'I've an open mind on the subject, but it's a feeling. If there was an injustice done, I want to write something about it. I'm not out to make money or cause bother but after all this time it's worth another look I reckon. If there's something to say, I'd like to record it, perhaps write the book of it, while people concerned are still walking the earth.'

Sykes liked the sound of that as he spoke the words. Perhaps he would write a book, although the better part of him had decided that Flaherty was most likely guilty, whatever the doctor's maiden aunt and Mrs Shackleton thought.

The police do not want to convict the innocent. Magistrates would not send a case to trial without sufficient evidence. Twelve good men and true heard the case and knew the finality of their verdict. The man's excuse was that of the boy in the playground. Wasn't me, sir, it was another lad who ran off. Don't know who he was.

Matt Walsh set his empty glass on the counter in a very definite way. 'How do you come to be interested in Joe Flaherty?'

Good question. It was an old standby of Sykes to invent a relation. His favourite was the cousin. 'I have an older cousin who knew Miss Simonson who spoke up for the man. They met in Southport as girls and kept up with each other over the years, letters and Christmas cards. My cousin was quite cut up when she heard about Miss Simonson's death. She told me all about her, and about the court case.'

The landlord returned to the bar. 'All done down below. Beer's as clear as Catrigg Foss.'

'Then another couple of pints, landlord, and one for yourself.'

'Thank you, sir.'

Sykes waited to hear whether his companion would let the landlord in on what they had been talking about. He did not, but picked up his pint. 'I'm for taking the weight off my feet.'

'I'll join you.' Sykes picked up his glass.

Matt Walsh led them to a table by the window, out of earshot of the landlord. He placed a beermat carefully and put down his drink. 'I don't want it all raking up again in here. It's not forgotten but it's passing into history and that suits me.'

They sat in silence for several moments. 'And I don't want to cause you upset, Mr Walsh.'

But neither did Sykes want the man to withdraw into silent reverie. Sykes waited, not offering a change of subject, not prompting, just waiting.

Eventually Walsh sighed. 'It'll always be an upset.'

'What was Mr Flaherty like?'

'His name was Joseph. I called him Joe but everyone at the works called him Paddy. He took it in good part. He was a comic, you see. Lads that make others laugh, well it's hard to take against them. He wouldn't have been out of place on the stage with his patter and his singing. Oh he was one for arguing the Irish cause, Home Rule, all that, but I wouldn't say he was mad for it. It was ninety percent the sound of his own voice he liked, and what he thought was expected. He said if there was a vote on Home Rule, he hoped they'd run it before the pubs opened or after they shut or there'd be a low turn-out. You've come across that kind of fellow. We'll start the revolution at chucking out time.'

'Yes, I've come across plenty like that. Was he a big drinker?'

'We all were. It's thirsty work in the lime kilns. But I'll tell you what, he never missed his mass on a Sunday, the eleven o'clock mass in St Mary and St Michael in Settle.'

'He was religious?'

'I wouldn't say so. I'm Catholic myself. Most of us, we're not mad for religion. We just want to steer clear of hell.'

'Did he carry a knife?'

'No, he did not. I said that in court. I've helped him

home often enough when he was unsteady. I've seen him strip off in the heat. I never saw him with a knife.' He took a drink. 'We were in the same lodgings, little old cottage on the main road, took us no time to get to work from there. There was one big bed and a little bed in that room. Him and me drew the short straw and shared the big un. None of us had nowt in them days. He had a Missal and a rosary. He had a book of poetry, Yeats, and he drove me mad with his reciting. Yeats and Omar Khayyám. He'd fall asleep reciting. If anyone should have committed a murder, it's me, on the grounds of his poetry. But I couldn't get mad at him because he was daft with it. Oh there was them wouldn't tolerate him because he was Irish, but my grand-dad was a tinker out of Scotland and there was Irish in him. Maybe that's why him and me rubbed along.'

'If people didn't like him . . . '

'Plenty of people have a down on the Irish, and plenty don't. Fellow shared with us, I never told Joe but he wouldn't share a bed with him and he wouldn't tolerate an Irishman having a bed to himself. That was why we had the arrangement.'

'Who was he, the other fellow who shared with you?'

'Oh rule him out if you're looking for new culprits. He was out courting and nowhere near that night.'

'What took you to the White Hart?'

'It was closest.'

'Was that the only reason?'

He waited a long time before answering. 'I didn't want us to go there. There'd been trouble with the landlord ever since that business in Dublin. Landlord's younger brother was stationed over there. Holroyd boasted that his brother had fired at the rebels, and that he'd got some of them.'

'Meaning?'

'Meaning he'd shot and killed them.'

'How did Mr Flaherty react?'

'How do you think?'

'I don't know.'

'He started singing a rebel song. We were chucked out and told not to go back.'

'All the same you did go back.'

'We reckoned our money was as good as anyone else's. Holroyd must have thought that, too, because he said, any more trouble, and you're out. We sat quiet as you like for I don't know how long and then it all blew up.'

'What blew up?'

'Joe stood up and started to sing. I'd gone out to the privy in the yard and I could hear him. When I came back, the singing had stopped. There was laughing, talking, and no Joe and no Holroyd. Holroyd wasn't a big fella but he was good at chucking out. When I went outside, thinking I'd have to pick Joe up and take him home, there was already a crowd there, circling Joe, saying someone had gone to fetch the constable. Holroyd was on the ground, bleeding. You know the rest.'

'Will you have another pint and a chaser?'

'I will.'

A waiter had come on. Sykes beckoned to him and placed the order.

Matt Walsh spoke quietly. 'If only I'd made him listen and we'd gone somewhere else that night.' He took a drink. 'When I looked at Joe in the dock, heard him being called the accused, and the prisoner, it was like a bad dream. I didn't think it could be happening. I went to see his family afterwards. They lived in Ormond Quays, Dublin. Joe's priest gave me the address. Miss Simonson paid my fare, and gave me money. It was the worst day of my life, handing Paddy's rosary back to his mother. She told me to keep the Yeats poems. Said they were no good to him now.'

'And you have no doubt Joe was innocent?'

'Innocent as the lamb of God. His mistake was to withdraw the knife from Mr Holroyd's body and leave his prints on the shaft. He was in a state of shock. That knife wasn't his any more than it was mine.'

'Then why was he found guilty?'

'Would you have believed him? No one else nearby, and him with the knife in his hand and blood on his shirt?'

Twenty-Four

Mrs Sugden and I sat together in the parlour. The amount of information she had gathered from Mrs Holroyd amazed me. I had seriously underestimated Mrs Sugden's abilities.

'How did you do it?'

'I worked her out. She is the kind of woman who must either look down on someone or look up. Having young women to stay suits her very well. She treats them as protégées and fills their heads with old wives' tales. You, Mrs Shackleton, made the mistake of being too friendly. You should have adopted your daughter of a titled lady stance. That would have found favour. But with me, it was a touch of fawning and being amazed at the marvels of Widow Holroyd's fascinating life.'

'All the same, she really told you things that . . . well . . . You have impressed me, Mrs Sugden.'

'You see, she is not a woman who will have many people to talk to. Meeting me, who is just here for a short time, was like talking to a stranger on the bus.'

'Not quite, because you know who she is.'

'I do indeed, and I suspect her.'

'Of what?'

'Of murder, Mrs Shackleton. Murder by proxy.'

'Explain.'

'She had a pig slaughtered to welcome the new minister. My reading of the situation is that she tipped the pig man an extra ten bob to do the job on poor Rufus.'

'That would be cheap.'

'Well, I'm guessing the amount. But the pig slaughterer was an itinerant, she gave me that impression. He waited for his opportunity, when someone else could be blamed. That would be her doing. She would have the cunning, he would have the knife.' Mrs Sugden warmed to her theme. 'She may even have done the deed herself.'

'I hadn't thought of her as a suspect.'

'Much as she hated the smell of ale, she came into the bar to make sure no one drank too much. If she saw trouble brewing, she might have gone into the back, donned her own husband's coat and hat, rushed out to stab him and hurried back in, hanging the coat and hat back on the hook. If the police already had a man with a knife in his hand, why would they look at her and her motives?'

A knock on the door prevented us from discussing this intriguing theory. Mrs Sugden went to answer. Through the window, I saw Lucian's car was parked next to mine.

I heard them talking in the hall. They are fond of each other. She was telling him about the rabbit pie, and he joked with her about having been out poaching.

After letting him in, Mrs Sugden went back to the kitchen.

'I'm glad to see Mrs Sugden has come to the rescue.' Lucian came in smiling.

'Yes, so am I, but don't tell her.'

He handed me a box of chocolates. 'Here you are.'

'Thank you! What's this in aid of? And you don't have to knock on your own door.'

'Can't a chap buy his sweetheart a box of chocolates without the third degree? I'm sorry I made a bit of a fuss about Sykes. If you do feel the need to investigate, I'd rather you send him off about the business than do it yourself.'

'I'm sorry, too. I should have told you before I began investigating.' I put the chocolates on the sideboard. 'Your aunt did hope the truth would come out. Look at her papers if you need confirmation.'

'Oh I believe you. But at the end of a person's life they're bound to dwell on what was left undone, or wish some things had turned out differently.'

'Yes and it would be comforting to think another person might later pick up the pieces and make sense of it all.'

'Aren't you going to open the chocolates?'

'Not with rabbit pies just waiting for Harriet and Martin to turn up. Will you stay and join us?'

'I will. Thank you. Friends again?'

'Of course.'

He looked around the room. 'You're right about this parlour. It could be a consulting room by day and a parlour by night. There's a screen in the cellar that I could bring up.'

'In theory and for a time it would work. You know what would happen in practice. It would soon be full of stethoscopes, thermometers, medical journals, patients' notes.'

'Well after a time I would expand, if successful.'

'I'm sure you will be.'

I took out the shoebox. 'You should look at what Aunt Freda wrote.'

'I'd rather not and, if I'm being honest, I have to say I hope you draw a blank, a big blank.'

'Why?'

'Think about it, about the impact on the village.'

'Will you let me try out an idea on you?'

'About the murder?'

'Yes.'

'Please do, especially if it saves you trying it out on someone else.'

'Mrs Holroyd had an insurance policy on her husband's life . . . '

'Oh come on! You're not suggesting . . . '

'Let me finish. She hated living at the White Hart, she was a teetotaller. Around the time of the murder, she had a pig slaughtered to welcome the new clergyman. What if the slaughterman did it?'

'Are you serious?'

'Why not?'

'And she instructed him?'

'It's possible. Rufus Holroyd was stabbed through the heart. A man who kills animals would know how to do it.'

'If he killed pigs, he would have been more likely to slit poor Holroyd's throat.'

'Too much blood.'

'Let's sit down and I'll tell why your theory doesn't hold up.'

We sat facing each other on opposite sides of the hearth. 'Go on then.'

'Mr Holroyd was murdered at the end of April.'

'Yes.'

'Wrong time of year to kill a pig. Pigs are slaughtered in the autumn, when the weather is cool, not in April. You certainly wouldn't kill a pig at Eastertime or hire a slaughterman at that time.'

'But Mrs Holroyd said a pig was slaughtered and they were donating some for a feast, for the new clergyman. It was around the time of the murder.'

'The Holroyds may have had a pig killed, but not in April. The meat would have been cured and kept for later. And it is ten years ago, Kate. People make mistakes, conflate events, confuse dates, you must know that.'

I was not prepared to show him the photograph that Sykes had brought that had the distinctive mark on the handle that I now knew was a kind of signature for Mr Young, Beth and Martin's father. Sykes would have obtained his information, including the photographs, in his usual intricate ways that were best kept quiet.

'All right, I take your point about the pig.' I showed Lucian the shoe box. 'This is full of information about the case.'

'Where did she keep it?'

'I don't know, just that Mr Wigglesworth brought it for me.'

'He shouldn't have. He had more sense than to give it to me. Aunt Freda may have appreciated that you've taken an interest, but believe me, she wouldn't want this business to consume your holiday.'

Lucian pressed the lid tightly on the shoebox. 'I think we should forget it now.'

'It wasn't Flaherty. The priest said so, too.'

'What does your precious Sykes think?'

'That the police wouldn't want to convict an innocent man, that a man with blood on his clothes and a knife in his hand will say anything to save his skin.'

'Then let it rest, Kate, if even Sykes takes that view.'

'He was bound to take that view, as a former policeman. He doesn't want to think there may have been a mistake. The man who wielded the knife, he knew where to run. He was ready to run.'

'Or he was a shadow on the wall, and a figment of Flaherty's imagination.'

'I'm going to get to the bottom of this, Lucian, and I know it may not sound like it but I have an open mind.'

He laughed. 'Then I hope I don't meet you when you feel you've come to a conclusion. You say you want to get to the bottom of it, but has it occurred to you that there may be no "bottom", like some deep whirlpool that could suck you in? Kate, please stop. Leave it alone now, for Harriet's sake if not for mine.'

'Then what is to be done? You could buy a strongbox. Deposit Aunt Freda's papers at the bank for posterity.'

'Is this what you're like when you are on a case, letting it take over?'

'I'm sleeping in your aunt's room, sitting in her chair, looking out on her garden – and yours. I owe it to her to find the truth if I possibly can.'

The outside door opened and Harriet and Martin tumbled in. I was glad Martin had gained the confidence to go out and about without fearing he would be dragged back to the farm.

Mrs Sugden called from the kitchen that the food was on the table and not to let it go cold.

Lucian and I stood up, ready to go through for our meal. He stopped me. 'Before we go in, I didn't just come to bring the chocolates.'

'What then?'

'Gouthwaite has confirmed that Murgatroyd visited the farmhouse on Saturday evening. They had a drink together. Murgatroyd wanted to wish Gouthwaite well and to say he hoped there would be no hard feelings between them. So Martin's statement at the inquest will be a simple straightforward account of what he saw.'

It occurred to me that Gouthwaite could have done little else than confirm Martin's account of Murgatroyd's visit to the farmhouse. After all, Murgatroyd arrived home alive. He could have told his wife about the visit to Raistrick Farm.

I wondered what the coroner would make of having two suspects: Mrs Murgatroyd with her knowledge of herbs and her reluctance to stay on her farm, and Mr Gouthwaite, about to be turned off his farm.

At the kitchen door, quietly enough for Martin not to hear, I asked Lucian, 'Is Mr Gouthwaite a well man, apart from his broken leg? Does he have a heart condition? Might he have had access to digoxin?'

'I don't know. Kate, it's up to the coroner and his officer to look into that. For heaven's sake, don't take on another case.'

'I won't.'

Not unless I have to.

After our meal, Lucian joined in a game of cards at the kitchen table, generously failing to win and thereby making himself popular with Harriet and Martin.

It was about eight o'clock when he left. I went to the gate with him.

'Well, Kate, it looks as if Sykes managed to book himself in at the Craven Heifer.'

'Yes I suppose he did. Oh and I forgot to say, I hope it's all right. He borrowed your bicycle to ride to Stainforth, so as not to use up his petrol.'

'That's fine.' He frowned. 'So, where has he parked his motor?'

'Somewhere out of sight.'

He smiled. 'Do you two think you are in the secret service?'

'If so we're not making the best job of it. I should think our motorcars and your frequent visits are providing a lot of interest. There was probably village speculation about the contents of my trunk.'

He kissed me and then climbed into his car. 'I'll see you tomorrow at the inquest. After that I hope you'll be able to relax and enjoy the holiday a little bit more. And if Mr Sykes does need petrol to get home, just let me know. I'll wangle some for him.'

I watched him drive away. It surprised me that he could not seem to understand that I felt the need to find out the truth when a crime had been committed. To me it seemed akin to his work. When a person came along with symptoms of an illness, he would need the correct diagnosis before prescribing a cure or something to ease the pain. Otherwise he might as well be a snake oil salesman, and I knew him to be a good doctor who did his best for his patients. He might not approve of or like what I did, but surely he could at least try and understand.

Twenty-Five

Sykes arrived back at Lilac Cottage around nine o'clock. I knew he had something to tell me or he would have waited until morning and not have suffered another bicycle ride. We were at the kitchen table playing Mrs Sugden's version of Canasta.

Although I could see that Sykes was bursting with information, with great restraint, he gave in to Harriet and Martin's pleas that he join in the game. We were playing for buttons. Being ridiculously competitive, Sykes accumulated most buttons in all sizes and colours and had the temerity to suggest big fat coat buttons were worth more than little pearl buttons. The fact that Harriet and Martin would have enjoyed some small success did not weigh a jot with him.

'It's luck and skill,' he announced magnanimously, raking in buttons. 'I was dealt good hands and made the most of them.'

Mrs Sugden opened the button tin and pushed it towards him, saying somewhat tartly, 'You came to this table with no buttons and you'll take none away.'

He sighed. 'You're a hard woman, Mrs Sugden.'

'And talking of that,' Mrs Sugden turned to Harriet, 'isn't it time some young people were in bed?'

Harriet returned the pack of playing cards to its box. 'My candle's burned down.'

Mrs Sugden produced two candles. 'You go up first, Martin. I expect you won't be as long in the bathroom as Harriet.'

Martin gave her an odd look. It had probably not occurred to him that he might visit the bathroom for a second time.

'At least brush your teeth.' Mrs Sugden lit a candle and handed it to him. 'Miss Simonson was a woman after my own heart. She hoarded candles as well as every item of clothing she ever bought.'

Harriet found lots of things to talk about before finally going to bed, taking her candle and a book borrowed from Susannah.

Mrs Sugden whisked away the button box. Sykes carried our cups to the sink. He pointed to the ceiling. Harriet's room was directly above. The three of us went into the parlour. There was no fire, but it was a mild evening.

Sykes lit the gas mantle.

We arranged ourselves around the hearth as though the fire was lit and we were taking some warmth from it.

He told us about meeting Matt Walsh at the Craven Heifer.

Mrs Sugden closed the curtains. 'I don't want to look at that murder spot. That poor woman, I wonder she didn't try and move house.'

For the first time, I showed Mrs Sugden the photograph of the knife that killed Mr Holroyd and explained why I thought it had belonged to Martin's father, pointing out the distinctive mark on the handle.

Mrs Sugden looked at the photograph. 'Wouldn't it be a shocker if that young lad's father was the murderer?'

Sykes leaned forward in his chair. 'A murderer wouldn't report his knives missing and that is just what Mr Young did.' Sykes had our attention and enjoyed the moment. 'I passed the police house several times earlier, hoping to bump into the local bobby. Luck was with me when I cycled back from Stainforth an hour or so ago. Constable Chapman was just taking off his bicycle clips. I introduced myself.'

Mrs Sugden raised her eyebrows. 'Did you now?'

'It's not so odd. I told him I'd been a bobby myself and had called to say hello. He was quite interested that I'm working privately now though of course I told him I was only here in the capacity of errand boy, bringing a trunk because of the railway strike.'

Sykes can be most exasperating. He would come to the point eventually but liked to build to a climax. I waited.

'He was impressed that the daughter of a high-ranking West Riding police officer is visiting Langcliffe. I hope you didn't mind my dropping that in, Mrs Shackleton.'

'It would be all the same if I did.'

'He invited me in and sent out for a gill of beer. His wife is with their daughter in Skipton. She's expecting. He was glad of a bit of company.'

Mrs Sugden gave in first. 'And what did you find out?'

'I'm just coming to that. Mr Chapman has been in post since late 1917. His predecessor had joined up so there was a good while when Langcliffe was without a police presence, including the night of the murder. They would have had to send to Settle police station for someone to come to the White Hart. Because I was so interested in the differences between town and country policing, Mr Chapman showed me how things work. I contrived a little look in the log book.'

'But if there was no copper in Langcliffe at the time of the murder, what was there to see?' Mrs Sugden disliked Sykes's insistence on setting the scene before imparting information.

'You're dead right, Mrs Sugden. But in October, 1915, one Michael Martin Young, giving his occupation as farm worker and travelling slaughterer, reported a set of knives missing. They were entered down as "tools of trade". The last place he had visited was Raistrick farm, where he'd slept in the barn.'

'That's the Gouthwaites' farm. Did Mr Young say the knives bore his mark?' I asked.

'More than that, he must have drawn it. There was the squiggle in the log book.'

'Why didn't anyone make the connection?'

'I suppose with the changeover in constables, by the time anyone paid attention – if they ever did – it was too late. The trial was over and done.'

We sat in silence for several moments. 'So now do you believe that Aunt Freda saw someone else? It's highly unlikely that the knife came into the hands of Joseph Flaherty. He lived in Langcliffe. He worked at the kilns. There would be no reason for him to go to the farm.'

'Who would take the knives?' Mrs Sugden looked from Sykes to me.

'Someone who wanted to place the blame for the murder elsewhere.'

Sykes sighed. 'The fact that Mr Young's knives went missing doesn't clear Flaherty, but it introduces doubt, and it suggests a good deal of forethought and planning.'

'It points to Gouthwaite.'

Sykes agreed with a nod.

'A barn on that farm was torched last night. One of the farm workers usually slept there. He could have been killed.'

'Arson?' Sykes asked.

'It would be hard to prove, but yes, I'm sure of it.' I told them about Gabriel Cherry and how he helped to find Martin and send him here. 'He moved out of the barn on the spur of the moment. That move saved his life. The Gouthwaites would have expected him to be there as usual.'

'Was it Gabriel Cherry who brought the rabbits?' Mrs Sugden asked.

'Yes.'

'What a kind man.'

'He may be in danger.'

Sykes looked grim. 'No "may" about it if someone tried to burn him alive.'

From the corner cupboard, I took out the envelope that Gabriel Cherry had given me for safe keeping. I handed the envelope to Mrs Sugden. 'I'd like your opinion, both of you.'

They each read the words on the envelope, pencilled in Gabriel Cherry's neat hand:

To be opened in the event something happens to me.

'That's not your writing,' Mrs Sugden said with evident relief.

'It's Gabriel Cherry's writing. He works at Catrigg Farm now.'

'The farm where the man died suddenly?' Mrs Sugden asked.

'Yes. Mr Murgatroyd, the man's whose inquest is tomorrow. Gabriel is working for Mrs Murgatroyd now. The Gouthwaites' lease won't be renewed. They will be leaving the area.'

Mrs Sugden raised her eyebrows. 'That'll put their nose out of joint.'

Sykes looked thoughtful. 'So, this sudden death – it benefits Gabriel Cherry?'

His comment surprised me. 'I suppose so.'

'Then we had better not rule him out, just because he is a kind man who brings rabbits.' Sykes smiled sweetly at Mrs Sugden.

I did not feel inclined to be diverted. 'Mr Sykes, we are looking into the murder of Rufus Holroyd. Gabriel Cherry was away fighting in April, 1916.'

Mrs Sugden stared at the envelope as though it might offer some clue. 'Someone in the butcher's said a passing tramp set fire to the barn. Does he know different, this Gabriel, is he naming the arsonist?'

'No. He wrote this before the fire. I saw him this morning and asked his permission to open the envelope. At first he was reluctant, saying he didn't see that my opening the envelope could help. I told him that if he felt he was in danger, prevention would be better than picking up the pieces afterwards. He saw the sense of that and he still did not say yes.'

'What did he say?' Mrs Sugden held the envelope to the light.

'He said I must do as I think fit. And then he said something very odd. "If you act on it, better do it at night." When I asked what he meant, he wouldn't say.'

'So was that a yes or no to your opening the letter?' Mrs Sugden pulled her cardigan tightly around her and the sleeves over her hands.

'He left it to me to open it if I thought it would help.'

'Help in what?'

'Justice? Saving him from a second arson attack? Or finding an answer to what happened in Langcliffe ten years ago. Now, do I open it, given his reluctance?'

Mrs Sugden snorted. 'People pretend reluctance when they want someone else to take responsibility.'

Sykes broke his silence. 'He has information that presents a threat to his former employers, the Gouthwaites.'

'Gabriel believes Mrs Gouthwaite set fire to the barn.'

'Is she in love with him?' Mrs Sugden asked.

'It's possible. It's also possible that she is afraid he will expose her in some way. She tried to blackmail someone and he prevented it.'

'So you do have some hint of what he knows.'

'I wish I did.' I picked up the letter. 'There has been so much going on in this village. Perhaps Gabriel Cherry knows he should have spoken up and did not. I'm inclined to open this envelope.'

Sykes is not a great one for debating niceties. He held out his hand. 'This calls for steam. If it's tittle tattle and nowt to do with owt, we'll seal it up again.' He looked at me for confirmation.

I nodded. 'With the inquest tomorrow, we should have as much information as possible.'

We trooped back into the kitchen.

Sykes had done this sort of thing before, that much was clear. He held the envelope above the kettle's spout, examined it and then brought it to the table. He placed the point of a pencil under the flap and drew it gently across.

He handed the envelope to me. I opened it and withdrew a single sheet of paper. I unfolded the paper.

It was not the letter of explanation I expected but was a drawing; a map, to be precise.

The names of the lanes were familiar from Aunt Freda's local map, the one I had consulted to find my way to the Gouthwaites' farm. There was the village of Stainforth, where Sykes had lodgings at the Craven Heifer. Goat Lane was neatly sketched, leading into Silverdale Road. A field was carefully marked: Lime Kiln Pasture. Gabriel had drawn in the small tower-like edifice that was the kiln. Behind this was an X.

I pushed the map towards Sykes.

He stared at it. 'Has he been reading *Treasure Island*?'

'Possibly.'

Mrs Sugden peered at the drawing. 'He is a man of few words, your Mr Cherry.'

'He wouldn't give me a map marked X unless he wanted me to know what's there.'

Mrs Sugden, always straight to the point, said, 'Is he all there, in his mind I mean. A lot of men coming back from the war turned very funny.'

'He's all there.'

'It's a bit of a puzzle this,' Sykes said. 'Either he's having a laugh or he seriously thinks something untoward might happen to him. Nothing has. Yet.'

'That's only because he wasn't in the barn when it burned down. I don't want to look at the sky on another night, see it red with fire, black smoke signalling some perverted success as his cottage burns. I'm sick of this village holding onto its secrets like a cat with familiar fleas.'

'What do you propose?' Sykes pushed the map back towards me.

'Farmers rise at the crack of dawn. We should go now if we want to learn what's hidden. That's why he said we must act at night.'

Mrs Sugden pulled her 'disgusted' face. 'Can't we just ask him to dig up whatever he has buried? Is he having a laugh at your expense? I feel like giving him a piece of my mind.'

'I'll go,' Sykes said. 'I can cycle with a spade across the handlebars.'

'You don't know the way.'

'It's clear enough.'

'It looks so from the map. I've driven there. It's further than you think, and you'll be hard pressed to make out the kiln from the rocks.'

'We'll alert the world if we go by car and besides . . .'

'I know. Petrol.'

Mrs Sugden looked from one to the other of us. 'Do you really think this chap's in danger, Mrs Shackleton?'

'I do, and I also believe that for the first time in his life he has the possibility of some kind of contentment, a home, a wife. He may be about to marry a barmaid from the Craven Heifer.'

'That seals the matter for me.' Sykes stood. 'I'll manage on the bicycle. Is there a spade in that shed out the back?'

307

I nodded. 'And there's another bicycle, Freda Simonson's. I'll just put on her divided skirt and I'll come with you.'

Mrs Sugden thought of protesting, and then gave up on the idea. 'I'm right glad I'm here to keep an eye on Harriet.'

'I wouldn't go otherwise.'

'Oh and among Miss Simonson's belongings, there's a very warm jacket.' Mrs Sugden and I went upstairs.

'Aunt Freda has not only provided the puzzle, she's given me the bicycle and the clothes to wear in order to tackle it.'

Ten minutes later we were ready to set off. Of course, Mrs Sugden had to follow us to the gate. 'Are them tyres pumped?'

'Yes.'

'Do you have a lamp?'

I had travelled the distance between Langcliffe and Stainforth by car with Harriet and Beth. To reach Stainforth and beyond by an elderly bicycle would be a new experience. I hoped local constables would be securely tucked up in bed.

The moon had diminished to the merest sliver. Without the lamp which Sykes had attached, our way would have been black as pitch. With the lamp, we could see just as far as the tiny pool of light inches ahead. For now, on this bumpy deserted road, that had to suffice.

We cycled side by side, blinking into the darkness, Sykes holding the spade across the handlebars.

I tried to see some indication of our whereabouts but all was blackness. Occasionally, shapes of buildings loomed, giving the reassurance that we were still on the main road but also creating the odd sensation that these houses might take a few steps towards each other and crush us.

'At least it isn't foggy,' Sykes called.

'Not yet.'

Our voices breaking the silence sounded huge and unnecessary, threatening to wake sleeping souls and send some irate villager running for a constable. Nah then, what's all this? Stop in the name of the law!

Sykes saw, or divined, the turning into Stainforth. He pedalled through the deserted village and I followed him. I recognised the shape of the Craven Heifer from my previous visit. I turned right, in the direction of the lanes that led to the moorland, our way rapidly growing steeper. Sykes followed. His pedalling slowed, his breathing increased.

'Stop the bicycle,' I called. 'We'll walk!'

'A bit further.'

'How do I explain to Rosie if you have a heart attack?'

Not until the cobbles ended and the dirt road began did he come to a halt. The way from here was far too steep.

We dismounted. Sykes stood with one foot on the ground, the other on the pedal. He detached the lamp and shone it around, looking for a place where we might leave the bicycles.

We wheeled them on a little way and left them by the side of the lane for when we came back. Sykes put a brave face on the job. 'That wasn't as bad as I expected. Beats the ride to Applewick I did a few years back.'

'Don't be over-enthusiastic, unless you want us to be the only enquiry agents in the country to go out and invest in a tandem.'

So far, we had kept to the main thoroughfares and paths.

In this pitch blackness we may lose our way. All it would take was a mist to descend, a fog to swirl in and what little sense of country direction we possessed would be blown away.

'At least no one will see us,' Sykes said.

'Not unless some midnight poacher mistakes us for game.'

Sykes shouldered the spade. I carried the lamp. Its dim flicker proved no great help but I could see my feet and the compacted earth of the path.

'How many miles do you reckon, Mrs Shackleton?'

'Two and half.'

'I like the half. You prefer not to say three.'

'All right, three. We pass a farm in about a mile and a half. There'll be a cluster of buildings on our right. Then it's about the same again to the lime kiln meadow.'

'Now I know how grave robbers felt on their way to work.'

'Grave robbers would be better prepared than we are.'

We spoke in low voices as if eavesdroppers crouched behind the dry stone walls, notebooks at the ready. The way became steep and steeper, leading as it did towards the hills.

Dotted about the fields were cattle and sheep, lying like stone sculptures, noticeable only when I stared into the darkness and saw the whiteness of a sheep against the black field.

The air was clear and cool, smelling of grass and dung. Holding the lantern, I had the advantage of spotting cow-pats. Sykes was not so fortunate and muttered under his breath every now and then.

We reached the halfway point, of Catrigg Farm. It was in

complete darkness. I imagined Mrs Murgatroyd, lying sleepless in her bed, and Jennifer tossing and turning in her sleep. Had they postponed the wedding? When would the funeral take place?

So many had lived and died here before us. This was the country where centuries ago Scots raiders had struck terror, raiding cattle, killing, burning. It was said that the village of Langcliffe had been so utterly destroyed that it had to be rebuilt in a different place.

We walked in silence, each with our own thoughts.

Would Rosie be wondering when Sykes would return, giving some pat reassuring answer when the children said, 'When's Dad coming home?'

Would Lucian be in bed yet, or making a list of what he needed to have done in order to turn Lilac Cottage into his, or our, home and a consulting room?

I felt glad he had let the place lie for a few months while he tended the garden and allowed time for his aunt's spirit to take her leave. Glad, too, that he entrusted me with sorting her belongings. That was what I should be doing. That and the care of Harriet. Instead, I was behaving like some juvenile character from a girl's story, heading for a spot marked X. All that was missing was the gnarled oak tree and the promise of treasure.

Sykes's thoughts were travelling along the same lines. 'I hope this Gabriel Cherry fellow is worth our exertions and that this isn't some bad joke of his.'

'He's worth it. He was a stretcher-bearer in the war. No one speaks of them now, but they were the real heroes.'

'I noticed the barmaid in the Craven Heifer chatting to a fellow from one of the farms. Might have been him.

Anyhow, he deserves happiness after living in a barn out this way. How did he not freeze to death?'

'He has a little dog called Nipper. I expect they cuddle up.'

'Oh that explains it. That makes a world of difference.'

'Don't get clever.'

'Why not, it makes a change.'

A cloud covered the moon entirely. We walked side by side. I held the lantern between us, for what little good it did.

After an age of walking, I saw the outline of the lime kiln. I stopped. 'It's there. Can you make out that shape in the field ahead? That's the old limekiln.'

He stared for several seconds. 'I expected it to be bigger.' We walked on. 'What's the way in?'

'I don't know. This wall goes on and on, and then there'll be a gate.'

'I'm not walking any further. We'll have to backtrack if we do. We'll climb the wall.'

'We risk knocking down the stones.'

'I won't tell if you don't.' He stopped. 'Come on, we can do this.' He took the lantern and placed it on the ground. 'Excuse the familiarity.' He put his hands on my waist and lifted me. I raised my legs as in some mad midnight high jump. Sykes leaned into the wall, setting me down on the other side.

'There's stones fallen already. That wasn't us.' He passed me the lantern which flickered as I took it.

Stay lit, lantern, we need every flicker you have for a while longer.

This was the field young Martin had limed. The ground

looked white where the lamp lit our steps. Beyond was darkness. I held onto the lamp.

Sykes held the spade like a rifle. 'I hope whatever lies under the spot is something we can reinter, or take away.'

'And I hope he hasn't buried it too deep.'

We reached the dilapidated kiln and walked round. The ground at the back of the kiln was a bigger stretch of earth than I had expected.

Sykes put the spade in the earth, pressing it with his foot. 'Did you bring the piece of paper?'

'No, but the cross was in the centre. He'd drawn pencil lines for the stones on the base of the kiln and it was dead centre.' I trod the space, heel-toe, heel-toe, counting my steps. 'Here. Dig here.'

'He'd drawn a line to show it wasn't exactly against the wall. Here, I'd say.' Sykes moved two stones. 'He will have covered the spot to disguise that it was newly dug. Let's notice where these stones are and return them.'

He began to dig.

If any pirate looking for buried treasure found his hoard as quickly as we did, he would be fortunate indeed. Sykes very soon hit something hard. He eased around the object until he could free it from the ground. The tin container he picked up was of the kind that may have held a gift of short-cake biscuits. If left in the ground much longer it would have rusted and lost its colour but as I lifted the lantern so that we could examine it, I saw that the bright green and red of leaves and berries, making me think this had contained some dainties or shortcake bought at Christmas time. A piece of twine had been tied round the box, holding the lid shut. I put down the lantern and held the tin while Sykes tackled the twine, murmuring, 'Full fist knot.'

I thought of the biscuit barrel in which Gabriel had kept Victoria Trevelyan's love letters. Did the man make a habit of burying containers across the countryside? And who gave him all the biscuits?

Sykes opened the lid. Something was wrapped in wax paper. I held the lantern aloft while he looked at papers. 'Certificates. Birth, Marriage, Death.'

He closed the lid. 'We've been lucky so far. Let's take it back.' He re-fastened the twine. From his inside pocket, he took a large linen evidence bag and slid the tin inside.

I took it from him and watched as he returned the soil to the hole and replaced the stones, leaving the area exactly as it had been.

We returned the way we had come, just as a light rain began to fall.

Mrs Sugden was waiting up for us, sitting by the front window. She came to the door. Sykes left his bicycle under the window and carried mine through the hall and into the back garden. Mrs Sugden took the spade. I carried the evidence bag through to the kitchen and placed the tin box on the table.

Mrs Sugden looked at it with reverence, as though it might contain the Holy Grail. 'You were that long. I thought you'd lost yourselves on the moors. Stand near the fire!'

I felt a sudden reluctance to open the tin. Birth certificates, but whose and why were they hidden?

Mrs Sugden had the kettle on the boil, and a pan of warm milk only slightly decorated with soot from the chimney.

She made mugs of cocoa for us. I held the mug with both hands, trying to bring life into my dead fingers. Only when I felt a little warmer did I take out the first certificate.

It was the birth certificate of Selina Gouthwaite, born on January 1, 1890 in Eggleswick to Abner and Sarah Gouthwaite.

I spread it on the table and passed it in the direction of Mrs Sugden and Mr Sykes.

'Where's Eggleswick?' Sykes asked me.

'I don't know, but I've heard the name.'

'Aye you've heard it from me today. It's the remote dale where Mr Holroyd hailed from.'

'Oh yes, that was it.' I looked at the second certificate. 'This is a marriage certificate. Abner Gouthwaite, bachelor aged twenty-three, farm labourer, and Sarah Brignall, spinster aged twenty-four, married at All Saints Church, Eggleswick in June, 1885. And the last certificate . . . that's a death certificate for Sarah Gouthwaite. She died of heart failure in 1913.'

I felt tired. Something was not making sense.

'So who exactly lives in that farmhouse?' Sykes scratched his head. 'One dead, two alive. Mother dead, father alive and the name of the woman living there?'

'Selina,' I said quietly.

'Ah,' Sykes let out a breath. 'At the Craven Heifer, they say it's Mr and Mrs Gouthwaite at the farm and that they make a poor fist of farming. According to these certificates . . . ' Sykes drew the papers towards him and looked at them. 'According to these certificates, Mr Gouthwaite and Miss Gouthwaite live there. You did say she was called Selina?'

'Yes. He calls her that. I thought it odd because most men refer to their wives as the missis or the wife. Most women refer to their men as the mister.'

Mrs Sugden scratched at her neck. 'Oh dear, we've found out summat that they'd rather nobody knew. She's his daughter. Do they live as man and wife?'

The cold night air and the exertion had left me feeling slightly stupefied. 'Yes they do.'

Slowly, Sykes stirred his cocoa. 'Incest.' He took a sip. 'No wonder someone tried to burn down the barn with Gabriel Cherry in it if they knew he had this little lot by him.'

'Why did they keep the certificates,' Mrs Sugden asked, 'if they knew someone might see them? They must have wanted to keep quiet about what they were up to. I expect that's why they moved from Eggleswick.'

'Well people do keep birth, marriage and death certificates. Everyone keeps their important papers. I'm guessing these were tucked well away and that Gabriel found them because he knew all the hiding places from when he was a curious lad.'

These papers explained so much. There was a good reason for Abner Gouthwaite to take his daughter away from the place where she knew people, had school friends that she grew up with, neighbours she might have turned to if she needed an escape. It gave me a chill to think how long Abner Gouthwaite may have been treating his daughter as a wife, perhaps long before her mother died of heart failure. Did that mother turn a blind eye, or not suspect? It was hard to believe she could not have suspected, but perhaps was too weak and ill to intervene, or would not have been able to. And Selina, was it all she had ever known?

Gabriel had said that he once pitied Selina and then he loathed her for taking the precious letters sent to him by his mistress.

The gross figure of Abner Gouthwaite seemed a presence at the table as Sykes, Mrs Sugden and I looked at the box.

We once more examined the documents, as if unable to believe the evidence of our own eyes.

'Little wonder they left Eggleswick,' Mrs Sugden said. 'People would have known them, known what was going on.'

Sykes tried to reduce the tension around the table. 'It happens. It happens more than you might imagine.'

'That's no excuse.' Mrs Sugden frowned. 'Incest. It's punishable by death.'

Sykes took a drink of cocoa. 'During the commonwealth it was a capital offence. Before that it was punishable by penance or excommunication.'

I did not speak, thinking of Selina, her greasy grey hair, her misery.

'Don't tell me, Mr Sykes, that an abomination in the eyes of God and man isn't against the law.'

'It is,' Sykes said wearily. 'It's a criminal offence under the Punishment of Incest Act 1908.' He looked at the dates. 'Selina was twenty-four when her mam died. Who knows how long it was going on before that? And the mother had a weak ticker.'

'That's no excuse.' Mrs Sugden could barely keep the outrage from her voice.

'Of course it's not,' Sykes said, 'but it doesn't take a lot of imagination to see how events moved on, and they had to leave Eggleswick.'

I made a great effort to banish the Gouthwaites from my mind's eye, Abner with his bandaged leg; Selina with her tears. I made myself focus on how this might change the case against Joseph James Flaherty. 'Mrs Sugden, when did you say that Mr Holroyd came to Langcliffe?'

'Sometime in 1915. He was invalided out of the army after losing an eye.'

'So he will have known the truth about Abner and Selina Gouthwaite.'

'That he will. It would have been one of the things he knew that he wouldn't confide to his wife, or anyone, being a reticent man who listened to everyone's secrets and kept them.'

'And theirs was the farm that Mr Young visited last, the place where he thought he left, or lost, his knives.'

'Or had them stolen,' Sykes added. 'That was the impression I got from my brief look of the entry where he reported them missing.'

'Gouthwaite found or stole the knives and chose one particular knife to silence Mr Holroyd. Aunt Freda saw the murder from her window, a big man, she said. He must have been waiting around the corner. I wonder how many Friday and Saturday nights Gouthwaite waited, waited for his chance to kill and run away.'

We sat quietly. Sykes stirred what was left of his cocoa. 'We'd never prove it. And it's too late.'

'But Aunt Freda was right. Joseph Flaherty was wrongly convicted and lost his life so that Abner and Selina's secret would be kept.'

Mrs Sugden patted my arm. 'Drink your cocoa before it goes cold.'

Sykes stood and stretched. 'I better get myself back to the Craven Heifer. The landlord gave me a key but he's bound to have an ear cocked for my coming back. They always do.'

Mrs Sugden picked up the tin and put the certificates back. 'I'll tuck these well away, until you know what you might do.'

I walked Sykes to the gate. 'We'll be able to think more clearly tomorrow.'

'Yes.' He wheeled out the bicycle and paused before mounting. 'You know, given that Dr Simonson doesn't like you investigating . . . '

'He has no objection whatsoever. He just wants me and Harriet to enjoy our holiday.'

'Then why did he tell you about this business? Did he have his own suspicions?'

'It was Mr Wigglesworth, Freda's friend, who told me.'

'But Dr Simonson did talk to you about it.'

'He told me how much the whole business upset his aunt.'

'Why didn't he bring you to meet her while she was still alive?'

'I don't know. I wish he had.'

'Goodnight then.'

'Goodnight.' I watched Sykes wobble off across the cobbles, gain his balance and make a beeline for the road.

Twenty-Six

In the early hours of the morning, I finally snuggled into bed. Mrs Sugden had declared the alcove bed in the kitchen to be very comfortable. We were a full house, with Martin in the loft and Harriet fast asleep in the bedroom she had taken a great fancy to. In spite of our unexpected activities, the holiday appeared to be doing her some good. She had eaten well, made friends, taken walks.

I had successfully put a stop to the window rattling but wind blew down the chimney once more. Through the open curtains I could watch the dark sky where a few bright stars multiplied as my eyes grew accustomed to the darkness.

In a few more hours the coroner would hold his enquiry into the death of William Murgatroyd. I would be called to give my statement, a simple enough matter on the face of it: *I called at Catrigg Farm and went with Mrs Murgatroyd into the bedroom she shared with her husband. I saw that Mr Murgatroyd was dead.*

That Bill Murgatroyd had drunk with Abner Gouthwaite hours before his death would soon be common knowledge. Gouthwaite had motives for wanting Murgatroyd out of the way – to prevent him from taking over Raistrick Farm, or simple vengeance, or jealousy.

Did Gouthwaite also have the means in the form of digoxin tablets? His late wife, Sarah, Selina's mother, died from her heart condition. There was a possibility that the Gouthwaites had kept digoxin tablets prescribed to Sarah to regulate her heart. Selina may have inherited that condition and have pills of her own, or a home-made remedy that contained digitalis. Unless the police had undertaken a search of the property – or even if they had – that information would not emerge at the inquest unless I revealed it.

There was something a touch mad about possessing such knowledge. 'How do you know this, Mrs Shackleton?' 'At darkest night, I was digging at a spot marked X, sir. There I discovered a biscuit tin containing evidence of incest. That is how I know about the real Mrs Gouthwaite's fatal heart condition.'

If tales of my exploits at Bolton Abbey had arrived in Langcliffe before me, what hope would there be for me, and for Lucian, if this came out? Sykes's and my exploits would rank only a little lower than grave robbing. I would be shrouded in notoriety, my personal morning mist never clearing except in far flung places where no one knew of Kate Shackleton and her itch for unravelling mysteries.

I closed my eyes, still seeing the night sky and stars that now unexpectedly took the shape of a dagger.

The coroner's jury had the power to return a verdict of murder, manslaughter, death by misadventure, or suicide. If they returned a verdict of murder or manslaughter, they had the duty of pointing a finger at the guilty party, if evidence led them in that direction.

321

I knew nothing about the police investigations, and therefore it was pointless to lose even more sleep by speculating, although that did not stop me.

When it was almost time to stir myself for the day that stretched ahead like a well-designed obstacle course, I fell asleep.

Harriet woke me with a cup of tea and the reminder that I had to be at the inquest. Quickly I washed and dressed. Glad that Mrs Sugden was there to take care of Harriet, I set off with my fellow witness, Martin Young, to walk to Settle.

Martin, his hair plastered into something like submission, stared at his boots. He wore three pairs of socks since the boots, which had once belonged to Lucian, were a size too big. He was nervous.

The day was fine and sunny, with the lightest of breezes. Under other circumstances this walk along the narrow track from Langcliffe to Settle would be a pleasurable experience. We passed trees in blossom. The hawthorn bloomed.

'What will they ask me?'

'You remember what you said when Lucian took you into the police station in Settle?'

'Yes, that I watched Mr Murgatroyd go into the farmhouse and then come out again, a bit tipsy.'

'That's what you will be asked to say.'

'But they know what I said. Why do I have to say it again?'

'Everything has to be confirmed officially, in public, and a conclusion reached as to the identity of the person and how he died.'

To our right, the copper dome of Giggleswick School dominated the skyline, shining in the sunlight. I pointed it out to Martin, trying to take his mind off what was to come. He was not to be diverted.

'Will old man Gouthwaite be there?'

'Probably, but you will sit between me and Dr Simonson and there will be nothing to worry about. All you have to do is stand up and tell the truth. You'll be under oath. Do you know what that means?'

'Yes. It means I swear to tell the truth.'

I managed to turn his thoughts elsewhere as we continued our walk. He told me about his home and the farm they once kept. He took two small carvings from his pockets. The goodbye presents he had whittled for Harriet and Susannah, a tortoise and a hare.

We were early but as we entered the town others were already making their way towards the court. Martin became silent. From the end of the street, I saw that Lucian was waiting for us at the entrance to the courtroom. A flight of steps led from the street to a heavy door.

A constable asked our names and let us through, directing where we should sit.

A long table drew the eye. It was covered with a white cloth giving it the appearance of an altar. To the left of the table was a row of chairs for the jury. To the right of the table a lectern, complete with Bible.

Because we were to give evidence, we had been told to sit on one of two benches near the front.

I went in first, followed by Martin and then Lucian. Mr Wigglesworth was already seated on the same bench and moved along to be beside me, bestowing his small, friendly smile.

'Are you giving evidence?' I whispered.

'No, but the ushers are used to me. I'm a regular you might say.'

I had the odd sensation of imagining him sitting beside Freda Simonson during the inquest into the death of Rufus Holroyd.

On the row in front of us were Mrs Murgatroyd and Jennifer. Next to Mrs Murgatroyd was a stout man with sparse grey hair and a florid complexion. I guessed this might be the seed merchant cousin who had offered Bill Murgatroyd a partnership but failed to tempt him away from the land.

Martin gave a small gasp. He was watching as people filed into the courtroom. When he heard the tap of a crutch he had turned to look and saw Abner Gouthwaite, dressed in a brown overcoat, carrying a battered trilby.

On the opposite side of the chamber were two pressmen with their notebooks. Alongside and behind them were members of the public, most prominently Mr and Mrs Trevelyan. More people trooped in. They squeezed into every available inch of bench space and then stood at the back quietly as ushers cleared the gangways.

The coroner's officer, Police Sergeant Dobson, directed the jurors to their place. It was an all-male jury, comprising a clergyman, a man with high stiff collar and the confidence of a bank manager, and a nervous young fellow who sucked in his cheeks. 'Retired headmaster,' Lucian whispered of the fourth. Two, in their best tweeds, might have been farmers. The last was exceptionally tall and wore a navy striped suit and the preoccupied air of a professor.

The coroner, a small, barrel-chested man, wore gold-rimmed spectacles, a little far down on his nose. In a sonorous voice, he opened the proceedings, by instructing his officer to swear in the jury.

Each of the jurors in turn repeated the oath. As they did so, a deeper hush descended so that I had the sensation of the very room being lowered several feet to somewhere quiet and deeply solemn.

The coroner glanced down at his papers and then into the room. 'We are here today to establish the cause of death of William Murgatroyd of Catrigg Farm whose identity is not in question, being confirmed by Sergeant Dobson and by Mr Brocksup, seed merchant of Settle and a relative by marriage. The pathologist is not able to be present, but I have his report. In summary, we know that Mr Murgatroyd died of poisoning with indications that the substance was digoxin.'

A startled murmur rumbled through the room. Mrs Murgatroyd bowed her head. She must already have been told about the cause of death.

Dr Lucian Simonson was called first and gave an account of his visit to the farm on Sunday. He had asked Mrs Murgatroyd questions and he reported what she said, including the last meal eaten by the deceased, a Sunday roast of mutton, potatoes and swede. No one else in the house had experienced nausea or discomfort.

The coroner looked at the papers in front of him. 'I have here a note of stomach contents including a corned beef sandwich, mustard and alcohol.'

On the bench in front of me, Mrs Murgatroyd and Jennifer leaned forward. Jennifer gave the slightest movement, like a cringe. Mrs Murgatroyd's, 'No!' was audible.

Lucian stood down, and Mrs Murgatroyd was called.

She was taken through the statement that was familiar to me: that she had thought her husband was sleeping, that perhaps it began to dawn on her that he was too still, but she did not want to think beyond that, and then a person came to the door.

She looked at me.

The coroner spoke in a kindly everyday sort of voice, as if discussing what he might like for supper. He asked her if she could say precisely when she realised her husband was dead. Was that before the arrival of the person who knocked on the door? She could not answer clearly. Her voice shook. She fought back tears, brought out her handkerchief and wiped her nose. She was offered and accepted a glass of water.

The coroner's voice was gentle when he asked, 'How long have you lived on a farm, Mrs Murgatroyd?'

'Since my marriage, thirty years ago.'

'You must have seen death a good many times during those years, of animals, and perhaps older members of your family.'

'Oh yes, many times.'

'Yet you did not know that your husband had died, until someone else told you.'

'I think I knew. I'm not sure what I thought.'

With the utmost delicacy, the coroner led her to describe what treatment she had given her husband the night before when he came home feeling so ill. Had she suspected that he might have had too much to drink?

'He does not drink.'

'And you did not smell drink on him?'

'No and he did not eat a corned beef sandwich. There

must be a mistake. He had eaten nothing since dinnertime, when we all ate together. I don't have corned beef in the house.'

'You did not ask, Have you been drinking?'

'No, I thought only of getting him to bed and keeping him warm. His breath was, well I did notice something strange.'

'Did he say where he had been?'

'He said he had been in the far field checking the livestock. They had not long been out, you see.'

'Out to graze you mean?'

'Yes.'

He took her back to the question of what remedies she had given to her husband and asked about her knowledge of herbal cures and useful plants.

She told him about the mustard plaster, morphia and laudanum.

Mrs Murgatroyd returned to her seat with the mist of puzzlement on her face. Something was wrong, she knew. As a widow she came across as correctly distressed, upset, and rocked by grief. As a witness she was unconvincing and had somehow managed to draw suspicion upon herself.

It was my turn.

The coroner took me through the statement that I had made at Settle police station. When asked about my impression of Mrs Murgatroyd, I said I thought she was in a state of shock and although she must have been aware that her husband was dead she had not been able to take it in and that her mind seemed to have become frozen by grief.

I do not know what Lucian whispered to Martin when he was called to the stand but he stood tall and very still. He gave his name, and age and said he was staying at Lilac Cottage since he had left Raistrick Farm where he had worked for Mr Gouthwaite.

If anyone on the jury, or the coroner himself, wondered why an underage boy had been employed on a farm, they gave no sign. The coroner spoke with courtesy as to an equal and asked Martin to tell what he had seen concerning Mr Murgatroyd on Saturday night. Martin obliged. He paused only briefly when the coroner asked him why he was watching the house from a distance.

'Because I was running away and wanted to be sure Farmer Gouthwaite had not killed himself when he chased me and fell.'

There was a swivel of eyes and a turning of heads as everyone in the courtroom looked at Abner Gouthwaite.

'Very well, Martin, you may stand down now.'

Sergeant Dobson gave Martin a prod and he made his way back to the bench and the safety of his place between Lucian and me.

I whispered, 'You did well, Martin.'

From the bench opposite, Mr Trevelyan caught my eye and gave an approving nod.

The coroner called Abner Gouthwaite. Gouthwaite, with the aid of his tap-tapping crutches, made his way to the stand. Martin tensed as the man walked by us, but Gouthwaite did not glance at him.

Sergeant Dobson held the crutch as Gouthwaite stepped up, holding the lectern for support. He had left off his top-coat and wore a brown suit jacket of indeterminate age and a pair of dark twill trousers.

He took the oath. Gouthwaite's contribution was one

part of the proceedings I could not anticipate. His manner was of the gallant loser mourning the good neighbour who had been set to take over his farm.

'Bill Murgatroyd and me had us ups and downs but there was no malice between us. I welcomed him when he called on Saturday. We had a drink together to show no hard feelings.'

'Did Mr Murgatroyd eat anything while he was with you?' the coroner asked.

Gouthwaite did not hesitate. The man did have sense, or cunning. 'He did. He was hungry, not having had anything since dinnertime. I made him a corned beef sandwich.'

A murmur rose in the room like a gentle hum. The coroner called for silence.

'You made this sandwich yourself, Mr Gouthwaite?'

'I did, Mrs Gouthwaite being out of the house attending to a lamb.'

'Did Mr Murgatroyd take anything else that you made for him?'

'He put his own dab of mustard on the corned beef.'

That was a clever stroke. Mustard would have disguised the taste of whatever may have been added. By claiming that Murgatroyd added the mustard, Gouthwaite tried to clear himself of blame.

'I see that you are using crutches. What happened to you?'

'I fell and hurt my knee and leg.' He looked at Martin. 'My farm lad wanted to go off to the May Day celebration in Langcliffe and when I told him he was needed on the farm, he ran off. I slipped in trying to call him back.'

'When was this?'

'On Saturday.'

'But on Sunday you were able to get about sufficiently to make a sandwich and pour drinks.'

'Aye, sir. I have to fettle when there's no one to fettle for me.'

'Quite. And how did Mr Murgatroyd seem to you?'

'He was cheerful enough, but would be sorry to see me leave the farm after so long. He said the only fly in the ointment was that his wife had a fancy to be a townswoman and live in Settle. We laughed about it.'

Mrs Murgatroyd leaped to her feet. 'Liar! He would not have laughed with you about me, never!'

There was a collective gasp in the room and a crescendo of whispers.

'Shhh, mother.' On either side of Mrs Murgatroyd, her daughter and her cousin restrained her, and she sat down.

The coroner spoke sharply, silencing the murmur of voices.

'Mrs Murgatroyd, I will overlook your disrespect to me and the court this time, but you must remain silent.'

Gouthwaite's demeanour was now of the deepest concern and sympathy. 'I am so sorry to have hurt your feelings, Mrs Murgatroyd.'

In a cold voice edged with impatience, the coroner reminded Gouthwaite that this was not a public meeting and that he must speak only when asked. 'So you parted on good terms?'

'We did, sir.'

There were no more questions. Why not, I wanted to ask.

The coroner adjourned the hearing, saying that the inquest would recommence at two o'clock.

We filed out.

People stepped aside to let Mrs Murgatroyd and her cousin pass.

'Am I done with?' Martin whispered.

His face lit with relief when I said yes.

He stuck limpet-like to Lucian who steered him towards the door.

Mr Trevelyan came to speak to us. 'Sad business. Sad business all round.' He caught up with Lucian and Martin. 'You'll be glad to hear, young Martin, that you are very much wanted back in Pendleton. The blacksmith has a place for you.'

'Thank you, sir.' He looked pleased enough to dance a jig.

There was now no sign of Mrs Murgatroyd, but I spotted Jennifer Murgatroyd, crying and trying not to as she disappeared into the ladies' lavatory. I excused myself and hurried after her. Mr Wigglesworth stayed close behind me. As I was about to go into the ladies' room, he whispered, 'Wait for you outside.'

Jennifer was at the wash basin, splashing her face, and sobbing quite loudly.

'Jennifer, you poor girl.' I gave her my handkerchief. 'Your mother was very brave.'

'Oh it's you. Yes she was brave and they all think she killed Dad.'

'No, no they don't.'

'Derek does, the Pickersgills do, that's why they're not here.'

For a moment I could not remember who Derek and the Pickersgills were, and then I did remember. Derek was the fiancé and the Pickersgills his parents.

'Surely not.'

'He's broken off our engagement. It's a scandal, you see. Oh they were all over us when Dad's death was natural causes but now . . . .' Her sobs grew deeper. 'He says I can be the one to break the engagement, to say I can't go through with it. He says that is the gentlemanly way to do it. How can I? How can I say anything?'

I put my arm around her. 'Then he's a cad and you're better off knowing what he's like before you marry him than after.'

This brought on a fresh bout of tears. 'But I'm not going to marry him, am I? And she has my dress, and my cake, and she says she will keep the cake for Christmas because she supposes we won't need it and there'll be no need to charge my mother for the ingredients.'

I put my arm around her. 'Then the woman's a monster. The family will breed monsters. You are well out of this engagement. You deserve much better.'

'But my dad, I want my dad.'

'Splash your face again. Dry your eyes. Your mother needs you to be strong.'

'Just because she knows about medicines . . . People think she poisoned Dad, so she could leave the farm and come and live in Settle.'

'Anyone who thinks that is stupid.'

'But what can we do?'

'Trust.'

'Trust what, trust who?'

'Just trust.'

I have never revealed this before, but I travel with a small bottle of smelling salts given to me by my aunt. I took it from my satchel and waved the bottle under Jennifer's red nose until her eyes watered with a different kind of tear.

'Come on now. Put on your brave face, Jenny. Think of Jenny Wren.'

'The bird?'

'Yes, and a character in Dickens who rises above.'

'Above what?'

I am not very good at cheering words.

'Come on,' I whispered as someone else came to avail herself of the facilities. 'Let's find your mother. Chin up.'

Outside, Mr Wigglesworth was waiting for me.

I left Jenny with her mother and the mother's cousin.

Mr Wigglesworth took my arm. 'Lucian said to tell you that he'll take Martin back to Langcliffe, and then needs to go to Embsay. He sends his apologies but I said I would give you lunch, if that is agreeable.'

'Most agreeable, thank you, Mr Wigglesworth, and I'm very glad because I need your help.'

Twenty-Seven

The clapper sounded as Mr Wigglesworth's assistant left the shop. He had sent her home for dinner and now turned the sign on the shop door to 'Closed'.

He led us into the room at the back which served as store and kitchen. 'Come through. We can talk while I make us a bite to eat.' He glanced at the counter by the wall and stroked a brown teapot. 'My assistant has left some tea in the pot. First things first, eh?' He poured deeply stewed tea into white mugs.

'Now how can I help?' He began to open a tin of baked beans.

'Mr Wigglesworth, you listened to Mrs Murgatroyd being questioned by the coroner this morning. She is suspected because she dosed her husband on Saturday night.'

'Yes, with morphia and laudanum. She is known for her knowledge of herbs and remedies.'

'And is suspected because of that.'

'That's ridiculous! The woman comes in here. She is a healer, not a poisoner.' He tipped the beans into a pan on the gas ring.

'That is not how it looks to people who don't know her. She wanted to leave the farm and move into Settle. Her husband would never have agreed. In some eyes, that is a motive for murder.'

He looked surprised. 'Really? You think that was how things were going in the courtroom? I did not see that at all. I agree that she gave a poor account of herself but that was because she was upset, naturally. Surely no one could think . . .'

'Yes they could. Her daughter's fiancé has broken off their engagement.'

He snorted. 'The Pickersgills. Legal men are forever cautious.'

'They fear a scandal. Mrs Murgatroyd is at risk of being accused of murder.'

He reached for two packets of potato crisps from the cupboard. 'It's true that a coroner's jury, if they return a verdict of murder, will always hope to back it up with a culprit. Will you . . . ?' Handing me two plates, he stirred the beans. I took the plates to the table.

He was looking thoughtful, and troubled. 'How can I help, other than to give a character witness for Mrs Murgatroyd?'

'You could alert the coroner to cross-question Abner Gouthwaite about what he put in the sandwich.'

'I don't see how that will do any good.'

'There is a history of heart disease in the Gouthwaite family. They will know all about digoxin.'

He brought the pan to the table, spooned the beans onto our plates and provided forks. 'What makes you think there is a history of heart disease in the Gouthwaites? I've never heard that said.'

I took Abner and Sarah's marriage certificate from my satchel and laid it on the table. He peered at it. I added Sarah's death certificate.

'Yes, I see. She died of heart failure. You think he kept his first wife's old medicines?

'They could have brought some of Sarah Gouthwaite's medication with them. Would it still be effective after several years?'

'Possibly yes, possibly no. It's difficult to say. By my reckoning they arrived in the area about eleven years ago.' He placed a packet of crisps by each of our plates. 'So Gouthwaite was a widower.'

'Not was a widower, he still is. The woman who passes as his wife is his daughter.' I set Selina Gouthwaite's birth certificate on the table. 'She may have inherited her mother's heart condition.'

'Shocking, shocking. Poor girl, his own daughter.' He gulped. 'Goodness, what a murky matter.'

'After his wife died, Abner Gouthwaite came from Eggleswick to Langcliffe with Selina. They do live as man and wife?'

'Oh yes.' He hesitated. 'I'm breaking a confidence but perhaps you should know. The poor woman was pregnant some years ago and lost the baby. I know the midwife who went to attend to her. From Eggleswick you say?'

'And if Selina has inherited her mother's heart condition . . . ?'

'Then I don't know about it, and I would if Dr McKinley had prescribed for her. Of course if she does have a weak heart, she may have enough knowledge to make her own concoctions. Many people do. That's how digoxin came to be known as a regulator for the heart, when it was identified as an ingredient in a folk remedy.'

He forked his beans and stared at the plate, as if it might offer a suggestion. After one more forkful of beans, he stood.

'This is sufficiently serious for me to speak to Sergeant Dobson, and to the coroner if necessary. He and I have known each other a long time, respect for each other, you know, it matters.'

He went to the sink and washed his hands. When he returned to the table, he picked up the certificates. 'May I? I won't produce them unless entirely necessary, but I believe that Abner and Selina Gouthwaite have questions to answer. I hate the thought of a shadow of suspicion falling on Mrs Murgatroyd.'

'Yes, take them.'

'I will speak to Sergeant Dobson straight away. I won't mention the incest unless it is absolutely necessary but I can assure him there is a history of heart disease in the Gouthwaite family and at the very least that will give cause for suspicion as to possible possession of digoxin.' He slid the documents into an inside pocket. 'If my assistant is not back by the time you leave, drop the latch. I will see you at the inquest at two o'clock.'

He ran his tongue around his teeth and smoothed his hair with his hands. 'You may finish my potato crisps, Mrs Shackleton.' At the door to the shop, he turned. 'You are like Freda in that you have sound instincts as to whom you trust.' He straightened his tie. 'I will not fail you.'

Twenty-Eight

The notice outside the courthouse caused something of a stir among those returning for the resumed inquest. It read:

INQUEST INTO THE DEATH OF WILLIAM MURGATROYD ADJOURNED UNTIL 2 pm WEDNESDAY 12 MAY

'Why?' someone asked. 'Why adjourn for a week?'

'New information?' said another.

'They like to drag things on and double their pay.'

Gouthwaite leaned against the wall, using one crutch to support himself. He threw away the cigarette he had been smoking, spat on the pavement and then began to hobble away.

The small crowd had become attentive. I looked to see what drew their interest. It was Sergeant Dobson, striding from the police station. He went up to Gouthwaite and put a hand on his shoulder.

They walked together back towards the police station.

Mr Wigglesworth strolled nonchalantly towards me, exchanging a greeting here and there as the crowd slowly dispersed. 'I have no idea,' he said to a woman who asked him if he knew why the inquest had been adjourned. He touched his hat to me. 'Mrs Shackleton?'

We walked back towards the main street. 'The deed is done. I have a very strong feeling that we have taken the right course of action.' Mr Wigglesworth cleared his throat. He looked about for eavesdroppers and saw none. 'It can be useful reaching the age where memory is not as powerful as it once was. The coroner's officer, Sergeant Dobson, you know he's a much younger chap than I and not surprised that I could not recall where I heard about the propensity towards heart disease in the Gouthwaite family. He will be questioning Abner Gouthwaite now. An inspector and constable are on their way from Skipton to interview Selina Gouthwaite and conduct a search.'

What would they find, I wondered, and why had they not searched Raistrick Farm before? There was plenty of time for Abner Gouthwaite to have destroyed any evidence there may have been. But say they had digoxin in the house and it was essential for Selina, how long might she live without it if Abner used it to poison Bill Murgatroyd? There was no point in speculating. I must wait helplessly on events, the hardest thing in the world.

We had walked a few yards in silence and then turned onto the main street – in the wrong direction for my walk back to Langcliffe.

'Do you have plans for this afternoon, Mrs Shackleton? Might you spare half an hour?'

'Other than walking back to Lilac Cottage, I have no plans so I'll be glad to. My housekeeper is with Harriet and I daresay they'll take care of Martin.'

A shopkeeper spotted Mr Wigglesworth and stepped out of his shop to ask about the inquest. This happened several times as he was a popular figure, drawing greetings as we walked towards the Market Place.

'Bear with me, Mrs Shackleton, there is something I feel you ought to know. Perhaps we might sit ourselves down on the bench in the square and watch the world for a short while.'

'Very well.'

'Also, I am curious as to how you came by the Gouthwaite marriage, birth and death certificates. Are you able to tell me?'

'It's a good question, but if I answered truthfully, I would betray a confidence, that's why I'm glad the constable took your word about the heart disease in the Gouthwaite family.'

We stood aside while two elderly women with shopping baskets bustled by.

'Then may I know if there is some connection between that information and your interest in Rufus Holroyd's murder?' He gave me a quick glance. 'I know you are interested. Your eyes you know, they give you away sometimes.'

'There may be. I did find out something, although it's too early to make inferences.'

Suddenly, he bristled with alertness. 'Yes, yes. What did you find out?'

'The knife that killed Rufus Holroyd was lost by, or stolen from, an itinerant slaughterman, who regularly came this way for work.'

'It was a distinctive knife, I remember thinking that at the time, during the trial.'

'This man reported the knives missing to the constable in Langcliffe but shortly afterwards Langcliffe was without a constable for some time. No one made the connection. I know the police had other priorities during wartime.'

'They were overstretched, and spent a great deal of time, more than they cared to admit, rounding up reluctant soldiers on leave, before they could be officially branded as deserters.'

'The fact that the man's knives – and there were several on a belt – were reported missing casts doubt on the conviction of Joseph Flaherty.'

'If only that had been picked up at the time. Did the man who lost them have any idea where?'

'His last port of call was Raistrick Farm.'

We came to a standstill. Mr Wigglesworth let out a deep noisy breath. 'Why didn't we know that? Why didn't I enquire myself?'

'You weren't to know, and I'm not sure it would have helped. The prosecutor was clever and determined. He could have made a case for Flaherty having found or stolen a knife, or bought it in a pub.'

'How did you discover all this?'

'With the help of my assistant, Mr Sykes.'

'I am much obliged to you.'

'We're at a dead end just now, but won't give up yet.'

As we reached the Market Place and made our way through the busy stalls, Mr Wigglesworth gave a satisfied smile. 'Good, the bench is free, especially for us. We can speak here, my words will float away, and if you wish you can forget I ever said them.'

A pigeon patrolled in front of the bench and stared up at us as we made our claim to the seat.

Mr Wigglesworth became suddenly silent, as if mesmerised by the scene before us, the woman and boy selling pots and pans; the man juggling plates to attract customers while his assistant did the wrapping and took payment; a vegetable seller calling out his bargains.

We sat in silence, watching the shoppers and the stall holders, the very ordinariness of it all, as if there was an invisible wall between here and the world where a man had been poisoned.

I waited, sensing Mr Wigglesworth's reluctance to speak.

And then it was too late. An elderly shopper came smiling towards us, clutching her basket. I budged up and she sat down, telling us she needed to take the weight off her feet and there weren't enough benches for a place the size of this and something ought to be done.

We agreed with her, always the best policy in such a situation.

Mr Wigglesworth rose, saying to the woman, 'Well we were just off. The bench is yours, madam.'

He took my arm. 'Would you like to see the photographic exhibition? You were kind enough to compliment me on my smoke and steam. There are better photographers than I whose work is on display.' There it was again, his nervous laugh. 'I'd like you to see Lucian's work.'

Viewing photographs was the last thing on my mind, but he seemed anxious that I go with him.

In the Town Hall, the entranceway was deserted, the

342

photographic exhibition not attracting as many people as had the inquest. He opened the door of the exhibition room. 'Come, Mrs Shackleton.'

The glamorous Mabel Nettleton sat at the table, ready to welcome visitors. She greeted us effusively.

'Hello, darlings. Is the inquest over? What was the outcome?'

'It has been adjourned, Miss Nettleton.'

'How trying for the widow.' Miss Nettleton has a most expressive face and showed powerful sadness and exasperation on the family's behalf.

An odd thought struck me. That was just the kind of expression that a doctor's patients, particularly those tending towards hypochondria, might appreciate.

Some entrepreneurial persons, including Miss Nettleton, had arranged for postcards to be printed from their photographs. These were spread on the table, with a tin nearby for the money. Miss Nettleton's photographs of a gipsy encampment and some of its inhabitants, singly and in groups, were very good indeed.

Mr Wigglesworth and I walked about the exhibition, looking again at his smoke and my portraits, and Miss Nettleton's Romany gipsies. Hers were the best in the exhibition, but of course she knew that.

It gave me a small shock to see Lucian's pictures, five in all. They were a tribute to his aunt. There she was in her late thirties. Lucian must have been aged about ten when he took this photograph. She was a little off-centre, but this added to the photograph's charm. She wore the divided skirt that I had borrowed and stood ready to mount a bicycle, looking serious, unsmiling as though anticipating a terrible collision. In the next photograph, she sat on a rock, legs outstretched, Catrigg Force in the background. The toes of her stout boots pointed to the sky. She smiled into the camera, a picnic basket by her side and a drink in her hand. One photograph was taken in the garden on the familiar bench. She held a bunch of flowers. The caption said that it was her forty-fifth birthday. On her fiftieth birthday, she was framed in the front doorway, seated in a chair, her head slightly to one side with an expression that suggested she wanted this photography business over and done so that the party might commence.

The camera liked Freda. In the most recent photograph, she stood with her back to the garden wall, near a trellis that supported wisteria.

Mr Wigglesworth smiled. 'She was sixty and said this would be the last photograph she allowed anyone to take. We laughed. I accused her of vanity and said she was only waiting for me to say she was as lovely as ever.'

'And did you?'

'Certainly not!' He laughed. 'She would have told me not to be so daft.'

Mr Wigglesworth and I gazed at her for a long time.

Finally, he turned away. 'There are others Lucian brought in. He photographed her every year, except 1916 and 1917, when he asked me to do it. When she took poorly, he said he would not take any more because she did not wish it and he could not bear to see her disintegrate.'

'Disintegrate?'

'I think that was his word. Lucian thought the world of

344

his aunt, you know, when he was a boy. He hated to see her suffer.' He did not look at me. 'We both loved her.'

'Yes.'

'I could have made her comfortable. She might have, should have, lived a few more months, and wanted to. She wanted to hear the carol singers on Christmas morning, and the bells chime in 1926. I thought she might live until April. She said she could put up with a certain amount of pain, you see, though she didn't refuse morphia, was glad of it, up to a point.'

He walked on and took one more look at his own pictures, at the smoke and steam rising from the train as it entered the viaduct.

There was a bench by the wall, placed where visitors might sit and admire Miss Nettleton's photographs.

We sat down.

He gave that laugh of his. 'I have old customers, people who have come to me for a long time. Occasionally one of them, one of the men, will say about his wife, "Mr Wigglesworth, I don't like the look of her." He will ask me if there is something could be done. I say, "She is not the girl you married." He will agree. She has changed and he definitely does not like the look of her. It's hard to see someone once so loved change before a person's eyes. Freda never changed for me, she was always Freda. When Lucian came back from the war, she had grown old, or at least he thought so.'

'I think you told me that you began to photograph smoke and steam after Freda became ill?'

He cleared his throat. 'Yes, yes I did. Starting that day that I visited her, and Lucian let me in and then he had to be off. The disease progressed. A nurse came, Dr McKinley visited. And of course she had Lucian. Everything was done. Everything. Perhaps too much.'

'Photographing smoke and steam is an interesting choice, something that is hard to see through, like fog.'

'Oh I wouldn't try to photograph fog. Technically that would present a difficulty.'

'You suspect something don't you?'

'I thought she would live longer.'

'Mr Wigglesworth, I need to know. Lucian wants to marry me.'

'Yes, yes he does.'

'You think he did something because he didn't like to see Freda suffer.'

'I'm not entirely saying he did.'

'But if you did say that?'

'There is a fine balance between not enough morphia and too much.'

We sat in silence for several moments.

'Did she ask him to, do you think?'

'Definitely not. She was protective of him, would not have put that burden on his shoulders. I am the one she would have asked. We had discussed it. I did not have to face that difficult choice. But she wanted to live. She wanted to hear the carol singers.'

'That is a serious allegation to make against a doctor.'

'Yes.'

'You truly think that?'

'I know it. I saw it in his eyes. She wanted to live for as long as possible.'

'To hear the carol singers and enter the New Year.'

'And the snowdrops, the daffodils, and you. She wanted to meet you, because of Joseph Flaherty.'

'Why have you told me this? Do you think he may do it again?'

'Of course not. He did it because he loved her.'

Twenty-Nine

It was late afternoon when I arrived back at Lilac Cottage. I had walked from Settle, glad of the time alone to think about everything that had happened; the postponement of the inquest, my talk with Mr Wigglesworth at the photography exhibition and his revelation of Lucian's actions.

Mrs Sugden was sitting in the back garden with a freshly made pot of tea. I took a cup and joined her.

'Where's Harriet?'

'She's with Susannah at the big house, being let in on some lessons with the governess, French of all things.'

'And what about Martin?'

'Young Martin said to say goodbye.'

'He's gone? That was quick.'

'When Dr Simonson brought the lad back and said Mr Trevelyan had given the all clear to go see this blacksmith chap, the kid was keen to be off, asking could he borrow a bicycle. Dr Simonson took pity on him and has taken him back to Pendleton. He said it was the least he could do when Martin had been plucky enough to give his statement at the inquest. He said he won't be more than a few hours, just wanted to be sure Martin was made welcome.'

'That was good of him.'

'Well he's a good man, isn't he, and very fond of you. It's just Mr Sykes he's taken against.'

A couple of blackbirds came into the garden and pecked at the earth. It was peaceful in the garden, with only the sound of birdsong to break the silence.

Mrs Sugden looked content. 'I like it here. A person might become used to it. Not Mr Sykes of course, he never would.'

'No I'm sure he wouldn't. Where is he, by the way?'

'Gone fishing.'

'Fishing? You mean for actual fish, or he's onto something?'

'I was doing a bit of clearing up, and I found fishing tackle in the cellar. He took himself off to the river saying he might catch something for tea. I'm not counting on it, mind you. Knowing Mr Sykes, there'll be some ulterior motive.'

'And knowing you, you've guessed what that motive is.'

'He told that local constable he is a keen angler. Going off with his rod and line will give Mr Sykes something to chat about, and then he can lead the constable on to other matters.'

'That sounds right for our Mr Sykes. And did Martin have time to say goodbye to Harriet and Susannah?'

'Yes, and gave them his little carvings.' She chuckled. 'Martin was apologetic about not having made a carving for me. He said there'd be one ready when we visit him in Pendleton.'

'What a nice boy.'

She took something from her apron pocket. 'This is yours, with his compliments.'

It was an owl. Although far from perfect in the symmetry of its feathers, he had spaced the eyes well. They seemed to look directly at me. 'How clever.'

'Aye, he's handy with a knife.' She poured us each another cup of tea. 'By the way, I found someone to take Miss Simonson's clothes.'

'Oh good.'

'It was the postmistress who advised. They usually know everything.' She stirred her tea. 'She even knew that the inquest had been adjourned till next week.'

'Yes. I believe the police are carrying out more investigations, centring on Abner Gouthwaite.'

'Are they by Jove?'

Mrs Sugden picked up my owl. 'How Martin knew what to give you, I don't know. There must be a bit of magician in the lad. Mind you, Pendleton is the land of witches.'

'Well I'm going to do something now that probably isn't very wise.'

'What's that?'

'Use up some petrol by going up onto the tops, to one of the farms.'

'The widow?'

'No, not Catrigg Farm, Raistrick Farm. I'm going to call on Selina Gouthwaite.'

'Don't waste time on her.'

'If you'd seen her, Mrs Sugden, you might pity her.'

'Aye and I might not. Folk make their beds and lie in them.'

'All the same, that's what I'm going to do.'

'Do you want me to come with you?'

'No. I won't be long.'

'Where have I heard that before?'

'Stay here, in case Harriet comes back while I'm gone.'

The ashes of the burned barn showed no smoulder. In places, rain had turned the ash to mush. A crow lighted on a burned piece of wood, looked about and flew away.

The farmhouse was empty. There were signs that the rooms had been clumsily searched, with drawers pulled out and cupboard doors left open. The fire in the grate had died.

No Selina. Had she been taken for questioning?

I went back outside, towards the barn where I had first seen her delivering a calf. A hush hung about the place. Only the smell of animals remained, and broken tools and trampled hay. And then I saw them.

In the stall where the cow had calved, Selina stood with a shotgun in her hand. She was pointing it at Bradley Wigglesworth who stood in the corner. As I came nearer, I saw that he looked bemused, and fearful.

'Go away,' Selina said to me, 'or I'll shoot him. I'll shoot you both.'

'Why?' I spoke calmly, though I did not feel in the least calm.

'Where is he? What have they done with Abner? He should have come back by now. He's hurt. His leg is hurt.'

'He's quite safe and in good hands.'

'Whose hands?'

'He's helping Sergeant Dobson. There were some things not understood about how Mr Murgatroyd died.' I risked moving a little closer to her. 'Selina, you look exhausted, worn out. Let Mr Wigglesworth go. He is a good man. We can help you.'

She gave a short laugh. 'He's here to thieve. They took my tablets. Then this nosy parker.' She jabbed the shotgun into Mr Wigglesworth's neck. 'What are you looking for?'

He tried to smile but it was a grimace. 'Just looking. I want to see you have everything you need.'

'Liar!'

'And I brought you a tonic, one of my own.' He took a dark bottle from his inside pocket. 'Special ingredients, a grand restorative.'

'Mr Wigglesworth is the apothecary, Selina.'

'I know who he is.'

'He could bring you the tablets you need.'

'When is Abner coming back?'

'I'll take you to see him if you like.'

'Why have they kept him?'

I decided to risk telling her the truth. If she was afraid of Abner, this would be her chance to break free. 'The police believe Abner poisoned Mr Murgatroyd's drink, or the sandwich he made for him.'

She stared at me in surprise, letting the gun drop a little. 'Abner, make a sandwich? Are you mad? Abner, slice a loaf, mash a pot of tea, stir his own sugar? You're crackers, you are.'

'Then was it you made the sandwich for Mr Murgatroyd?'

'Me? Me? I do everything, everything.'

Wigglesworth moved quickly, knocking the gun from her hand, moving to step from the stall. She was as quick, reaching for something behind them. A second later, she had a knife in her hand, its point at Wigglesworth's throat.

She had taken the knife from a belt that hung behind

Wigglesworth, on a hook in the wall. So that was why he was here. When he queried me about the Gouthwaites coming from Eggleswick, he had made the connection. He must have known that Rufus Holroyd came from there, and deduced as I had that Abner Gouthwaite had killed to keep his secret. Selina had spotted him prowling about.

A dot of blood appeared on his throat. He glanced at the knife, even in his fear wanting to see whether the handle bore the mark that would identify it as once belonging to the slaughterman whose weapon killed Rufus Holroyd.

Selina's fist covered the handle.

Yet Wigglesworth's eyes glowed with certainty and a fierce determination. He spoke quietly to me. 'Go, Mrs Shackleton. Go now. She can't kill two of us. Tell them what I've found, for poor Flaherty's sake, and Freda's.'

'I'm not leaving you. Selina, don't make things worse. It's all over.'

'Over?'

'Yes. You've done this before, haven't you? You once took a knife and went into Langcliffe one Saturday night.' I wanted to distract her sufficiently to make her shift her position, move the knife. 'Was it you who wore Abner's long coat and stabbed Rufus Holroyd? He wouldn't have told on you, he would have kept your secret, and so will Mr Wigglesworth.' I stared at Wigglesworth, willing him not to be foolish, and to coax her. The woman was at her wits' end.

He could not bring himself to go along with me, but seemed to put great faith in his gift of a bottle of tonic, that he waved at her as the blade of the rusty knife drew a drop more blood. 'You've had my tonic before, do you remember? I brought it to you when you lost your baby. No one knew. I told no one about that baby, and neither did the midwife. We felt for you, it was so very sad.'

I came closer. 'Give me the knife, Selina. Think what Abner will say if he comes back and finds you've done something terrible.'

'He'll laugh, and then he'll hit me.'

I was not getting through to her, and then I thought of Eggleswick, that most unlikely name, just the name, and how we all have a place we invest with a kind of magic. 'Perhaps you might want to visit Eggleswick, just once more. Would you like that?'

'I don't know.'

'Give me the knife, Selina.'

She shook her head, but she lowered the knife and put it in her pocket.

'I have my car here. I'll take you wherever you want to go. Away from here, somewhere you can rest.'

'Eggleswick.'

'Yes.'

Wigglesworth did not move. She stepped away from him.

I walked towards her, kicking the shotgun out of her way.

'A motorcar.' She stared at me. 'Is it true, I'm going in a motorcar to Eggleswick?'

'Yes.' I touched her elbow and led her towards the door.

'You came before, when I cried about the calf.'

'Yes.'

I turned back and looked at Wigglesworth, giving him the slightest signal – a warning to stay quiet. He nodded, rubbed at his throat and indicated that he would be all right.

In the yard, Selina clambered into the car, the driver's

seat. I edged her along and started the motor, hoping the diversion of the ride would quieten her. It did, until I had to stop and open a gate by the spot that led to Catrigg Falls.

She jumped out. 'I know where we are. I have to wash myself here, wash myself white as the sheep.'

From what I had seen of the sheep round here, that would be a fine sludge grey. Before I was able to dissuade her, she was hurrying towards the falls.

Slithering and sliding, she made her way to where the water formed a basin. Fearing she might do away with herself, I followed.

The rushing sound of water increased as I drew nearer, stepping down the stones. At first I could not see her. The overwhelming power of the falls took my attention and only slowly did other parts of the scene come into focus.

She was in the water, the great natural basin, splashing, singing something tuneless, a dirge. She sat down, laughing, and then she was holding something in her hand. The knife.

Slowly, I made my way towards her, ripping my stockings, expecting to fall and break my bones. How could she have slithered down there so easily? Practice. It was too late to kick off my shoes. I was in too deep. The water was bitterly cold, turning my legs to ice as I walked towards her.

'Selina!'

She swung round, wild-eyed, the knife in her hand. 'Leave me, leave me be.'

She was not threatening me. I could go back to the car, drive to Settle, seek help, but what might she do in the meantime? 'Come on, Selina.' I held out my hand. 'This water's so cold. I have a house with a big bath where hot water just comes out of the tap. You'll like it. And you can have something to eat, and a new dress.'

'Is that true?'

'Yes. You deserve it. Then you can go back to Eggleswick in style.' I held out my hand.

She gave me the knife.

It was about six inches long, with Mr Young's distinctive squiggle on the handle.

'Come to the bank.'

'I like this place. It's like the River Jordan. I sing about the River Jordan.'

'I'd like to hear you sing, but come with me now.'

'I baptise myself. It's not just for sheep, this place.'

'This way then.'

Slowly we walked up across the big flat stones and away from the sound of the water.

We were both soaked to the skin. She was shivering. I pushed the knife under the car seat, and took out my bag. I passed her the smelling salts. 'You can have these smelling salts if you like them.'

She took the bottle like a child takes a sweet, saying thank you, unscrewing the top, putting the bottle to her nose, taking a deep whiff.

'Come on then, it's time to go.'

She shook her head.

'Go on and I'll put this blanket round your shoulders.'

She climbed in the car.

I got in and started the engine, hoping the petrol would take us as far as Settle.

The journey was a blank. As we reached Settle, I had no memory of the trip we had just made. Selina said nothing.

Thankfully, we reached Duke Street without mishap.

Dr McKinley's housekeeper showed only momentary dismay when she opened the door and looked at me, dripping onto the step.

'Mrs Shackleton, whatever is the matter?'

'I have a patient for Dr McKinley. Her name is Selina Gouthwaite and she is deeply distressed.'

'Let me ask him . . .'

'Please, help me fetch her in. I don't know where else to take her.'

Thirty

When I arrived back at Lilac Cottage, Mrs Sugden took one look at me and ran the bath that I had boasted about to Selina Gouthwaite. I hoped by now Selina would have been given a sedative and be safe with Dr McKinley and Mrs Pontefract.

By the time Sykes returned from his fishing expedition, I was sitting by the parlour fire with a warm drink.

'What happened?' Sykes asked. 'You look like death.'

He sat quietly while I told him the story.

'How is Wigglesworth?'

'I hope he's arrived back at the pharmacy, but it would be good if you would go see.'

'Yes, I will. And you say she admitted to poisoning Mr Murgatroyd?'

I nodded.

'That could throw a spanner in the works.'

'How?'

'I've just spoken to my chum, the Langcliffe constable.'

'I'm glad you're on good terms with him.'

'It helps. Abner Gouthwaite has confessed to poisoning

William Murgatroyd. I wonder if they were in it together, or if she acted alone and then he realised what she had done.'

'It was her.'

'How can you be so sure?'

'She told me she does everything and I believe her. He's one of those men who won't stir his own tea. He wouldn't make a corned beef sandwich with mustard and digoxin.'

'And the murder of Rufus Holroyd?'

'I'm guessing she did it that too, fearing the shame of being found out. She's tall enough to match the figure that Freda described.'

'We should tell the police.'

'And let her take the blame, and Gouthwaite go scot free?'

'They would both be charged.'

'She's not in her right mind.'

'It seems to me she's entirely in her right mind when it comes to her own interests.'

'Mr Sykes, just now I haven't the energy to argue with you. Go see Bradley Wigglesworth. I hope he had the sense to leave the knives where they were hanging. Let him report to the police. He attended Joseph Flaherty's trial and will know what to say to Sergeant Dobson. Tell Mr Wigglesworth that Selina is with Dr McKinley, and ask him to have pity on her.'

We talked just a little longer. I told him that I wished I had been able to photograph the knives on the hook in the barn, for the purpose of evidence.

Sykes offered me a cigarette and though I rarely smoke, I took it.

He lit the cigarette. 'The police won't want photographic evidence about a case that's long closed.'

'You're probably right.'

'If the powers that be admit they were wrong about Flaherty, I'll be very surprised. But I'll tell my constable chum and let him know what you've found out, if that's agreeable.'

'Don't say Selina confessed. She really isn't in her right mind.'

'If you say so.'

'Just one other thing, Mr Sykes.'

'I thought there might be.'

'Give your friend the constable the titbits of information, about the missing knives and the links to Eggleswick. You'll know how to do it. See if he has the wit to work things out for himself. Then if Mr Wigglesworth is ignored when he reports to Sergeant Dobson, the truth might just leak out slowly into the village, in the way the fountain splashes onto the ground when it rains. I'll ask Mrs Sugden to drop a hint to the postmistress, the butcher and the baker. I'd like to leave here having set the seeds of doubt in the minds of the villagers, if only so they remember Freda Simonson as the woman who was right, rather than as the foolish creature taken in by shadows.'

'And then I suppose I'm done here, unless you have anything else for me?'

'I hope not. I think we've done enough.'

He nodded. 'Are you sure you'll be all right, Mrs Shackleton?'

'Yes. You go back to Leeds.'

'How much longer will you stay here?'

'We came for a fortnight, but I'll see. I want to do whatever is best for Harriet, so we'll most likely stay the course.'

'I'll say goodbye to Mrs Sugden. I'm glad she'll be here with you.'

'Oh by the way, did you catch any fish?'

'Not a bite, but you can't have everything.'

In the churchyard that evening I placed flowers in the vase on Freda Simonson's grave, lilac, apple blossom and carnations. She had wanted to live long enough to hear the carol singers, so although it was May, I considered singing my favourite childhood carol to her, 'Good King Wenceslas'. But there were passersby and someone had just come out of the church, so I kept quiet to avoid being carted off to Dr McKinley's and given a sedative.

But then I did whisper to Freda. 'You were right. You did see someone that night, a figure in a big black coat. It was Abner Gouthwaite or his poor mad daughter, Selina. On balance, I would say she was the one, caring more about the shame of being found out if Rufus Holroyd had said that he had known the two of them in Eggleswick. Also, he was lazy and she has a restlessness that would not let her be.'

Freda made no answer, but there was a sigh on the wind that blew down from the tops.

'What are you doing here?' The voice startled me. I turned to see Lucian.

'I brought your aunt some flowers.'

'I thought I heard you speaking.'

'You may have done. I was telling Freda she was right. Joseph Flaherty didn't kill Rufus Holroyd. It was most likely

Selina Gouthwaite, afraid that she and Abner would be talked about. She's his daughter, you see.'

'How do you know that?'

'I found out, let's just say that.'

He frowned. 'Kate, are you all right? I heard you brought Selina Gouthwaite to Dr McKinley. It's a good thing you did. We didn't know about her heart condition because she goes to Skipton for her medication. God knows how long she's been without it.'

'Perhaps not long enough, for her sake.'

'You're being mysterious. I expect you heard that Gouthwaite has admitted to poisoning William Murgatroyd?'

'Yes, and I thought he might. I suppose it's the least he could do, in the circumstances.'

'Is it over now? Have you finished your investigations?'

'Yes, it's all over.'

'You've changed. You weren't like this before, suspicious all the time, asking questions.'

'I was.' I turned to face him. 'Only not with you, that was the difference.'

'And now?'

I looked at the headstone that gave the dates of Freda's birth and death. 'Did she ask you to do it?'

'To do what?'

'She was your world, from when you were a frightened little boy of six years old. The thought of her suffering was more than you could bear. I'm right aren't I?'

He looked at the flowers. 'I love the scent of lilac.'

'So do I.'

'I saw such suffering in the war, Kate. You of all people know that.'

'Sometimes you would have been asked by a badly wounded man, Put an end to it for me, doctor.'

'Yes.'

'She didn't ask though, did she, Freda? She wanted to live a little longer.'

He did not answer for the longest time. 'That disease, it's so cruel, I have seen it many times, a ravaging torment.'

'Answer me. Did she ask you?'

'No.'

'I thought not.'

'Don't hold it against me. I did what I thought was right. We sat and talked that afternoon. She was cheerful. I'd brought her chrysanthemums. She had a glass of sherry and a slice of lemon cake. I thought . . . I thought it was for the best. She died full of hope. Wasn't that better than waiting until what we all know is inevitable? I couldn't bear it.' He looked away. 'You're judging me, aren't you?'

'She should have made the choice.'

'I knew her, you didn't. She would never have given in and would have died in pain and despair.'

We walked back to Lilac Cottage in silence. It was late when Lucian left. We parted in sadness. I was not the woman for him and I could not have settled with him, there in that village, playing the part of the good doctor's wife, knowing what I knew.

He made one last attempt to expiate himself, saying about the war and the suffering and how he could see she would suffer.

'We're not at war any more, Lucian. It's over.'

But of course, it would never be over.

It had been a pipe dream, this idyllic village, the country

doctor, his wife investigating the occasional theft from the railway.

'Stay on,' he said as he was leaving. 'I won't trouble you, but I would like you and Harriet and Mrs Sugden to stay for the rest of your holiday. Please.'

'Thank you. I'll stay for Harriet's sake.'

I walked him to the gate, and we said goodbye.

That night, Mrs Sugden and I swapped beds. I slept snugly in the kitchen alcove at Lilac Cottage, my first good night's sleep since arriving.

Epilogue

The invitation came from Mrs Murgatroyd, who had my address from Bradley Wigglesworth.

Jennifer was to marry Simon, second son of Ralph and Brenda Goodman of Hope Hill Farm. Simon was the boy who had sat behind Jennifer in school. They had walked out together before Derek Pickersgill turned her head.

On the same day, Gabriel Cherry and Winifred, widowed barmaid from the Craven Heifer, would make their vows in the same church. The couples would share a joint wedding spread in Langcliffe Village Institute.

How could I possibly refuse an invitation to a double wedding? Well easily, if Lucian was to be there. Victoria Trevelyan had thoughtfully written to tell me that he was away on a visit.

This time, I did not drive but took the train to Settle. The Trevelyans sent a car to meet me.

The church was full, the altar overflowing with flowers.

Mrs Murgatroyd had discarded her black for purple, 'For this one day,' she told me with a smile. 'Life must go on. We can't let wickedness stop the clocks. William wanted the match between Jennifer and Simon.'

Mr Wigglesworth, whom I now call Wiggy, sat beside me. 'That's the groom,' he said, which I might have guessed as a good-looking young man took his place in front of the altar alongside his best man.

Behind me, the familiar voice of Mrs Holroyd took advantage of the moment to give her lodgers advice. 'Marry someone you know to the bones. They're the only ones you can trust.'

Heads turned as Jennifer walked down the aisle on Mr Trevelyan's arm. He looked as proud as if she was his own daughter. She wore a white muslin dress and a garland of flowers above her veil.

Mr Trevelyan then took his place beside Victoria and Susannah.

Once again, Mrs Holroyd whispered a life lesson to her charges. 'She's lucky having Mr Trevelyan walk her down the aisle. They'll get a finer gift from him than from her brothers or that tight seed merchant she calls uncle.'

I felt so happy for Jennifer and her handsome young farmer that I foolishly and predictably began to cry.

Unusually, the married couple stayed in church, sitting on the front pew.

No one gave away Gabriel Cherry's intended, Winifred. She and Gabriel walked to the altar side by side. Gabriel looked a bobby dazzler in a decent dark suit, white shirt and red tie. Winifred smiling and dressed in the colours of butter and bluebells made me want to cheer. There was some whispered remark from Mrs Holroyd that I did not catch.

Where Jennifer and Simon's vows had been little above a whisper, Gabriel and Winifred's responses reached the rafters.

The couples left the church together, Jennifer and Simon followed by Winifred and Gabriel. Confetti and petals rained on them.

Wiggy took out his camera. There was much posing and clicking before the brides threw their bouquets. Beth Young let out a yelp of delight as she caught Jennifer's flowers.

There was power in Winifred's arm as she aimed her bouquet. Susannah caught it and laughed with pleasure. Gabriel gave Susannah a brilliant smile and she smiled back. She might not know that he was her father but she knew something. At the very least, she knew he was the man who brought the books.

We all set off for the Village Institute where the wedding feast was laid out. Victoria Trevelyan, a little subdued, put on a brave face. 'There are two wedding cakes,' she told me. 'I retrieved Jennifer's original cake from that miserly Mrs Pickersgill, for the price of ingredients and something for her trouble.'

'For Jennifer?'

'Goodness no. She has her own cake. I wanted to give them something, Gabriel and his cheerful, chubby barmaid. I hope she'll make him happy, but did you see how he glanced at me, that smile of his?'

I have now become Wiggy's regular correspondent. We sometimes meet and have occasionally visited Selina Gouthwaite in the asylum. She no longer remembers Abner, so there has been no need to tell her that he was convicted of William Murgatroyd's murder and paid the ultimate price.

Wiggy has not given up in his attempt to clear Joseph Flaherty's name, having sought an interview with his member of parliament. The letters he wrote to the Prime Minister and to the King he delivered in person, having travelled by train to London in order to call at 10 Downing Street and Buckingham Palace. He left his dossier to be presented to each personage, along with a complimentary bottle of his special tonic. He received a royal letter regarding the special tonic and the bottles displayed in his window now bear the inscription, 'By Appointment to His Majesty King George V'.

Mrs Trevelyan and I exchange occasional letters. She is a woman with time on her hands. Although she does not take a great deal of interest in their tenants' affairs, she told me that Jennifer and Simon Goodman have brought new life to the land since taking over Catrigg Farm. Mrs Murgatroyd moved to Settle where she efficiently manages the office work for her seed merchant cousin.

On a glorious Sunday morning at the crack of dawn, Mr Sykes acted as chauffeur, driving me and Mrs Sugden in the Rolls-Royce that was given to me at Bolton Abbey by a grateful Indian princess. In Langcliffe we collected Susannah, Beth and Beth's friend Madge and made the trip to Pendleton, astonishing the local population and delighting Martin and his new family, the blacksmith and his wife.

They treat him like a son. He is more interested in bicycles, cars and motorcycles than in horses, but I expect that will stand him in good stead.

On the way back from Pendleton, Beth told me that Mrs Holroyd has softened in her attitude towards Freda Simonson, so perhaps the hints that were spread so broadly have done their work.

No one told me of the engagement between Dr Lucian Simonson and Miss Mabel Nettleton but I saw the announcement in *The Times*, which I expect she insisted on.

Harriet and I are invited to join the Trevelyans when they visit their estate in Scotland this August. Harriet is very keen, I less so. I am not sure that holidays are a very good idea, for me at any rate.

Acknowledgements

Thanks to Sylvia Gill for our walks and talks in the Yorkshire Dales; author friend and Langcliffe resident Leah Fleming and the villagers who marked the millennium by producing *Glimpses of a Dales Village*; Phil and Rita Hudson of North Craven Historical Research Group; staff at Craven Museum; North Yorkshire Libraries in Skipton and Settle, and Settle Tourist Information Centre. You are the ones most likely to spot the liberties I have taken, so please keep schtum.

My sister Pat shared distant memories of being a patient at Killingbeck Hospital when she was ill with diphtheria. Expert witnesses are Charlie Holmes, who knows farming and the land; retired North Yorkshire police officer Ralph Lindley and pharmaceutical whiz Barry Strickland-Hodge. I'm grateful for their help. Any mistakes are mine.

If Gabriel Cherry's experience as a stretcher bearer interests you, do read Emily Mayhew's *Wounded*.

Special thanks to the team at Piatkus. Dominic Wakeford's insights and spot-on editing made finalising the book a pleasure. Thanks to Robin Seavill, valued copy editor on all the Kate Shackleton books.

Thanks also to Thomas Dunne Books Editor-in-Chief Pete Wolverton and the team at Minotaur Books who deftly oversee Kate's safe passage across the Atlantic. She and I are grateful.

As always, agents Judith Murdoch and Rebecca Winfield provided sterling support.

I'm fortunate to have the back-up of Roger Cornwell and Jean Rogers who take care of my website.

It's always a pleasure to hear from readers and so thanks to them, the booksellers, librarians, festival organisers, reviewers and all who support me and my work.